Hexes and Heartbreakers

A Hexed Valentine Romance

Yvonne Hamilton

Golden Light Publishing House

Contents

Trigger Warning

Hexes & Heartbreakers explores love under pressure—what happens when fate, family expectations, and magical systems collide with personal agency. The story delves into themes of emotional manipulation, gaslighting, and power imbalances within romantic dynamics, particularly when one person's choices are quietly overridden "for their own good." Characters grapple with inherited curses, toxic patterns dressed up as destiny, and the fallout of being managed instead of trusted. These elements are not romanticized; they are examined, challenged, and actively confronted within the narrative.

Readers will also encounter heightened emotional states, panic responses, and moments of anger or intimidation, including a brief non-graphic physical altercation. Family pressure, abandonment, and betrayal play significant roles, as does the struggle to reclaim autonomy after years of being overlooked or controlled. While the tone balances sharp humor with warmth, the book does not shy away from the messier sides of love and magic. There is no on-page sexual assault, no graphic violence, and no harm to animals or children—but the emotional stakes are real, and the healing is hard-won.

Dedication

For the ones who believe love should be chosen, not assigned.
For anyone who's ever been told to stay because it was "meant to be."
For those who learned—sometimes painfully—that walking away
can be an act of courage, not failure.
This book is for the hearts that refused to follow the script
and for the magic that answered anyway.

Playlist

Chapter 1
Love Of Your Life — RAYE

Chapter 2
Good as Hell — Lizzo

Chapter 3
NOBODY'S GIRL — Tate McRae

Chapter 4
The Fate of Ophelia — Taylor Swift

Chapter 5
Confident — Demi Lovato

Chapter 6
In the Dark — Selena Gomez

Prologue

Sayer

T he woman is crying before I even sit down.

Not quietly. Not gracefully. She's shaking so hard the water in the crystal glasses on the table trembles in sympathy, little ripples betraying what the wards are trying to smooth over. The man beside her keeps his hands folded, jaw locked, eyes fixed on a point somewhere just past my shoulder like if he doesn't look at either of us, this will become theoretical instead of real.

It won't.

I take my seat anyway, wings folding tight against my back out of habit rather than courtesy. The room is neutral by design—no windows, no symbols, no warmth. Headquarters likes these mediation chambers sterile. It's easier to discuss destiny when it doesn't feel alive.

"I asked for reassignment," the woman says, voice cracking on the word. "I asked three times."

The man flinches. Not at her pain—at the implication.

I don't interrupt. I've learned better than that. When people finally say the quiet part out loud, you let it land.

"She's been anxious," he says quickly, like he's correcting a clerical error. "That's all. The bond's been... intense."

Intense. That's the word they always use before the truth becomes inconvenient.

I glance down at the file between us, already knowing what it will say. Optimal compatibility. Clean alignment. No flags. The bond signature stamped so neatly it might as well be smug.

"How long has it been hurting?" I ask her.

She laughs—a short, brittle sound that doesn't belong in her throat. "Since the vows. Since the day it locked in and I stopped feeling like myself." Her eyes find mine, desperate and furious all at once. "Everyone told me that was normal. That love feels overwhelming at first."

The man finally looks at her then. There's irritation there. Fear, too. Not for her—but for what this conversation threatens.

I feel it before I see it: the way the bond between them tightens, not in comfort but in correction. Magic pulling her back into alignment when she strays too far from the shape it prefers.

That's new.

Or maybe it isn't, and I've just been pretending not to notice.

"Have there been incidents?" I ask, carefully.

She hesitates. He doesn't.

"She panics," he says. "She resists. Sometimes the bond reacts." He turns to me, exasperated. "You said that would pass."

I did say that.

Because that's what the system says. Because that's what we're trained to say when the data looks clean and the outcome is inconvenient.

"Define reacts," I say.

Her hands clench in her lap. "I can't sleep," she says softly. "If I think about leaving, my chest tightens until I can't breathe. If I get angry, I get sick. Last week, I couldn't cross the threshold of our apartment without collapsing." She swallows hard. "My body won't let me choose anything else."

The room goes very still.

I feel something cold settle in my gut, heavy and unwelcome.

"That's not how it's supposed to work," I say, more to myself than them.

"No," she agrees. "It's not."

I reach for the file, flipping through the pages with growing unease. I scan the compatibility charts again, the predictive modeling, the reinforcement protocols embedded so subtly they barely register unless you're looking for them.

There it is.

A corrective loop. A failsafe designed to stabilize wavering bonds by... discouraging deviation.

I look up sharply. "Who approved this?"

The man stiffens. "You're making it sound sinister."

"I'm making it sound like coercion," I reply.

"It's protection," he insists. "She would've walked away otherwise."

The woman's breath stutters. She doesn't deny it.

I close the file.

This is the moment. The one that keeps happening more often than it should. The one where I'm supposed to explain that love isn't always comfortable, that destiny has growing pains, that resistance is part of the process.

I don't say any of that.

Instead, I ask, "Do you want to leave?"

She answers immediately. "Yes."

The bond reacts.

Magic snaps tight in the room, pressure rolling off the walls as if reality itself disapproves. The woman gasps, folding forward, pain rippling through her like a physical blow. The man reaches for her instinctively—and stops when he realizes what's happening.

I'm on my feet before protocol can catch up with me, wings flaring despite myself as I sever the active channel with a sharp, practiced motion. The wards protest. Headquarters always does when you interfere mid-correction.

The pressure eases. Not gone—but loosened.

The woman sags back in her chair, shaking.

The man looks at me like I've committed a crime.

"You can't do that," he says. "That bond is sanctioned."

"So is free will," I snap.

It's a lie. Or at least, it's become one.

Security arrives moments later. They always do. I'm escorted out under the guise of "cooling off," the file confiscated for review, the couple reassigned to another mediator who will almost certainly smooth this over and send them home with reassurances and reinforced wards.

As I walk back to my office, my wings ache in a way they never used to. Not from strain—from resistance. Like even they know I crossed a line that can't be uncrossed.

Inside, my desk is stacked with new assignments.

On top sits a familiar seal.

Bellamy.

I don't open it.

I don't even touch it.

Bellamy cases are complicated, volatile, historically reassigned when things get messy. Someone else will handle it. Someone who still believes the system bends toward good if you give it enough time.

I sit down slowly, staring at the closed file, thinking of the way that woman's body betrayed her own choice. Thinking of how easily we call that love.

That's when it finally settles—not as anger, but as clarity.

We don't make matches.

We enforce outcomes.

I push the Bellamy file into the unresolved queue, tell myself it will be redistributed, and begin drafting my resignation. Not dramatic. Not angry. Just precise.

If love requires force, I want no part of it.

If leaving is treated like failure, then someone needs to stand on the other side and say it isn't.

I don't know whose life that file belongs to. I don't know that I've just delayed something instead of preventing it.

All I know is this:

I am done being the hand that tightens the bond. Let someone else carry that weight. I'm going to help people get out.

Chapter 1

Francesca

I wake to the soft crackle of magic—like a low hum under my skin—before I even open my eyes. January first. My birthday. And the exact moment the Bellamy curse likes to announce itself for the season.

I sit up slowly, obsidian hair falling out of the half-hearted bun I slept in. The strands are already picking up static, which is... well, not surprising. My magic tends to get twitchy on a good day. The first day of the Season is not a good day.

I drag myself into the bathroom, blink at the mirror, and watch as a faint smear of pink frosting appears across the glass—thin at first, then thickening into a single word:

Lovelorn.

I stare at it for a beat. The frosting wiggles guiltily and drips down the mirror.

"Happy birthday to me," I mumble, wiping the melted sugar off the mirror with my fingers. The curse is early today. Fantastic.

I make my way into the kitchen, bracing for something stupid to happen. The overhead light hums, the tile is cool beneath my feet, and the faint scent of last night's cinnamon batter still lingers in the air. For a moment, everything looks deceptively normal—until I notice my coffee mug trembling on the counter, vibrating in a tight little circle like it's trying to flag me down.

"Don't," I warn it.

It stops. For now.

I grind the beans, set up the pot, and let myself breathe for a moment. Thirty-five. Fifteen years of dodging love like it's a poorly aimed firework. Fifteen years of keeping the curse manageable by helping other people in Bramblewick stumble into their happily-ever-afters—because nothing keeps the magic calmer than playing matchmaker for everyone except myself.

Ironic, honestly.

My phone buzzes with the morning orders. The first name on the list pulls a tired smile out of me.

Sayer Valentine – 7:30 a.m. Everything bagel with what he calls "a respectable amount of cream cheese," what I call "a crime scene." Large caramel latte, one dollop of whipped cream. And if it's a bad morning? He adds an apple fritter.

The fritter is his tell. He doesn't know that I know that, but I do. He also doesn't know that every time he orders an extra espresso shot,

I slip a thread of Bellamy Luck into his latte—just enough to keep the day from chewing him up.

It's not meddling. It's... preventative damage control. The man runs a divorce practice. He needs all the luck he can get.

I take a long breath, letting the quiet morning settle around me. The curse flickers again beneath my skin, that restless magic stretching like it's been waiting all year for this moment.

It always gets stronger on my birthday. It always reminds me that another year has passed without "true love," whatever that's supposed to mean. My sisters found theirs early. I found a bakery, purpose and a lot of work to keep me busy. I'm fine with that. Mostly.

I tie my apron and check the clock. One hour until opening. One hour until the first rush of hopefuls looking for "something sweet to start the new year right."

One hour until Sayer Valentine walks through my door, pretending he hates the holidays while ordering a latte that tastes like melted candy.

I rub my hands together, warming the air with a small spark of magic, and roll my shoulders back.

"Alright," I say to the empty room." Let's try not to blow anything up this year."

The curse twitches again like it disagrees.

And—yeah. That tracks.

I grab my keys from the hook by the door, shrug on my fleece-lined jacket, and step into the narrow stairwell that leads down to the bakery. The walls are the same soft sage my grandmother painted them decades ago, and even half-asleep, I can feel the magic threaded through every grain of wood. Bellamy Bakery isn't just a business—it's a living thing. A temperamental one. Like a cat that occasionally bursts into seasonal chaos.

The scent hits me halfway down the stairs. Warm sugar. Buttery dough. Fresh cinnamon. A hint of citrus. The building practically exhales around me, like it knows the Season has started and is stretching into its busiest time of year.

I push open the door into the back kitchen, and the blast of heat from the ovens wraps around me like a hug.

Harper—our head pastry chef, a night owl by choice and by temperament—is already elbow-deep in a massive bowl of dough. She's been here since midnight and looks exactly the same at six a.m. as she does at three in the afternoon: focused, steady, and vaguely judging the entire world.

Her copper curls are piled on top of her head in a lopsided bun, flour smudged across one cheek like a battle stripe, and her dark eyes narrow in concentration as she folds the dough with the unyielding precision of someone who fears neither gods nor gluten.

"Morning, boss," she says without looking up. "Your magic woke up before you did."

"It usually does," I admit, hanging my jacket on the peg. "Did anything spontaneously combust?"

"Only the lemon curd, but that happens every year. I've accepted it."

Fair.

I move through the kitchen, checking the trays already proofing, feeling the air buzz faintly as the curse stretches itself through the floors. The ovens hum with it. The mixers twitch. The enchanted temperature wards flicker like they're adjusting to my presence.

Miguel arrives at three a.m. every morning, mostly because he claims "this bakery has the best sunrise lighting in the city," which is a lie—he just likes the peace before the rush and thinks I don't notice.

He's tall and lean, always in soft flannels rolled to the elbows, dark hair pulled into a short tie at the nape of his neck. His eyes are warm brown, perpetually half-lidded in a way that makes him look serene even when he's juggling ten drink tickets. Tattoos curl along his forearms—coffee beans, constellations, a whisk, a tiny grinning skull—each one a story he only tells after three cups of espresso.

This morning he's manning the espresso machine, calibrating the grind with the focus of a man diffusing a bomb. The machine hisses its greeting just as he glances over at the sound of my footsteps.

"Morning, Fran," he says, mouth curving in that slow, unhurried smile of his. "Happy birthday."

"Don't remind me," I say, though I can't help smiling a little.

"We saved you a cinnamon roll," he says. "The curse already ate the first two."

Of course it did.

I move to the prep station, brushing my fingers lightly over the countertop. My magic settles the way a restless animal settles beside someone it trusts—still twitchy, still not fully under control, but calmer. These mornings are always like this. A negotiation, not a harmony.

Harper finally looks up at me, wiping her hands on her apron. "You feeling it worse than last year?"

"Too early to tell," I say. "The mirror wrote me a love letter."

Miguel snorts. "Let me guess—something subtle and respectful, like 'find a man' or 'your ovaries are bored'?"

"Close. It went with *lovelorn*."

Harper grimaces in sympathy. "It's going to be a fun season."

The front of the bakery is still dark, but through the half wall I can see the silhouette of our display cases—empty for now but soon to be filled with the usual magic-laced staples: Lemon Sugar Cookies for clarity, Caramel Espresso Cupcakes for courage, Pineapple Upside-Down Cakes for turning your life right-side up again, Chocolate-Dipped Strawberries for... well, obvious reasons.

Today we'll prep the first Valentine's run of the year, and by this afternoon, half the city will be waiting in line for them.

I breathe it in. This chaotic, ridiculous, enchanted place. My place.

And then, because fate likes to keep things interesting, my phone buzzes again.

Reminder: 7:30 a.m. — Sayer Valentine. Bagel. Latte. Possible fritter. The ritual begins.

Harper follows my gaze. "He's coming in today?"

"He always comes in on the first," I say, tightening my apron strings. "Like clockwork."

Miguel arches a brow. "Think he'll get the fritter?"

I stop, think about the way Sayer's shoulders tense whenever he's bracing for something hard, the way his voice gets clipped when he's dealing with particularly messy cases, the way he tries to pretend the world isn't exhausted by his cynicism.

"...I'd bet on it," I say.

The curse flickers again beneath my skin—predictable as sunrise.

I steady myself with a long breath, turning toward the front of the bakery as the first glimmer of morning light slides across the floor.

"Alright," I say quietly. "Let's get ready."

And somewhere behind me, one of the ovens pings in agreement.

By the time the clock creeps toward 7:30, the bakery has settled into that familiar pre-opening tension. The ovens hum in steady rhythm. The cinnamon rolls rise obediently for once. My magic paces under my skin, restless, coiling and uncoiling like it's waiting for someone to throw a switch.

The back door swings open at precisely 6:45—as it always does—and a gust of cold air sweeps in along with Ellie.

If Harper is a storm cloud—steady, dry humor, a little brooding—Ellie is the sunrise behind it. All brightness and bounce and the type of optimism only someone immune to the Bellamy curse could maintain.

"Happy birthday!" she chirps the moment she sees me, practically skipping across the tile. Her ponytail—messy, blonde, and aggressively enthusiastic—swings behind her like it also got the pep-talk memo.

Before I can even respond, she holds out a small velvet pouch. "I made you something!"

Oh no.

Ellie's magical gifts are... well-intentioned. Always. Effective? Rarely. Safe? Debatable.

I open the pouch and find a delicate necklace made of rose quartz, moonstone, and something that looks suspiciously like enchanted glass beads.

"It's a love frequency charm," she says, beaming proudly. "It attracts aligned romantic energy and repels emotionally unavailable men."

I blink at her. "That's... oddly specific."

Harper, without looking up from her dough, mutters, "She based it on her last three exes."

Ellie glares at her sister like a cat hissing at a much larger cat. "It works! Probably. I mean—don't wear it while boiling water or actively casting anything above level two, and definitely don't sleep with it on, but besides that, it should totally help your love life."

"My love life is a rumor," I say dryly.

"That's why this will help!"

She clasps the necklace around my throat before I can protest. The moment the cool stones touch my skin, a soft pulse of energy ripples outward—subtle, but noticeable. Not dangerous. At least not immediately.

"Ellie," I say gently, "does this react to the curse?"

"Probably not!" she says brightly.

Which means: definitely yes.

But before I can question her further, she drops her bag behind the counter and moves to the front window. She peeks out through the curtains—and lets out a low whistle.

"You're gonna love this," she says. "There's a line around the block already."

Harper groans. "It's the first day of January. People should be in bed regretting last night's decisions."

"People regret last night," Ellie agrees cheerfully. "But they also want cupcakes that fix their relationships."

I move to the door, sliding the curtain aside just an inch. And she's right.

There's already a crowd forming—coats pulled tight, breath fogging in the cold morning air, hands wrapped around thermoses as they chat excitedly. Several look like they've been there since dawn. One girl holds a travel mug that says LOVE SPELL COOKIES OR RIOT.

Miguel murmurs, "Ah, yes. Another peaceful Season."

The clock flips from 6:59 to 7:00.

And the moment it does, the front bell rings like the bakery has a built-in sense of timing. Ellie swings the door open with her usual flourish.

"Good morning! Happy New Year! Welcome to Bellamy Bakery!" she sings out, voice bright enough to make half the line perk up.

The first wave pours in—twenty, maybe thirty people—voices eager, scarves damp with melted frost, the whole place filling instantly with warmth and chatter.

Harper moves back to her dough in the kitchen. Miguel starts pulling espresso shots like a man gearing up for war. I take my place at the center island, ready for whatever mix of magic and madness the Season throws at me.

Ellie leans close as the crowd rushes forward.

"Your favorite grumpy heart-hater is going to be here soon," she whispers conspiratorially.

I feel the necklace hum once—low, warm—like it's reacting to the name alone.

"Yep," I say, fixing my messy bun. "Let the season officially begin."

And somewhere deep in the bakery walls, the curse stirs in agreement.

Chapter 2

Sayer

Mornings in January always show up with the same heavy silence, like the world is finally sobering up after a month-long bender. I stare at the ceiling for a long moment, listening to the last dying pops of illegal fireworks and wondering why people insist on celebrating a holiday they'll regret in six to eight weeks.

Most of the city is still asleep. I should be. But the Season starts now, and the Season doesn't care about my feelings.

A new year means couples everywhere are waking up beside someone they're suddenly not convinced about. The shine wears off, reality creeps in, and three months from now I'll be sorting out who gets the air fryer and who gets the dog they both "rescued."

It shouldn't entertain me. But it does. Quietly. Consistently. I understand the rhythm of human disappointment better than most.

I roll out of bed, stretch, and ignore the faint pull between my shoulder blades—just a leftover reminder of a job I have absolutely no interest in revisiting. The apartment is cold enough to make me grit my teeth as I cross to the closet. My suits hang in precise order, the closest thing I have to religion these days.

I choose a charcoal one, put it on, button it up. The ritual is calming. Predictable. Nothing like the rest of this month will be.

The mirror catches my eye. I don't bother looking at myself for long. I already know what I'll see—the man who figured out that calling and purpose are not the same thing, and that passion is overrated when your bills aren't paid. I smooth down my tie and breathe out once.

"Here comes the circus," I mutter.

Another round of declarations and promises, another round of breakups and reconciliations. Another cycle of people realizing that love is a lot easier to start than maintain. If experience has taught me anything, it's that most people underestimate how much actual work it takes to not crash their lives into each other.

Coat on, briefcase secured, I step into the hallway and accept that the day is already judging me. The building smells faintly of old wood and radiator heat—and, because the universe enjoys taunting me before caffeine, the unmistakable drift of cinnamon and sugar from across the street. Bellamy Bakery is already awake, its morning magic leaking into the air like a scented reminder that I'm running late for my own routine.

Of course it is. Those people operate on a schedule that violates natural law.

I check the time. If I leave now, I can hit my office first, drop my things, then head over before the next wave of hopefuls floods the door. I lock up and head down the street, the cold biting enough to feel like a warning.

My office sits across the street, tucked into the ground floor of a narrow brick building that's been around long enough to develop both character and a permanent draft. The place has tall windows, old ironwork framing the door, and a plaque that looks far more dignified than anything happening inside. It's wedged right beside the bakery—close enough that the smell of sugar and fresh bread leaks into the hallway year-round.

It isn't far, just a quick crosswalk and a stretch of pavement, but on a morning like this it feels longer. The world's still half-asleep, early risers trudging past with the grim determination of people who made too many resolutions last night and already regret all of them.

I unlock the door to Valentine & Associates and flick on the lights, letting the familiar scent of stale coffee, toner, and quiet legal despair settle around me like a reluctant handshake. Everything is exactly where I left it—neat, structured, untouched. The way I prefer it. The lobby lights hum awake as I cross the lobby, and my footsteps echo down the short hallway toward my office in the back, safely removed from the noise of the street.

By the time I reach my office, the familiar quiet settles around me. I drop the briefcase beside my chair, hang my coat on the hook by the door, and hit the power button on my computer. The screen flares to life with the enthusiasm of someone eager to ruin my morning—clients panicking about holiday mistakes, opposing counsel pretending they've found religion and deadlines, and a flood of cheerful new-year emails from companies I've never willingly engaged with.

January never arrives gently. It shows up with bags under its eyes and a stack of problems.

I skim through my schedule. Nothing catastrophic today, though January is when people start realizing that a holiday proposal will not magically fix a relationship built on duct tape and delusion.

I close the program. I'm not caffeinated enough to deal with people's feelings yet.

Through the shared wall, I can hear the bakery—muffled chatter, laughter, the telltale clatter of too many customers at once. They run on some cursed internal clock over there. Always have.

I grab my wallet. No point pretending I'll get any work done before coffee. I learned years ago that legal analysis without caffeine ends in malpractice.

I take a last look around the lobby—quiet, orderly, waiting for the chaos of the season to really kick in—then switch off the lights and lock the door behind me.

The line outside the bakery hasn't fully disappeared, but it's manageable. I weave past the remaining customers without making eye contact, shove my hands into my pockets, and aim myself at the warm glow coming from behind the glass.

Routine. That's all it is. Not comfort. Not habit. Routine.

Just caffeine. Just a bagel.

Taking a breath, I reach for the bakery door, push it open, and step inside.

Warmth washes over me first—the kind that makes the cold outside feel like a bad decision. Then the smell hits: fresh bread, citrus glaze, cinnamon, too much enthusiasm in the air for seven in the morning. The place is loud, busy, packed with people who look like they think a pastry is going to fix the existential crisis they woke up with.

Maybe it will. Stranger things have happened.

I move off to the side to stay out of the stampede. Ellie spots me immediately—as usual—and waves like we're old friends instead of two people who see each other at ungodly hours several times a week.

"Morning, Sayer! Happy New Year!" she says with enough cheer to give someone a migraine.

I nod back. Anything more enthusiastic would require lying, and I have a strict no-lying-before-coffee policy. "Morning, Ellie."

The noise settles into the background as I scan the counter. It doesn't take long to find her.

Francesca Bellamy stands behind the display case, sleeves rolled up, hair shoved into a bun that looks like it's barely clinging to its purpose. There's a streak of flour on her cheek and a look in her eyes that tells me she's been awake far longer than any responsible human should be.

She's mid-conversation with a customer who appears to be having a meltdown over which muffin will bring him more luck in the new year. She handles him with patient efficiency—just firm enough to steer him, just soft enough to keep him from spiraling.

When she finally hands him his box and turns, her gaze flicks toward me. Pinned instantly. Like she could locate me in a room with her eyes closed.

No smile. No greeting. Just that assessing look she always gives me—the one that makes it feel like she's sizing up my mood before deciding how to approach.

"You're early," she says, wiping her hands on her apron as she comes closer. "Didn't think you'd risk the first-day-of-January crowd."

"It's either face it early or suffer through it later," I say, leaning an elbow against the counter. "I prefer to choose my battles."

She lets out a sound that lands somewhere between a laugh and outright disbelief, then turns toward the espresso bar. She doesn't ask what I want—never has—and despite myself, that small certainty loosens something in my chest.

In a world built on predictable disasters, this is one detail that reliably behaves. She reaches for the portafilter, movements already calibrated to whatever mood I've dragged in with me, and something in me stirs—petty, tired, and far too aware of how much that quiet familiarity matters.

"So," I say, shifting just enough that she glances back at me, "how's the first morning of the Season treating you? Still convincing people that baked goods will solve their relationship problems?"

Her eyes narrow just a fraction, the corner of her mouth lifting in that unimpressed way she does when she's deciding whether I'm worth responding to.

"It's called hope," she says, turning back to tamp the espresso. "Some people like having it."

"Mm," I hum, noncommittal. "Right up until they're in my office explaining how the 'sudden spiritual connection' they felt over a box of cupcakes turned out to be indigestion."

She doesn't pause, but I can practically feel her decide to ignore that one. Which, honestly, only encourages me.

"You know," I add, adjusting my cufflinks, "you could save yourself a lot of time if you just put a disclaimer on the door. Something like: 'These pastries may lead to temporary delusions of compatibility. Consult a legal professional before committing to anything long-term.' I'd even help you format the fine print. Consider it a birthday present."

She stops then—just long enough to give me one sharp, sideways look over her shoulder.

"Good morning to you too, Valentine," she deadpans.

"I'm just saying," I continue, because I haven't had coffee yet and restraint is not available to me at this hour, "the turnover rate is impressive. I admire the optimism it takes to keep peddling desserts like emotional life preservers when statistically speaking—"

"Sayer Valentine," she cuts in, voice flat, "if you recite divorce statistics at me before seven-thirty, I'm charging you double."

That almost gets a smile out of me. Almost. I settle for leaning an elbow on the counter and watching her work—because watching her get mildly irritated at me is more effective than caffeine.

"It's nothing personal," I say, not bothering to hide the dry amusement in my tone. "It's just fascinating how many people walk in here thinking sugar will fix their love life. Then they come running to me with the fallout."

"Maybe," she says, sliding a cup under the espresso spout, "maybe if people talked to actual human beings instead of emotionally repressing themselves like it's an Olympic sport, they wouldn't need either of us."

I arch a brow. "You think talking fixes everything?"

"No," she says calmly, "but it usually avoids crying in a lawyer's office on a Tuesday morning."

"I don't mind the crying," I say. "It's billable."

She lets out a soft breath that might be a laugh, might be frustration—it's always hard to tell with her. She reaches for the caramel syrup, and the scent hits the air between us, warm and sweet in a way I refuse to examine too closely.

She glances up at me again, eyes sharper now. "You enjoy this way too much."

I shrug one shoulder. "Someone has to balance out all the optimism in here."

"Right," she says, "because you're a natural candidate for that."

I open my mouth to respond, something appropriately acerbic already forming, when she finishes the drink, sets it on the counter with a practiced motion, and steps back just slightly. Not much. Just enough to signal she's still not putting up with my nonsense today.

"Here," she says. "Maybe this'll soften your personality a little."

"Doubtful," I say, but I take the cup anyway.

And despite every cynical thing I just said, the first sip hits exactly right.

I'll never admit that out loud.

Chapter 3

Francesca

I watch him take that first sip—trying not to look like I'm watching, because Sayer Valentine noticing me watching him would be unbearable on principle alone. His expression doesn't change much, but his shoulders ease the tiniest bit, and that's how I know I got it right.

He never says thank you out loud. He says it with posture.

He lifts the cup in a small, almost reluctant gesture of acknowledgment, like it pains him to admit the coffee did something positive for his soul. The man could win an award for emotional minimalism.

"Try not to terrorize anyone before noon," I say lightly as he starts to step back from the counter.

He gives me a look—dry, unimpressed, but not unkind. "I make no promises."

"Then at least—" I wipe my hands on my apron and nod toward the door, "—have the day you deserve."

It slips out sharper than intended, but not hostile. Just... accurate.

His mouth twitches, the closest thing Sayer has to a smirk. He raises his cup again, a silent concession to the moment, and turns toward the exit.

I watch him weave through the lingering customers, the door chiming softly as he pushes it open. Cold morning air spills inside for half a second, brushing over my arms, and then the door shuts behind him.

And in the heartbeat after it closes, the bakery's magic—my magic—seizes on something in the air and makes its opinion known.

The whipped cream canister I'd set on the counter gives one innocent little wobble.

"Oh, don't you—"

It explodes.

White foam bursts out in a spectacular fountain, spraying across the counter, the floor, the display case, and, most impressively, my entire upper half.

I stand there in stunned silence, coated in a sticky layer of whipped cream, feeling droplets run down my hairline and drip off my chin. The necklace Ellie gave me hums like it's personally offended.

From the far end of the counter, Ellie gasps. Harper mutters, "Called it." Miguel steps out from behind the other espresso machine, takes one look at me, and nods like this is exactly the kind of morning he expected.

I close my eyes for a long, slow inhale. I open my eyes again, staring through the haze of whipped cream clinging to my lashes.

Fantastic start to the morning.

I don't bother trying to clean the counter yet. Miguel and Ellie can manage the front for a few minutes, and Harper won't look up from her dough unless the building is on fire. I head straight for the staff locker room, closing the door behind me with a quiet thud that feels like the first breath I've had since the whipped cream incident.

The fluorescent light flickers on, revealing the full scope of the disaster. I'm absolutely covered. There's whipped cream in places whipped cream has no business being.

With a resigned sigh, I grab a towel from the shelf. The moment I start wiping my face, my phone starts buzzing aggressively in my apron pocket. I already know that ringtone—my sisters. All of them.

"Of course," I mutter, accepting the call.

Their faces pop onto the screen at the same time: Cassia positioned perfectly in her office already, Juniper curled up in pajamas with her mug of tea, and Daphne leaning so close to her camera that I can see every eyelash she owns.

"Happy birthday!" all three shout at once.

Then they go silent.

Cassia tilts her head, brow furrowing. "Francesca... why do you look like you were mugged by a dessert cart?"

"I wasn't mugged," I say, rubbing a smear of cream down my cheek. "Technically speaking, it was an explosion."

Juniper lowers her mug, staring. "Is that whipped cream in your hair?"

"Yes," I reply, trying to dislodge a glob near my ear. "And elsewhere."

Daphne laughs, delighted. "You look like a cupcake that gave up halfway through icing itself."

"Wonderful," I say dryly. "Exactly the aesthetic I was going for at seven in the morning."

Cassia folds her arms, her voice shifting into that calm, managerial tone she uses when she's about to problem-solve my life. "Do you need one of us to come down and help? I'm free between meetings."

"I'm fine," I insist. "Really. Just the usual magical misfire."

Juniper gives me a sympathetic look. "It's only January first. Everything's probably going to be heightened for a bit."

"Don't remind me," I say, scrubbing at the cream along my jawline.

Daphne squints at the screen. "Hold still. I think there's a blob behind your ear."

I check. She's right. Of course she's right.

I clean it off, toss the towel into the hamper, and reach for a fresh one.

Cassia softens a little. "At least tell me you made a wish this morning."

"I did," I reply, pulling whipped cream off my bun. "I wished for twenty more minutes of sleep."

Daphne laughs. "Optimistic."

"It was," I admit. "And it didn't happen."

All three sisters pause, and for a moment the teasing falls away.

Juniper clears her throat. "Did Sayer come in yet?"

I freeze just long enough for Daphne to catch it.

"Oh my God," Daphne says, pointing at the screen. "He did. I can hear it in your face."

"That is not a thing," I tell her.

Cassia raises an eyebrow. "You don't have to pretend. It's January first. He's nothing if not a creature of habit."

Juniper smiles over her tea. "Did he at least behave?"

"As much as he ever behaves," I say, though the corner of my mouth twitches before I can stop it. "Which is to say, not particularly."

Daphne gasps. "Did you two argue already?"

"We didn't argue," I say firmly.

All three of them respond immediately:

Cassia says, "Mm-hm."

Juniper murmurs, "Sure."

Daphne says, "Right. Totally believable."

I glare at them, but it's half-hearted. "I'm hanging up now."

Juniper waves her mug. "Happy birthday, sweet sister."

Cassia gives me a warm smile. "We love you."

Daphne blows an exaggerated kiss. "Go scrape the dairy off your soul."

"I'll do my best," I say, ending the call.

I drop the phone onto the bench with a soft clatter and take another look in the mirror. Clean enough. Presentable if the lighting is forgiving. My bun is still hanging on out of sheer spite. I tie my apron again, roll my shoulders once, and head back toward the kitchen.

Whatever's waiting out front, it can't possibly be worse than what I just survived.

Probably.

By the time I make it back toward the kitchen doorway, most of the whipped cream has been cleaned off the front counter. Ellie is wiping down the display case while humming far too cheerfully for someone who witnessed dairy-based violence. Harper hasn't moved an inch from her workstation. Miguel glances up only long enough to confirm I'm no longer a walking dessert.

I'm halfway through tying my apron tighter when the front bell rings again.

Ellie brightens. "Francesca's your parents are here!"

Of course they are.

I step out from behind the half-wall and see them immediately—my mother standing at the counter, waving like she's signaling ships from the shore and my father standing beside her with the patient endurance of a man who has been married to a Bellamy long enough to surrender to the chaos.

"Happy birthday, sweetheart," my mother says, leaning over the counter to kiss my cheek. "You didn't answer your texts."

I gesture to my hair. "I was dealing with... this."

She studies the remnants of whipped cream with a sigh thick with maternal resignation. "You really should consider wearing a hairnet during The Season, Francesca."

"I'm not wearing a hairnet," I say. "I still have dignity."

"You lost dignity somewhere around the moment you chose a career next to citrus-flavored magic," she replies.

My father lets out a soft huff that might be a laugh. "We just came to see if you wanted to join us for lunch later," he says. His voice is calm, always calm, no matter what's happening around him. "Your mom made reservations."

"She made reservations," I repeat, narrowing my eyes slightly. "Dad, it's January first. You can't get reservations anywhere today."

He clears his throat. "She... may have made them last November."

"That sounds correct," my mother says proudly.

Before I can respond, one of the pastry carts that Ellie just restocked gives a suspicious shudder. I turn toward it just in time to see two cinnamon-twist pastries lift off the tray as if caught by invisible hands.

"Please don't," I whisper at them.

They ignore me. Of course they do.

The pastries sail through the air—not maliciously, just enthusiastically misguided—heading straight toward my parents. My mother gasps, bringing her hands up too late.

But my father simply steps forward, snatching both pastries out of the air without blinking. One in each hand. Smooth. Efficient. Like a man who has been dodging Bellamy-related magical incidents his entire adult life.

He offers one pastry to my mother without ceremony.

She takes it delicately. "Thank you, dear."

Then he holds the second one up to me. "Breakfast?"

I pinch the bridge of my nose. "Dad, that pastry just tried to commit a felony."

He shrugs, taking a bite. "Tastes fine."

My mother brushes crumbs from her blouse and smiles at me like none of this is strange. "So, lunch at one? You're coming, yes?"

I open my mouth to answer, then glance behind me as another tray wobbles in warning. I grab it quickly before the pastries get ideas.

"Yes," I say, steadying the cart. "I'll be there. I promise."

My father nods once, satisfied. "Good. We'll pick you up."

My mother pats my cheek again. "And wear something nice. Nothing enchanted this time."

"That was one time," I protest.

"That was three times," she corrects.

Dad finishes his pastry, wipes his fingers on a napkin Ellie hands him, and rests a warm, steady hand on my shoulder. "Happy birthday, sweetheart."

There's something grounding in the weight of it—something that makes the chaos around us feel briefly manageable.

"Thanks, Dad," I say softly.

They head toward the door, waving to Ellie and Miguel on their way out. As the bell jingles behind them, another cart shifts, threatening rebellion.

I set my hands on my hips.

"Absolutely not," I warn the pastries. "We are done with theatrics until at least ten."

The cart settles.

For now.

Chapter 4

Sayer

The office is exactly the way I left it—silent, orderly, and blissfully free of anyone attempting to discuss their feelings. I set my coat on the back of the chair, and take another slow sip of the latte the bakery witch made.

It's perfect.

I won't say that out loud. But it is.

The warmth spreads through me in a way I can't attribute entirely to caffeine, and I let out a quiet breath. Mornings are tolerable when they start like this. Predictable. Reliable. No one crying into legal documents yet.

I reach into the paper bag and pull out my everything bagel, still warm. The aroma hits immediately—salt, toasted dough, and an indecent amount of cream cheese. Exactly what I wanted. Exactly what I needed.

For the first time today, something like contentment settles in my chest. Not joy—Gods forbid—but something adjacent to "not awful." I sit down, unwrapping the bagel with the reverence of a man who knows this might be the high point of his day.

I take a bite. It's perfect too.

Of course it is. She always gets it right.

I'm halfway through chewing—and, yes, possibly smiling the smallest, most private smile a grown man can manage—when the front door of the office swings open with absolutely no regard for the fact that it is barely eight in the morning.

"Sayer?" Jackson's voice booms through the building like he's announcing a raid. "You alive in here or have you withered into a husk of bitterness and paperwork?"

I close my eyes briefly. There goes the peace.

Footsteps cross the floor outside my office—heavy, unhurried strides followed by the lighter, sharper cadence I've learned to associate with Leona. They appear in the doorway a moment later, Jackson filling most of the frame with his height and broad shoulders, his demon heritage close to the surface today in the faint ember-freckled glow scattered across his olive skin. Leona stands at his side, a full foot shorter and far more composed, her posture elegant and assessing, witch-gold catching subtly in her irises whenever the light hits just right.

They look like they stepped out of a chaotic rom-com where the side characters exist solely to annoy the protagonist. Which, unfortunately, is accurate.

"Oh good," Leona says, smiling in that deceptively sweet way she uses before delivering a verbal blow. "You're not dead. We'd have to close for the day, and that would ruin my schedule."

Jackson looks at the bagel in my hand, then at the coffee, then at my expression. His grin spreads slow and wide. "Is that... happiness? On your face?"

"No," I say flatly.

"It looks like happiness," Leona adds as she moves to hang up her coat. "Or what passes for happiness in your species."

"It's indigestion," I reply. "Go away."

Jackson laughs, dropping into the chair opposite my desk with the dramatic sigh of a man who enjoys ignoring boundaries. "You know, for someone who hates love, you sure spend a lot of time lingering next door."

"I do not linger," I correct him. "I acquire breakfast. And caffeine."

Leona raises a brow. "Every single morning."

"It's called consistency."

"It's called denial," she says smoothly.

Jackson leans forward, clasping his hands like he's about to deliver a sermon. "Anyway, we found someone for you."

"No," I say immediately.

"You haven't even heard the description yet," Leona argues.

"I don't need to. The answer is no."

Jackson's mouth quirks. "Interesting. You didn't say *absolutely not*. That's a softer no."

I glare at him. "Do not psychoanalyze my refusal."

Leona hops up to perch on the corner of my desk, nudging a perfectly aligned file out of place just to irritate me. "You can't keep rejecting blind dates on principle. It's deeply unnatural."

"I'm not rejecting them on principle," I say flatly. "I'm rejecting them because I don't want to go."

Jackson nods, delighted. "See? That's different. Before, it was 'this is a bad idea.' Now it's 'I personally object.' Emotional growth."

"There is no growth," I snap. "There is only refusal."

Leona smiles like she's already won. "Great. Then this one will be perfect practice."

"What's unnatural," I say, "is the idea that I need my employees matchmaking for me."

Jackson shrugs. "It's a hobby."

Leona gestures at him. "It keeps him out of trouble."

"That is demonstrably false," I mutter.

They both ignore me.

Leona softens slightly—just enough to look earnest without actually backing down. "Sayer, you're impossible, but you're not hopeless. You just need... practice."

"Love is not something one practices," I say. "It's a catastrophe people willingly sign up for."

Jackson slaps his knee like he's been told the funniest joke in the world. "This is why we love him."

"That is not mutual," I reply.

"You say that," Leona says, "but we both know you'd be lost without us."

I take another slow sip of my latte, because the alternative is admitting she's right.

Jackson glances toward the door. "Did you at least wish the bakery witch a happy New Year?"

"No," I say.

Leona smiles, knowing damn well why I didn't. "Of course you didn't. Heaven forbid you act like a human being."

"She doesn't need small talk," I say, returning to my bagel. "She needs efficiency."

"That woman needs a vacation," Jackson mutters.

"That woman," Leona adds, "tolerates you more than a rational person should."

"She tolerates my money," I correct. "And I tolerate her baked goods. It's a mutually beneficial arrangement."

Jackson leans back, looking entirely too pleased with himself. "I bet you smiled when you walked in."

"I did not," I say.

"You absolutely did," Leona counters.

"I assure you," I reply, "I am incapable of such a thing at this hour."

Jackson smirks. "You keep telling yourself that, boss."

I take another bite of my bagel, refusing to dignify that with a response.

Because the truth is, if I smile at anything, it's usually this moment right here—before the clients arrive, before the problems start, when my office is warm, my breakfast is perfect, and my staff is insufferable in the exact ways I've come to rely on.

Not that I'd ever tell them that.

Jackson opens his mouth—dangerously—and I know exactly where the conversation is going before he even starts.

"So, when you did talk to Francesca. You didn't wish her a happy new year. What about a happy birthd—"

He doesn't even finish speaking before every pen in the cup on my desk rattles like a small earthquake is happening only in my office.

All three of us stare at the pen cup.

The pens continue vibrating.

Leona blinks. "Is... that new?"

"No," I say sharply. "It's nothing."

Jackson squints at them. "It looks like something."

"It is *airflow*," I lie, reaching out to steady the cup. The moment my hand touches the desk, the pens stop like they weren't just reenacting a mild possession.

Leona crosses her arms. "That only happens when we bring her up."

"Coincidence," I snap.

Jackson snaps his fingers. "Maybe you two have—"

"Stop talking," I interrupt, holding up a hand.

He grins. "You're no fun."

"I'm not paid to be fun," I reply. "I'm paid to be competent, efficient, and unamused. Which brings me to my next point—Leona, we need to review the schedule."

She straightens automatically, shifting into professional mode. "Of course. You've got your settlement conference at eleven, then a client consultation at one. We need signatures on the Worthington file by end of day. And the deposition prep for tomorrow still needs your final review."

"Good," I say, nodding. "Print everything I'll need for the afternoon, organize the files by priority, and check if opposing counsel sent over the revised terms. They won't have, but we'll pretend optimism for thirty seconds."

Leona smirks but doesn't argue. "I'll get it done."

I turn to Jackson. "And you—research for the Worthington case, pull social media history, gather anything public that can be weaponized, and file the pretrial motions. You're also covering the preliminary hearing at three."

Jackson gives a mock salute. "On it, boss."

"Excellent," I say. "Now can we please have one morning without talking—"

"—about Fran?" he finishes, grinning like the demon half of him finds this deeply entertaining.

The second her name leaves his mouth, the lamp on the side table flickers violently. Once, twice—then the light bulb pops with a sharp crack.

Jackson jumps. "Okay, that one was definitely not airflow."

Leona lifts a brow. "Want to try that excuse again?"

I grit my teeth. "Old wiring."

Leona gestures toward the ceiling. "In a building renovated four years ago?"

"Faulty craftsmanship."

Jackson snorts. "Sure. Totally unrelated to the fact that the bakery witch sets off your office like a broken sorcerer's alarm every time she crosses your mind."

"She does *not* cross my mind," I huff.

The overhead light flickers.

All three of us look up.

"This is absurd," I say tightly.

Leona gives me a gentle, patronizing pat on the shoulder. "Of course it is, Sayer. That's a completely normal amount of denial."

Before I can argue—not that I have a coherent argument—a sharp knock hits the front door.

Jackson glances at the clock. "Uh-oh. It's eight-thirty. Who's scheduled this early?"

"No one," Leona says with a frown. "Your first appointment was supposed to be a phone consult at ten."

The knock comes again, more urgent.

"Perfect," I mutter. "That's never a good sign."

Leona opens the door, and a middle-aged man practically stumbles inside. His shirt is half buttoned, his hair is doing something desperate, and his eyes have the wild shine of someone on the brink.

"Mr. Valentine?" he gasps. "I need help. Immediately. My wife—she—she left this morning. New Year's Day. She said she wants a divorce. She took the dog. She took *our dog*."

Jackson whispers, "And so it begins."

The man barrels on, panicked. "She met someone. At a juice retreat. He teaches goat yoga. GOAT. YOGA."

I inhale slowly, letting the last thread of peace slip away. Leona gestures toward one of the chairs in the waiting area with professional calm. "Sir, if you'll have a seat, Mr. Valentine will be with you shortly."

He drops into the chair and immediately starts tearing through the complimentary mints from the bowl on the side table, popping them into his mouth like they're prescribed.

Jackson murmurs, "Happy New Year, boss."

I take another sip of my latte, savoring the brief illusion of control before setting the cup aside and straightening my jacket. From the doorway, I get a clear look at our first client of the year, still slumped in the waiting chair like gravity has personally offended him. He looks as though he hasn't slept since last year, which is technically true, but the hollowness under his eyes suggests the problem started well before midnight.

Leona rises smoothly from behind the desk and gestures down the short hall toward my office, already flipping open a fresh notepad as she walks. "Mr. Valentine is ready for you now," she says, her tone calm and professional in a way that immediately signals both competence and judgment.

The man scrambles to his feet, pockets half-full of crumpled receipts and poor decisions, while Jackson slips past us to retrieve the intake file. I step aside to let the client go first, following him toward my office and bracing myself for whatever version of holiday regret he's about to unload.

I take my seat across from the man and fold my hands on the desk.

"Alright," I say, keeping my tone steady, "let's start with the basics. Tell me your name."

The man straightens a little, chest still heaving with leftover panic. "Oh—yes. Sorry. I'm Dillon Harper."

"Good," I say with a nod. "And Dillon, I need you to start from the beginning. Take your time and walk me through everything that happened this morning."

Leona's pen hovers over the page, ready.

Dillon exhales shakily, rubs both hands over his face, and begins.

And just like that, the first official disaster of the new year is underway.

Chapter 5

Francesca

By the time my parents pull up in front of the bakery, I've already showered twice.

The first shower was to get rid of the whipped cream. The second was to remove the powdered sugar that detonated like a confectionary land mine thirty minutes later.

And the third disaster—an eclair catastrophe that somehow launched pastry cream across half the kitchen—was the final sign from the universe that I needed to evacuate the premises before something actually caught fire.

So yes, I showered. Thoroughly.

And now my hair is down, still damp at the ends, curling in places it only curls when it feels like mocking me. I don't normally wear it this way for family outings, but after this morning's parade of humiliation I don't have the energy to wrestle it into anything more complicated than "loose and barely functional."

My mother's eyes immediately widen when I slide into the back seat.

"Oh, Francesca." She presses a hand to her chest, looking delighted. "Your hair looks lovely."

"Thank you," I say, fastening my seat belt. "It's called 'I surrende red.'"

My father glances at me in the rearview mirror with a sympathetic grin. "Tough morning?"

"That depends," I say. "If the rubric is 'Did I survive?' then yes, wildly successful. If the rubric is anything else, less so."

"That bad?" he asks.

"Let's see," I reply, ticking items off on my fingers. "We had the whipped cream explosion, the powdered sugar bomb, an eclair firing squad, and a tray of raspberry scones that tried to make a break for the exit."

My mother turns, scandalized. "Why didn't you call?"

"What were you going to do?" I ask. "Bring holy water? Stage an intervention?"

She considers this. "Possibly."

Dad pulls away from the curb, merging into light traffic. "Maybe the magic's just acting up early this year."

"Maybe," I mutter. "Or maybe the universe is personally invested in making thirty-five as memorable as possible."

Mom pats my knee. "It's not all bad. You get lunch with us."

"That is the highlight," I admit.

"And," she adds casually, too casually, "I may have invited your sisters to join us."

I blink. "All of them?"

She nods like she's just announced the arrival of honored guests. "They insisted."

"Wonderful," I sigh. "Nothing like a birthday lunch where I'm the entertainment."

Dad chuckles under his breath. "You'll be fine. We're going somewhere quiet. Neutral territory."

I lean back in the seat, letting the tension slide off my shoulders as the city passes by outside the window. I didn't realize how loud the morning had been until I wasn't in it anymore. The bakery feels like a living thing this time of year—pulsing, buzzing, misbehaving like it's got a personal vendetta.

My phone buzzes with a message from Ellie. *We're okay! No more explosions so far! Lots of wiggling, though.*

Great. Wiggling. That's comforting.

Mom notices me checking my phone. "Everything alright at the bakery?"

"As long as nothing starts levitating in synchronization, we're fine."

My father glances back again. "You sure you don't want us to swing by after lunch?"

"I'm sure," I say. "If anything catastrophic happens, Harper will text me a single emoji of disapproval."

"And you'll know exactly what it means," Mom says, nodding with satisfaction.

She's not wrong.

Dad parks outside a small, cozy restaurant tucked on a quiet side street—a place my family's been going to since I was a teenager. Familiar. Warm. No pastries with intent to harm.

I open the door and step out, inhaling the calmer air. My hair shifts around my shoulders, still loose, still not fully dry. Mom beams at it like I've personally bestowed a gift upon her.

"You should wear it down more often," she says.

"I should survive my workdays more often," I reply.

She laughs, linking her arm through mine as we head toward the entrance.

"Let's at least start your birthday lunch without anything exploding," she says.

"That," I agree, "would be ideal."

The moment my parents and I step inside the restaurant, I spot my sisters at a round booth near the back. They're impossible to miss—Daphne waving both arms like she's trying to flag down a plane, Juniper cradling a steaming mug of tea the size of her face, and Cassia already halfway through organizing the salt and pepper shakers into some kind of tactical formation.

Great. They're in rare form.

"Birthday girl!" Daphne calls out, sliding over to make room. The motion jostles the entire table and a lemon slice promptly falls out of Juniper's tea. Juniper catches it midair without looking up.

I squeeze into the booth while Mom and Dad take the chairs opposite us. Menus are scattered everywhere. A basket of dinner rolls sits in the center—hovering about two inches off the table like it's considering a career change.

No one acknowledges it.

Cassia simply presses the basket down with the edge of the butter knife, and it settles like that's just what bread does.

Mom smiles warmly. "See? This is cozy."

"That basket levitated," I remind her.

She waves a hand. "Barely."

Daphne leans into me playfully. "Happy thirty-five, Fran. You look good. A little tired. A little traumatized. Very on-brand."

"Thank you," I reply dryly.

Juniper passes me a napkin. "You still have a little powdered sugar in your hair."

I run a hand through my curls and find, yes, there is indeed one last stubborn crystal. "Of course I do."

Dad opens his menu. "Alright, what is everyone having?"

Before anyone can answer, a fork just... slides off the table on its own and clinks to the floor. Cassia picks it up, sets it back, and then places her water glass on top of the napkin as if that's going to prevent it from wandering off again.

She doesn't comment. No one does. This is normal.

Mom glances around the table with a too-bright smile. "Now. We're here to celebrate Francesca's birthday—"

"And also," Cassia cuts in, "to establish that your magical incidents have officially hit concerning levels."

Juniper nods. "You've had more mishaps this morning than you usually have in the first two weeks."

Daphne adds, "You nearly died by pastry."

"I did not nearly die," I protest.

"A tray of raspberry scones attempted an escape," Daphne says, pointing at me. "That is intent."

Dad reaches for one of the rolls. The entire basket tries to dodge his hand like a startled cat. He simply grabs it out of the air, tears one open, and passes it to Mom without missing a beat.

Mom butters hers calmly. "Your father's right. Something is a little... heightened this year."

"I'm aware," I say, sitting straighter. "You don't need to stage an intervention."

Cassia looks pointedly at me. "Then consider this a birthday check-in."

"A forced one," Daphne clarifies.

"A caring one," Juniper amends.

"An unavoidable one," Mom finishes.

Dad clears his throat. "We love you, sweetheart, but your bakery has been acting like it's been on a sugar bender since dawn."

"And you nearly got drowned in whipped cream," Daphne reminds me again.

"That was one incident."

"It was three," Juniper corrects gently.

Cassia rests her elbows on the table, studying me with that sharp, analytical sister-sense she has. "Is anything bothering you? Are you overwhelmed? Overworked? Avoiding something?"

I take a long drink of my water. "My magic is just acting up, that's all. It's January. Happens every year."

Cassia lifts a brow. "Not like this."

A waiter arrives with a pitcher of water. As he pours into Daphne's glass, the stream briefly curves sideways toward me—like the water itself changed its mind halfway through—and Juniper guide's Daphne's cup beneath it without blinking.

The waiter doesn't notice. My family doesn't stop talking.

This is my life.

Daphne sighs loudly and leans her head on my shoulder. "We're not judging you. We're just worried."

"I'm fine," I insist.

Cassia tilts her head. "If you feel out of balance, your magic is going to respond accordingly."

Juniper sets her mug down carefully. "And lately your magic has been responding like it's trying to file a complaint."

Mom reaches across the table and pats my hand. "We just want to make sure you're happy, sweetheart."

I open my mouth to answer, but the basket of rolls lifts again—just a few inches—like it's nosy and wants to eavesdrop.

Dad snatches it mid-float and sets it firmly between the butter knife and the salt shaker.

"Stay," he orders the bread.

It obeys.

For now.

I blow out a breath. "I appreciate the concern. Really. But I'm okay. Just... dealing with the usual January chaos."

My sisters exchange looks—the kind that mean they don't believe me for a second.

They don't push. Juniper hooks her arm through mine, Daphne immediately steals a fry, and Cassia launches into a story about a client who tried to outmaneuver their own spell work. The levitating bread basket drifts quietly between us, unnoticed, like it knows better than to interrupt.

The table finds its balance. Daphne keeps sampling my plate. Juniper slips extra lemon slices into my water with quiet, purposeful intent. Cassia steers the conversation like a meeting she already controls. When a spoon inches toward freedom, Dad intercepts it without looking up. Mom continues buttering her roll. No one reacts.

Normal. Unfortunately.

We're halfway through dessert when Cassia finally sets her fork down and levels a look at me that makes my shoulders square on instinct. It's the look that means the casual part of the meal is over, and whatever comes next will be handled with charts, concern, and absolutely no mercy.

"Francesca," she says, tone edging into dangerous-big-sister territory, "we've been trying to be subtle—"

"You really haven't," I mutter.

"—but let's not pretend we don't all know what's happening."

Juniper nods sympathetically. "Your magic always spikes this time of year, but this morning? That was... *intense*."

"That was a cry for help," Daphne adds, licking frosting off her spoon.

Dad folds his hands calmly. "You're thirty-five today. That means the curse is getting stronger."

Mom sighs, soft but firm. "Sweetheart... the magic is reacting to you. To your choices. To your avoidance."

I blink slowly. "Avoidance of what?"

Cassia gives me a pointed stare that could cut through steel. "Dating."

Juniper smiles kindly. "Meeting someone."

Daphne leans forward, eyes bright. "Letting a person within one emotional zip code of you."

"I date," I protest.

All three of them answer in perfect, horrifying unison.

"No, you don't."

Juniper stirs her tea. "You cancel half the time, and when you don't cancel, you pick people who don't stand a chance."

"That's not true," I say.

Cassia lifts one brow. "Name the last date you went on."

I open my mouth. Nothing comes out.

Across from us, Mom gives me the gentlest, most devastating smile.

"Honey," she says, "no Bellamy has ever made it to thirty-five without finding their true love. The family curse gets worse the longer we avoid real connection. You know this."

Dad nods, adding quietly, "It's time you stop pretending you can outrun it."

Daphne points her spoon at me like she's delivering a verdict. "It is high time you stop avoiding dating."

Cassia nods. "The magic isn't subtle anymore."

Juniper squeezes my hand. "And neither are we."

I sink back against the booth, the weight of five Bellamys staring at me like they already have a spreadsheet titled *Operation Fix Francesca's Love Life.*

The basket of rolls rises an inch. Dad slams it gently back down.

My eye twitches.

"Fine," I say rolling my eyes, because arguing will only get me tackled emotionally. "I'll consider it."

Mom beams like I've just announced I'm getting married next week.

"That's all we ask," she says.

But the glint in Daphne's eyes tells me they're already planning something.

And for the first time today, I'm not entirely sure which is more dangerous— the magic...

...or my family.

Chapter 6

Sayer

By the time the fourth unexpected client leaves my office, I'm two minutes away from locking the door, turning off the lights, and letting everyone assume I fled the country. The stack of paperwork on my desk has evolved into something sentient. Motionless, but deeply threatening.

I lean back in my chair, pinch the bridge of my nose, and take a slow breath that does absolutely nothing to restore sanity. Today was supposed to be straightforward—one settlement conference, one consult, maybe a nap during lunch if the universe felt kind.

Instead, it turned into a revolving door of marital disasters.

Client Number Two arrived crying. Client Number Three arrived *together*, which should be illegal without prior notice. Client Number Four brought homemade muffins as a bribe, which I did not accept because I know better than to ingest baked goods from people who met during a sound bath.

My inbox is a graveyard. My calendar looks like a threat. And the pen I've been using keeps rolling an inch to the left every time I think about the bakery, which I am *not* thinking about.

I drop my forehead onto the stack of forms, debating whether it's too early in the year for a burnout-induced existential crisis.

A soft thud lands in front of me.

I lift my head just enough to see a familiar white to-go cup being placed on my desk with gentle finality.

Leona straightens, offering a mildly smug smile. "You looked like you were about to commit paperwork-related violence. Thought this might be safer."

I blink at the cup. "Is that—?"

"From next door," she says cheerfully. "Extra shot. Apparently you 'looked like you needed it.' Their words, not mine."

Magic shifts through the room like a breeze only I can feel. My pen jitters once—like it's excited.

I glare at it until it stops.

Leona watches me, amused. "You know, most people would just say thank you."

"I do thank you," I reply, reaching for the cup. "Internally."

She snorts. "For the record, internally is useless to the people who bring you coffee and manage your chaos."

I open the lid and breathe in the caramel and espresso—stronger this time, richer, the exact kind of thing capable of dragging me back from the brink. One sip and the frustration in my chest loosens just enough to feel human again.

Leona's eyes soften. "Long day?"

"Long year," I mutter.

"It's January first."

"Exactly."

She laughs under her breath, then moves a few stray folders into a neat stack because my stress levels apparently offend her sense of visual order. "Jackson and I can handle the Worthington paperwork. You need to step away from the desk before you start yelling at inanimate objects."

"I don't yell at—"

The pen rolls again.

I point at it. "Don't."

Leona gives me a knowing look. "Uh-huh. Completely stable."

I take another sip of coffee, ignoring both her tone and the fact that the cup is *suspiciously perfect*. A little too perfect. I know exactly who made it, and the thought alone is enough to make the lamp flicker once in warning.

Leona raises a brow. "Should I... get an electrician?"

"No."

"Should I call the landlord?"

"No."

She tilts her head. "Should I pretend I don't notice that the office acts possessed whenever the bakery witch comes up?"

"Yes," I say. "You should do exactly that."

She pats my desk twice. "Great talk, boss. Jackson and I will finish the filing."

As she heads for the door, she pauses and glances back.

"Hey, Sayer?"

I look up.

"You can keep pretending lunch, coffee, and casual human emotion don't affect you. But your office keeps tattling."

I stare at her and narrow my eyes in warning. "Go do your job."

She grins and disappears into the hallway.

I lean back in my chair, take a long, steady sip of the drink I definitely do not appreciate as much as I absolutely do, and close my eyes for a moment.

Just one moment.

The pen rolls another inch.

I consider throwing it out the window.

I'm halfway through the cup—finally feeling the caffeine settle into my bloodstream like a peacekeeping treaty—when the door to my office swings open again.

Jackson enters first, followed by Leona. They both look too composed, which is never a good sign.

Leona clears her throat. "Now that you've had your coffee..."

"Oh God," I mutter. "What now?"

Jackson closes the door behind them, which is an even worse sign. He crosses his arms, Leona clasps her notepad to her chest, and they stand in front of my desk like they're preparing to break national news.

Leona asks, "Do you want the bad news or the worse news first?"

"Neither," I say.

Jackson nods once. "Bad news it is."

Leona sighs dramatically. "You have a dinner date tonight."

I stare at them. "No. I do not."

"Yes, you do," Jackson says, far too cheerfully. "Seven o'clock. Reservations already confirmed."

"With whom?" I ask, already regretting the question.

Leona flips a page on her notepad. "A perfectly respectable person with a stable income, good hygiene, and no history of throwing drinks during arguments. At least, according to the file Jackson compiled."

"I am not going on a date," I say, enunciating each word. "Cancel it."

Jackson grins. "Already tried. They said the reservation is under *your* name and requires *your* voice to cancel it."

I rub my temples. "Of course it does."

Leona brightens with false optimism. "Look at it this way—you get a free dinner."

"I don't want a free dinner."

"You want to not be miserable," she says. "These are sometimes the same thing."

I open my mouth to argue, but Jackson holds up a hand.

"That's the lesser evil," he says. "Now for the actual problem."

"Fantastic," I mutter.

Leona reaches into her folder and pulls out a thick envelope—cream-colored, wax-sealed in shimmering gold. That kind of gold. The kind that makes my teeth clench on instinct.

She sets it gently on my desk like it might explode.

Jackson says, "This came by courier."

I go very still.

Leona folds her arms. "From Cupid Headquarters."

I stare at the seal. The temperature in the room seems to drop a degree.

"No," I say flatly. "Absolutely not."

Jackson winces. "We didn't open it."

"Good," I say. "Because I don't want it in here."

Leona uses the tip of her pen and nudges it an inch closer to me. "Unfortunately, it's addressed to you."

"I refuse delivery," I announce nudging back towards her.

"You can't," Jackson says. "The courier said it binds once it's placed in your possession."

"It binds?" I repeat. "Since when?"

Leona gestures to the envelope. "Since whatever you ran from fifteen years ago decided to find you again."

Magic shifts in the corners of the room like a draft through a closed window.

My pen rolls. My lamp flickers. The envelope glows faintly.

I glare at it with the full force of a man who absolutely does not want the past returning with bureaucratic enthusiasm.

Jackson takes a cautious step back. "So... dinner date or interdimensional summons. Those were your two choices. And you got both."

I pinch the bridge of my nose. "I hate this day."

Leona pats the corner of my desk. "We know."

Jackson nods solemnly. "We truly do."

"And yet you brought me both pieces of information."

Leona shrugs. "We're efficient."

The envelope pulses once.

I swear under my breath and grab my coffee like it's the only thing keeping me tethered to reality.

Of course. Of course the Season of Love would drag the past back by the throat.

And of course it would happen today.

The envelope sits in the middle of my desk with the smug confidence of something that knows it has already won. The wax seal glints faintly in the light, and a soft hum vibrates through the paper—just enough to raise the hair along my arms.

Leona and Jackson have migrated toward the door, giving me space like I'm about to detonate. Which, considering the glowing mail, is not an unreasonable precaution.

Leona folds her arms. "You don't have to open it right this second."

Jackson adds, "Though if you don't, it might escalate. The courier seemed extremely clear on that part."

They both look at me expectantly.

I drag a hand down my face. "For the record, if this…this thing pulls me into some magical vortex, I'm blaming both of you."

Leona nods solemnly. "That's fair."

Jackson gestures to the envelope. "It's humming now. I feel like that's a sign."

The hum deepens, and the golden seal pulses like a heartbeat.

Perfect. Just perfect.

With a muttered curse, I break the seal.

The glow erupts, swallowing the room in a bright surge of gold. The air compresses around me, tugging hard enough to knock the breath from my chest.

"Oh, hell—"

The world tilts sharply.

My office dissolves.

For a split second, I'm suspended in a swirl of light and pressure, the kind of magical transportation that always feels like someone grabbed the back of my skull and yanked. My stomach rolls in protest. My balance vanishes.

And then my feet slam down onto solid ground.

I catch myself against the nearest object—a marble cherub statue wearing rhinestone sunglasses—because of course even the décor here is obnoxious.

When the spinning in my head settles, I straighten and take in my surroundings.

Cupid Headquarters.

Everything is aggressively pink. Pink marble floors polished to a mirror shine, pink quartz columns rising in sweeping arcs, pink clouds floating lazily overhead like the ceiling itself has a sweet tooth. Glitter spills gently from nowhere, settling on my shoulders like a deeply unwanted welcome.

A familiar voice rings out behind me.

"Well. Look what the karmic cat dragged in."

I turn to find Lorian Everhold standing a few steps away, wings unfolded in a showy display he absolutely practiced. His suit is a pastel nightmare. His smile is worse.

"Sayer Valentine," he says, drawing my name out with theatrical delight. "Welcome back."

"I'm not back," I tell him. "I was kidnapped by stationary."

He waves a hand. "Details."

I dust glitter off my coat. It refills instantly. Of course it does. "Why am I here, Lorian?"

His expression brightens like he's been waiting all morning to deliver the punchline. "Because you abandoned an assignment fifteen years ago, and the Council finally noticed."

My jaw tightens. "Which assignment?"

"The last file you received before you quit." His smile turns sharp. "The one you didn't complete."

My stomach drops.

Of course it would be *that* file. The Bellamy assignment—the one I ignored for fifteen years, shoved into the bottom drawer the day I walked out, and pretended never existed.

Lorian clasps his hands together, positively glowing with self-satisfaction. "The High Council would like an explanation. Preferably something better than 'I quit mid-mission to become a divorce atto rney.'"

He turns toward the towering heart-shaped doors ahead, which part with a wash of unnecessary, shimmering drama.

"Come on," he says over his shoulder. "They're eager to hear why you left a Bellamy unresolved."

I inhale slowly, bracing myself.

Of course. As if today wasn't already doing its best impression of a cosmic joke.

Chapter 7

Francesca

By Friday night, I'm convinced the universe has been testing the structural limits of my sanity.

It's been a full week of magical nonsense—nothing catastrophic, but enough small disasters to keep me on edge. A mixer that turned itself on and tried to march off the counter. A batch of scones that rotated like a lazy Susan every time I looked away. A tray of macarons that hummed in harmony for an entire hour. And every time something happened, my well-meaning family brought it back to the same conversation.

"No Bellamy has ever made it to thirty-five without meeting their cupid." "Are you sure no one contacted you at twenty?" "It's strange you didn't get a match file." "Maybe the universe is improvising…" "You need to start dating, Fran. Something's clearly building."

By Thursday, I seriously considered faking a retreat to a silent monastery.

But no. Instead, I'm here. At a restaurant Daphne picked. Wearing a red sweater that miraculously survived the week without being set on fire, stained, or animated. And because Ellie insisted my "heart chakra needed grounding," I'm wearing the crystal necklace she gifted me—a piece that has already tangled itself twice since I left the house.

My date, Brandon, stands as I approach the table. He's neat, well-dressed, and polite in that steady, old-fashioned way that suggests he was raised by people who still send thank-you cards. He pulls out my chair with a small smile.

"Fran?" he asks. "That's me," I say, returning the smile as I sit. "Thanks for waiting. The bakery was a little… eventful."

He chuckles, and before I can elaborate, my water glass slides exactly two inches to the left.

Brandon glances at it, then calmly moves it back without a flicker of alarm.

I blink. Most strangers panic when the magic gets playful. He doesn't even hesitate.

We talk through the drink order and appetizer, and for the first few minutes everything feels almost peaceful. Then my silverware rearranges itself into precise parallel lines, like it's preparing for a military inspection.

Brandon observes it with mild interest and then looks up at me.

"Does that happen often?" he asks.

"Only during a very special time of year," I say. "January and mid February, my magic likes to... express itself."

"Family thing?"

"You could call it that."

He considers this, then nods as if it all makes perfect sense. Meanwhile, my bread plate rotates a full quarter turn like a lazy carousel, and he doesn't even blink. Our food arrives—miraculously without incident—and I find myself relaxing a little. Brandon is easy to talk to. He listens more than he interrupts. He smiles often enough that it feels genuine, not performative. And above all, he doesn't react to the magical ripples around us as though I'm possessed.

When the candle flickers, flares, and dies with a dramatic puff of smoke, he only lifts one brow.

"Should I be concerned?" he asks.

"That depends," I say, "on your definition of normal."

"My definition is very flexible tonight."

"Then no. You're fine."

The lights above our table choose that exact moment to go out—only our table, of course—and the rest of the restaurant continues unaffected, bathed in warm ambient glow. Our small pocket of darkness feels intentional, like the magic is trying to be subtle and failing miserably.

Brandon laughs softly. "I'll take that as a yes."

I cover my face with my hands for a moment, torn between embarrassment and resignation. "This is just the curse acting up. It's been a week."

"A curse?" he asked, his eyes locking on mine.

"A family one," I explained. "It's a long story. Lots of dramatic history."

Between sips, he mentions, "I like dramatic history."

This earns an involuntary laugh out of me, the first real one I've had in days. The waiter replaces our lightbulb with the kind of weary smile that suggests this is not his first Bellamy-adjacent shift. Brandon carries on as though nothing at all is unusual.

For a moment, I let myself enjoy it—the company, the conversation, the unexpected comfort of someone who doesn't flinch at the chaos orbiting me. Maybe this date won't end in a magical outburst or a polite "I had a great time" followed by ghosting.

But then, beneath the table, my chair gives a small, unmistakable shudder, like it's about to reenact an earthquake drill. I plant both heels firmly on the floor before it can escalate.

Brandon notices, eyes warming. "You sure you're alright?"

"I'm fine," I say, forcing a smile. "This is basically a normal Friday for me now."

He laughs gently. "I'm glad you still came."

I settle back, letting myself breathe for a moment. He really is sweet. Steady. Kind. And I want this to feel right. I want to stop disappointing my family. I want the curse to stop escalating like it's preparing for doomsday.

But under the table, a slow, creeping prickle builds along my skin—an instinctive tug that feels like the magic is listening.

It reminds me of what my family kept repeating:

No Bellamy ever makes it to thirty-five without their cupid showing up.

Something's off this year.

If your magic is acting like this, it's reacting to something.

I try to push the thoughts away, but they linger like the hum of electricity. And as Brandon continues telling me about his job—something about finance or event planning, I can't remember—an uneasy truth settles in my stomach.

He's pleasant, charming and remarkably normal.

But deep down, beneath the candlelight and the polite conversation, I can feel it. My magic isn't paying attention to him at all.

Conversation carries us comfortably through the first half of the meal. Brandon is easy to talk to—pleasant, attentive, unfazed by the occasional magical twitch that keeps slipping through the cracks of my control. For the first time all week, the air around me feels a little less tense.

Then his phone vibrates against the table.

He glances down, and in that brief moment something in his expression shifts. It's nothing dramatic—a flicker in his eyes, the quick tightening of his jaw—but noticeable enough that it pulls my attention. Whatever he sees, it stops him cold.

When he looks up again, the change is gone. Smoothed over. Replaced with a practiced smile that feels a touch too deliberate.

"You alright?" I ask lightly, giving him an out if he needs it.

"Everything's perfect," he replies, and though the answer comes easily, something in his voice doesn't quite match it.

Before I can say anything else, the phone buzzes again. Then again. A steady, insistent rhythm that makes the water in his glass tremble. Brandon doesn't reach for it this time—he simply turns it over, face-down, and presses his palm against it to muffle the sound.

"You can take the call," I offer, because ignoring something that persistent feels... strange.

He shakes his head, eyes still on me rather than the phone. "It's nothing urgent. I'm here."

But the phone has other opinions. It lights up repeatedly beneath his hand, glowing through the thin layer of linen like a heartbeat trying to get his attention. The magic around me prickles in quiet response—as if it, too, senses the tension he's trying to hide.

The device rings next. Not a vibration this time, but a sudden, bright sound that cuts through the restaurant's soft background chatter. Brandon silences it immediately, jaw tightening just enough that I know he's holding something back.

The moment hangs between us—not uncomfortable, but undeniably odd—until the waiter arrives with our entrees. The interruption snaps the tension, drawing both our attention to plates that look beautifully normal, gloriously uneventful.

The flickering stops as the lights above our table settle. The magic surrounding me relaxes, like a person easing their shoulders after pretending to be unaware of what just happened.

Brandon thanks the waiter, picks up his fork, and resumes the conversation as if nothing unusual has happened. And to his credit, he shifts back into that same easy rhythm he had earlier—asking about my sisters, the bakery, the curse, all with genuine curiosity. His smile seems real this time. His voice steady.

If I hadn't seen that first moment—the initial flick of worry, the too-bright recovery—I might have let myself relax completely.

But his phone keeps lighting up silently beside him. One call. Then another. Then another.

He doesn't reach for the phone again. It stays face down beside his plate, his fingers resting on it with casual restraint, as if proximity alone might keep it quiet. Whatever tension flickered earlier smooths back into the same composed ease he's carried all evening, his attention apparently fixed on me and the meal between us.

Still, the longer the screen pulses faintly beneath his hand, the more something stirs under my skin. It's a low, familiar awareness—less alarm than instinct—like the curse clearing its throat. Dinner carries on without disruption, conversation easy, the room warm and unremarkable, but beneath it all I feel a steady tug in my chest. Bellamys learn early to listen to that sensation. Whatever's demanding his attention isn't nothing, and it isn't finished with us yet.

We're halfway through the entrée when the first woman approaches the table.

She's stunning—silky dark hair, sleek dress, the sort of confidence that announces itself long before she reaches us. She stops beside Brandon with a tight smile that doesn't come anywhere close to her eyes.

"There you are," she says, ignoring me completely. "I've been calling you."

Brandon stiffens. "Not now, Marcy."

My fork pauses halfway to my mouth.

Before I can process her name, another woman appears behind her. This one is tall, elegant, blonde—movie star cheekbones and a glare sharp enough to slice citrus.

"Unbelievable," she snaps. "I told you not to stand me up again."

Brandon inhales, slow and pained. "Chloe, I really don't—"

A third woman arrives, practically vibrating with outrage.

"Are you kidding me? You said we were exclusive!"

The restaurant freezes. Conversations falter. A glass clinks somewhere and is immediately set down again, like no one wants to be caught holding evidence.

Brandon leans back, rubbing a hand over his face with the resigned focus of a man mentally drafting his own obituary. "Ladies," he says carefully, "I can explain."

"Oh, I'm sure you can," Marcy replies, her smile sharpening.

"Yes," Chloe adds, folding her arms. "Please. Enlighten us."

The third woman gestures wildly. "Same."

Brandon looks between them, then glances at me with an apologetic wince that does *nothing* to soften the absurdity unfolding in front of me.

"Well," he says dryly, "if one more shows up, I'll have the full week."

I stare at him.

They stare at him.

The *entire restaurant* stares at him.

My magic, already simmering from earlier, gives a sharp tug in my chest like it's offended on principle.

Chloe gasps. "Is he... joking about this?"

"He is," I say quietly, "and I'm starting to understand why his phone was having a meltdown."

Brandon lifts his hands in surrender. "In my defense—"

But none of the women are interested in hearing it. They all start talking at once—accusations, demands, disbelief—while Brandon attempts to negotiate in the verbal equivalent of a hurricane.

I sit very still, watching the storm hit.

A fork slides off the table by itself and clatters to the floor. My candle sputters. My chair shifts half an inch like it's trying to drag me away from the disaster for my own protection.

And honestly? It has a point.

Brandon tries to stand. All three women block him with synchronized fury. One of them even snaps, "You told me we were married in spirit!"

He chokes on his own breath. "I say a lot of things in spirit."

Of all the magic-related catastrophes I've ever experienced during a date, this one is... refreshingly mundane.

But also incredibly humiliating. And possibly dangerous, depending on which one of these women owns a taser.

I clear my throat. "Brandon, I think this is where I leave."

He turns to me with something like desperation. "Francesca—wait—"

But the universe, my magic, and basic human self-preservation all agree for once.

Nope.

I rise from my seat, carefully step over the fork that has now skittered halfway across the floor, and give the group a polite smile that takes absolutely all of my emotional energy.

"Good luck sorting out... whatever this is."

Then my candle abruptly flares, sending a thin ribbon of flame straight upward like it wants to punctuate the moment with dramatic lighting.

One of the women gasps. Brandon flinches. The surrounding tables take a collective step back.

I murmur, "Sorry. That's just me," and make a swift, dignified escape before the magic decides to escalate.

Chapter 8

Sayer

The Council chamber hasn't changed in fifteen years, which is deeply unfortunate. The massive circular room is carved from rose quartz polished within an inch of its existence, haloed by floating lanterns shaped like soft, glowing hearts. The lanterns pulse in perfect unison—an unnecessary flourish that feels aggressively smug.

The Council themselves sit behind a sweeping dais of gold-veined marble, wings unfurled in varying degrees of sanctimonious self-importance. I recognize each one. I had hoped they'd retired. Or died. Or been smited by particularly poetic irony.

No such luck.

Lorian escorts me to the center of the room with the triumphant air of someone delivering a captured fugitive.

"Sayer Valentine," coos Councilor Aurelia, her voice dripping honey over steel. "Welcome back."

I school my expression into something that resembles professionalism. "To be clear, I did not return voluntarily. Your summons teleported me mid-day and in direct violation of workplace safety standards."

Lorian elbows me discreetly. "You're not helping."

"Not trying to."

Councilor Vesper steeples his fingers. "We have reviewed your former caseload, Valentine. It appears one file remains unresolved."

My jaw tightens. "So I've been told."

"The Bellamy assignment," Aurelia says, as if the name alone carries weight. "A highly time-sensitive, deeply magical line with a long history of celestial entanglement. And you abandoned it."

"I left the entire organization," I remind them. "A full resignation should have discharged all open files."

"It would have," Vesper says, "had the assignment not been marked as a priority convergence case."

My stomach knots. "A convergence case? You're telling me you withheld that information fifteen years ago?"

Aurelia's wings flutter faintly. "Would it have changed your decision to flee?"

"Yes."

"No."

Lorian and I answer at the same time. Only one of us is lying and it's not Lorian.

Vesper clears his throat. "Regardless, the situation has escalated. The cursed bloodline in question has reached a critical threshold. We require the match resolved."

I drag a hand down my face. "Why now? It's been fifteen years."

Aurelia tilts her head with serene menace. "The Bellamy girl has reached thirty-five."

I freeze.

Thirty-five. The upper limit before the curse turns unpredictable. The age no Bellamy has crossed without intervention.

Perfect.

"So what exactly are you demanding?" I ask, already irritated by the answer.

Vesper lifts a scroll—thin, official, glowing faintly with enforcement magic. "You have until midnight on February fourteenth to complete the match."

A soft ringing fills the room—the chime of binding magic being invoked.

"And if I don't?"

Aurelia smiles the way some people smile before delivering tragic news they've been looking forward to. "Then you will be reinstated into active duty."

The room feels suddenly smaller. "Absolutely not."

"You will also," Vesper continues, "have every divorce case you've filed in your mortal career nullified."

I stare at him. "You're joking."

"We do not joke," Aurelia says primly.

"So what? You want to... undo fifteen years of legal work?"

Vesper nods. "Their marriages will revert to the state they were in on the Valentine's Day preceding their divorce filings."

My vision goes flat with horror.

"You'd revert their lives?" I ask. "Their finances? Their custody arrangements? Some of these people have remarried!"

Aurelia clasps her hands. "All the more reason to finish your task."

"This is extortion," I mutter.

"This is incentive," Vesper corrects.

I take a slow breath, trying to rein in the sudden surge of anger shoving up my spine. "You're threatening to unravel hundreds of lives because I didn't want to be your magical errand boy anymore."

Aurelia's expression doesn't waver. "Magic is balance, Valentine. You left an imbalance. It is time to correct it."

I want to argue. To fight. To point out how catastrophically irresponsible it would be to rewind the lives of people who came to me desperate, broken, and trying to rebuild.

But the enforcement magic already hums through the air, circling me like a barely leashed storm.

"If I complete this assignment," I say slowly, "my cases remain untouched?"

"Correct."

"And I don't get dragged back into service?"

Aurelia nods. "You may return to your mortal profession unimpeded."

I hate this. I hate every inch of this place. I hate that the one file I abandoned is now the linchpin to hundreds of people's happiness.

And I hate—truly hate—that the Bellamy assignment is the one waiting for me.

Because Bellamys are complicated. Because their magic is volatile. Because fate loves them a little too loudly.

And because I already know exactly which Bellamy this file belongs to.

I exhale slowly. "Fine. I'll take the timeline. But after that, I'm done."

Aurelia smiles like she's already won. "We never doubted you."

Lorian pats my arm. "Congratulations. You're back on the clock."

If my glare held physical force, he'd be ash.

I should have known the conversation wasn't over. The Council never dismisses anyone gracefully; they prefer pomp, ceremony, and some deeply unnecessary display of power.

Aurelia glances at Vesper, and he gives a subtle nod. The lanterns overhead brighten, casting the chamber in a rose–gold shimmer that raises every alarm I have.

Lorian steps closer, expression softening. "Sayer... you should brace yourself."

"For what?" I ask, already irritated.

Aurelia lifts her hand.

Magic snaps through the room like a whip.

A sharp, electric pressure clamps between my shoulder blades—so sudden and so intense I stagger forward, catching myself on the edge of the dais. For a heartbeat, the sensation is simply pain, hot and deep and old. Then something beneath my skin shifts.

Locks unfasten. Bindings I forced there fifteen years ago begin to give. Magic I refused to touch stirs like a beast waking up. As I grit my teeth, a low sound ripping out of my throat.

"Stop—" But the word breaks apart as a white-hot bolt radiates down my spine.

Lorian murmurs, "Just breathe, alright? You can't keep them folded forever."

"My wings are none of—"

Pain lances through me again, cutting the sentence short. It isn't sharp, not exactly—it's the deep, bone-heavy ache of something cramped for too long being forced out of confinement. Like someone cracking every vertebrae of my spine at once after years of immobility.

A violent shudder rips through my back. Then another.

And then—with a sound like tearing silk and shattering glass—my wings unfurl.

They snap open in a rush of light and force, flooding the air with a surge of power I haven't felt since the day I walked away. The release is overwhelming—pain, yes, sharp and biting—but there's relief braided through it too, a flood of breath I didn't realize I'd been holding for over a decade. Air moves around them, through them, across feathers that haven't tasted magic in years.

I brace both palms on my knees, breathing hard. Sweat beads along my temple. The wings stretch again, instinctively, shaking off the stiffness of long imprisonment.

Lorian winces sympathetically. "Yeah... that part hurts."

Aurelia watches, serene as an executioner. "You sealed them forcibly when you abandoned your post. You couldn't maintain that suppression under a Council summons."

"Then you should consider redesigning your summons," I say, voice rough. "Not everyone enjoys involuntary spinal explosions."

Vesper ignores the complaint entirely. "Now that you are restored to full capacity, we can proceed."

I glare at all of them. "For the record, that was a violation of at least three celestial labor codes."

Aurelia's smile is pleasant and utterly insincere. "And yet here you stand. Whole."

"Debatable." I snarl.

My wings twitch, stretching behind me like they're testing whether they still exist. I want nothing more than to fold them away again, bury them back under skin and stubbornness—but they refuse to obey. They're awake now. Alert. Irritated.

And they remember this place as well as I do.

I straighten slowly, shoulders still tense. "If you expect me to agree to your terms, I want them in writing."

The Council shares a collective look. Offended. Surprised. Maybe impressed.

Vesper arches a brow. "Writing?"

"Yes," I say flatly. "A binding contract. Signed. Sealed. No hidden clauses, no open-ended language. If you want this resolved, I want proof you won't yank me back into service the moment it's convenient."

Aurelia sighs as if I've asked her to handwrite an essay. "Mortals and their paperwork."

"I'm not mortal," I remind her. "But I am an attorney. Humor me."

Lorian mutters under his breath, "Oh, this is going to be fun."

Vesper reaches into the shimmering air and pulls out a scroll—fresh, blank, humming with enforcement magic. "Then let us craft the terms."

The lanterns dim. The chamber shifts. The contract hovers between us, parchment glowing faintly, waiting to be written.

And with my wings still aching and spread behind me, every feather bristling with old resentment, I prepare to negotiate with the very institution I ran from.

Because if they think they're getting one more ounce of compliance from me without ironclad documentation?

They've forgotten exactly how stubborn I am.

The Council straightens with the kind of collective focus that suggests they expected me to sign whatever they handed me without question.

Idiots.

I crack my knuckles, wings stretching behind me with a stiff, irritated sweep. "Let's get started."

For the next stretch of time—minutes, hours, or possibly whole geological eras judging by my mounting annoyance—we negotiate.

And when I say *negotiate*, I mean I drag the High Council of Celestial Matchmaking through the kind of point-by-point legal dissection most mortals only see in nightmares.

Aurelia begins with sweeping, lofty phrasing about "reinstatement of cosmic balance" and "the sacred duty of rekindling destined bonds."

I rewrite it to: "Sayer Valentine will complete the assigned match, singular, not plural."

Vesper attempts to slip in the phrase "and all associated threads of alignment."

I cross it out. "No vague destiny nonsense."

Lorian snorts behind the Council table. "This is why he was terrible at the job."

"And spectacular at my job now," I shoot back.

We move on.

Aurelia dictates a line about me returning to service "should the Council find performance lacking."

"No," I say immediately. "Absolutely not. You get one match. One. And you don't get to grade me afterward like this is some celestial performance review."

"That clause is standard," Vesper insists.

"And in my contract, it's gone."

The scroll adjusts accordingly.

They try again.

"Failure to perform assigned duties," Aurelia begins, "will result in reinstatement—"

"Put a pin in reinstatement," I say. "That's threat language. We're not using threat language."

Vesper scowls. "It is not a threat. It is a consequence."

"Then write it like a consequence, not an ultimatum."

We debate compensatory terms next—something the Council apparently never imagined a cupid would request. I add protections for my legal caseload, my mortal identity, and my office. I insist on immunity from recall outside the specific parameters of this assignment.

Aurelia's left eye twitches.

Finally, Vesper rolls his shoulders and tries again, slower this time. "In the event that the Bellamy case—"

"*The* Bellamy case," I correct. "Singular."

He exhales. "Fine. The singular case... if it remains unresolved by midnight, February fourteenth, you will be returned to active service."

I don't like the phrasing, but it's at least clear. "And all divorces I have handled remain binding?"

"Yes," Aurelia says with an edge of impatience. "Assuming you fulfill your obligation."

Good. Good. This is almost tolerable.

The scroll reconfigures itself, words weaving into place in shimmering ink.

And then—just as we're finalizing the last page—Vesper clears his throat in that deeply suspicious way only bureaucrats possess.

"There is one final clause," he says. "Simply a formality."

My eyes narrow. "Define formality."

"An availability provision," he replies smoothly. "Should *other* Bellamy cases arise with direct relevance to the one at hand, you may be consulted."

My jaw tightens. "Consulted. Not conscripted."

"Of course," Aurelia says in a tone that absolutely means nothing of the sort. "A brief, ancillary responsibility. Nothing more."

Lorian shoots me a warning look, but I'm focused on the words forming across the scroll.

"...and he shall remain available for auxiliary matters pertaining to Bellamy lineage alignments, where such matters directly support the successful completion of the primary assignment."

It sounds reasonable. Too reasonable. But right now, I'm juggling wings I haven't used in fifteen years, a deadline that could unravel hundreds of mortal lives, and a Council that delights in being vague. I don't have the luxury of fighting over a clause that reads like logistical support.

"If it's strictly related to this case," I say slowly, "fine."

Aurelia beams. "Wonderful."

The scroll seals itself with a soft flare of gold, then floats into my hands. The magic binds. The contract is set. And somewhere deep in the room, a bell chimes.

The Council rises in unison.

"Your assignment begins immediately," Vesper announces.

My wings flex in irritation, catching the glow of the lanterns. "Then send me back."

Lorian opens a portal, shimmering and heart-shaped with entirely too much theatrical flair.

"Brace yourself," he says. "Re-entry's never elegant."

I step toward the light, contract in hand, wings aching and unfurled.

"Don't worry," I mutter. "I don't expect elegance from any of you."

And then the magic surges, pulling me home.

Chapter 9

Francesca

Walking through my front door feels like stepping out of someone else's life and back into my own. The air inside is warm and familiar, touched with the faint sweetness of vanilla from the batch of test cookies I left cooling this morning. My shoes get kicked off somewhere near the entryway, the kind of graceless toss that says I am absolutely done being a functioning adult.

The cute date outfit goes straight onto the closest chair. Pajamas replace it—my softest flannel bottoms and a sweatshirt so broken-in it's practically a second skin. My hair comes down, then goes up again into a messy bun that mirrors my emotional state: unstable, but holding for now.

The microwave hums, warming last night's pasta until garlic fills the small space. The couch welcomes me like an old friend, blanket waiting in a crumpled heap, cushions molded to the shape of every Bellamy meltdown I've ever had. I curl into my preferred corner and inhale the first forkful of pasta like it's therapy.

Naturally, that's when my phone chooses to buzz.

A group video request flashes onto the screen. My sisters. Because of course they'd schedule themselves around my date like it was a sporting event.

I accept.

Three faces pop up instantly, each a different brand of chaos.

Daphne reclines across her couch wearing a teal face mask that glows under her lamp. Popcorn litters the cushions like confetti. Her cat, who may or may not be in a coma, sleeps at her feet.

Juniper looks like a cozy woodland creature—wrapped in a thick knitted blanket, tea steaming beside her, soft amber light behind her creating a halo effect she absolutely doesn't need.

Cassia sits upright at her desk, hair pinned neatly, posture militant. Her background is a shrine to organization: labeled bins, straightened books, a planner already open to a page titled *Francesca Debrief.*

Daphne leans close enough for her nose to dominate the screen. "You're home already. This smells like drama. Talk."

"Alright," I say, twirling pasta. "He had three girlfriends."

Cassia inhales her water and immediately regrets it. Juniper splashes tea onto her blanket. Daphne drops an entire handful of popcorn.

"Three?" Daphne shrieks. "As in—plural? Catch-them-all levels of plural?"

"Yes," I say. "All of them gorgeous. All furious. All convinced they were his one-and-only. One told said they were 'married in spirit,' which honestly explains more than I wish it did."

Cassia rubs her temples, already emotionally exhausted on my behalf. "Tell me you didn't get caught in the fallout."

"Only long enough to realize they all knew his schedule better than his calendar app. And then I escaped before my magic decided to contribute."

Juniper's voice softens. "How bad was the magic?"

The memory drifts back—flickering lights, a candle that tried to audition for a pyrotechnics show, cutlery vibrating like tuning forks.

"Not disastrous," I say. "But... aware. Restless. Like it was listening for something outside the room."

Daphne raises a brow. "Maybe your cupid finally woke up from a fifteen-year nap. Like... 'Oops, missed my cue by a decade.'"

Cassia is already typing with frightening speed. "Or the original match assignment was interrupted. There's precedent for cosmic interference, and if the curse is escalating—"

"Cass," I warn.

She holds up a hand. "I'm just gathering data."

Juniper tucks her blanket closer, worry softening her features. "Your magic doesn't usually behave like this without a reason."

"I know," I admit quietly. "It feels different this year. Stronger. Sharper. Like it's waiting for something."

"Or someone," Daphne singsongs in the least helpful tone possible.

"Absolutely not," I mutter.

"That wasn't a denial," Cassia notes.

"It wasn't an invitation either." I retort.

The three of them exchange looks—sister-silent looks that communicate volumes and promise future meddling.

Daphne claps her hands together. "Okay, regroup. New strategy. Tomorrow we—"

"No," I cut in immediately.

"Yes," all three of them reply with terrifying synchronicity.

Cassia taps her keyboard. "I've already made a spreadsheet for candidate screening."

Juniper smiles sweetly. "We just want you to be happy, love."

Heat flushes my cheeks—not embarrassment exactly, but the soft ache of being known too well. The blanket slides against my legs, comforting and familiar. The steam from my pasta curls into the air like a warm sigh.

Before I can get a word in, my phone buzzes again—one of those sharp, insistent vibrations that cuts straight through the noise of my sisters' overlapping voices. A banner flashes across the top of the screen from a number I've never seen before, and something in my chest pulls tight.

"Hold on," I say, shifting the phone slightly. "I just got a message."

Daphne leans so far into her camera I can see the individual sparkles in her face mask. "If that man is texting to apologize, I swear I will personally ghostwrite your reply."

Cassia lifts a brow. "Check if it's Calamity Ben. He's overdue for one of his... reappearances."

Juniper tilts her head gently. "It wouldn't be surprising."

"Let's just... see," I murmur, swiping open the notification.

The moment the message expands across the screen, everything in me stills.

A delicate, iridescent crest glows at the top—elegant lines woven together in a pattern I haven't seen since childhood stories and whispered warnings. The lettering beneath it gleams faintly, as if lit from within.

This isn't a prank. This isn't mortal.

A cold ripple moves across my skin.

Daphne squints. "Okay, what is that face? Did he send something gross? Do we need to bleach your phone?"

"It's not him." My voice sounds distant, even to me. "And it's not Ben."

Cassia sits straighter. "Then who is it?"

A breath steadies in my lungs. "The Celestial Matchmaking Headquarters."

The reaction is instant, but not explosive—not yet. It's the quiet kind of shock, the kind that makes three very different women fall completely still at the same time.

Juniper blinks slowly, as if waiting for me to add a "just kidding."

Cassia's mouth parts, surprise slipping through the cracks in her usual composure.

Daphne goes very quiet, which is frankly more alarming than her screaming.

I clear my throat and read the message aloud, hoping it will somehow make more sense spoken:

"Your file has been reviewed and updated by CMHQ. Please expect contact from your assigned Cupid within 48 hours. We apologize for the delay and are committed to resolving your match as quickly as possible."

The words hang there a moment, suspended between all of us.

And then the Bellamy household chain reaction hits.

Daphne lets out a sound so sharp and startled that her husband, Leo, appears in the doorway behind her wearing pajama pants and concern. "Honey? What happened? Did someone die or is this just family magic?"

Juniper's husband, Rowan, appears just as quickly, moving into frame with the cautious energy of a man accustomed to magical surprises. "Everything okay in here? I felt a surge."

Cassia's wife, Martha, leans over her chair, sandwich in hand, looking more confused than alarmed. "Do I need to get the emergency binder?"

"No binder," Cassia says, though she hasn't taken her eyes off me.

The spouses hover in the background, trying to gauge whether they should call reinforcements or simply let the Bellamy women deal with their own storm. Meanwhile, my sisters look at me the way Bellamys always look when the curse shifts—equal parts love, worry, and the unspoken promise that they'll handle whatever comes next with me.

I draw in a breath, pulling the blanket a little tighter around myself. "So... that happened."

Juniper's gaze softens. "Fran... they only send a message like that when a match is officially activated."

Cassia nods slowly, logic already clicking into place behind her eyes. "Something must have delayed it. Something significant."

Daphne presses a hand to her chest. "A Cupid is actually coming? After all this time?"

I don't answer right away, because the truth is still settling into my bones. My magic has been restless all evening—sharper, quicker, humming beneath my skin like it's been waiting for something I didn't have a name for.

Now I do.

And it feels like the air shifts around me just a little, the faintest tremor of something old and inevitable waking up.

"I guess," I say softly, "we're about to find out."

The moment the last word leaves my mouth, the air in my apartment changes.

It isn't dramatic at first—just a subtle tightening, like the room is inhaling. The lights flicker, the faintest shimmer rippling along the walls, and the hair on my arms rises as if brushed by static.

"Fran..." Juniper murmurs, sitting up straighter. "Is your magic—?"

Before she can finish, the surge hits.

A pulse of energy bursts outward from my chest, warm and bright and far too strong to be accidental. It sweeps through the apartment in a shimmering wave, rattling the pictures on my wall and making the blanket around my legs lift as if caught in a soft gust of wind.

On their screens, my sisters' cameras jolt as their own wards react.

Daphne flinches as silver sparks crackle across the top of her fireplace mantle. "Uh—Fran? My protection charm just lit up like a Christmas tree!"

Juniper's tea ripples violently in her mug. Behind her, Rowan steps closer as a translucent sigil burns gold above their doorway. "Our wards just flared—full alert level."

Cassia's carefully organized shelves rattle, a soft chime ringing at the edge of her audio. Martha looks up at the ceiling. "And ours just activated too."

Then, faint through all the feeds, another tone joins in:

The Bellamy ancestral ward.

Even across the distance, I feel it like a tug in my ribcage—an old, bone-deep echo, the kind only family magic can summon.

Cassia inhales sharply. "That was Mom's house."

"Oh good," Daphne groans, covering her face. "We've alarmed the matriarch."

As if on cue, another call tries to come through—Mom. Her name flashes across the top of my screen like a divine judgment.

Daphne squawks. "Don't leave her hanging! She'll astral-project right into my living room if we ignore her."

Cassia hits the "merge call" button before anyone can discuss consequences.

Suddenly, our mother's face fills a new square on the screen—hair pulled back, glasses on, wrapped in her favorite maroon robe that she absolutely pretends is not enchanted against spills.

Her expression is... exactly what you'd expect from a woman who lived through raising four magically volatile daughters.

"What," Mom says, her voice the perfect mix of concern and threat, "just set off the wards in all five households?"

Daphne immediately points at me. "Francesca did it!"

"I did not!" I protest. "Okay—I might have. But not on purpose."

Mom peers at me over her glasses. "Francesca. Your magic surged hard enough that I dropped my casserole."

Juniper winces sympathetically. "Sorry, Mom."

Cassia lifts her notepad. "We have an explanation."

Mom folds her arms. "It better be a good one."

Everyone looks at me.

"Okay," I say, steadying myself, "so… I got a message tonight."

Mom's eyes narrow with the speed of a woman ready to take on fate itself. "From who?"

Not *who*. *What,* actually.

I swallow. "Celestial Matchmaking Headquarters."

Silence.

Not the shocked kind from earlier.

The Bellamy kind.

The heavy, ancient, magically resonant stillness of a curse old enough to have its own opinions.

Mom finally speaks, slow and careful: "Fran. Did you say CMHQ contacted you directly?"

"Yes."

"And your file was updated?"

"Yes."

"And a Cupid has been assigned?"

"Within forty-eight hours," I say quietly.

Mom exhales through her nose, sits back in her chair, and mutters something in Italian that she only uses for weddings or catastrophes.

Daphne leans into her husband's shoulder as if bracing for impact. Juniper clutches Rowan's hand. Cassia starts making furious notes while Martha looks over her shoulder like she's studying hieroglyphics.

Mom adjusts her glasses. "Alright, girls. Everyone stay calm."

"We are calm," Daphne insists.

Mom gives her a look so dry it could dehydrate a cactus.

"Fine," Daphne sighs. "We're calm-adjacent."

Mom's eyes settle back on me. "Francesca, sweetheart... this is big."

The magic beneath my skin thrums again—this time steadier, more certain, like it recognizes the path finally opening.

"I know," I whisper.

And even though the room is quiet again, the wards hum faintly in the air like a chorus of unseen bells.

Because the curse felt the message. The magic felt the message. And the family?

Oh, the family definitely felt the message.

The moment is still settling when Mom speaks again, softer now:

"Looks like your Cupid's finally coming."

Chapter 10

Sayer

The portal drops me without ceremony.

One moment I'm standing under vaulted celestial arches, surrounded by people who speak in riddles and glowing legal clauses; the next, the world snaps sideways and the floor of my apartment slams up to meet me. Hard.

The impact knocks the air out of my lungs. My wings, newly freed and still hypersensitive, flare wide behind me, catching the edge of the couch and scattering a stack of case files across the rug. The collision rings through every bone like someone struck a tuning fork against my spine.

For a long moment, I just lie there—half sprawled across the hardwood, one hand braced against the leg of the coffee table, wings twitching in painful protest. The apartment around me is dim and quiet, lit only by the glow of a streetlamp filtering through the blinds and the faint shimmer still clinging to the feathers I didn't ask to have back.

The room smells faintly of old books and citrus cleaner. It's grounding in a way that makes the ache behind my ribs ease a little.

"That," I mutter into the floor, "was uncalled for."

The wings don't fold entirely, but they settle, rustling like they're making their displeasure known. I push myself up slowly—carefully—trying not to pull anything I actually need for mortal living. Everything feels stiff, stretched, unfamiliar. It's like wearing a suit I haven't tailored in years, except the suit is attached to my spine and apparently holds grudges.

I make my way to the kitchen by muscle memory alone. No lights. No need. The whiskey bottle waits exactly where I left it, the glass beside it already cold from the draft that settles in this place after midnight.

The pour is steady. Familiar. The sound is low and reassuring, a soft glug that fills more than just the glass. I take a long, quiet sip. The burn rolls through my chest, smoothing out the lingering celestial static. My shoulders loosen. My breathing evens.

Better.

Whiskey in hand, I turn toward the bookshelf.

It sits in the corner like it always does—unassuming, practical, the exact kind of furniture no one looks at twice. But I know what's hidden behind the bottom shelf. The body remembers the things it swore it would never touch again.

I cross the room slowly, each step stirring the air enough that my wings shift behind me in restless arcs. They brush faintly against the back of my arms, feathers catching the soft glow spilling in from the window. It's strange—feeling them again. Heavy and familiar and foreign all at once. Like a language I once spoke fluently but lost through stubbornness.

The floor creaks beneath my feet as I kneel.

My fingers trace the underside of the shelf until they find the seam—smooth, nearly invisible, worn only by years of denial. A small catch gives under my thumb. The panel clicks, soft as a breath, and shifts open.

Light spills out.

Not bright or blinding. Just a faint, cool shimmer that washes over my hands and paints the edges of the shelf in a subtle halo. Celestial magic never loses its shine, no matter how long you try to bury it.

And there it is.

The file.

Thin. Pale. Gently glowing. Untouched by dust or time. Waiting in the exact place I left it fifteen years ago. Its edges pulse once—recognition, resentment, or maybe both—before settling back into a steady glow.

I reach for it slowly, the whiskey warm in my free hand, the room steady around me. The wings flare a fraction as my fingers close over the cover, as if even they remember what this file cost me.

Standing again feels heavier, not physically but in a way that settles behind the breastbone. I take another slow sip, letting the warmth bleed into the ache spreading across my back.

The file hums quietly.

Like it's breathing.

Like it's been waiting for this moment to exhale.

I carry it to the desk, a place lit only by the soft, amber glow of the lamp I left on earlier. The light catches on the celestial sigil, making it shimmer faintly, and when I lower myself into the chair, everything around me feels too still.

Too quiet.

I smooth a hand across the cover.

"Alright," I whisper to the room, to myself, to whatever cosmic nonsense just yanked me back into this. "Let's see what I've been avoiding."

And with the wings stretching behind me in a slow, uneasy arc, I open the file I swore I'd never touch again.

The file unfolds with a soft shiver of magic. My wings lift slightly—not on purpose—just a reflex, the way an old instinct wakes when something familiar brushes past it.

Then the surge hits.

Not mine. Not celestial.

Hers.

A wave of raw, untamed magic ripples across the room—bright, warm, undeniably mortal and absolutely not subtle. It rushes over my skin with the sensation of stepping too close to a bonfire: heat, static, a spark of something alive that doesn't care about boundaries.

I inhale sharply.

Of course I'd feel it. Of course her magic would flare the moment I opened the file.

"Dammit," I mutter under my breath, rubbing the heel of my palm against my sternum as the last of the surge fades. "You've got to be kidding me."

My eyes skim the document until they land on the name on the first page: Francesca Bellamy.

This entire time. Fifteen years. Fifteen *years* of denial and avoidance and building a career rooted in the exact opposite of what I once did—and the Bellamy match was right fucking next door.

Right next door, sharing the wall with my office this whole time. I close my eyes for a beat and drop my head back against the chair, letting out a low groan. "Unbelievable. Absolutely unbelievable."

Of all the places in the city I could have rented. Of all the buildings I could've moved into. Of all the bakeries that could've set up shop beside my office with the smell of cinnamon and citrus seeping through the walls every damn morning.

Of course it had to be hers.

When I look back down, the file has finished updating. The top page glows with a soft, steady pulse. A photograph settles into focus—one that definitely wasn't there fifteen years ago. Celestial files don't use staged portraits; they use truth. Moments caught in real time, unfiltered, unposed.

The picture shows Francesca standing behind her bakery counter, head thrown back in laughter at something out of frame. Hair escaping her bun in wild curls, flour smudged across her wrist, eyes bright and warm in a way that knocks the air out of me. It's a rare, unguarded happiness—radiant, effortless.

Real.

My chest tightens—not the pleasant kind. More like someone hooks a fist under my ribs and pulls. There's a pressure there I haven't felt in years, maybe longer, something old and unwelcome and entirely too human.

"This is going to be hell," I mutter quietly.

Because I know how these assignments work. I know the signs. I know what it means when a file updates with a photo like *that*.

And I know—deep down, beneath the cynicism and the irritation and the long-practiced resignation—that this assignment isn't just overdue. It's going to be the most difficult match of my life.

I rest my fingers on the edge of the page, staring at her captured mid-laugh, unaware that somewhere in the city her magic just reached out like it recognized me.

Totally oblivious to the fact that her Cupid is finally—unfortunately—back.

The wings behind me shift, restless.

And for the first time since I walked out of headquarters fifteen years ago, I feel it:

Fate closing in. Closing the file feels heavier than it should.

The cover presses shut with a soft, resonant glow, the kind that lingers in the air long after the parchment settles. It pulses once beneath my palm—faint, warm, unmistakably alive—before the light recedes to a low thrum, like the magic is exhaling after I've disturbed it.

I rest my hand there for another quiet moment. Part disbelief. Part resignation. Part something else I don't have the energy to name.

Slowly, I slide the file to the corner of the desk, squared neatly, precisely, as if organization can neutralize the truth of what's inside it. It can't. The wings behind me know it too—they unfurl a fraction, unsettled, brushing the air with a restless sweep that sends a ripple of tension down my spine.

"Not tonight," I murmur, more to myself than to them.

I take another slow sip of whiskey, letting the warmth settle through the tightness in my chest, and make my way toward the couch. The apartment is dim, lit only by the muted glow of the city outside, but it's enough to navigate without effort. The space smells faintly of paper, citrus cleaner, and the whisper of espresso that seems permanently embedded in the building's bones.

Lowering myself onto the couch should feel grounding, but the wings jolt awkwardly behind me, half-open and unfamiliar, knocking against the back cushions as if they don't quite belong to me yet. I breathe through the discomfort and close my eyes, fingers pressing at the ache in the muscles along my shoulder blades.

Focus. Remember. Control.

The wings resist at first, stiff from disuse, the magic in them still thrumming with the remnants of that surge from the file. But I draw in a slow breath and reach inward—toward the old pathways I used to command without thinking, the instincts I buried under law degrees and client meetings and a very intentional denial of all things celestial.

It takes a moment. Longer than it should.

Then the feathers settle, folding in toward my spine with a slow, grudging sweep that aches all the way down my back. Not forced. Not sealed. Just... resting. Free, but quiet.

"I'm not locking you away again," I say softly into the dim room. "But I need some peace tonight."

They calm at that—still present, still humming faintly beneath the skin, but no longer bristling against the edges of the space. A compromise, uneasy but accepted.

I lean back into the couch and let the silence fill the room. The ice in the glass clinks softly. The streetlamp outside casts thin bars of gold across the floor. Somewhere in the distance, someone laughs; a car door shuts; the city settles into its midnight rhythm.

But none of it lulls me.

My mind keeps drifting—to the surge of magic that hit the moment I opened the file, warm and fierce and unmistakably hers. To the realization that she'd been beside me for years. To the photograph still burning behind my eyes: the bakery witch caught mid-laugh, lit from within, radiant in a way no assignment ever should be.

The kind of candid joy you don't fake. The kind I've never seen in any file, ever.

I try lying down eventually, but the wings make the bed feel too narrow, the sheets too confining. No position feels right. Every turn pulls something tight. Every moment of stillness makes my thoughts louder.

Sleep refuses to come, no matter how long I sit there waiting for it. I end up perched on the edge of the mattress with a glass in my hand, staring at the faint glow spilling from the desk where the file waits—too deliberate to ignore, too charged to pretend it's just paper and ink.

A slow breath leaves me, heavy enough to drag my shoulders down with it. I rub my hand over my face, caught between exhaustion that sinks into my bones and a restless alertness that refuses to loosen its grip. There's no relief in either state, just the growing certainty that this is already bigger than I want it to be.

"This is going to be a disaster," I murmur, and the room offers no argument.

Whatever lies on the far side of this assignment has already started moving. Ready or not, it's no longer content to wait.

Chapter 11

Francesca

Morning arrives far too soon.

The alarm drags me out of sleep like it's annoyed I dared to close my eyes at all, and every part of me feels weighted—like my magic kept pacing long after the rest of me slid under. My hair is a disaster, my pillowcase smells faintly of lavender and stress, and the faint hum under my skin hasn't settled even a little.

Perfect.

I pull on leggings, an oversized sweatshirt, and the thick socks I keep specifically for mornings when life feels unreasonably complicated, then tie my hair into a bun that is more wishful thinking than structural integrity. The air in the apartment has that charged feeling, as if the walls remember the magical surge from last night even more vividly than I do.

The moment I open the door to the stairs that lead down to the bakery, warmth hits me—vanilla, cinnamon, butter. The familiar scent should be soothing, but everything in me is still buzzing, restless, almost jittery.

By the time I step through the backdoor, Harper is waiting at the edge of the prep table, arms crossed, eyebrows raised so high they might detach. Her short chestnut curls are pulled back with two mismatched clips, and flour dusts her apron like she wrestled a bag of it to the ground.

"Morning," I say, voice still rough with sleep.

She doesn't say "morning" back. Instead, she levels me with a look that could curdle cream.

"What," she demands, "the hell happened last night?"

I blink at her, caught off guard. "Uh… what do you mean?"

Harper gestures broadly at the kitchen like she's presenting Exhibit A, B, and C of a magical crime scene. "The wards went off when you came in. Not a little shimmer—not one of your usual birthday sparkles. I'm talking full sirens. My protection charm nearly slapped me."

I open my mouth, but she barrels forward.

"And then—" She points toward the other tables, where trays of covered dough are overflowing like yeasty monsters trying to escape captivity. "All of *that* happened."

"Define 'that,'" I try, though the evidence is fairly unsubtle.

"Oh sure," Harper says dryly. "Let me clarify. All of your doughs—and I mean *all* of them—quadrupled during proofing. Quadrupled, Fran. The brioche tried to climb out of its bowl. The cinnamon roll dough inflated so much it knocked over two sheet pans."

I wince. "Okay... that's new."

"That's terrifying," she corrects. "New is when the spell labels misprint or the frosting changes color. This—" She gestures wildly again. "—this is the kind of magical nonsense that makes the ancestors start whispering in the walls."

I pinch the bridge of my nose. "It wasn't intentional."

"Oh, I know that," Harper says, hands landing on her hips. "If it were intentional, we wouldn't be having this conversation—you'd have left a note that said 'sorry about the sentient brioche' and moved to the mountains."

Fair. Completely fair.

"Something else happened," I say eventually, leaning back against the counter and watching the brioche swell another half inch like it's testing boundaries.

Harper pauses mid-adjustment of the proofing rack. Very slowly, she turns to look at me. "Like what?"

That's when the back hallway door slams open hard enough to rattle the pans.

Ellie barrels in like a human exclamation point—pink sweater, glitter eyeliner, ponytail swinging, a box of macarons tucked under one arm. She skids to a stop the second she sees me.

"Oh thank gods," she announces. "You're alive. Now tell me everything."

Harper exhales through her nose. "Ellie, she hasn't even had caffeine."

Right on cue, Miguel appears from the front like a man answering a silent distress call and hands me a latte without comment. I take it with both hands and sip like my life depends on it.

Ellie leans forward, eyes bright. "Okay. You have caffeine now, so start talking. Was he hot? Was he weird? Was there crying? Were there other women?"

I rub my forehead. "The date was fine. Almost pleasant and then it wasn't."

Harper doesn't even look surprised. "Define wasn't."

"He had three girlfriends."

Ellie gasps. Harper shuts her eyes.

"Let me guess, they showed up," Harper says flatly.

"Like an emotionally coordinated task force."

Ellie presses a hand to her chest. "I *knew* it. Men who moisturize are never to be trusted."

"And then," I add, setting the latte down carefully, "something else happened."

That gets their attention.

Ellie stills. Harper turns fully toward me this time.

"What," Harper asks quietly, "does 'something else' mean?"

I swallow. "I got a message."

Ellie's grin snaps back into place. "Ohhh. Redemption arc. Did he apologize?"

"It wasn't him."

The air shifts.

Harper's shoulders tense. Ellie blinks. Even the dough seems to pause.

"It was from the Celestial Matchmaking Headquarters."

Ellie's mouth drops open. Harper presses a hand to the counter like she needs it to stay upright.

"No," Ellie whispers. "They wouldn't."

"They did," I say. "Last night. Apparently, my file updated."

Harper stares at me, then at the ceiling, then back again. "That explains the wards."

"And the dough," Ellie adds faintly.

"My Cupid is coming," I finish. "Within forty-eight hours."

Ellie lets out a sound somewhere between a squeal and a spell misfire. "The necklace worked!"

"Ellie—"

"I charged it," she insists. "With intent."

Harper closes her eyes. "Of course you did."

The weight of it settles deep in my chest, heavier than nerves, heavier than excitement. This isn't just news. It's a turning point.

"Okay," I say finally, lifting my latte like a referee calling a time-out. "Enough. We open in an hour, the brioche is staging a coup, and I refuse to face destiny without croissants."

Harper straightens immediately. "Preheat everything. Reinforce containment."

Miguel peers into the kitchen. "The cinnamon rolls hissed at me."

"That's normal," Harper says. "Assert dominance."

Ellie grins. "It's dough, not a raccoon."

"With Francesca's magic," Harper replies, "the distinction is thin."

I set my empty cup down and pull my apron over my head, tying it tight. The motion steadies me—something about routine always has. Even with the magic thrumming under my skin, there's a rhythm in this place I've always known how to step into.

We fall into motion.

Harper starts tackling the overgrown dough, muttering under her breath like a baker facing a personal betrayal. Ellie re-stocks the display case with the efficiency of a caffeinated hummingbird. Miguel lines trays for the first batch of scones, moving with the resigned calm of a man who is very used to our family's magical fallout.

And me? I start building the espresso bar for opening—fresh beans, clean pitchers, towels folded, syrups restocked. The normalcy of it grounds me, even as that electric hum inside me refuses to settle.

By the time the clock hits six-fifty, the bakery looks less like a magical disaster zone and more like... well, us. Cozy, warm, glowing. Ready for people who need pastries and coffee more than oxygen.

Ellie slips up beside me and nudges my shoulder. "You okay?"

"I have approximately thirty-seven emotions running around like squirrels at a rave ," I say. "But yes."

Harper snorts. "We'll take it."

And just as Ellie is about to say something undoubtedly loud, the door chimes. Right on cue. Because the universe has a sense of timing I do not appreciate today.

Sayer Valentine steps inside—the morning chill still clinging to his coat, hair slightly mussed, expression carved into its usual early-hours scowl. He looks like he slept badly, which is comforting because I also slept badly. Symmetry, I guess.

The bakery softens around him the way it always does—lights warming just a touch, the air shifting subtly, like the building itself recognizes him.

"Morning," he says, voice still rough from lack of caffeine.

"Morning," I echo, moving to the espresso machine without needing to ask what he wants.

He watches me set up the shot, his gaze sharp but not unfriendly.

"Extra shot today," he says. "And an apple fritter."

I blink at him. That's his "bad case day" order. I hesitate just a second too long, hands stilling over the portafilter.

"You okay?" he asks.

The tone isn't gentle. It's matter-of-fact, blunt, like he's asking if the sky intends to fall soon and wants fair warning.

"Long night," I admit, turning back to the machine. "Yours?"

He huffs out something that isn't quite a laugh. "You could say that."

The espresso begins to pour—dark, rich, steady—and the steam curls upward between us like a quiet punctuation mark neither of us acknowledges.

I reach for the caramel syrup, and as my hand brushes the bottle...

My magic flares. Not a little. Not subtly.

A spark skitters across my fingertips and dances up the side of the espresso machine.

Sayer's eyes flick to the glow. He notices—he *definitely* notices—but doesn't say a word.

Instead, he leans slightly against the counter, watching with a careful, steady gaze that feels far more perceptive than anyone should be at seven in the morning. He doesn't flinch. Doesn't comment. Just absorbs it with that lawyerly stillness of his, as if cataloguing details he's not quite ready to admit he's noticing.

I slide the finished latte toward him, the caramel ribboned perfectly through the foam. He wraps his fingers around the cup but doesn't step away just yet.

"Francesca," he says quietly, lowering his voice so Ellie's chatter and Harper's grumbling don't drown him out.

I straighten a little. "Yeah?"

He studies me for a heartbeat—too intent, too measuring, like he's choosing his words with surgical precision. "When you get a moment today, could you stop by my office?"

My pulse jumps in that annoying, traitorous way that only happens when the curse is paying very close attention.

"Why?" I ask, keeping my tone light. "Did I finally violate some obscure pastry ordinance?"

A corner of his mouth tugs—almost a smile, but not quite. "No laws broken. Yet." He shifts the cup in his hand, expression settling into something more serious. "I just... had something come across my desk. Something I need to discuss with you."

My stomach goes faintly weightless. "Is everything okay?"

"I'll explain when you come by." He straightens from the counter, all business once again. "It's not urgent this second. But today, if you can."

The bell over the door rings as the next customer steps inside, and that seems to snap whatever strange moment was stretching between us. He nods once, crisp and final, then turns toward the exit.

"Thanks for the coffee," he says over his shoulder.

And then he's gone—coat trailing the scent of winter chill behind him, the door swinging shut, leaving me staring at the empty space he occupied and wondering why the air feels different now.

Chapter 12

Sayer

By the time I reach my office, the latte is doing its best to drag me into full consciousness, but the morning is still wearing its teeth. The air inside Valentine & Associates feels colder than usual, like the building itself knows I'm avoiding the conversation chained metaphorically—and magically—to my existence.

I set my briefcase down, shrug out of my coat, and finally lower myself into the chair. The leather creaks, familiar and grounding. Good. Normal. Predictable. Everything the rest of my life is currently refusing to be.

The fritter goes on the corner of the desk. Right next to the file.

The file that glows—subtly, but unmistakably—like it's trying to hum itself into my peripheral vision.

"Not now," I mutter at it.

It does not care.

I unwrap the bagel, fully committed to enjoying at least one moment of peace, and take a bite. Perfect crisp edges. Obnoxious amount of cream cheese. Exactly what a man on the brink of celestial ruin deserves.

It lasts eight seconds.

The office door swings open with the force of a minor natural disaster. Leona sweeps in first— tablet already in hand, the faint scent of fire magic trailing her like expensive perfume. Jackson follows, taller, broader, carrying two coffees and looking like he's already survived one argument today.

They both stop mid-stride.

Leona's gaze locks onto the glowing file. Then the apple fritter beside it. Then the glowing file again.

"Oh," she says, drawing the word out like she's examining a crime scene. "Well. That explains the energy in the building."

Jackson sets the coffees down, eyes widening. "Is that the file?"

I take another bite of my bagel with the deliberate calm of a man who refuses to acknowledge the impending catastrophe on his desk. "It appears so."

Leona tilts her head, studying the gentle thrum of magic radiating from the parchment. "And you put a pastry *next* to it. Bold choice. Risky. Potentially stupid."

"It's a fritter," I reply. "Not a bomb."

"It's glowing," she counters, gesturing sharply. "It's glowing like it wants to unionize with the paperwork and overthrow your sanity."

Jackson leans closer, cautious. "Boss... is this the Bellamy file?"

I set my bagel down slowly, close enough to civility that no one can accuse me of snapping, and rest my arms on the desk. "Yes, Jackson. It is the Bellamy file."

Leona whistles low. "And here I thought today would be boring."

I close my eyes for a brief, prayer-like moment. "Please don't start."

"Start what?" Leona asks, all faux innocence. "Preparing for the inevitable chaos? Rewriting your schedule so we can fit in celestial fallout? Calling housekeeping to let them know magical flare damage isn't covered under our insurance?"

Jackson nods sympathetically. "She's right. The file does look... *angry*."

"It isn't angry," I say flatly. "It's sentient. There's a difference."

Leona lifts a brow. "Sentient. Glowing. And sitting beside a sugar-based offering like it's waiting to negotiate."

I open my eyes again, sip my latte, and admit with profound irritation: "Fine. Maybe today will not be my best morning."

Jackson snorts. "Boss... today's going to be a *mess*."

Leona points at the file. "And it starts with that."

And I... do not disagree.

Leona circles the desk like a predator assessing prey—or paperwork, which for her is essentially the same thing. The file continues to glow in that steady, insistent way, as if it's taking attendance and has noticed I'm trying to ignore it.

"All right," she says, planting both palms on the desk. "Let's cut to the part where you stop brooding like an under-caffeinated gargoyle and tell us which Bellamy this is for."

Jackson straightens beside her, eyes widening. "Oh—yeah. That's important. The Bellamy coven is huge. This could be for *anyone.*"

Leona lifts her brows meaningfully. "So? Who is it? One of the cousins? One of the aunts? The matriarch? The pastry rebels? Which magical chaos gremlin are we dealing with?"

I hesitate.

Just for a breath. Just long enough for Leona's gaze to sharpen into something feral and triumphant.

"Oh no," she says, recognizing the pause instantly. "No no no—don't you dare. Don't you even *think* about being vague with me. Which Bellamy is it?"

"It's—"

The front door chimes, sharp and bright in the quiet of the lobby.

All three of us look up at once.

A heartbeat later, Francesca appears at the far end of the short hallway, framed by the narrow stretch between the front door and the office proper. She steps into view like she's crossing a threshold instead of a corridor, the winter chill still clinging to her as she adjusts the cardboard drink carrier balanced carefully in both hands. Four cups. Perfectly steady.

Her cheeks are flushed pink from the cold, her hair pulled back into a half-tucked braid that looks like it gave up halfway through the morning. She shifts her weight slightly as she walks, boots quiet against the floor, and with her comes the unmistakable warmth of the bakery—vanilla and citrus and something brighter beneath it, the kind of scent that doesn't just linger but *announces itself.*

The magic in the room reacts immediately. Not flaring. Not exploding. Just snapping awake, like every circuit has been switched on at once.

She reaches the edge of the office, lifts her gaze, and gives a small, unapologetic smile. "Morning," she says, as if she hasn't just brought half my carefully controlled world to attention with a paper carrier and a cup of coffee.

"Morning," she says, lifting the drinks a little. "I brought coffee. For everyone. Thought you might need it."

Leona inhales sharply. Jackson mutters something that sounds suspiciously like *oh shit.* The file glows brighter.

And me?

I can feel my wings pull tight beneath my shirt in a way that is completely, cosmically unhelpful.

Because of course.

Of course this would be the moment she walks in. Cupids have timing; curses have timing; Bellamys have timing.

But the universe? The universe likes to see me suffer.

Francesca crosses the threshold with the kind of unassuming confidence that makes the entire room shift.

"Morning, Leona," she says brightly, handing over a cup with a little flourish. "One lavender oat milk latte with a dash of honey. Extra foam, because I know you pretend you don't like it but you absolutely do."

Leona blinks, caught completely off guard. "I—thank you. Yes. Correct. I do." She takes the cup like it might explode with magic or joy, neither of which she is equipped to process before nine.

"And Jackson," Francesca continues, offering him the next cup, "your cinnamon mocha with the extra shot of espresso and the nutmeg sprinkle."

Jackson's face lights up. "You remembered the nutmeg."

"You're very unmistakable for someone who needs nutmeg," she says with a half smile.

Then she turns toward me.

"And for you—your usual," she says, handing me the last cup. "Caramel latte, extra shot, dollop of whipped cream."

Her gaze flicks toward the fritter still sitting on the desk. "And I assume the day is... fritter-level bad?"

"It's approaching that," I admit.

She gives a small sympathetic hum, setting the now-empty drink carrier aside. There's a nervous energy under her calm—subtle, but there. A faint buzz of magic that prickles along my arms like static wanting a place to land.

I gesture to the chair across from my desk. "If you have a minute, please—sit. We should talk."

Francesca hesitates only a heartbeat before sitting, her eyes scanning the glowing file without recognition. She probably thinks it's just another weird magical office thing.

Leona, however, springs into motion like someone just fired a starting pistol. She snatches her notepad off the bookshelf and moves toward the chair beside Francesca, poised to take minutes like this is a board meeting about to erupt into scandal.

"No," I say firmly, without looking at her.

Leona freezes mid-step, pen hovering dramatically over the page. "But—this could be important."

"It is important," I say, tone even. "Which is why I need you to clear my schedule for the next two hours. And then help Jackson with that research request at the courthouse."

Jackson frowns. "The custody case or the property dispute?"

"Both," I say.

"At the same time?" he asks.

"Yes."

Leona lets out a sound halfway between indignation and admiration. "Fine. But if you need backup—"

"I don't," I reply.

Jackson nudges her. "He really doesn't."

They gather their cups and retreat toward the hallway with the speed of people who desperately want to eavesdrop but have enough self-preservation instincts not to.

Leona pauses at the doorway, arching a brow. "If you need us, yell."

"Go," I repeat.

She disappears, muttering something about cosmic timing and poor life choices. And then the door clicks shut.

Leaving me alone with Francesca. And the glowing file. And the inexplicable hum of magic that fills the air like a held breath.

"Okay," she says softly, shifting in the chair. "What's going on?"

And for the first time in fifteen years, I have absolutely no idea how to answer.

Francesca settles into the chair with her hands wrapped around her drink, posture straight but eyes cautious. The kind of caution people use when they're not sure if they're here for legal trouble, a misunderstanding, or an extremely awkward conversation neither of us wants to have.

I clear my throat. Professionally. Or... as professionally as a former Cupid with wings cramping under his shirt can manage.

"First," I begin, folding my hands on the desk in the exact pose they teach you in mediation seminars, "I want to apologize."

Her brows lift. "For what?"

The directness hits harder than it should. I hold up a hand, trying to keep the conversation from derailing before it even starts.

"I'm getting there," I say, or attempt to say with composed lawyerly authority. It comes out more like someone trying desperately to maintain dignity while his spine is full of celestial pins and needles. "I simply mean that recent... developments... have made me aware that certain actions—or inactions—may have been... less than ideal."

Francesca blinks at me.

I push forward. "And that a lapse in... correspondence... might have caused unintended inconveniences."

She tilts her head slowly, expression sharpening. "Sayer."

"Yes?" Gods, my voice is too crisp. Too tight.

"What exactly are you apologizing for?"

The question lands with surgical precision.

I falter—not visibly, I hope, but enough that the file on the desk gives a smug little pulse of light. Traitor.

"I'm apologizing," I say carefully, "for the... delay."

"In what?"

The room feels suddenly, catastrophically small.

I exhale and attempt a tactful pivot. "For something that requires... delicacy."

"Sayer."

Her tone is polite. Her eyes are not.

She leans forward slightly, elbow resting on the arm of the chair, coffee cradled in her other hand like she's settling in to watch a show she didn't buy tickets for.

"You're apologizing," she says slowly, "for something I don't know happened. I can't decide if that's suspicious or just badly phrased. So I'll ask again."

She sets her cup down on the desk with a soft click.

"What. Are. You. Apologizing. For?"

The wings press tight against my back like they're bracing for impact.

I open my mouth. Close it. Open it again.

Because there are many ways to deliver this truth.

None of them good.

And absolutely none of them professional.

Chapter 13

Francesca

Sayer looks like he's trying to sit perfectly still inside a room that stopped cooperating with him the moment I walked in. His shoulders are set, his hands folded neatly, but there's something restless in the way he watches me—something he keeps trying to tuck behind professionalism that keeps slipping.

"You started to apologize," I say, keeping my voice steady. "But you didn't actually say what for."

He lets out a quiet breath, measured and annoyingly composed. "I was building up to it."

"No, you were dodging it," I counter.

"I was giving context."

"You were giving *nothing*."

His eyes narrow just slightly, the only sign he's losing the argument—and not enjoying it. "This isn't simple."

"Then start with the part that is."

He sits back, clearly regrouping. "Francesca, the file that showed up on my desk... it wasn't something I expected. At all."

"Fine," I say. "What does that have to do with your apology?"

He looks at the glowing file again—brief, reflexive, guilty—and I follow his gaze because the thing might as well be screaming my name at this point.

"Is it my file?" I ask.

He doesn't answer immediately.

Which is an answer.

"Sayer," I push, "look at me. Did that file come from Celestial Matchmaking Headquarters?"

His attention snaps back to me, expression guarded, but not cold. "Yes."

"And is it mine?"

A muscle in his jaw ticks, the kind that betrays reluctant truth. "I didn't know it was yours."

The words land sharp, unexpected.

He leans forward slightly, elbows braced on the desk. "Not until last night."

That pulls the air out of my lungs—not dramatically, just enough to make my magic stir under my skin in that low, restless hum that always warns me when something important is unfolding.

"You didn't know," I repeat, trying to make sense of it.

"No," he says, firm enough that I believe him. "The file was sealed. Assigned, but sealed. I never opened it. Never saw the name." His gaze flicks to the parchment again, then back to me with a tightness that wasn't there a moment ago. "I shelved it. Permanently. Or so I thought."

My heart does a funny, unwelcome twist. "And last night?"

"The seal broke," he says quietly. "And it updated."

The buzzing under my skin sharpens—heat, pressure, something old and instinctual tugging at the edges of my senses. The same feeling I got when the message hit my phone. The same pulse that shook the bakery this morning.

"And when it updated," I say, voice lower, "you saw my name."

"Yes."

There's no hesitation, no waffling. Just a simple acknowledgment of a truth he clearly hates having to deliver.

"And that's why you're apologizing?" I ask.

He shifts in his chair. "I'm apologizing," he says slowly, "because I know how it looks. Like I knew something about your situation and kept it from you."

"But you didn't know it was me."

His gaze holds mine, steady. "Not until last night."

Something in me loosens—just a fraction—but it doesn't stop the magic from humming louder, sharp enough that I'm surprised the lights aren't flickering.

"And now?" I ask softly. "What are you supposed to do now?"

Sayer's mouth opens, then closes, like he's choosing words with surgical precision again. Whatever he's about to say, I can already feel it pressing at the edges of the room.

"I'm supposed to—" he begins.

And the file gives a soft, insistent pulse of light, like it's tired of waiting for him to finish the sentence.

The glow from the file pulses again, warm enough that I can feel it across the desk, and that's the moment the absurdity finally snaps inside me.

"Okay, no," I say, lifting a hand. "Pause. Back up. Explain this like I'm a person who hasn't slept and currently has three doughs plotting a coup in my kitchen."

Sayer looks like he wants to rub his temples but is restraining himself out of sheer professionalism.

"Fran—"

"No." I lean forward, brows raised. "Why the hell does a *divorce attorney* have my celestial matchmaking file? HQ said my Cupid would be reaching out. Cupid. As in winged romantic meddler. Not... you."

He sits a little straighter, bracing. "It's not a mistake."

"That's hilarious," I say, gesturing at him and the glowing file and the entire ridiculous room. "Because it feels like the universe is stacking cosmic jokes just to see how much I can take before I spontaneously combust."

His jaw tightens. "I quit," he says, voice low. "A long time ago. That's why the file was sealed. It was frozen when I walked away."

I stare at him. "You quit being a Cupid. To become a divorce attorney."

"Yes."

"That's not an upgrade."

"It is when you consider the paperwork."

My eye twitches. "And where are these supposed Cupid wings? Because you don't exactly strike me as the 'flutter around spreading joy' type."

Something shifts in his expression—something resigned, reluctant, inevitable.

"They were bound," he says. "Sealed. Until last night."

I blink once. Then again. "You expect me to believe that you, Mister Everything-is-terrible-until-I-have-coffee, have wings?"

"Yes."

"I don't believe you."

He exhales—the long-suffering kind—and stands.

Not abruptly. Not dramatically. But with the quiet finality of someone stepping into a truth he's avoided for years.

His shoulders roll back, his posture adjusts, and then—

The shirt he's wearing—black, fitted, clearly not standard office attire—separates along invisible seams. Not tearing. Opening.

And the wings unfurl.

Not angelic, not soft. They're sharp-lined and celestial, rich with feathered texture that catches the light just enough to make them look real in a way my brain refuses to process. They stretch wide, filling the space behind him, the motion impossibly smooth for something that hasn't seen daylight in fifteen years.

I grip the arms of my chair because my knees suddenly aren't trustworthy.

"That..." My voice wavers. "That can't be real."

He flexes them once, the faint whisper of feathers stirring the air between us. "They're real."

Shock hits first. Then confusion. Then the slow, dawning horror that this—*this man*—is the one the universe assigned to help me survive the curse currently upending my life.

"Oh absolutely fucking not," I say, finding my voice again. "This cannot be happening."

He folds the wings halfway, cautious, as if trying not to overwhelm the room. "It is."

"This is ridiculous." I point at him, wings and all. "You are literally the last person alive who should be in charge of anything involving romantic outcomes."

He doesn't flinch. "You're not wrong."

"Then how," I demand, gesturing wildly now because my brain refuses to move without my hands, "are *you*—a man who quit the job—who hates the holiday—who physically recoils at heart-shaped candy—supposed to help me?"

He doesn't give me a polished answer. Or a diplomatic one. Or a magically reassuring one.

He just meets my stare and says, with a dry honesty that lands harder than it should:

"I'm still figuring that part out." I stare at him, wings half-unfurled like some celestial punchline, and for a moment all I can manage is a quiet, incredulous breath.

"Well," I say, "that inspires absolutely zero confidence."

He huffs out a sound that is not quite a laugh. More like the exhausted exhale of a man who agrees with me but refuses to admit how much.

"There's a catch," he says, and the way he lowers himself back into his chair tells me it's not a small one.

Of course there is.

"There always is," I mutter.

He folds the wings in with visible effort, the feathers adjusting until they rest against his back in what is clearly their version of neutral. The shirt reseals seamlessly—magic, tailored arrogance, or both—and he braces his forearms on the desk, expression shifting into the kind of controlled seriousness.

"Given the... considerable delay," he begins, choosing the phrase carefully, "there were additional provisions added to your case."

"My case," I repeat, because hearing it phrased that way does something unpleasant to my stomach. "Like I'm a legal nightmare."

"You're not," he says quickly—too quickly—then adds, "The situation is."

"Oh, that's comforting."

He ignores the comment, which means it's absolutely true.

"There's now a deadline," he continues. "One imposed by the High Council when they released the file. I have until midnight on February fourteenth."

My heart drops. "Valentine's Day."

"Yes."

"Of course," I say, because why not add thematic cruelty to my week?

He rubs the bridge of his nose, something tight settling into his voice. "If I don't resolve your case by then—successfully—they'll forcibly return me to active duty."

I blink. "Meaning?"

"Meaning," he says, and the words come out colder, quieter, "I stop being a divorce attorney. Permanently. Wings out. Back in the field. No choice."

Something flickers in his eyes—resentment, resignation, the ghost of old obligations that clearly still have teeth.

"That's terrible," I say before I can stop myself.

"You haven't heard the rest."

"Oh, good," I mutter. "There's more terrible."

He gives me a look that says he'd apologize again if he thought I'd let him.

"If I fail," he says, "every single divorce I've handled since leaving will be nullified. Completely undone. The couples will be magically reset to the state they were in the Valentine's Day before their divorce filings."

I stare at him.

That isn't terrible. That's catastrophic.

"That's hundreds of people," I whisper.

"More," he corrects quietly. "And the magic involved won't be clean. They won't remember why things broke apart. Or how they healed afterward. Their lives would be... scrambled."

I lean back slowly, trying to absorb the scale of it. "Sayer, that's—"

"I know," he says softly. "Trust me, I know."

"And they put that... entire disaster... on whether you fix my file by Valentine's Day?"

"They did."

"Why?"

He hesitates. Just long enough for the file between us to pulse with warm, infuriating awareness.

Sayer draws in a slow breath, eyes flicking briefly to the glowing file before returning to me. There's no theatrics in his voice now—just the fatigue of a man who knows he's delivering news that will land exactly how I think it will.

"Your case isn't simple," he says. "Not because of anything you did. Because of your family line. The Bellamy curse... it isn't a myth. Not to HQ."

A chill rolls through me that has nothing to do with the room temperature.

He continues, careful but not evasive. "I don't know every detail—Celestial files are intentionally vague when it comes to generational magic—but yours isn't treated like a routine match. It's flagged. Prioritized. And now that you've hit thirty-five..." He shakes his head slightly. "That's a threshold no Bellamy woman has reached before. Not without intervention."

My heart gives a slow, uneasy thud. "Meaning what, exactly?"

"Meaning the longer a Bellamy goes without a completed bond, the more volatile the magic becomes. HQ doesn't like volatile magic." His jaw tightens. "And they really don't like cases that have been unresolved for this long."

I sit back, absorbing that. The magic beneath my skin reacts immediately—like the curse itself is listening in and has opinions about being publicly called volatile.

"So let me get this straight," I say, voice quieter than before because the weight of all this is starting to settle in. "If you fail, your entire life gets ripped apart and a few hundred married couples get magically shoved back together without consent."

"Unfortunately, yes."

"And if you succeed?" I ask, forcing myself to meet his eyes. "What happens to me?"

He doesn't look away. Doesn't try to soften it. Doesn't wrap it in cosmic destiny sparkles.

"That," he says, steady and maddeningly honest, "is what we're going to have to figure out. Together."

The word *together* lands in my chest with a strange mix of dread and inevitability—like my magic recognizes it long before my brain does.

Sayer lets out a slow breath, the last pieces of whatever he's been holding back settling into place. The file's glow softens, almost expectant, and he looks at me with a steadiness that wasn't there when I walked in.

"We're not going to figure all of this out in one morning," he says. "Let's meet for dinner tonight. Somewhere quiet. We can make a plan and go from there."

It's practical. Direct. Almost normal—if I ignore the wings and the cosmic implications sitting between us like an extra chair.

"Dinner's fine," I say. "Text me when you pick a place."

He nods once, something like relief passing through his expression. "I will."

I rise from the chair, and he does the same out of habit, the faint rustle of feathers under his shirt reminding me this isn't just a complicated conversation—it's the start of something much bigger.

"I'll see you tonight," I say.

"Tonight," he confirms.

And that's how we leave it—simple, unfinished, and hanging with the kind of tension you don't admit out loud.

Chapter 14

Sayer

Francesca's steps fade down the hallway, the faintest echo of her boots drifting through the open door before it closes with a soft click. The moment she's gone, something in me tugs—low, annoying, insistent. A quiet pull right beneath the breastbone, like a thread snapping taut in a direction I have absolutely no intention of following.

Nope. Absolutely not.

I lean back in my chair and give myself a single, pointed thought:

Do not get attached to the Bellamy.

It does about as much good as telling fire not to burn.

The room still smells faintly of the coffee she brought—a warm blend of caramel and espresso that hangs in the air longer than it should. The glow from the damn file paints the corner of the desk a soft gold, pulsing like a heartbeat. My wings itch under my shirt, restless as if they're reacting to her departure in ways I refuse to examine.

"Ridiculous," I mutter, reaching for my bagel. "She's a client. A cosmic bureaucratic nightmare. A walking target for magical chaos. She is not—"

I stop myself. The bagel helps. Barely. The moment is grounded and almost calm—right up until the office door slams open and blows that illusion apart, ushering in an entirely different kind of chaos.

Leona storms in first, boots clacking sharply against the hardwood. The scent of sulfur and patchouli trails her, a signature blend of half-demon ancestry and expensive enchantments. Her dark curls are pinned back with a dagger-shaped hair clip that matches her expression perfectly.

"Hell itself couldn't prepare me for that courthouse," she announces, dropping her tablet onto the nearest chair. "Someone tried to smuggle a spell-jammed quill through security. The metal detector nearly had a stroke."

Jackson enters behind her, snow still dusting his shoulders, holding two battered folders and looking like he's aged ten years in the last ninety minutes. His magic always tastes like cold iron and burnt sugar, a strange mix that settles into the room as he shuts the door behind them.

"The clerk declared a 'no enchanted ink' policy." Jackson rolls his eyes. "You ever tried filling out form C-17 without enchanted ink? Took me twenty minutes to write a single paragraph. My hand still hurts."

Leona points toward him. "He forgot how to spell his own last name halfway through."

"I was under pressure," Jackson protests.

I raise a hand to stop the bickering. "New policy."

Both freeze mid-argument, eyes snapping to me with identical looks of wary curiosity.

"No new clients," I say. "None. Not until this situation is dealt with."

Leona follows the line of my gaze straight to the glowing file on my desk. Her expression morphs immediately—part dread, part fascination, part I-told-you-so.

"Oh," she breathes. "So it's officially bad."

"Worse," Jackson adds, stepping closer. The file throws warm light onto his shirt, making him look like a tourist standing too close to a holy relic. "It's humming." He leans in, frowning. "Why is it humming?"

"It likes to do that," I say, taking a steady drink of my coffee, as if that explains anything.

Leona plants a hand on her hip, eyes narrowing. "All right. Define 'dealt with.' Are we talking days? Weeks? Or the type of cosmic timeline measured in romantic disasters?"

"Hopefully before Valentine's Day," I reply.

Their twin groans vibrate the walls.

"And the existing clients?" Jackson asks.

"Push them to March," I say. "Anyone without a hearing date waits. Everything else gets postponed unless a judge orders otherwise."

They exchange a look of mutual dread.

"March is going to be a bloodbath," Leona says.

"Better March than now," I reply.

The office feels fuller suddenly—magic reacting to the tension, the warmth of the heating vent brushing my ankles while a cold draft curls along the window behind me. The muscles on my wings tug tight, a reminder they're still adjusting to freedom after too many years bound.

Leona's gaze sharpens. "She's coming back, isn't she?"

I keep my voice flat. "We're meeting for dinner."

Jackson whistles under his breath. "Dinner, huh."

"Planning," I clarify. "A work-related discussion."

Leona arches a brow. "At night."

"How scandalous," Jackson adds.

I glare. "You're both impossible."

"And you," Leona says, stepping closer, her magic crackling faintly like heat lightning, "are radiating celestial interference every time her name gets mentioned. The wards flickered earlier. Don't pretend you didn't feel that."

My wings twitch. I pointedly ignore the wings.

"We're handling it," I say.

Jackson snorts. "Your back says otherwise."

"My back is fine."

It is absolutely not fine. Nothing is fine. And the Council's deadline is ticking closer with each passing hour.

But that is not a conversation I'm having with either of them.

Leona sighs and grabs her tablet again. "Fine. I'll rearrange the schedule. Jackson, you help me shift filings."

"On it," he says. "And if anyone asks, we're on a temporary administrative hiatus."

"Magical fallout sabbatical," Leona corrects with a grim nod.

"Same thing."

They turn to go, and the file pulses a warm, smug glow across my desk.

Leona lifts a finger toward it. "That thing thinks it's running the show."

It might be. But I'll never admit that out loud.

The Registry opens the way ancient magic always does—slowly, deliberately, with a shimmer that settles into the room like the pressure drop before a storm. Gold light spills across my desk, catching on the edges of the Bellamy file and the half-eaten bagel, painting everything with that faint celestial light I've been trying to avoid for fifteen years.

Leona moves closer, her expression sharpening as the interface settles into the space between us. Runes drift upward in soft waves, curling around the ceiling beams before dissolving. The whole office seems to lean toward the display, the wards shifting subtly in response to the Bellamy magic threaded through the file.

"All right," she murmurs. "Show us what the next six weeks look like."

I brace myself as the Registry begins to unfurl the coming events—not as neat entries or calendar squares, but as living memory fragments. The system prefers symbolism: impressions, atmospheres, flashes of what magic will demand.

The images sweep past like scenes glimpsed through a half-open doorway.

Lanterns floating above a packed street, lighting faces lit with enchantment. A ballroom drenched in gold and rose magic, music swelling as dancers twist through glittering illusions. A bonfire crackling high into the night sky, its flames shaped by ancestral rites older than any modern spell book. A labyrinth of shifting walls that looks deceptively elegant until the light bends wrong inside it. Masks with eyes that spark like embers. A shadowed hall carved from obsidian, glowing sigils breathing across its floor.

And in the center of it all, lingering just long enough to announce itself: a crimson seal carved in infernal script, unmistakably Lucifer's.

Leona sucks in a breath. "Is that *his* ball?"

"Unfortunately," I say, watching the sigil pulse like a heartbeat. "He sends the invitation whether you want it or not. It's a cornerstone event. All celestial-adjacent matches have to attend."

Jackson leans over her shoulder, the color draining from his face. "So you and the bakery witch are expected to show up there. Together."

"Among several other places," I reply, because that's the problem: the Registry is still moving, still revealing glimpses of the Lupercalia cycle as the magic evaluates Francesca's curse and what it needs in order to stabilize.

This is not a choose-your-own-adventure. It's a gauntlet.

Leona traces a finger through the light and more impressions rise—ribbons threaded with charm work, festival crowds buzzing with love magic, a masquerade glittering with too much glamour to be safe for anyone unstable. Some moments glow warmly, others bristle with tension that even the Registry can't disguise.

"These aren't suggestions," she says quietly.

"No," I answer. "The Council will treat each one as a marker of progress."

"And all of them require you and Francesca to be present." She doesn't phrase it like a question. She doesn't need to.

The Registry shifts again, this time bringing forward the match data. It doesn't present it as a list, but as a constellation of magical signatures—small swirling lights, each hovering with a faint aura and a single name tied to it. They rotate slowly, like stars being considered by the universe itself.

The first signature flickers—an intense, sharp-edged magic that snaps at the edges of the screen. Overly volatile. Fire-heavy. A terrible fit for a Bellamy curse. The next is dim, barely stable, its magic too weak to balance hers. Another is so flirtation-charm infused the Registry gives an audible disapproving chime.

One after another, eleven signatures rotate through the air, each illuminating for a few seconds—some disastrous, some merely inconvenient, one or two that might survive a first date but would crumble under any magical pressure.

Leona watches the swirl with a tension that settles between her shoulders. "These are her alternatives."

"Technically," I say, drumming my fingers against the desk.

"Technically," Jackson echoes, "most of these men would spontaneously combust in her presence."

He's not wrong.

The twelfth candidate gleams a steadier silver—strong enough to catch the Registry's interest, not strong enough to settle the curse. A temporary fix at best.

"Seventy-five percent," Leona murmurs, reading the margin. "That's the closest match she has besides—"

Her voice falters as the final signature drifts forward.

It doesn't glow like the others. It flares, gold and warm and unmistakable.

My name. My magic. My bond.

The Registry reacts to it immediately, its runes brightening until the whole system feels like it's reverberating through the office walls.

Leona's voice softens. "There it is."

Jackson lets out a low whistle. "One hundred percent match."

The wings at my back tighten before I can stop them. "Yes."

"Pre-birth alignment," Leona adds, reading the data that spins around the gold light. "Assigned before either of you existed."

"I didn't know." The truth lands heavier than I expect. "Not until last night."

The Registry pulses again, reacting to my voice, to Francesca's name shimmering through the bond. The air thickens with Bellamy magic—warm, electric, threaded with a spark of her I'm starting to recognize.

Leona lowers her hands. "So that's what we're dealing with. A whole cycle of escalating events, culminating in whatever the Council expects on Valentine's night… and a match system that's telling us Francesca has eleven options that will make her life miserable and one that won't."

Her gaze lands on me.

I don't look away.

"This doesn't change the plan," I say. "It just means we start tonight."

The Registry dims slowly, leaving the office lit only by the golden pulse of Francesca's file.

Her magic dances through the air again—restless, bright, impossible to ignore.

"Dinner," I repeat, more to myself than anyone else. "And then we figure out how to walk straight into all of that without setting the city on fire."

Chapter 15

Francesca

By the time I reach the corner pizzeria, my magic has fully committed to behaving like an overeager smoke alarm. Every time I think about Sayer—his wings, that impossible file, the way he said *tonight*—a little spark flicks along my skin like someone is teasing my nerves with warm static.

The place smells incredible: yeasty dough, roasted garlic, tomato simmered in herbs. It's cozy too, with string lights looping across the ceiling and the kind of booths that swallow you whole. I tell myself the environment will help settle me.

It does not.

Because Sayer is already here, sitting in the back booth with all the posture of a man preparing for cross-examination. The ambient lighting does unsettlingly flattering things to his cheekbones. He looks up as I approach, and something in his expression eases—barely, but enough for me to notice.

"Evening," he says, voice warm and controlled in a way that sends my magic fluttering again.

I slide into the booth across from him. "Evening. Good choice of place."

"It's neutral," he replies, closing the menu. "Less risk of magical casualties."

"I appreciate your optimism," I say, right as the salt shaker trembles a half inch toward the pepper.

He notices. Of course he notices.

And that's when it hits—the sharp, bright flare beneath my skin. It comes fast, a rush of heat and pressure like my magic has decided *this* is the moment to surge, and for one horrifying second the silverware rattles, the sugar caddy shifts, and the table flickers with a faint shimmer.

I grip the edge of my seat, trying to breathe through it.

"Fran—"

"I'm fine," I start, but my voice catches, because the spark is climbing, turning into a hot, crawling wave behind my ribs, and I'm going to embarrass myself in a very public place.

The flare spikes—

And Sayer reaches across the table without thinking.

His hand finds mine—warm, steady, grounding like someone dropping a stone into water trouble enough to pull it back into place. The magic stops mid-surge. Not fades. Not settles.

It listens.

A soft thrum moves through my palm where his fingers touch mine, like two currents locking into the same frequency. The air stills. The tremor stops. The tension in my chest unwinds so abruptly it almost hurts.

I look up.

He's already looking at me.

And that moment—quiet, charged, far too intimate for a table covered in laminated menus—stretches just long enough for something in my magic to lean toward him.

His eyes widen.

He jerks his hand back like the table just caught fire.

The magic doesn't surge again, but it ripples, almost... pleased. I, on the other hand, am trying not to implode.

"Sorry," he says quickly, adjusting his cuffs like that explains anything. "You looked like you were about to... combust."

I clear my throat, trying to summon dignity. "Well. Thank you. For the... intervention."

"That wasn't planned," he mutters, clearly annoyed with himself. "It was instinct."

"Is that... a Cupid thing?" I ask, eyes narrowing.

His jaw works. "It's a bond thing."

My pulse nearly forgets its job.

The server arrives just in time to save me from spiraling, dropping off two waters and promising to return for our order. I'm grateful for the interruption; I need the moment to gather whatever composure I have left.

Sayer leans back slightly, watching me with a level of awareness that's both irritating and impossible to ignore. "If your magic keeps flaring like that," he says, "we'll need to add grounding techniques to our plan."

"Oh, good," I say dryly. "A curriculum."

His mouth twitches—almost a smile, almost not.

"It's going to be a long dinner," he says.

And somehow, that doesn't sound like a complaint.

The tension between us shifts—not lighter, not heavier, just... real. Tangible. The kind of thing you feel behind your ribs and try very hard not to acknowledge.

But for the first time all week, the knot in my chest eases. The flare quiets. And even with everything swirling around us—curses, wings, deadlines—I feel something I haven't felt in days. A little bit of calm.

Sayer is studying the menu like it personally insulted him. He glances up, that composed, almost annoyingly collected expression already in place.

"Before I order," he says, "do you have a preference? This place does half-and-half better than anyone, and I'm not wasting the opportunity."

I lift an eyebrow. "I'm flexible. Just no anchovies, mushrooms, or pineapple on red sauce."

"That," he says dryly, "is not flexibility. That is a list of vetoes."

"It's called having standards."

The faintest flicker of amusement touches his mouth. "All right. Fair enough." Then, to the waiter who appears at his elbow: "Large pizza, extra cheese, extra garlic. Half supreme, half margherita."

The waiter nods and disappears.

I blink at him. "Extra garlic?"

"It dampens magical feedback," he says, as if ordering food for magical safety is the most normal thing in the world.

"For me or you?"

"Yes," he replies without hesitation.

I open my mouth to argue, but he's already sliding a leather folio onto the table between us. It looks official enough to audit my soul. The kind of folder that screams *please panic responsibly.*

But before he opens it, he asks, "What are you actually looking for, Francesca?"

I freeze. "Excuse me?"

"In a partner," he clarifies. "The Council assigned the match array, but they don't know you. We should start with what you want."

I look down at my hands, at the soft glow of the garlic knots warming the air, at the silverware gently tapping in response to my quickened heartbeat.

"I guess..." I begin slowly, "I want someone steady. Who knows how to ground a situation instead of inflaming it. Someone who can meet my sarcasm without getting defensive. Someone who's patient but not passive, who listens and pushes back when I need it. Someone who doesn't treat my magic like a problem to fix, or a spectacle, or a tool."

When I finally lift my gaze, he's already watching me.

And his expression... shifts. Something small. Something that says he recognizes the description whether he wants to or not.

My magic hums in my chest, warm and traitorous, as if it has the audacity to agree with what I just said. Sayer clears his throat—sharp, defensive, like my honesty reached across the table and poked him between the ribs—and he gives the folio in his hands far too much attention.

"Right," he says, straightening one cuff as if it personally offended him. "That's... useful."

He flips open the folio, and the air above the table brightens as five glowing photographs rise out of the pages. They drift upward in a loose arc, hovering like enchanted snapshots waiting to be judged.

"These," he says, with all the enthusiasm of someone reading aloud from a parking violation, "are the five least combustible options."

"Such a romantic category," I reply, and I don't even try to hide the sarcasm.

He ignores that—gracefully, which somehow makes it worse—and nudges the nearest photo toward me. The man captured in the glow looks soft around the edges, cardiganed and gentle, like he has never spoken above a polite indoor voice.

"He's very... polite," I say, watching his awkward half-smile.

"That's Elliot," Sayer says, tone even. "Earth-aligned magic. Stable. Predictable. Very low chance of igniting anything—emotionally or literally."

"Wow," I murmur. "Be still my heart."

Sayer pretends he didn't hear that and taps the next photograph forward. This one shows a broad-shouldered man with warm brown skin and flour dusted across his hands. His smile is shy in a sweet way.

"Jonas," Sayer explains. "Minimal magical output. High patience. Solid grounding presence."

"He looks like he brings casseroles to people having a bad day."

"Accurate," Sayer says, not sounding thrilled about it. "He also gifts baked goods on holidays."

The next photo drifts in—messy curls, round glasses, a slightly rumpled sweater embroidered with tiny cauldrons. The man is clutching a stack of books to his chest like they're emotional support animals.

"Quentin," Sayer says. "Potion scholar. Intelligent. Kind. Very careful."

"Careful how?"

"The kind who would ask before holding your hand or hugging you."

"That's... sweet?"

"Or slow," Sayer counters.

I roll my eyes and look to the next face. This one is... striking. Sandy hair, bright smile, confident posture. He looks like the human equivalent of hot chocolate on a cold day—warm and easy and maybe slightly too good to be true.

"That's Calum," Sayer says, voice tightening in a way he definitely doesn't want me to notice. "High compatibility. Adaptable magic. Good communication skills."

My magic gives a faint, curious flutter.

Sayer's jaw flexes. Just a little. Just enough for me to catch it.

Before he has to clear his throat again, the last photo tilts forward. A polished man with neatly trimmed facial hair and a gaze that says he alphabetizes his bookshelf and everyone else's.

"And that's Dorian," Sayer says. "Structured. Intelligent. Handles pressure well."

"He looks like he'd critique people's life choices at brunch."

"He would," Sayer confirms.

I let myself lean back, watching the photos drift lazily between us, glowing soft and expectant, as if they're waiting for me to declare a winner.

"These are my options?"

"These," he corrects without hesitation, "are your safest."

"Which is not the same thing as best."

"Correct."

My sigh is long and theatrical, the kind that could win awards. "Okay. So how does this go?"

Sayer shifts into business mode so smoothly it might as well be a spell. "Originally, I'd have spaced this out. Coffee dates. Gentle pacing. Low magical risk."

"That sounds sane. Let's do that."

"We don't have time for sane," he says flatly.

"Fantastic. Love that for me."

He folds his hands, leaning in a little. "I've arranged something else for tomorrow. A private dining room. Lunch. Controlled environment. Five candidates, one location."

I blink. "You scheduled a—what?—romantic speed-interrogation?"

"It's not an interrogation," he says, which is absolutely a lie. "It's an efficiency measure."

"Sayer. That's a speed-dating gauntlet."

"It's structured," he corrects. "Each of them will get individual time with you. Fifteen minutes apiece. Enough to get a sense of resonance without letting anything escalate."

"That sounds like a hostage situation with appetizers."

"It's better than five separate chaotic encounters in public, where any one of them might trigger your magic into detonating a bread basket."

I stare at him. "You say that like it's happened before."

"Hasn't it?"

"...once," I mutter.

He nods like he's made a very compelling point. "Exactly. This keeps things contained."

"And after this magical Thunderdome of lunch?"

"Then we narrow down the most viable candidates."

"And viable means...?"

"Resilient enough to handle your magic," he says, utterly unbothered. "And compatible enough to survive the first event."

I squint. "Event as in... what kind? Please say it's a cooking competition. Or mini golf."

"It's a ball."

I blink. "A ball. Like... gowns and dancing and too much perfume?"

"Yes."

I scrub a hand down my face and let my head fall forward. "Sayer, the last ball I went to—other than my family's—I was twenty, and my magic tried to set fire to the table linens."

"Which is exactly why we need to prepare."

"For dancing?"

"For survival," he repeats.

I peek at him between my fingers. "And how do we prepare for that?"

"Clothing," he says, far too calmly. "You'll need appropriate attire. Charm-resistant fabrics. Glamour-safe stitching. Fire protection. At least two gowns. Preferably three."

I lower my hands and stare. "You want me to have magical body armor."

"It's traditional."

"It sounds ridiculous."

"It's remarkably effective."

I sigh. Deeply. "And do I still own any of these gowns?"

"Given your recent magical incidents?" he asks, giving me a pointed look. "Highly unlikely."

"So I need new ones."

"Yes."

"We're going shopping."

"Yes."

I grimace. "Fashion with a side of magical risk assessment."

A slow exhale leaves him. "It will increase your odds."

"Of what?"

"Yes," he says.

I glare at him again. He does not blink.

The waiter arrives, setting the steaming pizza between us—the extra cheese glistening, the extra garlic wafting aggressively through the air, the supreme side practically shimmering with toppings.

"Here you are, lovebirds," he chirps.

We both choke—simultaneously, violently, with matching indignation.

"We're not—" I start.

"Official," Sayer finishes, pinching his nose.

"Sure," the waiter replies with a knowing grin before walking away.

Sayer stares down at the pizza like it's responsible for everything wrong in his life.

"This month," I say, grabbing a slice, "is going to be absolute chaos."

"It is," he agrees, taking his own slice with resigned precision. "But we'll plan for the chaos."

My magic purrs—warm and annoyingly pleased.

And somehow, despite the folder full of glowing suitors between us, I can't shake the feeling that the universe is planning something very different.

Chapter 16

Sayer

The private dining room is supposed to look elegant, but the longer Jackson and I fuss with it, the more it feels like a courtroom disguised as a bistro. Sunlight spills through the frosted windows, soft and harmless, trying its best to brighten the tension simmering in the walls. The table stretches down the length of the room, polished so thoroughly I can see my reflection bending in the grain.

Jackson steps back from adjusting the place settings with a flourish that definitely doesn't match the task. "You know," he says, gesturing at the immaculate table, "this all feels like a cross between a corporate luncheon and a wedding rehearsal."

"It's a controlled environment," I remind him, not for the first time. "Chaos needs boundaries."

"Chaos laughs at boundaries," he counters. "Normally while throwing dinner rolls."

I ignore that because he's right, and because acknowledgment only encourages him. Instead, I focus on the seating: my chair at the head, angled slightly toward the room; Leona's place on my right side, Jackson's on my left, both seats reserved for oversight; and directly across from me, the chair we've designated for Francesca. It's positioned cleanly at the opposite end, the natural focal point of the table—the place of honor, scrutiny, or possibly both.

The candidates' chairs line the long sides of the table, spaced evenly so neither proximity nor magic can give anyone unfair advantage. Across the room, near the windows, we've placed a small two-person table—angled just enough to offer privacy, not enough to hide anyone's expression. It's intimate by design, but not romantic. Practical. Efficient.

"It's too neat," Jackson says, watching me run my hand along the table's edge. "They're going to walk in and know something is up."

"Something is up," I remind him. "I'm not hiding that."

"You're *never* hiding that," he mutters under his breath.

He's not entirely wrong.

The candidates begin to arrive before I can respond. Elliot is first, stepping in with that careful, soft-footed courtesy that makes me wonder if he apologizes before he knocks on doors. Jonas follows, smelling faintly of cinnamon and bakery ovens. Quentin hovers at the threshold, clutching a small notebook like he's waiting to be called on in class. Calum strolls in without a hint of hesitation, confidence radiating off him like a summer breeze that didn't ask for permission. And last, Dorian adjusts his cufflinks as though the fate of the afternoon depends on symmetry alone.

They cluster near the entrance, taking in the room, the layout, the side table—all without speaking. The air thickens with expectation, or dread, or both.

Jackson leans toward me. "They're nervous."

"Good," I say quietly.

"Is that because nervous people behave better, or because you're enjoying this too much?" Jackson asks.

"Yes," I answer, and he mutters something theatrical while I turn toward the group of men hovering near the table. They're trying very hard to look casual and failing in five completely different ways.

"All right," I say, stepping closer before their collective anxiety turns into a problem. "Before Francesca arrives, we need to go over how this works."

Elliot shifts his weight carefully, shoulders a little tense but his expression open—ready to cooperate, ready to listen. Jonas stands beside him with the calm, grounded presence of someone who's spent years kneading dough and managing chaos without announcing it. Quentin fidgets with the edge of his notebook, glancing up at me like he's waiting for instructions he can memorize. Calum rests one hand on the back of a chair, relaxed to the point of arrogance, wearing a smirk that says he already thinks he'll ace this. Dorian holds himself with measured precision, his posture crisp, his gaze assessing every detail he can catalog.

"We'll start with a shared meal here at the main table," I explain. "Nothing dramatic. Nothing competitive. Polite conversation only."

Calum tilts his head, amusement sparking. "Polite is relative."

"Not today," I reply, and his grin sharpens just a little before he leans back again, conceding the point.

Jonas gives a quiet hum of agreement. "A shared meal sounds reasonable."

Quentin raises his hand halfway, quickly dropping it when Calum gives him a look. "And after lunch?" he asks. "We... rotate?"

"Yes," I say, gesturing toward the smaller table near the window. "Each of you will have a private conversation with Francesca over there. Fifteen minutes apiece. She'll decide the order."

Dorian's chin lifts as he studies the space. "Are we being evaluated individually or comparatively?"

"You're being evaluated," Jackson says before I can answer, and the dry finality in his tone settles that question instantly.

"Remember," I add, "this is not a competition. There is no 'winning.' This is simply to determine compatibility and safety for the coming events. No magic. No influence spells. No glamouring. Conversation only."

"That's disappointing," Calum murmurs.

"I'm sure you'll manage," I say.

He chuckles under his breath.

Before anyone can ask anything else, the room's wards shiver—subtle but unmistakable. A wash of warm, bright energy curls along the edges of the table, resonating with restless familiarity.

"She's here," Jackson says quietly.

The candidates all turn slightly toward the door, each in their own way trying to look composed.

A moment later, the door opens and Leona steps inside, guiding Francesca with a steady hand and a look that dares anyone to make this more complicated than it already is. And Francesca—wearing soft waves in her hair, a flush warming her cheeks, and a faint shimmer of magic rippling under her skin—carries the entire room's attention without even trying.

She lets her eyes travel over the setup before finding me at the head of the table. Her shoulders square a little, determination overshadowing the flicker of nerves in her magic.

Leona nudges her lightly. "Go on."

Francesca moves toward the far end of the main table—her seat, the one directly opposite mine—and settles into it with a mix of caution and resolve. The grounding charm woven into the chair hums softly in response, a barely visible pulse that steadies her magic the second she sits.

"Okay," she says, folding her hands and giving the room a look that dares it to misbehave. "Let's get this over with before something actually explodes."

I take my seat at the head of the table. Jackson sits to my left, Leona to my right. The candidates slide into their places along the sides of the table, the scrape of chairs blending with the quiet pulse of the wards as everything locks into position.

A soft knock at the door breaks the quiet tension balancing over the table, and the restaurant staff sweeps in with the kind of practiced choreography that only comes from years of navigating small dining rooms and volatile magical signatures.

Trays float ahead of them—enchanted gently, nothing flashy—before settling onto the table with the barest whisper of displaced air.

The aromas bloom instantly.

Warm rosemary and browned butter drift up from a platter of roasted chicken, the skin crisp and laced with herbs. Steam curls off bowls of wild mushroom risotto, creamy and rich, carrying that earthy scent that settles low in the chest. There's a platter of charred vegetables—zucchini, peppers, onions—glazed with maple and lemon, sending ribbons of sweet citrus through the air. And near the center, a basket of fresh bread makes the wards pulse in warning, the scent of toasted crust and melted garlic butter curling around the edges of the table like a temptation.

Francesca's magic reacts first—of course it does—lifting beneath her skin with a faint, curious shimmer as though even *her curse* appreciates good food. She inhales once, barely noticeable unless, apparently, you are me, and her fingers relax slightly against the tablecloth.

Jonas sits up straighter, the scent of the roasted chicken clearly appealing to him. Elliot gives a quiet, impressed hum. Quentin makes a soft note in his notebook as if cataloging aromas is part of his coping mechanism. Calum eyes the bread like it might be his competitive edge. And Dorian studies the spread with a level of scrutiny typically reserved for hostile contracts.

The lead server clears his throat gently and sets down a large bowl of mixed greens dressed with a vinaigrette so fragrant—honey, shallots, black pepper—that even Jackson pauses long enough to inhale appreciatively.

"Lunch is ready," the server says, offering a polite bow to Francesca first, then the rest of us. "Please let us know if you need anything."

He exits, the door whispering shut behind him, leaving the room swathed in warmth, herbs, garlic, citrus, and a thread of cinnamon from the charmed breadbasket that—the universe help me—is probably one strong emotion away from levitating.

She glances at the spread, then at me. "This smells incredible."

"It's meant to keep things grounded," I say, though my voice comes out a little lower than intended. "Warm scents counterbalance magical agitation."

Jackson leans back with a grin. "Translation: good food keeps people from doing stupid things."

Calum reaches for the bread. "Works for me."

Dorian intercepts the basket with the passive-aggressive efficiency of someone accustomed to controlling the room. "Bread passes right, not left."

Calum raises his brows. "Says who?"

"Etiquette," Dorian replies with the conviction of a man who has read the full manual.

Quentin tilts his head. "Wait—bread has a direction?"

Jonas quietly takes the bowl from Dorian's side and passes it the opposite way, smiling. "There are multiple schools of thought."

Francesca stifles a laugh, the corner of her mouth quirking, and her magic flickers warmly before settling again. The grounding charm under her chair pulses a steady counter-beat to match it.

I watch the men for a moment—the way they're already revealing themselves in small, telling ways—and then let my gaze drift back to Francesca's who is watching all of this unfold with a mixture of amusement, tension, and something softer I can't quite name yet.

The dishes glow lightly under the floating candles above, and the hum of magic curls through the room like it's waiting for what comes next.

"Shall we eat?" I ask.

Francesca nods, steadying herself with a breath, and the luncheon finally—officially—begins.

Chapter 17

Francesca

The moment the door shuts behind the servers, the dining room settles into a warm, fragrant haze—garlic butter drifting up from the breadbasket, rosemary softening the air around the roasted chicken, citrus glaze glowing sweetly over the vegetables. Everything smells rich and comforting, the kind of meal that tries to anchor a person whether they want to be anchored or not.

And my magic, traitorous little menace that it is, reacts to absolutely everything.

It hums at the bread like it remembers centuries of Bellamys charming loaves too enthusiastically. It shivers at the steam rising from the risotto—as if glutinous rice is somehow suspicious. And when my eyes slide across the table and catch on Sayer—steady posture, shirt fitted just so, watching the room like he's assessing witnesses instead of possible suitors—something in my magic curls warm and tight under my ribs.

I force myself to look away before it does anything dramatic.

The men begin serving themselves, each movement revealing more than their actual words.

Elliot, sitting closest to me on the right, handles the serving spoon with careful deliberation, his brow drawn with concern that the chicken might not line up perfectly on his plate. When he glances at me, his smile is genuine—sweet, even—and my magic hums politely but without interest. More of a gentle "oh, he's nice" vibration than anything else.

Quentin fumbles the tongs for the roasted vegetables and mutters an apology to the air, to the table, to the tongs themselves, then to me for good measure. His earnestness makes me smile, which makes him blush, which makes my magic give an embarrassed flicker that mirrors him too closely for comfort.

Dorian has already cut his chicken into uniform, mathematically consistent bites. When the breadbasket comes his way, he evaluates each piece like he's inspecting gemstones. My magic gives him a once-over and promptly settles back down in absolute disinterest.

Calum? He's exactly what he looks like—charming, bright, a walking sunbeam with extremely suspicious confidence. He scoops risotto onto his plate with a grin that feels practiced but not malicious. When he catches me looking, he tips his chin in a silent "gotcha," and my magic flares—not romantically, not uncomfortably... but with the same chaos-energy it gives fireworks and broken lightbulbs.

Calum is a walking hazard. My magic seems delighted.

And then there's Jonas, quiet and warm, who sits slightly back in his chair like he's trying not to take up too much space. He passes me the breadbasket without flourish, simply murmuring, "Careful, it's warm," as if that tiny kindness is instinct rather than intention. His eyes, when they meet mine, are steady in a way that makes something deep in my magic stir—soft, warm, curious.

Unexpected. Comfortable. Almost grounding.

The scent of cinnamon clings to him like he walked through a bakery on his way here... which, honestly, he might have. My magic leans toward him the way plants lean toward sunlight.

Well. That's inconvenient.

I reach for a piece of bread, trying to appear unaffected. The spell woven into the basket shivers at my touch, but Jonas steadies it with a light tap of his thumb, and the charm settles instantly. He doesn't comment on it, doesn't even look smug—just gives me a small nod like it's normal to calm down someone's semi-sentient bread.

And suddenly I understand why Sayer's jaw flexed when he showed me Jonas's picture.

His gaze flicks toward me at that exact moment—quick, sharp, entirely too perceptive. My magic snaps to attention in my chest, warm and bright, and I have to reach for my water glass to break eye contact before something levitates.

"Everyone comfortable?" he asks, tone mild but lined with lawyer authority.

"Very," Calum says, leaning back with a grin. "Good food, good company, high stakes. What's not to like?"

Dorian presses a cloth napkin to his mouth, unimpressed. "Some of us are here to take this seriously."

Jonas takes a sip of water, voice low. "Being relaxed doesn't mean you're not serious."

Quentin nods eagerly. "Right! Right. Serious. Relaxed. We can be both."

Elliot clears his throat. "This is a lovely meal, Francesca. Thank you for inviting us."

"I didn't invite you," I say before I can soften it. "But thank you for being here anyway."

That earns a quiet laugh from Jackson. "Honest. I like that."

My magic pulses again, a warm wave that brushes the wards, and Sayer reacts before anyone else—his fingers tightening briefly on his fork, posture sharpening a fraction, the subtle twitch along his shoulders giving away the wings he's trying not to flare in public.

I look away immediately, cheeks warming.

The conversation continues, weaving between the men like threads of their personalities tangling and tugging. I answer questions when they're directed at me, attempt polite responses, and do my best to keep my magic from dramatizing my emotions. But the whole table feels alive, expectant, humming with competing energies.

Two men keep drawing my attention:

Calum, bright and bold and impossible to ignore— and Jonas, quiet and steady and unexpectedly magnetic.

And then there's the third pull I refuse to acknowledge:

Sayer, watching all of this like he's measuring the shape of my fate with his bare hands.

The risotto is warm, the chicken tender, but the air is thick with tension and magic and the subtle, relentless hum beneath my ribs that reacts every time Sayer speaks.

I take another sip of water to steady myself.

As I do, Sayer's voice cuts gently through the room. "When you're ready, Francesca, we'll begin the individual conversations."

The small table near the window waits quietly, sunlight catching the rim of its plates. And my magic—traitorous, unpredictable, too loud for its own good—gives a bright, anticipatory flicker.

The moment everyone's attention shifts toward me, the pressure lands all at once, and of course that's the exact second my magic decides to make an entrance. The rosemary sprig in the little glass vase gives a faint tremor, like it's bracing for impact. The breadbasket inches subtly in my direction, as if my magic is trying to claim emotional support carbs. Even the wards along the windows respond with a faint shimmer, catching the light in a way I really hope no one else is paying attention to.

Harper would call this "adorably dramatic." Personally, I call it "please, not in the restaurant."

I press my palm lightly against the table and try to steady the warmth building in my chest. Choosing should be simple. Pick a man, walk to the side table, proceed with structured awkwardness. Instead, my magic swells the moment I consider any of them—bright, eager, far too involved—like it wants to make the choice for me. The surge pushes upward, tightening beneath my ribs, and I know if I don't resolve this quickly something in the room is going to react in a way that requires a mop, a charm reversal, or both.

Before I can make a decision—or accidentally trigger a spontaneous indoor breeze—Jonas clears his throat softly. He stands with a calm I wish I could borrow. "If it helps, I can go first."

The relief that moves through my chest is instant and palpable, and my magic settles so quickly it feels like someone lowered a window sash. "That... would actually help a lot," I admit, giving him a grateful look.

He nods and waits for me to rise before heading toward the small table by the window, steady and quiet in a way that doesn't draw attention yet manages to ground the entire room.

Jonas sets the tone without meaning to. Our talk at the little window table is warm and unhurried, full of quiet steadiness that feels like a soft quilt laid over fresh snow. He listens well, asks thoughtful questions, and tells me, almost shyly, about his obsession with heirloom baking molds. It's sweet and unexpectedly endearing. But somewhere in the middle of explaining the science of perfect crumb texture—the fourth tangent in fifteen minutes—my magic begins to tug back, growing restless. By the time we wrap up, I'm both charmed and quietly overwhelmed, like too much cinnamon on an already sweet pastry.

The rest of the afternoon moves in a warm, indistinct blur, each man stepping into that little sunlit space and leaving behind a brief impression—something pleasant, something jarring, something that tells me my magic is paying closer attention than I am.

Elliot sits next. He carries gentleness like it's sewn into his clothes, offering easy conversation about music, city parks, and the quieter corners of town he retreats to when life feels too loud. I find myself liking the calm of him. But then he mentions his five-year plan—which includes living somewhere remote, ideally a cabin in the mountains—and the moment he says the word *secluded,* my magic stiffens like someone pulled a thread too hard. Being alone in the woods with a man who plans his future with bullet points and color-coded charts? Probably not.

Quentin follows, and I barely have time to reset my breath before he sits down with a notebook so earnest it practically glows. He asks if I prefer cats or dogs, then apologizes for asking, then apologizes for apologizing. It's cute for the first ten minutes. It's exhausting the moment he starts rewriting his questions mid-sentence. Still, when he talks about his favorite fantasy novels, sparks light in his eyes, and it's impossible not to enjoy that kind of passion—until he mentions he's never traveled farther than two hours outside the city. My magic folds its metaphorical arms in absolute silence.

Then Calum takes his turn. He carries himself like he was born knowing the room will love him, and I hate that my magic reacts before I do. It flares warm and bright the moment he smiles, which is rude because half his charm feels practiced, like he's spent years perfecting it. He talks about marathons and city festivals and his uncanny ability to win free drinks at trivia nights. It's fun—really fun—but midway through describing a bar brawl involving enchanted billiard balls, it hits me that his life is approximately ninety percent chaos and ten percent cardio. My magic buzzes like it wants to join the chaos. I do not.

Which leaves Dorian.

He sits across from me with a stare so intent it feels like an audit. He asks smart questions—sharp, probing, analytical—and there's something compelling about a man who wants every variable laid out clearly. But when he starts reciting the legal statutes surrounding magical licensing, I feel myself drifting. My magic drifts too, fluttering around us with no real interest, as if even the curse can't keep up with footnotes.

When I finally return to the long table, the afternoon light has softened along the windows, and the men have slipped into an easy conversation among themselves while they wait. They shift chairs, pass the breadbasket, laugh quietly at something I didn't hear. And somewhere in that shifting orbit, two of them draw into the same gravitational pull.

Calum leans toward Quentin with his usual effortless charm, and Quentin—normally tight-shouldered and self-conscious—relaxes in a way I never saw with me. They start comparing running routes, then favorite cafés, then novel recommendations. The more they talk, the brighter they both seem, as if they're reflecting each other without thinking about it.

It's subtle at first—a smile exchanged too easily, a shared laugh that softens the whole table—but it sharpens when Quentin says something about marathon training. Calum sits up with a little spark in his eyes, grin widening. The connection between them clicks like a key turning in a lock.

It's not directed at me. It's not *about* me. And for the first time all day, my magic actually settles in content agreement.

When Quentin pauses, flustered, as if he's revealed too much, I tilt my head and gently nudge the moment. "You know," I tell him, "there's a running group that meets on Thursdays near the river. They're always looking for new people."

Calum glances toward Quentin, expression brightening. "Funny. I run that group."

Quentin blinks. "You... what? Really?"

"Really," Calum says, nudging his shoulder against Quentin's with easy familiarity. "You should come by. I mean—if you want to."

The warmth that flares between them is unmistakable, and my magic hums its approval like it's been waiting for someone to get a clue.

By the time Sayer clears his throat to refocus the room, Calum and Quentin are exchanging numbers, smiling in that quiet, expectant way people do when something unexpected and hopeful has taken root.

And somehow, in the midst of all the nerves and interviews and magic that refuses to mind its business, I feel the first sliver of the day that feels like actual progress.

This curse might be a nightmare. The timeline is definitely going to kill me. But at least two people are leaving with a win.

And for the first time in days, the magic under my skin softens into something almost gentle.

Chapter 18

Sayer

The moment the meal winds down, the energy in the room shifts. Plates are cleared, chairs scrape back, and the candidates linger in that uncertain space between polite dismissal and hope. Francesca is still at the long table, gathering her things with a soft, distracted focus; her magic flickers around her like warm static, and every now and then it tugs at something under my ribs I wish it would leave alone.

Calum and Quentin are deep in conversation by the door—too deep, in fact—and when Francesca catches sight of them comparing phone screens and laughing with an ease that never surfaced with her, she lifts a brow in my direction, equal parts amused and resigned. The smallest ghost of a smile touches her mouth before she turns to slip her bag over her shoulder.

"I'm heading back to the bakery," she says, brushing a loose strand of hair behind her ear. "Prep for the evening rush waits for no one."

Leona moves in to hand her a to-go pastry box, murmuring an affectionate reminder to eat something real later. Francesca thanks her, offers Jackson a quick wave, and gives me a look that's equal parts guarded curiosity and weary humor—one I haven't found a name for yet. Then she steps out, the door closing behind her in a gentle click that somehow feels louder than the room deserves.

Once she's gone, I turn my attention back to the remaining candidates. Jonas has already left with a quiet nod. Calum and Quentin are clearly drifting toward plans of their own. That leaves Elliot and Dorian—both standing a little apart from one another, waiting to be dismissed or instructed, not sure yet which way the wind is blowing.

I gesture for them to stay where they are, then step forward enough to make the moment formal. "I need a few minutes of your time," I say, keeping my voice even. "You both handled yourselves well today, and I'd like to move forward with one-on-one dates."

Elliot straightens with a relieved exhale, while Dorian gives a small, assessing nod, already filing details away in that relentlessly structured mind of his.

I turn slightly, enough that Leona and Jackson can hear me. "We need two dates set. One tomorrow afternoon, one Sunday evening."

Leona flips open her planner with a flourish that could rival a stage magician. "All right. Who's tomorrow?"

"Elliot," I say. "Something calm. Neutral space. Somewhere he won't feel pressured and her magic won't feel challenged."

She taps her pen twice on the page. "I have ideas."

I believe her, which is either comforting or dangerous, depending on the hour.

Jackson is already pulling out his phone when I look at him. "Sunday for Dorian," I say. "Something structured. Quiet. No surprises that might trigger the curse."

He smirks. "A date that feels like a well-written contract. Got it."

Dorian considers that with absolute seriousness, then nods. "That would be ideal."

I ignore the way Jackson's mouth twitches.

"When your appointments come," I continue, "you'll both meet at my office first. I'll go over logistics with you, and you'll pick Francesca up after that. Timeliness matters."

Elliot promises he'll be early. Dorian assures me he's never late. Neither point surprises me.

When they finally leave—quietly, politely, each with the air of a man heading into some kind of exam—the room exhales. Chairs get pushed in, stray napkins collected, lingering magic tamped down by habit. I gather the files and tuck them into my briefcase, but my thoughts refuse to settle as neatly.

Leona watches me with a knowing look, the kind she probably thinks is subtle. "She did well," she says lightly, adjusting the stack of menus into perfect alignment. "You did too. For someone pretending not to hover."

I give her a flat stare that only makes her smile widen.

Jackson nudges her as he lifts the leftover breadbasket. "You think he hovered? I think he brooded. Big difference."

I could argue the point, but there's no point pretending otherwise. They're right, and we all know it. The room still carries a faint hint of rosemary from the table and that warm, subtle scent Francesca always brings with her, something bright beneath the flour and sugar that lingers longer than it should. Her laugh has been echoing in the back of my mind since she walked out, looping far too easily for a man who prides himself on emotional discipline.

I remind myself of the role I'm supposed to play—professional, focused, the impartial hand guiding a complicated case—but the truth settles in with a weight I can't quite ignore. If I'm going to keep that line intact, I'll need to get a handle on this long before those dates start. I finish giving Leona and Jackson the final round of instructions—what needs to be confirmed, which protective wards to refresh, and how to keep the next two dates from turning into magical emergencies. They listen with the patient focus of people who have long accepted that micromanaging is my love language, even when I refuse to call it that.

When I'm done, Leona tucks the remaining menus under her arm and gives me a look that lands somewhere between satisfaction and amusement, while Jackson barely hides his grin behind the breadbasket he's emptying. Their expressions make it clear they think I'm invested more than I should be, but instead of correcting them, I gather my briefcase and head for the door before either decides to be clever about it.

The winter air outside is sharp enough to sting, but it clears my head in a way the restaurant never could. The city has settled into that lull between afternoon and evening; traffic is light, the sidewalks thinned out, and every breath burns cold before dissolving into a faint trail of fog. I start walking automatically, telling myself I'm heading home, though the thought rings false even before I reach the corner. Home would leave me alone with a glowing file, an impossible deadline, and far too much space to replay the sound of Francesca's laugh or the way her magic kept brushing against my awareness like it had forgotten I don't want it there. That combination never leads anywhere good.

So I turn down the side street instead, the one lined with older buildings that lean toward each other as if sharing stories. The lamps here give off a deeper golden glow, warm enough to soften the brick walls and chase the worst of the cold from my coat. My pace settles into something measured as I follow the familiar path, and beneath the quiet rhythm of my steps I can feel the old instinct pulling me forward, the one I've tried for years to ignore. It's stronger tonight, threaded with the kind of tension that comes from knowing I've already crossed a line simply by opening that damn file.

The townhouse waits at the end of the block, red brick weathered but dignified, its windows glowing with the steady light of someone who prefers to be left alone but always knows when company is coming anyway. The door is cracked open by just an inch—a very pointed invitation from a man who doesn't make accidents.

I pause at the threshold long enough to gather myself, then push it open and step inside. The warmth hits immediately, wrapping around me with the familiar hum of old magic woven into the frame, the same signature he's carried through every place he's lived over the centuries.

"Come in, Sayer," my mentor calls from deeper in the house, his voice warm in that aggravatingly perceptive way of his. "I've been expecting you."

And just like that, the pretense of avoiding this conversation dissolves. I let the door latch behind me and move toward the sound of his voice, the weight of the last few days settling across my shoulders in a way even the cold couldn't shake loose.

My mentor waits in the glow of the fire, settled into that deep green armchair with a kind of ageless steadiness that always makes it difficult to remember just how old he actually is. Lucian Marrow hasn't changed in the fifteen years since I stormed out of Headquarters—same silver-streaked hair pulled back neatly at the nape, same angular features softened only by time and an almost scholarly curiosity, same eyes the exact shade of amber glass warmed by candlelight. His presence has always carried the quiet weight of old magic, the kind woven into bones and bloodlines rather than conjured on a whim.

Most people see only a refined academic when they first meet him. They don't see the former Guardian, the one who brokered peace treaties between enchanted factions three centuries before I ever existed, or the man who personally trained the last three generations of Cupids until the Council decided his methods were "too intuitive" to be standardized. He retired only officially; in practice, Lucian simply moved his guidance off the record and into whatever home he chose to inhabit that decade.

This townhouse—worn brick, tall windows, walls lined with books rescued from dying magical archives—is merely the latest in a long list. It suits him, though. Everything here smells faintly of cedarwood and old spell ink, a scent that always felt like permission to breathe.

He watches me now with that layered gaze—part mentor, part archivist of mistakes I haven't admitted yet. "You look older," he says quietly, not unkindly. "But also more yourself than when you left."

"I'm not sure that's a compliment," I reply, taking the seat across from him.

"It is," he answers, lifting his teacup again. "You were half-shadow and half-expectation when you trained under me. Now at least you've chosen who you want to be. Even if you chose poorly."

I huff out a laugh despite myself. "Law isn't a poor choice."

"It isn't," he agrees, "but running from a calling is."

The fire pops as if punctuating the truth of it. I settle deeper into the chair, letting its familiar worn edges steady me. "Lucian... I need your advice."

He sets his cup down with deliberate care, fingers long and steady. "Then you finally came to the right place. Start from the beginning."

"It's Francesca Bellamy," I say, and the shift in his expression tells me everything I need to know. Lucian doesn't pale or stiffen; he simply becomes sharply present, the way he used to before stepping into any battlefield or negotiation chamber. That quiet stillness is its own warning.

"I suspected," he murmurs. "The magic around you changed the second you crossed my wards."

"She's my unresolved assignment," I say. "The file I buried."

"You were barely more than a fledgling when they gave her to you," he replies. "No one should have been surprised when you broke under that pressure."

"I didn't break."

"You did," he counters softly. "You just redirected the collapse into a different path."

I bristle, then force myself to breathe through it, because he isn't wrong. He has never been wrong about me, which is the most infuriating thing about him.

"The Council gave me a deadline," I say. "Midnight on the fourteenth. If I fail, everything I've built collapses. Every divorce I facilitated reverses. Every life I helped restructure gets rewound."

Lucian exhales slowly, the sound layered with centuries of understanding. "And if you succeed?"

"That's the part that isn't clear yet."

His gaze sharpens. "Tell me what you've felt."

I hesitate a fraction too long, and he sees it immediately. He always sees it.

"She responds to my presence," I say. "Her magic does. Stronger than it should."

Lucian leans forward, elbows resting lightly on his knees. The firelight casts soft shadows along the markings on his jaw, evidence of the old pact-magics his line is known for. "A Bellamy's magic will always react to the Cupid assigned to them. That bond isn't ephemeral or emotional. It's structural. Foundational. Ancient. You were tied the moment her name was written onto your docket."

I swallow once, hard, because the truth tastes like inevitability.

"And you," he adds gently, "are reacting to her far more than you want to admit."

I drag a hand through my hair and let my head fall back against the chair. "I didn't come here for sentimental analysis."

"No," Lucian agrees with a faint smile, "but you came for truth. So here it is: if her magic is flaring at your presence already, the bond is reawakening. And if the bond is reawakening, then your role in her story isn't just professional."

"That's exactly what I was afraid of," I mutter.

He tilts his head slightly, studying me in that deeply patient way of his. "Then ask the real question, Sayer. What are you afraid it means?"

And that—more than the file, more than the deadline, more than the looming chaos ahead—is the part I haven't let myself confront.

Not yet. But I'm going to have to.

Chapter 19

Francesca

The late-morning light in my apartment has that warm, forgiving quality that makes everything look softer than it feels. I'm halfway through curling my hair, trying to convince both myself and my magic that this lunch date is nothing to be nervous about, when my phone buzzes against the counter. The caller ID flashes all three names at once: Daphne, Juniper, Cassia.

Perfect timing. Or terrible timing. With my sisters, those are usually the same thing.

I accept the call, propping the phone against my mirror.

Daphne appears first, sitting cross-legged at her kitchen island with a bowl of cereal big enough to feed a small village. Her long hair is piled on top of her head in a loose knot, and she's multitasking in the most Daphne way possible—scrolling on her tablet with one hand while spooning cereal with the other. Sunlight pours in behind her, catching on the faint dusting of flour across her shirt, evidence that she's either been baking or stress-snacking. With Daphne, the line is thin.

Juniper's frame comes next. She's in her plant room—the sunniest corner of her house—surrounded by greenery that climbs the shelves behind her. She's trimming the leaves of a pothos plant, her movements unhurried, her expression calm in that instinctive, grounded way that always makes me feel like she could talk a lightning storm into taking a deep breath.

Cassia appears last, already seated at her desk with her planner open, color-coded tabs arranged like a rainbow of judgment. Her hair is pinned neatly, her glasses perched low on her nose, and her background is immaculate—as if the room itself starts organizing the moment she enters it.

All three of them take one look at me—hair half done, dress not yet zipped, makeup in progress—and inhale sharply in unison.

Daphne's cereal spoon stops midair. "Okay, that's not your bakery face. What's going on?"

Juniper sets down her shears and leans closer, eyes softening. "You look... anticipatory."

Cassia clicks her pen once, the sound sharp. "Date today?"

I exhale, adjusting the phone so they can see me more clearly. "Yes. Lunch with Elliot."

Daphne brightens instantly. "He sounded sweet. A little nervous. But sweet."

Cassia already has her pen moving. "Walk us through what we need to know. Brief summary."

I smooth a curl that refuses to cooperate. "There's not much to tell. He's punctual, polite, and he didn't flinch when a pastry tray tried to roll itself off the cart yesterday."

Juniper smiles behind a curtain of trailing leaves. "That's a good sign. Stability matters."

"It does," I agree, even though my stomach hasn't fully caught up with the sentiment. "But my magic's been... off. Restless. Like it's hovering too close to the surface."

Cassia looks up sharply. "Restless in which direction? Flare, surge, or premature attunement?"

"Not a flare," I say, pressing a hand over the slow current beneath my skin. "More like it's... listening. Paying attention to things I wish it wouldn't."

Daphne narrows her eyes at me. "Listening to who?"

The mascara wand suddenly feels heavier. "We are not doing this."

Juniper's voice is gentle but firm. "Francesca. The curse intensifies with emotional instability. If your magic is reacting, we need to know what or who triggered it."

I breathe out slowly, watching the morning sun drift across my dresser. "It reacted during the gauntlet yesterday. But it wasn't with Elliot."

Cassia freezes. "Then who?"

My silence says everything.

Daphne makes a low sound like she's just uncovered a scandal in one of her dramas. "Jonas. It was Jonas, wasn't it?"

Juniper's smile warms. "He did have a grounding presence."

Cassia writes something down immediately, probably a flowchart titled Potential Magical Resonance Indicators.

"Just because my magic reacted doesn't mean anything," I say, tightening the zipper on the back of my dress. "Right now, I need to get through lunch without setting off the restaurant's fire suppression system."

Juniper nods, tucking a strand of hair behind her ear. "Then focus on grounding. Eat something before you go."

Daphne shovels another spoonful of cereal into her mouth. "And text us if the date is a disaster. Or if it's great. Or if it's medium. Actually just text regardless."

Cassia closes her planner with a soft snap. "We're here if something shifts. Even something small."

"I know," I say, slipping into my coat. "And I appreciate it."

Juniper lifts her plant shears in a small, encouraging gesture. "You've got this."

Daphne grins around her cereal. "Go be charming. Or at least go be fed."

Cassia gives one decisive nod. "Report back."

The call disconnects, leaving the apartment in its earlier quiet. My magic swirls beneath my ribcage—not volatile, not calm, just present. A reminder that time is not on my side.

I take one steadying breath and head downstairs. By the time I reach the bottom of the stairs, I've convinced myself that today might actually go well. Elliott stands near the front counter, hands clasped politely, posture a little too straight—as if he rehearsed it. But the smile he gives me is warm, earnest, and completely unthreatening in a way that settles something low and hopeful inside my ribs.

My magic reacts softly—a gentle little flutter, curious but not chaotic. It feels like a door cracking open instead of blowing off the hinges, which honestly counts as progress.

"You look lovely," Elliott says, offering an arm.

"Thank you," I answer, looping mine through his and letting myself take that peaceful breath I've been chasing all week. "Ready for lunch?"

"Absolutely."

We walk through the crisp, late-morning air toward the restaurant Sayer arranged, and the first few minutes feel... good. Comfortable. The kind of ease I've been trying to find, the kind of spark-adjacent flutter that could maybe grow into something with the right nudge.

He talks about his morning at the conservatory—replanting a stubborn rosemary shrub, prepping soil mixtures for winter herbs—and there's something soothing about the way he describes things. Gentle. Steady. Thoughtful.

I catch myself leaning toward that steadiness, searching for that deeper tug the curse is supposed to respond to. It doesn't come—but the absence doesn't feel like a red flag yet. Just... early.

Once we're seated, menus open between us, Elliott smiles a little shyly. "Tell me about you. Outside the bakery. Outside magic. What does Francesca Bellamy love?"

God, it's been a while since anyone asked me that.

"I used to paint," I say, smoothing the napkin into my lap. "Read a lot. Drag my cousins on road trips they didn't ask for. But lately it feels like the bakery and the curse ate entire years while I wasn't paying attention."

"That happens," he says softly. "Especially when you're taking care of everyone else."

His tone is warm enough that some small part of me tries to rise to meet it. My magic hums, testing the air, as if uncertain whether to lean in or pull back.

I'm still trying to coax that spark when the conversation shifts—naturally, easily—toward family.

"Do you all work in the bakery together?" he asks. "Your cousins, I mean?"

"Oh—some of them." I laugh lightly. "Harper works the midnight shift. She's the one who gets the dough prepped for morning. Flour ends up everywhere when she's on rotation, but she's a genius with pastries."

Elliott's whole face brightens in a way that takes me off guard. "Really? What kind of pastries does she make?"

"Chaotic ones," I say fondly. "She once made a blackberry-lavender brioche that shouldn't have worked, but somehow it was the best thing I'd eaten all year. She insists dough 'talks' to her."

His eyes spark—just a little. "That's... incredible."

The warmth in his voice shifts in a way I feel before I fully register it—something soft, bright, and unmistakably curious. And for the first time all afternoon, I realize that glow isn't aimed at me at all. It settles somewhere else entirely, something in the space where I'd mentioned Harper's name. The moment stretches, subtle but undeniable, and the whole date rearranges itself in my mind with quiet, startling clarity. He *is* a good match—just not in the direction I'd hoped. Not for me.

We continue talking anyway, both of us pretending we don't feel the shift. Elliott asks kind questions, listens attentively, smiles in ways that should tug at me... but don't. At least, not like they should. My magic stays calm. Not reaching. Not sparking. Just... observing. Almost relieved.

And every time conversation drifts toward something personal, something tender, Elliott responds with warmth—but it's warmth that doesn't land the way I hope it would. Not on me. But when I mention Harper again—casually, unintentionally—his expression lifts in a way I don't think he even notices. And that's when I realize I've spent the last ten minutes describing her without meaning to.

And the entire time?

The one name my magic keeps circling back to is Sayer Valentine.

But with Sayer—just the thought of him—my magic draws tight beneath my skin, a quick, traitorous pull like someone catching a thread that shouldn't be tugged. I try to shake it off, try to focus on the man sitting across from me, but the shift is there, pulsing quietly.

Elliott finishes a sip of water, sets the glass down, then studies me with a level of gentle observation that makes me straighten a little.

"Can I ask you something?" he says.

"Of course."

"It's about Sayer."

My fork pauses midair. "What about him?"

He hesitates—not in discomfort, but in the careful way someone chooses their words when they want to be respectful. "I don't know him well," he begins, "but he's... attentive to you."

A subtle heat pricks low in my throat. "Attentive?"

"Yes," he says, leaning back slightly, thoughtful rather than prying. "Not possessive. Not jealous. Just... aware of you in a way people don't bother to be unless they care how something turns out."

I blink, unsure whether to laugh or ask for examples. "You got all that from one afternoon?"

Elliott smiles, a little sheepish. "I pay attention for a living," he says. "And he watches you like he's tracking more than your schedule. When your magic shifted during the introductions? He noticed before anyone else."

My stomach dips, slow and warm, like the floor tilting beneath me. "You're reading too much into it."

"Maybe," he allows. "But I saw the way his posture changed when you walked into the restaurant. Like he was bracing for impact and relieved at the same time."

That tenderness I am absolutely not ready for flickers through me, immediate and unwelcome.

"And," Elliott adds carefully, "I saw the way *you* reacted when he spoke to you yesterday. You looked at him like you were trying very hard not to."

I set my fork down before I drop it. "Not to what?"

He gives a soft, knowing laugh. "Not to feel something."

My magic purrs in agreement—annoyingly, smugly—and I wish I could shove it under the table with my purse.

Elliott raises both hands slightly, palms out. "No pressure from me. Truly. But if you're trying to force a spark somewhere it doesn't live, maybe the place you're avoiding is where the real answer is."

I open my mouth to argue, to dismiss, to redirect, but he cuts in gently.

"I like you, Francesca," he says, warmth steady and uncomplicated. "But not in the way the curse needs. And that's okay. There's nothing wrong with discovering we're better suited in other directions. But whatever is going on with you and Sayer..." he gestures vaguely toward my chest, where the magic is currently doing an interpretive dance, "...it's not nothing."

I exhale slowly, the truth settling in like a weight I can't quite shift.

Elliott's smile softens. "And for what it's worth? He's far more rattled by you than he'd ever admit."

My thoughts slip—inevitably—back to the way Sayer had looked at me earlier this week, the tension in his shoulders, the sharp attention in his eyes, the way his wings had unfurled as if reacting to something he couldn't help.

Tightened thread, indeed.

"Let's just survive lunch first," I murmur, picking up my fork again.

Elliott laughs, warm and easy. "Deal."

Chapter 20

Sayer

Jackson walks Elliott out with a cheerful "right this way," and the moment the door closes behind them, the office feels too quiet in a way that presses at the back of my neck. I start pacing the lobby, hands in my pockets, trying very hard not to think about the fact that Francesca Bellamy is about to go on a finalist date with someone who isn't me.

Leona watches me over the top of a case file, unimpressed. "You're doing that thing again."

"What thing?"

"The thing where you pace like you're waiting for a verdict from the Underworld."

"I'm monitoring," I say, adjusting my cuffs more sharply than necessary.

"Monitoring," she repeats, deadpan. "Sure."

Before I can fire back, the door opens and Jackson strides in—coat dusted with snow, cheeks flushed from the cold.

"Alright," he says, rubbing his hands together. "Elliott's next door waiting for Francesca. She should be down any—"

He stops mid-sentence, following Leona's gaze to the window.

Francesca and Elliott have just stepped onto the sidewalk together, her arm linked through his. She's smiling—wide, bright, open in a way that sends something sharp through my chest. Elliott leans in to say something, and she tips her head toward him like the moment is easy, familiar, comfortable.

My wings twitch under my shirt, a quick, involuntary flash of heat down my spine.

Jackson lets out a low whistle. "Well. That's a look."

Leona folds her arms. "He's doing emotional math in real time."

"I'm not," I mutter.

They both stare at me like I've started speaking in tongues.

Jackson smirks. "Buddy, your shoulder blades are glowing."

I yank my coat tighter. "Residual HQ magic."

"Uh-huh," Leona says. "And I'm an archangel."

I brush past them into my office, shutting the door before my face gives away anything else. Of course, neither of them respects boundaries enough to stay out; they trail in after me like nosy familiars.

I pull Francesca's glowing file to the center of my desk. Her signature magic flickers along the surface—warm, gold, annoyingly responsive to my touch. The glyph pulses once, syncing to the beat of my pulse before I can stop it.

"We need to finalize the next forty-eight hours," I say, forcing my voice steady. "Two finalists. Two evaluations. One today. One tomorrow. After dinner with Dorian, we decide who attends the major events with her."

Leona takes the seat opposite me, flipping open a notebook. "And how are *you* doing with that?"

"I'm fine."

Jackson drops into the chair beside her. "He says, while actively radiating thunderstorm energy."

"I'm not—" I pinch the bridge of my nose. "Elliott first. Lunch date today. Dorian tomorrow. We need the compatibility projections updated, surge patterns rechecked, and event-readiness outlined."

Leona lifts a brow. "You mean you're going to drown yourself in research so you don't have to think about what you felt watching her walk off with someone else."

"That's not—"

The lights flicker. My wings thrum. Jackson makes a triumphant sound.

"See?" he says. "Emotional tsunami."

I glare at both of them and shove the glowing file forward, opening the next phase: timeline markers, resonance patterns, event protocols. Every thread twists back to her—her magic, her name, the ripple she creates without meaning to.

"We stay objective," I say. "We stay on task. No personal involvement. At ALL."

Leona's smile is all teeth. "You keep saying that like repetition will make it true."

Jackson leans back. "I give it two dates before he cracks."

I snap the file shut, jaw tight. "We are done discussing my emotional state. Update the projections. Prep the event outlines. And for the love of everything, do not bring up my wings."

They exchange a wordless, wickedly amused glance.

"Sure, boss," Jackson says. "Absolutely."

"Whatever you say, dear," Leona adds sweetly.

I ignore them both and dive into the work, telling myself the burn under my skin is just stress, just pressure, just the job.

It's not jealousy, I tell myself. It's not longing, or whatever that sharp little pull was when I saw her hand resting so easily on someone else's arm. It's pressure. Responsibility. The weight of a case that's already more complicated than it should be.

Just the assignment.

The alert flickers across the projection just as I'm trying to convince myself that rereading Francesca's compatibility strands for the fifth time counts as productive. A soft chime follows, delicate enough to be polite but insistent enough to demand attention. I tap my fingers against the edge of the holograph, angling it toward me as the update expands into full view. Elliot's name rises to the top of the chart, accompanied by an elegant line of script noting a sudden shift in availability.

"Interesting," I say, keeping my voice neutral purely out of spite. "It looks like Elliot's been offered a research fellowship."

Leona glances up from her notes, suspicious but curious. "A fellowship? Where?"

"Bell Haven College of Enchanted Sciences. East Coast." I scroll through the details—funding, housing, a three-year appointment, all wrapped in enough academic prestige to make even the most grounded mortal reconsider their immediate plans. "It's an impressive offer. The kind people uproot their lives for."

Jackson returns from the break room with fresh coffee, catches the shift in my expression, and leans forward like he's tuning into a soap opera. "That sounds like a game changer."

"It certainly complicates things," I reply, pulling the projection closer and pretending the faint sense of relief unspooling in my chest is irritation instead. "If he accepts—and he probably will—it removes him from the finalist track before he even gets to the second evaluation."

Leona's gaze sharpens, studying not the screen, but me. "You're remarkably calm about this."

"I'm being professional."

"That's not what I said."

I ignore the remark and fold the projection down to its next layer, reviewing the timeline adjustments. Removing one finalist shifts the entire pacing, compressing evaluation structure, placing more pressure on Dorian's dinner tomorrow, and thrusting Francesca straight into the major events without a chance to ease into the rituals. It's an inefficient plan, messy and unnecessarily abrupt; I'd argue against it even if I didn't have personal feelings to deny.

Leona watches the calculations flick across the screen, then taps her pen against her knee. "If Elliot's out, Dorian becomes the primary candidate by default. That's risky."

"Which is why we'll prepare him accordingly," I say, adjusting the event-readiness metrics.

She tilts her head. "Or—and hear me out—you could stop pretending you're just running spreadsheets and actually help Francesca prepare yourself."

Jackson laughs under his breath. "She's advocating practice dates. I love this for us."

I straighten, narrowing my eyes at both of them. "Practice dates?"

Leona lifts her chin with that infuriating confidence she gets when she knows she's right. "Yes. Warm-ups. Rehearsals. Call them whatever makes you feel less flustered. She needs someone who knows the pacing of the events, the magical etiquette, the emotional pressure points. If she goes into the major gatherings cold, her magic will detonate the decorations before they dim the lights."

Jackson gestures toward the glowing file. "And you're the only one who's actually trained for this stuff. Might as well put that ancient Cupid knowledge to work."

I try for indignation. It comes out closer to weary resignation. "That's not how this assignment works. I'm the evaluator, not the participant."

Leona doesn't blink. "You're also the only person whose presence stabilizes her magic instead of igniting it."

That lands harder than I expect. I feel the truth of it in the slow ripple beneath my skin, a hum I've been ignoring since she walked into my office days ago. I clear my throat, adjusting the projections again to buy myself a second. "If Elliot leaves—and he should—then yes, we'll need a plan to help her acclimate before the first major event. But this is still a structured process. There are rules."

"Rules you already broke the moment she stepped into your office," Jackson says, far too pleased with himself.

I shoot him a look sharp enough to cut paper, but he only sips his coffee with a satisfied grin.

Leona leans forward, folding her hands atop her notebook. "Sayer, you can call it preparation, training, calibration—whatever helps you sleep at night. But she trusts you. Her magic responds to you. If she's going to walk into those events without panicking, she needs a partner she won't accidentally set on fire. That's you. Whether you like it or not."

The room goes quiet around us, filled with the low hum of the magical database and the soft glow of amber light pulsing along the edges of Francesca's file. I tap the corner of the projection and watch the event icons rearrange themselves, sliding seamlessly into a new timeline that would, admittedly, run far more smoothly with the additional preparation she'd get working directly with me.

It's not jealousy, I remind myself. It's not longing or possessiveness or anything remotely problematic. It's strategy. Planning. The responsible approach. If Elliot is leaving, Francesca needs stability and support during the most volatile part of the season.

Practice events make sense.

Leona sees the exact moment I accept the logic. Of course she does. "Should I schedule a few warm-up outings? Something small to start with—a dance walkthrough, a charm rehearsal, maybe even a mock dinner?"

Jackson grins. "Look at that. We just volunteered you for dating drills."

I close out the projection and straighten in my chair, composing myself with what dignity I can muster. "Schedule whatever is necessary to ensure she's prepared. This is still about the assignment."

Leona's smile is far too knowing. "Naturally."

Jackson lifts his mug. "For the assignment."

I return to the file, grateful for the distraction of glowing glyphs and neat timelines, even as some quiet part of me acknowledges the truth I'm not touching yet.

If I say it's just the assignment enough times, maybe it will feel true.

And if it doesn't... I'll deal with that when I run out of excuses.

Leona has that look she gets when a plan locks into place—sharp, satisfied, and just a little too pleased with herself. She flips her notebook to a fresh page and uncaps her pen like a weapon.

"Alright," she says, tone brisk. "I'll block off this Monday. Morning is dance practice with Francesca. Afternoon is shopping."

I blink at her. "You aren't serious?"

"Deadly," she says without missing a beat. "She's going to need proper formal wear for the events, and she can't go into those dances blind. The curse is already touchy; the last thing we need is a misstep triggering a binding waltz because no one briefed her on the choreography."

Jackson leans back in his chair, clearly enjoying this far too much. "Besides, you're the only one here who's done these circuits from the inside. You know where the enchantments are layered, where the pressure spikes, when the music cues the magic."

I try, very briefly, to find a reasonable objection and come up empty. "And you two? Where will you be while I'm apparently coaching and personal shopping?"

Leona's mouth curves, slow and unapologetic. "Conveniently summoned. We got notice this morning—Lucifer wants us in the underworld on Monday for a review session. Something about cross-departmental compliance and 'ongoing demonic-human interface standards.'"

Jackson grimaces. "He said there would be slides. Plural. With animations."

I stare at them. "So while you're doing compliance theater in Hell, I'm expected to escort a cursed Bellamy through dance drills and formalwear fittings."

"Exactly," Leona replies, jotting something in her planner. "You're the one the Council trusts with her case. This falls under that umbrella."

Jackson lifts his coffee in a half-toast. "Look at it this way—it's quality time with your favorite assignment."

I ignore that. "Does she know about any of this yet?"

"Not yet," Leona says, already closing her notebook with a decisive snap. "We'll frame it as preparation. Which it is. You don't send someone into a magical ballroom without a rehearsal. That's how tragedies happen. Or worse, spontaneous engagements."

She stands, smoothing her skirt like the matter is settled, because as far as she's concerned, it is. Jackson grabs his coat, still amused, like he's leaving at the best possible part of the show.

"We'll finalize the details and drop them in your schedule," Leona adds, heading for the door. "Make sure you rest at some point tonight. You're no good to her exhausted."

Jackson pulls the door open and glances back. "Try not to overthink it, boss. It's just practice."

They step out into the hall, voices fading as the door swings shut behind them. The office goes quiet.

Francesca's file still glows on my desk, her name haloed in warm amber light, the pulse of her magic threaded through every glyph like a heartbeat I can't quite tune out. Monday now stretches in my mind—dance steps, spellbound music, crowded shops, her magic brushing against mine in spaces that are far less controlled than this office.

I tell myself it's logistics. Training. Sensible preparation for a dangerous season.

Nothing more.

The file hums under my fingertips when I close it, as if it knows better. I sit back, exhale slowly, and decide I'll lie to myself about this for as long as I can get away with it.

Chapter 21

Francesca

I'm slipping on my second shoe—fingers still working the buckle—when a firm knock echoes through my apartment. The sound startles my magic enough to send a faint shimmer along the hallway lights, nothing catastrophic, just a soft reminder that the curse is listening. I smooth a hand down my black dress, inhale once, and open the door.

Dorian stands there like he stepped out of a magazine spread titled *Effortless Confidence in Knitwear*. He's dressed casually, but the kind of casual that still looks intentional—dark jeans that fit far too well, a soft charcoal sweater that makes his shoulders look unfairly broad, and an undercurrent of quiet cologne that hits warm and expensive the moment the door swings open. I feel the reaction before I can rein it in, a flutter low in my chest that my magic catches and mirrors in a subtle hum along my skin.

He's holding a bouquet of cookie flowers, each one shaped and iced into delicate roses and peonies, arranged in a small woven basket that looks like it belongs in a pastry fairytale.

"For you," Dorian says, offering them with a smile that softens the sharp lines of his face. "I wasn't sure if you liked traditional flowers, but I figured I couldn't go wrong with edible ones."

A surprised laugh escapes me. "You brought me dessert disguised as plants. That's... unexpectedly perfect."

"Good," he says, the corner of his mouth lifting with a quiet sort of pride. "I wanted to start this off properly. And I was raised to pick up my dates, not make them find me."

It's old-fashioned. Charming. A little disarming, honestly. I step back to let him in long enough to set the basket on my kitchen counter, and the moment I move toward the sink for a vase, he stops me gently.

"No need," he says. "They're meant to be eaten, not displayed."

My magic flutters again—curious, warm—and the traitor whispers maybe.

Dorian gives the apartment a polite sweep with his gaze, not prying, just observing, the way people do when they're genuinely interested in the person in front of them. His posture is easy but confident, hands in his pockets, shoulders relaxed as if nerves aren't something he remembers experiencing. That steadiness settles into the air between us, and for a moment I wonder if maybe I'd misjudged him the first time. There's something quietly compelling about him up close, something assured without being arrogant, like a man who knows exactly who he is and doesn't need the room to applaud it.

"Ready?" he asks, gesturing toward the hallway.

"As I'll ever be," I say, grabbing my coat.

I lock up behind us and lead the way into the interior hallway, the overhead lights casting a soft, familiar hum as we descend the narrow staircase. Dorian stays at my side with an ease that feels intentional—his stride adjusted to mine, his attention warm without crowding. By the time we step through the front door and out onto the sidewalk, the winter air sweeps over us in a crisp rush that fogs my first breath.

"I'm glad you agreed to tonight," he says as we reach the last step. "First impressions aren't always reliable."

"Are you implying I judged you," I ask, "or that you judged me?"

"Both," he admits with a quiet laugh. "But I'm open to being wrong if you are."

The banter slides between us smoothly, almost instinctive, and it pulls a reluctant smile from me as we step toward the curb. That's when I see it—his car. Sleek. Midnight blue. The kind of sports car that looks like it should be driven by someone with a multi-million-dollar watch collection, not a man who just brought cookie flowers to a date. The vehicle glints beneath the streetlights, elegant without being showy.

"Oh," I say under my breath. "You're one of those."

"Only on weekends," he says, opening the passenger door with a flourish that somehow comes off sincere rather than theatrical. "And on dates I'd prefer to go well."

I settle into the seat, the leather warm and impossibly soft, while my magic shifts through my chest like it's testing the air, curious but not chaotic. Dorian rounds the front of the car, sliding into the driver's seat with fluid ease, and for a moment the interior fills with the subtle scent of cedar and something darker—amber? smoke?—that mixes dangerously well with the warmth of his body.

He glances at me, one hand on the wheel, the other settling on the gearshift. "Comfortable?"

"Yes," I say, maybe too quickly.

"Good," he replies, voice low and steady enough to make the temperature feel several degrees warmer. "Then let's see if we can make tonight memorable."

The car glides into motion, quiet and smooth, the kind of machine that barely acknowledges the road beneath it. Streetlights slip across the windshield in slow, amber strokes, casting soft highlights along Dorian's jaw. He glances my way as we merge onto the main road, and his gaze lingers just long enough for my skin to register it before my brain does.

"You look... stunning tonight," he says, tone even, but there's an undercurrent in it that hits deep and warm. "The black dress with the red accents—it suits you."

I'm suddenly very aware of the way the red heels press against the floor mat, the way my lipstick matches them perfectly, the subtle shift of my smoky eyeshadow when I blink. Heat curls low in my stomach before I can talk myself out of reacting, and my magic answers with a slow shimmer beneath my ribs.

"Thank you," I manage, hoping the car is too dim for him to see the flush creeping along my collarbone.

He smiles as though he did, in fact, see it—and approves.

The city lights fall away as we take a turn I absolutely know wasn't on Sayer's plan. The roads grow quieter, dusted with frost, the trees thinning as we head toward the outskirts of town.

"So..." I say, watching the unfamiliar scenery slide by, "we're not going where Sayer booked the reservation."

"No," Dorian says, completely unapologetic. "I prefer to choose my own date locations."

There's something almost rebellious in the way he says it—gentle rebellion, quiet but firmly rooted. It makes something tighten pleasantly in my chest.

"And where exactly are you taking me?"

He nods toward the windshield, where soft white lights begin to twinkle between the bare branches ahead. "A winter festival. Small. Local. My sister teaches at the high school—they host it every year. I grew up going to it."

A winter festival. Not what I expected at all.

The closer we get, the more the air changes—brighter, sweeter, tinged with the scent of kettle corn and hot chocolate drifting on the wind. Strands of warm lights crisscross between tents, casting golden halos against the snow-packed ground. Families and couples move from booth to booth, bundled in scarves, breath fogging like lazy ghosts above their heads.

Dorian parks near the edge of the lot. When he steps out and circles the car to open my door, I catch the faintest ripple of nerves beneath my magic—anticipation, maybe, or something that wants to step closer to him just to see how it feels.

He offers his hand. Not presumptuous, simply polite. But the moment my fingers brush his, something in the air shifts—an unexpected flicker of heat, a subtle pull low in my stomach that I definitely wasn't prepared to experience with anyone tonight.

If he feels it, he hides it well.

"My sister's working the volunteer booth," he says as we fall into step together. "I thought you might like something simple and a little nostalgic before the chaos of the larger events."

"That's... actually thoughtful," I admit.

"Don't look so surprised," he murmurs, a teasing edge slipping into his voice. "I have my moments."

We pass beneath the arch of twinkling lights, the cold air sparkling faintly with frost. My magic lifts in a soft hum, not misbehaving but alert—curious, as if it's testing the edges of Dorian's presence beside me.

He glances at me again, eyes lit gold by the overhead bulbs. "Francesca?"

"Hmm?"

"Relax," he says, quieter now. "Tonight's supposed to be effortless."

And the ridiculous part is... standing here with him, surrounded by lights and laughter and winter air, it almost feels like it might be.

The festival unfolds around us in a warm, bustling swirl—glowing lights strung between booths, kids dragging parents toward games, the smell of caramelized sugar and woodsmoke drifting through the cold air like some seasonal enchantment. Dorian walks beside me with an easy confidence, hands in his pockets, watching the crowd as if he's cataloging the energy of the night and deciding exactly how much of it he plans to conquer.

We stop at the first booth—a ring toss—and he lifts one eyebrow, a sort of quiet dare wrapped in a smile. "Care to test your odds?"

"Only if you promise not to pretend you're terrible and then win the whole booth," I say, narrowing my eyes at him.

His laugh is low and warm in a way that hits deeper than it should. "I don't sandbag. I win fairly."

"Oh, I'm sure that's completely unbiased."

"It absolutely is," he says as he hands me the first ring. "Ladies first."

The plastic ring is icy against my fingers, my magic stirring just enough to warm the tips as I line up my shot. I toss it, watching it arc through the cold air, and it lands perfectly around the center peg.

Dorian lets out a slow whistle. "Beginner's luck."

"Please," I say, brushing a loose strand of hair behind my ear. "Goddess-given talent."

He picks up his ring, steps forward like the universe itself owes him accuracy, and tosses it with a fluid flick of his wrist. It lands dead center.

"See?" he says, smug but charming. "Fair."

We go back and forth until we've each landed three perfect shots, the volunteer running the booth growing increasingly impressed—or concerned—before Dorian lifts the last ring between his fingers like it's a peace treaty.

"This feels like a stalemate," he says. "Which is unacceptable."

"So what do you propose?"

"A wager."

My magic stirs. Wagers always get its attention.

"A wager," I echo slowly, like I'm testing the weight of the word.

He steps a fraction closer, just enough for his breath to fog the air near my cheek, but not enough for anyone watching to call it forward. "Winner of the night gets to claim a truth... or a dare."

My heartbeat does a confused little hop before I can stop it. The space between us tightens subtly, charged in a way that makes the lights around us feel warmer.

"That's bold of you," I say, lifting my chin. "What makes you think you'll win?"

"I don't," he says with a warm, unbothered confidence. "I think it'll be close. Which makes the risk more interesting."

He tosses the final ring, almost lazy in the movement, but it lands skewed—touching the peg, then bouncing off. He smiles like he meant to do it, because of course he does.

"Your turn," he says.

The ring is cool against my palm, my magic humming like it has opinions. I take a breath, aim, and—

It misses by an inch.

Dorian's smile grows slow and pleased. "Well. Looks like we need another game."

We wander to the dart booth next, then the milk bottle toss, then a ridiculous challenge involving rubber ducks and fishing poles. At each one, the pattern repeats: neither of us lets the other win, neither pulls punches, and the boil of tension grows more intriguing than the games themselves. I learn he likes strategy games and secretly hates winter but loves the way festivals make it feel softer. He learns I color-code my spice cabinet and have a talent for making dough rise faster than it should. We laugh, we challenge, we lean a little closer than necessary to survey the scoreboard—close enough for my shoulder to graze his arm, close enough for his breath to tickle the tip of my ear when he teases me about missing a shot by a mile.

"That didn't count," I say, heat blooming along my throat.

"You missed the entire board," he replies, fighting a grin. "Pretty sure it counted."

We move on again, hand brushing hand as we reach for tickets at the same moment. The contact is brief but electric, a soft spark that travels up my arm in a way that makes my magic flutter like an overeager bird.

He feels it—I know he does—even though he masks it behind a smooth inhale and a suddenly too-focused look at the next booth.

"You alright?" I ask.

"Perfectly," he says, but his voice dips just enough that I know I've rattled him.

We end up at the high striker—the giant strength test with the hammer and the bell. Dorian takes the hammer first, holding it like it's made for him, and swings with a clean, powerful motion that sends the puck slamming upward. It hits the bell with a triumphant clang that echoes across the snow.

The crowd nearby cheers, because apparently this is a spectator sport now.

Dorian turns to me with that quiet, confident, maddening smile. "Beat that."

I take the hammer, ignoring the warmth of his hand lingering on the handle. I brace my stance, lift, swing—and the puck shoots up, not all the way, but close enough to prove that I have a respectable amount of strength for someone whose job revolves around pastries.

He steps closer, leaning in as if he's inspecting the score. "Not bad."

"Not bad?" I say, nudging him with my shoulder. "That was excellent."

"Mm. Acceptable."

"You're impossible."

"So I've been told."

The banter is effortless, the energy easy and warm, and somewhere between booth four and five, I realize we're not just talking—we're learning each other's rhythms. The way he leans in when he's amused. The way his voice drops when he's genuinely curious. The way he watches my hands when I gesture, like he's mapping every movement to memory.

We slip into a quieter stretch of the festival where the lanterns hang low, their warm glow caught in the frost like tiny suspended suns. The crowds thin behind us, replaced by soft laughter in the distance, the muffled crackle of a fire pit, the rhythmic hush of winter settling into the bare trees. My breath curls into the air, mingling with Dorian's as we stop beneath an arch of golden lights.

He turns toward me, his expression easier than it should be for a man who nearly beat me at every booth. "So who's winning our wager?" I ask, my voice a little softer than I intend.

"That depends," he says, taking a slow step closer. The cold fades under the heat that rolls off him, subtle but unmistakable. "Do you want the truth?"

"Yes," I breathe, and the sound barely feels like mine.

The lantern light paints warm amber across his cheekbones as he studies me—really studies me—as if he wants to learn the shape of my reaction before I even have it. There's nothing rushed in the way he leans in, nothing careless; it's deliberate, thoughtful, the kind of movement that asks for permission without a single word. My pulse stumbles. My magic stirs in a low, rising hum beneath my skin, cresting like a tide that's been waiting for exactly this angle of his mouth, this distance, this moment.

"I think," he murmurs, and his breath brushes my cheek like a whispered dare, "we're tied."

The words linger between us, warm and fragile, catching in the thin space that's left. I don't know who leans in first—him or me—but the shift is unmistakable. His hand lifts slightly, hovering near my waist the way someone does when they're fighting not to touch too soon. My magic answers before I do, flaring in a sudden, bright rush that tingles down my arms and lights the air with a faint shimmer only someone attuned would notice.

Dorian notices.

His jaw tightens almost imperceptibly, not in discomfort but in the kind of restraint that sends a slow ache of awareness through my ribs. The pull between us sharpens, a single breath of distance from becoming something reckless and wonderful.

Then, right as the space between us tightens to a single breath, my phone erupts with a cheerful, utterly unwanted notification—bright, insistent, and about as subtle as a fire alarm in a cathedral.

The surge of magic flickers, startled, scattering the lantern light around us like a handful of glitter tossed against the night. I step back just enough to break the spell, blinking hard as I dig into my coat pocket. Dorian exhales slowly—controlled, deliberate—straightening in a way that tells me he feels every inch of the reality snapping back into place.

"Important?" he asks, voice lower, steadier than I expect.

I glance at the screen. A new notification from Leona.

> **MONDAY: 10 AM — Dance practice.11:30 — Formalwear shopping. Mandatory attendance. Bring caffeine.**

I groan. "It's tomorrow's schedule."

Dorian's eyebrow lifts, amusement sliding through the tension like a warm blade. "Ah. The infamous preparation phase."

"You have no idea."

"I might," he says, a faint smile tugging at the corner of his mouth. "I'm one of the finalists, remember?"

My magic pulses again—conflicted, curious, entirely unhelpful.

We stand beneath the lanterns for a long, suspended moment, the almost-kiss hanging between us like breath on the air.

And for the first time tonight, I'm not entirely sure which one of us stepped away first.

Chapter 22

Sayer

The community center smells faintly of varnished floors and old heating vents—the sort of place where a million awkward high school recitals have lived and died. I stand near the wall of mirrors, dressed in gray sweats and a fitted black shirt that feels more revealing than the suit armor I'm used to. Casual isn't my preferred mode; it leaves too much to chance, too much room for interpretation. But Leona insisted, and Francesca agreed, and apparently I'm the one with the most to prove today.

The room is warm enough that I roll my shoulders back, trying to decide if the tension sitting between my shoulder blades is leftover from Cupid HQ or anticipation. Probably both. The wings aren't out—not here, not now—but they're awake under the skin, restless in a way that would annoy me if I didn't understand exactly why.

Her magic has been brushing against mine for days.

The door opens, and the warm buzz under my skin sharpens instantly.

Francesca steps inside, cheeks flushed from the cold, gym bag slung over one shoulder. She's wearing black leggings and an oversized T-shirt that absolutely fails at being oversized—soft fabric skimming over the curve of her hips, dipping against her waist just enough to make looking away a test I'm suddenly not prepared for. Her hair is braided over one shoulder, long and glossy, a dark river tied neatly for practicality.

She carries two cups of coffee. One is clearly for me.

I swallow once, quietly, before my brain can embarrass me.

She spots me and her expression shifts—soft, surprised, and then something else beneath it, something immediate and warm that hits harder than it should. Her magic rolls through the air in a subtle wave, brushing against mine in a way that feels almost like someone running fingers down my spine. It steadies almost instantly, but not before I feel it.

"Morning," she says as she crosses the room, offering one of the cups. "Leona said you take it with too much caramel and not enough common sense."

"That's slander," I reply, taking the cup anyway. "And accurate."

A smile flickers across her mouth—quick, involuntary, bright enough to tighten something in my ribs. She sets her gym bag down, stretching her arms overhead in a slow, absent arc that pulls her shirt up just enough for my gaze to betray me. I look away before she notices, pretending to check the playlist on my phone.

"This is a terrible idea," I mutter, mostly to myself.

Her brow lifts. "Dancing?"

"No," I say, lifting my cup in a mock toast. "Us. In a room. Together. With my coordination on display."

She laughs, and it hits warm and direct, right through the sternum. "Relax, counselor. It's practice, not a performance."

"Tell that to my pride."

"Oh, I plan to," she says, sipping her coffee.

Her lips are a deep wine-red today—slightly smudged from the cup's lid, and I hate how fast my attention drops to that. The lipstick combined with the leggings and the flushed cheeks and the braid is... dangerous. Entirely too distracting. And the most ridiculous part is that she has no idea how much she's unraveling my equilibrium simply by existing in the same room.

I clear my throat, intending to regain control of this moment. "We should probably start."

She steps closer—close enough that I feel the warmth of her body radiating through the mirror-bright air of the room—and my magic reacts before I do. A subtle hum flickers down my spine, old instincts stretching, testing the space between us.

"What kind of dance is this supposed to be?" she asks, tone light but edged with challenge.

"Formal," I say. "Basic waltz style. The balls aren't... casual. They expect a certain level of fluency."

She gives me a slow look. "And you think I don't have fluency?"

My throat warms. "I think I haven't seen what you can do yet."

"Then you're about to."

I step forward, offering my hand. She hesitates—not because she's unsure, but because something in the air between us thickens, warm and charged enough to tug at both our breaths. When her fingers finally slide against mine, the magic snaps in place like two currents locking together. It's subtle. Soft. Immediate.

And if this is what holding her hand feels like, the dances, the balls, the entire next two weeks?

I'm in far more trouble than I planned for.

She rests her hand lightly in mine, settling into position as though she's done this a thousand times. Which... apparently, she has.

"You do know," she says as she steps closer, aligning her body with mine in a way that sends a steady thrum along my nerves, "that the Bellamy family hosts the *final* ball of the season every year. Dancing isn't a new concept to me."

"That's different," I reply, trying for confidence. "Hosting a ball doesn't automatically mean you—"

She places her free hand on my shoulder with a featherlight touch that derails every coherent thought I had. Her gaze lifts to mine, warm and faintly amused.

"Sayer. We were taught to dance before we were taught to drive. Before taxes. Before basic geometry. Believe me, I can keep up."

The room tilts a little. I'm not intimidated—just... very aware. I clear my throat, nod, and start the first step of the basic waltz. Or at least, that was the plan.

My foot catches on absolutely nothing.

I stumble.

Me.

The man who once navigated celestial combat without tripping over his own shadow.

Her grip tightens instinctively, steady but gentle. Her eyes widen—not mocking, but startled—and then her lips curve, slow and wickedly delighted.

"Did you just... trip?" she asks.

"No," I say immediately.

She lifts an eyebrow.

"It was a strategic misstep. To evaluate physics."

"That's adorable," she says, voice warm enough to make it worse. "Breathe, counselor. You're wound tighter than my grandmother's yarn basket."

"I'm perfectly calm."

"You're vibrating."

"I'm not vibrating," I say, right as my magic flares under my skin in a traitorous ripple that brushes against hers. She gives me a look so knowing it should be illegal.

"Loosen up," she murmurs, adjusting our hold. "Leave the over-thinking for the courtroom."

I inhale—slow, intentional, grounding—and something shifts. The tension in my shoulders eases. My grip steadies. The room widens around us.

She feels it.

"There you go," she says softly. "That's better."

We fall into motion again, and this time my body remembers how to move. She glides into each step with a fluidity that makes guiding her feel less like instruction and more like instinct. Her hand fits comfortably in mine, her breath warm against my throat when we turn. The music pulsing from the overhead speakers threads between us until it's impossible to tell where her rhythm ends and mine begins.

Minutes slide into something softer.

She switches effortlessly between forms—waltz, swing, slow turn, a flirtatious spin that catches the hem of her shirt and sends my pulse stumbling for entirely different reasons. She laughs when I overcorrect; I bite back a smile when she challenges me with an unexpected pivot.

Time loosens its grip as we move, the steps blending into something seamless—her braid sweeping over her shoulder when she turns, my hand finding the small of her back with growing confidence, the quiet pulse of her magic brushing against mine in warm, responsive waves. The mirrors catch glimpses of us as we pass: bodies aligned, expressions focused but open, an ease settling in that neither of us invited but both of us fall into anyway.

Before long—whether it's fifteen minutes or closer to thirty—the practice shifts into something far more natural. The choreography fades; instinct takes over. Our movements sync without effort, our shapes fitting into the music as though we've done this together a hundred times instead of just once. The tension that held me tight at the beginning unravels into something fluid, almost electric, a connection that builds quietly until it's impossible to ignore.

When we finally slow, stepping apart with breath still mingling in the warm space between us, I glance toward the clock on the far wall. The realization hits with a strange jolt of disbelief. Two hours have vanished, and neither of us noticed.

I reach for the small stack of supplies Leona left on the bench—two towels, two bottles of water—and walk them over to her, still trying to steady the way my breath insists on catching whenever she looks at me. Her cheeks are flushed, skin glowing from the exertion, braid slightly loosened at the end from all the turns. The magic curling around her feels warmer now, content in a way I've never felt in this room before.

"Here," I say, offering her the towel first.

Her fingers brush mine as she takes it, a light contact that sends a faint spark down my arm. She pretends not to feel it, or maybe she's too busy catching her breath, but the magic between us hums with the awareness anyway.

"Thanks," she says, pressing the towel to the side of her neck. Her hair sticks in a few damp places along her temple, and for one reckless heartbeat I have to force my gaze higher—away from the line of her jaw, away from her mouth, away from a dozen things my thoughts have no business cataloging.

I hand her the water next, and she twists the cap with a grateful exhale before taking a long drink. The movement reveals the curve of her throat, and I have to ground myself all over again.

"The locker room's down that hall," I manage, nodding toward the side corridor. "Second door on the left. Yours is the one with the charm on the handle—Leona insisted on privacy wards."

She smiles at that, faint but genuine. "Of course she did."

"I'll take the one on the right," I say. "Change, cool down, try to remind myself my legs were not, in fact, replaced with overcooked pasta."

She snorts, covering it with an exaggerated sip of water. "Oh yes, very intimidating counselor energy."

"We can't all be cursed with perfect rhythm," I mutter, though it comes out warmer than I intend.

"Well," she says, lifting the towel to blot her cheek, "you're not bad."

The compliment hits harder than it should, settling somewhere low and unmistakable.

"We'll head to our next stop once we're changed," I say, trying to summon a tone that resembles professionalism. "It's... important."

Her eyebrows lift in wary curiosity. "Important how?"

"You'll see," I tell her, stepping back before I hover any closer. "Go get changed before I forget what the word boundaries means."

She gives me one more look—soft, charged, utterly unaware of how much it undoes me—and turns toward the hallway, braid swinging lightly with each step. The magic she leaves behind trails after her like warm static.

I gather my things slowly, giving myself a moment to let the room settle back into something that resembles sanity. The lingering warmth of her magic still clings to the air, humming faintly against the mirrors like an afterimage. I'm halfway to the bench when my phone buzzes in my pocket.

Jackson's name flashes across the screen, followed by a short message:

Elliott's leaving this afternoon. Fellowship accepted. He asked me to pass along his regards.

I stare at the words a moment longer than I should, the quiet shift of fate settling into place with a weight I'm not entirely prepared to acknowledge.

Chapter 23

Francesca

The ride to the dress shop is quieter than I expect, but not in a strained way. More like we've both surrendered to the warm hum of leftover magic trailing between us from the dance studio, something soft and wordless settling in the space we share. Sayer drives a sleek black sedan—expensive enough to make a statement but understated enough that he never would. The city slides past the windows in a muted blur of winter light and drifting frost, and for most of the drive I'm caught somewhere between replaying the way his hands fit at my waist and trying very, very hard not to replay the way his breath brushed my cheek.

He doesn't push conversation. Doesn't fill the silence with unnecessary noise. And somehow, that makes the air between us feel strangely intimate, like a shared secret neither of us has the nerve to examine yet.

When he finally pulls up to the shop, my chest tightens with a ripple of excitement I can't quite hide.

The Atelier of Thorne & Thimble.

The letters gleam in swirling bronze script above the entrance, each one threaded with faint enchantment that makes them shimmer between hues—rose gold, champagne, soft amber. I've walked past their storefront more times than I'd ever admit. They dress the elite: coven matriarchs, high-ranking fae, the kind of witches whose names carry weight before they ever step into a room.

I've admired their work from afar, always half-convinced I'd never have a reason—or enough disposable income—to cross the threshold.

And now I'm here because a Cupid-turned-divorce-attorney needs me to be... stunning enough to solve a magical curse.

Not the trajectory I imagined for my Saturday.

Sayer parks with effortless precision, then rounds the car to open my door. The gesture is old-fashioned in a way that should annoy me but instead sends a small warmth through my chest. I step out, smoothing a hand down my clean leggings—Leona insisted on an outfit that could "transition"—and lift my gaze to the shimmering shop window.

Mannequins float inside the glass display, draped in gowns that ripple like water and catch the light in impossible ways. It feels like walking into a fairy tale with a credit limit.

"Lost in thought?" Sayer asks softly.

I blink, trying not to get caught staring at the reflection of the two of us standing far too close. "Just... admiring. I've always wanted to come here."

He studies me for a moment, something warm flickering in his expression. "Then today's your day."

The door opens before either of us touches it—two attendants sweeping into existence like conjured greeters, their smiles warm, their eyes sharp enough to catalog every detail of my life story in five seconds or less.

Magic thrums through the air as the interior reveals itself. The floors are polished stone veined with subtle luminescence, the ceiling strung with floating candles that glow in soft rose tones. Bolts of enchanted fabric float along the walls, shimmering between colors as though undecided which emotion they want to project.

And right in the center of all that luxury, I stop breathing.

"This place is... incredible," I whisper, unable to help myself.

"It's functional," Sayer replies, though his voice has that quiet shift he gets when he's trying not to admit he's impressed too. "They create attire specifically attuned to magical signatures. For the balls, that's essential."

"Have you done this before?" I ask.

"Not as a client," he murmurs. "But I've escorted people who needed the right presence. You'd be surprised how much difference fabric can make in fate." He nods toward me. "And you deserve something worthy of the events ahead."

The words hit deeper than he intends, enough that I have to look away before I give him a reaction he hasn't earned yet.

A seamstress sweeps toward us, tall and ethereal, measuring tape draped around her neck like a silver serpent. Her eyes widen just slightly when she takes me in—my magic, my nerves, my lineage—and she claps her hands once, delighted.

"Oh, she's a Bellamy," she says, voice bright and musical. "And not just any Bellamy. This one's humming."

Sayer clears his throat gently beside me. "We're here for a full consultation. Multiple events."

"Of course you are." She beams at me. "Come, darling. Let's get your measurements. And don't worry about anything—Bellamy magic and couture go together beautifully when handled correctly."

Sayer gives me a small, steady nod as the seamstress guides me deeper into the shop.

And for the first time since this entire disaster began, I feel something that doesn't quite resemble dread.

The seamstress—Maribel, according to her name pin written in glittering cursive—ushers me onto a small raised platform surrounded by mirrors. The lights above shift to a warm blush tone as if greeting my magic, and something in the air lifts, curious and alert in the way only enchanted spaces can be. Maribel circles me, measuring tape flicking from one hand to the other with charming menace, and the moment she gets close enough to feel the magic running along my skin, she lets out a delighted hum.

"Oh yes," she says, already sliding the first measurement around my ribs. "A Bellamy in full flare. Exquisite. Volatile. Possibly combustible. But exquisite."

Behind her reflection in the mirror, I catch Sayer leaning against a column—casual, composed, too handsome for my peace of mind—observing everything with that quiet intensity he reserves for things he doesn't want to admit matter to him.

His gaze flicks up when mine catches him in the mirror.

Heat skims the back of my neck immediately.

Maribel notices.

"Oh dear, the resonance spike is adorable," she murmurs. "Try not to combust on my platform, please. You'll ruin the finish."

"I'm not combusting," I say.

Sayer's voice drifts over, low and maddeningly calm. "You're absolutely combusting."

"Counselor," Maribel says without looking at him, "if you intend to challenge my assessment, at least have the decency to blush as well."

The choking sound Sayer makes is... deeply satisfying.

She finishes the measurements with a final swish of the tape, then gestures to the racks of enchanted fabric hovering along the back wall. Each bolt glimmers with subtle magic—silks whispering their own colors, velvets shifting from shadow to light depending on my breath, gossamer materials shimmering like auroras.

"Your lineage responds strongly to fire-based enchantments," Maribel explains as she walks. "But also moon-threading, which is unusual. Very few families harmonize with both. Bellamys... well. You're a unique case."

"She is," Sayer says quietly behind us.

My pulse jumps.

He doesn't try to take it back.

Maribel pulls three dress forms forward, each one shimmering to life with the faint outline of gowns that haven't manifested yet. She examines them, muttering to herself, adjusting the magic around the silhouettes until one flickers brighter than the others—deep red with ember light undertones.

"This one likes you," she announces. "And I suspect you'll like it."

The gown materializes with a soft shimmer—dark crimson silk threaded with subtle charline that glows like banked embers beneath the fabric. It draws the eye the way flame does: warm, mesmerizing, slightly dangerous.

My breath catches.

"So," Maribel says, turning to me with a gleeful little clap, "shall we test it?"

I step behind the screen, change, and when I emerge, the room shifts.

The mirrors flash, catching the red in a dozen angles. The fabric clings in all the right places without being scandalous; it flows at the hips like smoke, resting against my collarbones with delicate embroidery that shimmer-flares when my magic answers it.

Maribel beams.

Then I look at Sayer.

And the magic slams through my body so hard I grip the edge of the platform to steady myself.

He's not leaning anymore. He's standing—completely upright, shoulders tight, jaw set, expression doing absolutely nothing to hide the way he's staring at me like he just forgot what language is.

Maribel observes him for half a second, utterly delighted. "Ah. Excellent. We have confirmation."

"Confirmation of what?" I ask, but I already feel the heat rising in my chest.

"That the dress chose correctly," she says, waving a dismissive hand. "And that your magic agrees." Her eyes flick to Sayer. "His does too."

He clears his throat sharply—too sharply. "We should... continue with the selections."

I should tease him. I should say something snarky. Instead, I feel heat pooling under my skin in a way I'm not entirely prepared to admit out loud.

As Maribel adjusts the hem, Sayer steps closer—still keeping distance, still trying for professional—but his voice is softer now.

"How was your date last night?" he asks.

The question catches me off guard. "It was good. Different from the first. We ended up going somewhere else, not the reservation."

His eyes narrow slightly. "He changed the location without telling me?"

"Relax," I say. "It was a winter festival. His sister teaches at the high school."

Sayer processes that. Not angry. Not dismissive. Just... something thoughtful threading through his expression like he's recalibrating his understanding of the situation.

"And Elliott?" I ask, watching him in the mirror as Maribel flutters around the hem. "You said there was something I needed to know."

Sayer exhales. "He left. The fellowship up the coast. He asked Jackson to pass along his regards."

"Oh." I swallow. Not sadness—just clarity settling into place. "So that's one finalist down."

"Yes," Sayer says, and there's something unreadable in the way he says it. "One down."

"And one remaining."

His gaze lifts to mine in the mirror, steady and unguarded for the briefest heartbeat.

"Two," he corrects quietly.

The room feels suddenly smaller. Warmer. Charged.

Maribel claps once, breaking the spell. "Wonderful! This gown is approved. Now let's discuss the accessories and enchantments appropriate for the first event."

But Sayer and I don't look away immediately.

Not this time. Not quickly enough.

By the time Maribel is satisfied—and Maribel is only satisfied when every detail has been tailored, charmed, tested, and approved—we've accumulated enough garments to supply a small aristocratic rebellion. Gowns for each event, enchanted wraps, gloves threaded with subtle protection spells, three pairs of heels that adjust height depending on the dance, even a daywear collection she insisted I needed "for balance and energy alignment."

Sayer tries to keep his expression neutral through the entire process, but each time another bag levitates to the counter, his jaw tightens just a fraction. Not annoyed—more... resigned to the reality that Bellamy preparation is not a minimalist sport.

By the time we reach the register, the final total glows in the air like a floating omen. Sayer pays without a blink, though I catch the faint clench of his hand before he signs the charm slate. Maribel kisses both my cheeks, tells me she expects photographic evidence, and sweeps us out the door as though we just survived a spiritual pilgrimage.

Sayer carries the bulk of the bags to the sedan, arms full of shimmering garment covers and delicate boxes that hum with enchantment. I take the lighter pieces—scarves, jewelry pouches, a sleek clutch that matches the ember-threaded gown—and load them carefully into the back seat.

Once everything is tucked in safely, we slide into the car, both of us letting out identical slow exhales at the same time. The synchronicity pulls a small smile from me. His fingers tighten around the steering wheel, subtle but noticeable, before he starts the engine.

"We'll go over everything tonight," he says, his voice a shade lower than before. "Leona and I will finalize which events I'm escorting you to and which ones Dorian will handle."

"So it's not just a simple 'pick the best match and hope for the best' situation?"

His lips twitch. "Not when the Bellamy curse is involved. Each event influences the trajectory. The alignment matters."

"Alignment," I repeat, amused. "You're sounding very celestial for someone who now prefers paperwork over prophecy."

A breath of laughter escapes him—quiet, but warm. "Don't remind me."

We pull onto the main road, the rhythmic passing of winter-slicked storefronts reflecting across the windshield. The car settles into a comfortable hum, the quiet between us less heavy than earlier, more charged, like the dance practice left its imprint somewhere in the air.

My phone vibrates in my pocket. Once. Twice.

I glance down.

Dorian: *I had a really good time last night. Would you like to grab lunch later this week? My schedule is flexible.*

My stomach does this strange swoop—part flutter, part confusion, part something warmer than I expect.

Sayer's eyes flick from the road to me, just for a second. "Everything alright?"

"Mm-hm," I say, though my magic stirs in a restless ripple beneath my skin. "Just... an invitation."

"From him," Sayer says—less question, more quiet certainty.

"Yes."

He nods once, professional, composed, the picture of neutrality. Except the air in the car tightens almost imperceptibly, the faintest shift of energy that skims down my arms. He hides it well, but my magic doesn't.

"Do you want to go?" he asks.

The directness catches me off guard.

"I think so," I answer honestly. "I'd like to see where it goes."

He exhales slowly, and it isn't disappointment exactly—more like he's rearranging his expectations without complaint.

"Then it's a good sign," he says softly. "It means the alignment is taking shape."

Alignment again. Fate. Duty. Whatever cosmic nonsense we're tangled in.

But the truth is far murkier, humming beneath my ribs with every quiet mile of the drive.

I want lunch with Dorian.

And I also can't stop thinking about the way Sayer looked at me in that dress.

And I'm not sure what that means yet.

Chapter 24

Sayer

Three days have crawled by since the dress shop, and I've spent every one of them carefully avoiding the Bellamy Bakery like it's booby-trapped. It shouldn't take tactical precision to sidestep a morning coffee run, yet here I am, sending Leona and Jackson to fetch my order as if venturing inside would detonate something I'm not equipped to survive. They've handled this responsibility with maddening enthusiasm—Jackson returning each morning with the reverence of a pilgrim bringing home holy artifacts, and Leona arriving with commentary sharp enough to slice through my attempted neutrality.

The first morning, she set the cup on my desk and informed me that the bakery witch had asked where I'd been, her tone softened just enough to make me feel the guilt sliding beneath my ribs. The second morning, Jackson delivered my latte along with a warm apple fritter, explaining that she had sent it "because something must be wrong if Sayer Valentine isn't asking for extra caramel in person." By day three, Leona showed up carrying *two* fritters, announcing that Francesca had recruited half her staff into a game of emotional telephone to check on me. According to Ellie's version—filtered through Harper, then Miguel, then Jackson—Francesca now believes I'm either catastrophically ill or hiding an impending disaster, because "there's no other reason for this man to avoid free sugar."

Avoidance was supposed to help me regain focus. Instead, it's only sharpened every detail I've been trying not to examine. The way she laughed during dance practice. The way her braid swung against her shoulder when she turned. The way the red gown chose her as if it knew exactly who she needed to be. Every attempt at distance has only agitated the restless magic under my skin, which seems determined to remind me that ignoring her presence solves none of my problems.

And now the first formal event is nearly here—this weekend—and she'll be going with Dorian. Dorian, who checks every polite, promising box on paper. Dorian, who is calm, attentive, well-spoken, confident without being theatrical... and still manages to set every one of my instincts on edge. Old instincts—the ones I buried when I walked away from Cupid HQ—have begun flickering like embers trying to catch flame. It's not jealousy, though admitting that doesn't make the tightness in my chest any less irritating. It's something else.

Something familiar in a way that puts my guard up. Something that doesn't match the neatness of his file. And yet the moment I try to examine it too closely, my own feelings muddy the clarity I used to pride myself on.

I lean back in my chair and study the glowing Bellamy file resting on my desk, its soft red pulse a quiet reminder that this situation is no longer something I can compartmentalize. Her magic brushed mine the last time I touched the file, and even now the echo sits in the air—a lingering warmth that shouldn't be possible in a room as cold and practical as my office.

Leona knocks once and walks in without waiting for permission, crossing her arms like she's been waiting all morning to deliver bad news with flair. She tells me I'm wearing the "broody, world-weary, self-sabotaging expression" again and should probably fix it if I want potential clients—or anyone, really—to take me seriously. I tell her she's imagining things. She tells me she never imagines anything where my emotional incompetence is concerned.

I ignore all of that and ask her to run a background check.

Her eyebrow lifts, smug and knowing, but she doesn't argue. "On who?" she asks, despite clearly knowing the answer.

"Dorian Hale."

She tries—she *tries*—to keep a straight face, but the grin leaks through anyway. Jackson, having absolutely no boundaries, chooses that exact moment to poke his head around the doorframe, nodding like he's been waiting days for me to crack. They both needle me with comments about jealousy and conflict of interest until I threaten to invoke HR policies, which do not exist in this office but should, solely for moments like these.

Once they've left, the silence settles thick and uncomfortable around me. I reopen the magical database, scanning through Dorian's metrics—lineage charts, event alignments, compatibility predictions. Everything reads perfectly. Too perfectly. Clean lines where there should be discrepancies. Smooth energy patterns where a real person's life leaves the occasional fracture. He feels curated, not lived.

Leona's voice floats down the hallway as she calls in favors, promising me subtlety. Jackson mentions cross-checking public and magical records so quietly no one will notice. Their competence would be reassuring if the knot between my ribs would ease.

It doesn't.

The truth presses heavier now, settling into the room with the weight of something I can't rationalize away. I drag a hand over my face, exhaling slowly as the realization forms with irritating clarity.

Distance isn't helping. Logic isn't helping. And pretending I don't care is the least effective strategy I've ever attempted.

I'm still staring at the glowing metrics on Dorian's file—still trying to convince myself the unease twisting through my ribs is imagination—when Leona reappears in the doorway with a tablet balanced on her hip and a look that tells me she's about to make my life difficult on purpose.

"You're spiraling," she announces.

"I'm analyzing."

"You're spiraling while pretending to analyze. Completely different thing."

I push away from the desk, forcing my voice into something steady. "If Francesca is attending the first event with Dorian, I need to be able to observe the room. Quietly. Objectively."

She raises an eyebrow. "You mean you need an excuse to be in the same ballroom so you don't implode at home wondering what's happening."

"I didn't say that."

"You didn't have to."

She crosses her arms, waiting for me to say the thing I've been circling without admitting. The magic in the Bellamy file hums faintly beside me, pulsing like it knows I'm one step away from making a decision that could either stabilize everything—or blow up the remaining illusion of neutrality I've been clinging to.

I take a slow breath. "I'll need a plus one."

Leona blinks. Her smile spreads slowly, brilliantly, like sunlight dripping into the room. "Oh. Oh, this is delicious."

"It's practical," I correct, though my voice wavers just enough to betray me. "If I show up alone, Dorian will notice. Francesca will notice. People talk. A companion makes it easier to blend into the crowd."

"And," she says, drawing out the word, "it gives you something to do instead of pacing the perimeter like a sulking gargoyle."

"That is not what I would be doing."

"Sayer, that is *exactly* what you would be doing."

She taps her tablet once, scrolling through contacts with quick, purposeful swipes. "Fine. You need a plus one. Preferably someone unobtrusive, charming enough to keep you from glowering holes in the drapes, and competent enough that they won't accidentally get enchanted by the crowd."

"That's... specific."

"That's *necessary*. Especially for a Lupercalia event." She hums thoughtfully, eyes narrowing. "But I already have someone in mind."

I straighten, wary. "Define someone."

"Human," she says. "Mostly. Clever. Self-sufficient. Not easily intimidated by supernatural nonsense. And—this is important—not even remotely interested in you romantically, so you can stop panicking about the moral implications."

"I am not panicking."

"You are absolutely panicking. It's adorable."

I pinch the bridge of my nose. "Who is it, Leona?"

She closes her tablet with a satisfied snap. "Arden."

I blink. "Arden. Your cousin Arden?"

"Yes. She's perfect."

"She hexed her last date because he said cilantro tasted like soap."

"That's called having standards."

"She also started a fistfight with a cupid at the summer festival because he insulted her handwriting."

"That cupid deserved worse." She retorts shrugging.

I stare at her, torn between horror and inevitability. "You want me to bring *Arden* as my date."

"She checks every box," Leona says brightly. "She's immune to the insanity of these events. She can keep up appearances. She will absolutely not let you brood yourself into an early grave. And most importantly, she's available."

"This is a terrible idea."

"Which is precisely why it will work."

She steps closer, tapping the back of her knuckles against the glowing Bellamy file on my desk. "You want to protect her. You want to watch for danger. And you want to pretend you're not emotionally entangled while doing it. So fine. Bring Arden. She'll run interference so you don't accidentally broadcast the wrong thing."

"...the wrong thing?"

"Oh please." She rolls her eyes. "Your face is starting to betray you, counselor. You need backup."

The knot behind my ribs tightens, not painfully—more like something bracing itself.

"Fine," I say, though the word tastes like inevitable disaster. "Set it up."

"I already did," she says, already halfway out the door. "She'll meet you at the office an hour before the ball."

I inhale sharply. "Leona—"

"You're welcome!"

And then she's gone, leaving me alone with the glowing file, the weighted silence of the room, and the unmistakable sinking feeling that I just agreed to something that will complicate everything I've been trying—and failing—to keep simple.

Arden arrives exactly on time—because of course she does—and steps into my office like she owns not just the room but whatever universe it's attached to.

She's striking in the way a blade is striking: sharp, elegant, and carrying just enough danger to make the sensible part of my brain sit up straight. Her dark hair is braided into a crown that circles her head before falling into a loose, glossy sweep over one shoulder. Her dress is deep wine-red, fitted at the waist, flowing at the hem, slit high enough that she could kick someone and still look like she'd done it with grace. Gold cuffs gleam around her wrists, runic etchings catching the light each time she moves.

Arden has always radiated confidence, but tonight she's dialed it into a kind of poised, effortless power that makes even the office wards perk up.

She skims her gaze over me—black suit, tailored cleanly, wings hidden beneath structured enchantments—and smirks. "Not bad, Valentine. You almost look like you won't emotionally combust if someone flirts with you tonight."

"I'm fine," I say, which earns me a slow, unblinking stare that suggests she has already diagnosed twelve different ways that statement is a lie.

"Leona warned me about your denial issues."

"Of course she did."

Arden steps closer, tugging lightly on my lapel as if testing whether my suit will survive the night. "Relax. I'm here to keep you from glaring holes through your own assignment. You observe. I provide cover. And if someone decides to be an idiot, I will handle it before you can."

"That's... not actually comforting."

"Good," she says, patting my chest once before turning toward the door. "Terror helps you make better choices."

I follow her out of the office, locking up behind us. Jackson gives us a wave; Leona beams like she's watching a plan unfold exactly as she predicted—which is probably true. The wards hum softly as we pass, picking up on Arden's magic, which crackles warm and contained, like embers banked under velvet.

Outside, the sun has begun its slow descent, bathing the street in a copper glow. My car waits at the curb, polished to a shine that suggests Jackson bribed someone to detail it.

Arden slides into the passenger seat with graceful efficiency. "All right," she says, fastening her seatbelt, "let's go watch your Bellamy try to survive the first big trial."

I grip the wheel, ignoring the way my pulse jumps at the word *your*, and navigate toward the historic district—toward the Hall of Echoes, where the first Lupercalia Ball always unfolds like a spectacle wrapped in enchantments.

As we turn down the final street, the building comes into view, glowing with lanternlight: grand arched windows casting warm gold across the snow-dusted pavement, spell-forged sigils drifting lazily above the entrance like floating constellations. Carriages and sleek enchanted sedans line the front, guests shimmering with glamour as they walk inside.

Arden leans forward, eyes bright with anticipation. "Well," she murmurs, lips curving, "this is going to be entertaining."

I pull up to the valet, heart beating harder than I want to admit, because somewhere inside that glittering mess of magic and obligation—

Francesca is waiting. And the night is about to start.

Chapter 25

Francesca

Dorian steps out first, offering his hand as the valet closes the passenger door behind me. The winter air grazes my shoulders, cool against the midnight-blue satin of my gown. The dress fits like it was stitched with spells—structured bodice, soft flowing skirt, the kind of fabric that catches the lanternlight in shifting shades of indigo and silver. I smoothed the skirt twice in the car without meaning to, nerves winding themselves into quiet little knots beneath my ribs.

We've spent time together every day this week—long walks, phone calls, laughter that surprised both of us. Dorian is steady in a way that invites trust, warm in a way that coaxes comfort, and respectful in a way that feels almost old-world. And yet, despite all of that, something in my chest keeps pulling sideways, tugging toward a shadow at the edges of my thoughts.

Sayer Valentine.

Always just out of reach, like a scent or a chord or a half-finished thought I can't quite shake.

Dorian squeezes my hand gently as we start up the steps. "Ready?" he asks, his voice pitched low, warmth curling through the syllables.

"As I'll ever be," I answer, lifting my chin.

The Hall of Echoes glows ahead of us, lanterns shimmering like captured starlight, sigils drifting lazily across the stone archway. Magic hums against my skin the moment we cross the threshold—an immediate, unmistakable awareness that I've stepped into something ancient and enchanted.

Inside, the ballroom unfolds in a sweep of gilded balconies and glittering chandeliers. Enchanted snow falls in a soft spiral from the ceiling before dissolving into harmless sparks. A string ensemble plays near the dais, their instruments glowing faintly with spell work that makes the notes feel richer, deeper, almost touchable.

Dorian keeps his hand at the small of my back, guiding me with a confidence that feels practiced but not possessive. He leans in as we pause at the entrance, and his breath warms my cheek. "You look stunning tonight," he murmurs. "Like this room was built to show you off."

The compliment lands in my chest with a flustered flutter I pretend not to feel. "Careful," I say, forcing a smile. "I might start thinking you're trying to win the wager from the festival."

"Who says I'm not?" His grin is quick but charming, and for a moment I let myself sink into the ease of it.

We move further inside, weaving between guests in velvet robes, shimmering gowns, elaborate suits with runic threads sewn through their lapels. Magic glides through the crowd—little pulses of enchantment riding every gesture, every laugh, every clink of glass.

My own magic stirs in response, subtle at first, then more insistently. It's not misbehaving yet, but it's awake, restless, sensing something in the air that sets every Bellamy nerve humming.

"Familiar faces?" Dorian asks, scanning the room.

"A few," I say, catching glimpses of distant cousins and acquaintances from old family events. "Nothing I can't handle."

His hand presses lightly to my elbow. "If anything—or anyone—makes you uncomfortable tonight, tell me. I'm here for you."

It's sweet. And safe. And exactly what I should want.

But despite his warmth beside me, despite the comfort in his tone, a faint tightening spirals through my magic like a thread pulled taut.

I draw a steady breath and let the music settle along my spine, but something in the room shifts before I can exhale—a subtle change in pressure, a spark of awareness that skims across my skin like a fingertip tracing the back of my neck. Lanternlight drifts over the dance floor in warm, shimmering waves, but beneath all that brightness, the magic in the air realigns itself, almost as if the ballroom has quietly acknowledged a new arrival. The sensation is unmistakable, a familiar pull I haven't felt in years, one that stirs before I have time to question it.

Someone familiar just stepped inside.

I don't turn, don't scan the room, don't give myself away, but my pulse betrays me anyway, quick and traitorous. Dorian leans in, unaware of the sudden current running under my skin. "Ready to dance?" he asks, his voice warm, steady, exactly what I thought I wanted to hear tonight.

I gather myself with a practiced steadiness and offer a small nod, forcing my attention to stay anchored to him. "Let's make tonight count," I say, even though a quiet part of me already doubts whether I'll be able to hold onto the moment.

My magic stirs the instant we step toward the dance floor—a low, rippling current that tightens beneath my ribs as if waking abruptly. It isn't dramatic, but it's sharp enough that I slow without meaning to, breath catching as warmth coils through my palms and the neckline of my gown. The sensation is unmistakable: awareness. Recognition. A pull strong enough to trip my steps.

Dorian's hand settles lightly at the small of my back, and the flare dims—too quickly, too smoothly. His steadiness pours over my senses like cool water, soothing what shouldn't be soothed, quieting what shouldn't quiet. For a heartbeat, I wonder if maybe I imagined the intensity.

Then the crowd parts just enough for me to see the source.

Sayer Valentine stands across the ballroom near the second tier of tables, dressed in obsidian-black formal wear that fits him too well, tension wrapped through his shoulders in a way only I would notice. And beside him—just a step too close, her hand resting on his arm—is a woman with sharp cheekbones, dark coils of hair, and the kind of confidence that settles around her like expensive perfume.

The flare inside me twists, brighter this time, almost reactive.

Dorian's thumb moves in one slow, grounding arc against my spine, and the magic quiets again—obedient, unnatural, as if responding to someone who isn't meant to have that kind of sway over it. Something about the ease of it doesn't sit right, the way my own power yields to his touch too fast, too willingly.

I draw a breath, steady on the outside, far less so beneath my skin.

"Well," Dorian murmurs, following my gaze just long enough to take the measure of what he sees. "Looks like we've found the first complication of the evening."

He says it lightly. My magic knows better.

I shake off the prickle beneath my skin, telling myself it's nerves, or the curse stretching its claws now that the ballroom is full and the energy is thick enough to taste. The uneasiness settles into something I can almost ignore—almost—so I let Dorian guide us toward the heart of the evening. The music swells, soft candlelight catches in the folds of gowns as dancers turn, and little by little I let myself drift into the rhythm he offers.

He's careful with me. Confident. Present in a way that makes it easy to forget everything else. We laugh over a spilled drink that narrowly misses my skirt, navigate the crowd arm-in-arm, accept compliments from distant relatives and acquaintances who suddenly remember my name because the Season has a way of making everyone overly attentive. I'm not used to being sought out at events like this, but Dorian moves with such comfortable assurance that I find myself matching his ease.

Eventually, we circle close enough to cross paths with Sayer and the woman he brought with him. The magic under my skin gives a small lurch—sharp, immediate—but Dorian's hand tightens gently around mine, and the feeling folds back in on itself before it can gain momentum.

Sayer's expression is perfectly polite, impeccably detached, but something there feels too measured to be natural. The woman on his arm—Arden, I think—greets us with the poised warmth of someone trained to make impeccable first impressions. Dorian is gracious, introducing himself with that low, composed charm he wields so effortlessly. I manage a greeting that doesn't betray the spark thrashing under my ribs.

We don't linger long, but the moment stays with me even after we move on, clinging to the edges of my awareness like a shadow refusing to dissolve.

I push it aside. Nerves. Curse. Ballroom energy. Too much everything.

My parents arrive a little later—my mother elegant in deep garnet, my father looking like he stepped straight out of a prestige drama where he plays "distinguished patriarch with chaotic daughters." Dorian handles them beautifully, offering a warm greeting, engaging my father in conversation about something historical and obscure while my mother assesses him with the kind of quiet scrutiny only she can get away with.

They like him. I can see it immediately. That realization does strange things to my chest.

The night deepens. Music softens into a slower, more intimate tempo. Lanterns drift lower, casting a warm gold haze across the floor. Dorian leans in just enough for his breath to brush my cheek.

"Would you like some air?" he asks. "There's a garden off the west terrace. It's beautiful at night."

I hesitate only long enough to catch the pull of my magic trying to gauge something it doesn't understand. But the warmth in his voice tugs me forward, and I let him guide me through one of the side doors into the crisp evening air.

The garden is strung with floating lights that drift between the hedges like fireflies, illuminating the frost-touched petals of winter roses. The path curves beneath our feet, crunching softly with each step. The cold should sting, but Dorian shrugs off his jacket and settles it over my shoulders before I can protest.

"It suits you," he murmurs, eyes warm in the moonlight.

We walk a little farther, the quiet stretching pleasantly between us, the world narrowing to the brush of our hands, the faint glow of enchanted lanterns, the steady pulse of magic humming at the edges of my awareness. When he stops, it's in a small clearing where the hedges open just enough for moonlight to pool like silver ink on the ground.

He turns toward me slowly, one hand lifting to brush a stray strand of hair from my cheek. His fingers are warm, deliberate, a touch that asks rather than takes.

"Francesca," he says, my name low and careful, as if speaking it too loudly might break the moment. "May I?"

Something in my breath stumbles. My heart answers before my mind fully catches up.

I nod.

Dorian leans in, unhurried and certain, and the kiss that follows is warm and steady, more invitation than claim. My magic flickers—bright, unsettled, curious—but instead of spiraling out of control, it settles into a soft shimmer beneath my skin, as if unsure what to do with the gentleness of this connection.

For a few long, suspended seconds, the world is only moonlight, breath, the press of his lips, and the whisper of winter roses shifting in the breeze.

And for the first time all night, I stop trying to figure out what anything means and let myself feel it.

Chapter 26

Sayer

By midweek the office should feel calm—Victorian calm, library calm, the kind that comes after a crisis has safely passed and you get to pretend you planned it that way all along. Instead, everything feels off-kilter, like someone nudged the universe half an inch to the left when I wasn't looking.

The first event went flawlessly. Painfully flawlessly. On paper, this is where I should be celebrating—internally, quietly, with a small, satisfied smirk no one gets to see. Even without the Bellamy complication, even without the curse thrumming like a second heart in the background, it was a textbook execution. Everything fell into place. No magical meltdowns. No interpersonal catastrophes. No unexpected cosmic interference.

Which is exactly the problem.

Perfect never means perfect in my world. Perfect means I missed something.

And I hate missing things.

I stare at the open ledger on my desk, the neat columns of projected outcomes and compatibility branching that should make sense. Instead, the numbers press against my temples like a headache waiting for permission. Every instinct I've spent decades sharpening keeps tugging me toward the same conclusion: Dorian should not be this smooth of a fit. Not for Francesca. Not for the curse. Not for the season.

Yet there he is, sliding through every obstacle like he was pre-approved by fate itself.

Jackson drops a stack of files on the corner of my desk, and the noise snaps through my irritation like a pebble hitting glass. He gives me a quick nod before disappearing into the war room, leaving me alone with the quiet hum of warded walls and my steadily worsening mood.

I lean back in my chair and exhale, letting the frustration settle low in my chest. Losing sight of them at the ball still grates—one moment I was monitoring their position from across the room, and the next they slipped into the garden like the shadows swallowed them. I combed the crowd for a solid ten minutes, convincing myself it was observational necessity, not some absurd, unprofessional spike of anxious curiosity. Still, it felt wrong. Too difficult to track. Too easy for him to move her out of sight.

I rub at the tension in my jaw, irritated at how easily this—*she*—has started to get under my skin.

The next Ball is days away, and for the first time since the High Council slammed responsibility back onto my shoulders, I feel the pressure shifting. Not the looming deadline. Not the curse.

Something else tightening around the edges of the assignment. Something I can't name.

Leona taps lightly on the door before slipping inside, a folder tucked under one arm and suspicion written all over her face.

"You're thinking too loudly," she says, dropping the folder in front of me. "It's making the wards twitch."

"That's not a thing," I mutter.

"It is today," she shoots back, sliding into the chair across from me. "So. Are you going to tell me what's wrong, or should I start guessing and make it very, very weird?"

I don't immediately respond. Partly because I'm stubborn, partly because she'll drag it out of me anyway.

Finally, I sigh. "The projections aren't lining up."

"With Dorian?"

"Yes."

"And you think you missed something."

"I know I did," I admit, the words heavier than they should be. "Everything went too smoothly."

She studies me, eyes sharp, far too perceptive for someone who claims she "just vibes" with magical anomalies.

"Is this your gut talking," she asks, "or your... complicated feelings?"

I glare.

She smiles. "Right," she says. "Both."

I shut the ledger and push it aside, that restless, crawling energy still working its way under my skin. "This still isn't right," I say, more to myself than to Leona. "You and Jackson pulled everything that's publicly available?"

"We did," she replies, tapping the folder she brought in. "On paper, he's spotless. Employment history checks out. Family records are extra boring. No flagged contracts, no off-the-book bindings, no disciplinary actions that anyone will admit to. If you want the technical answer, Dorian Hale is exactly who he says he is."

"Technically," I repeat.

Her mouth tilts. "Technically. Which is why my contact at the Archives is still digging. Old sealed files, restricted match reports, any hint he's been redirected or reassigned before. Jackson's cross-checking magical registries and private contracts on the back end. If there's a crack in the façade, we'll find it—but so far, nothing obvious."

When she leaves and the door clicks shut behind her, the room feels too quiet. I sit there for a long moment, staring at the space where that folder rests, trying to convince my shoulders to unclench. They don't. Everything about this situation is refusing to behave the way it should—not the curse, not the pattern of the match pathways, not the way Francesca is responding to all of it, and sure as hell not whatever is happening in my own chest every time her name crosses my mind. The next event is closing in, and with each passing day it feels less like I'm guiding the process and more like I'm being funneled toward the edge of something I can't quite see yet.

A soft pulse of ward light flickers along the doorframe—just enough warning for me to look up before the door swings open without so much as a courtesy tap. Francesca steps inside like she owns the place, the scent of espresso drifting in with her, two to-go bags hooked over her wrist and a coffee carrier balanced neatly in one hand. Her braid hangs over her shoulder in a loose sweep, cheeks warmed from the cold outside, magic humming around her like it's got opinions it's dying to share.

She closes the door with her hip and lifts the coffee carrier a little higher. "I come bearing peace offerings," she announces, crossing the room with far too much confidence for someone who bypassed every boundary spell I have. "Because rumor has it"—her eyes flick to mine, dry as a desert—"you're having a very difficult time finding my perfect match. Strange, really, since Dorian and I seem to be getting along beautifully."

There's a smile on her lips, but underneath it something coils—curiosity sharpened by challenge, interest wrapped in something warmer, something she's pretending not to examine too closely.

I sit back in my chair, steepling my fingers because if I don't, I might do something unprofessional like stare at her mouth. "Rumor, hm?" I say. "Let me guess. Leona."

"She didn't need to say anything," Francesca replies, setting the coffee carrier on my desk and sliding one cup toward me with casual precision. "It's written all over your face. That 'I can't believe the universe is doing this to me' look you get."

"I don't have a look," I counter.

"You have several," she says, passing me a napkin as if this is a regular Tuesday. "That one's my favorite."

She sets the lunches down next—something warm and fragrant that fills the office within seconds. Lemon and garlic. Toasted bread.

Roasted herbs. I shouldn't register any of it, but my stomach clearly didn't get the memo that we're in the middle of a professional crisis.

I take the coffee she pushed in front of me—my order, of course she knows my order—and the heat seeps through the cup into my hand like an accusation.

Francesca watches me with that Bellamy intuition that sees far too much. "Since everything is going so well with Dorian," she says, lifting her brows, "I thought you might want a little... encouragement. Or a break. Or carbs."

"Encouragement," I echo, because I need a second to get my heartbeat under control.

She shrugs, the braid sliding against her chest. "You're working too hard. You look like you're trying to beat fate with spreadsheets."

It's meant to be a joke. It hits nowhere near lightly.

Something tightens in my chest, and I cover it by taking a long, deliberately casual sip of coffee. "Dorian is... fine."

Her eyes narrow. "That sounded like the least convincing endorsement in history."

"He's fine," I repeat. "Your compatibility scores are decent."

"'Decent,'" she says, leaning against the edge of my desk, crossing her arms. "Not the most glowing phrase."

"You want glowing? That's not how this works."

"You're evading," she fires back gently. "Which is even more suspicious."

There it is again—that flicker of magic that responds to every shift in my breathing, every change in my tone. The air feels warmer, closer, like the room is shrinking around the two of us.

I clear my throat. "Your lunch is going to get cold."

"That was an evasion too."

"It was," I admit. "A strategic one."

Her laugh softens the tension, but doesn't dissolve it. "So tell me, Valentine. Am I interrupting some very important brooding?"

"Extremely important," I say. "But I suppose I can spare a few minutes for someone who barges into my office without knocking."

"If I knocked," she says, pushing off the desk and taking the chair across from me, "you might have said no."

And just like that, the air between us shifts again—familiar, charged, tinged with something neither of us has any business touching yet.

I take another slow sip of coffee.

She unwraps her sandwich, watching me over the top of the paper.

Dorian might be her date.

But she brought lunch here.

To me.

And the magic in the room is very aware of that fact.

I take another slow drink of coffee, letting the warmth settle through my chest before I speak. "If things with Dorian aren't lining up the way we hoped," I begin carefully, measuring every syllable, "I can widen the field again. There are still viable matches we haven't explored. You're not locked into anything."

The reaction is immediate—her shoulders draw back, her posture straightens, and her eyes flash with something sharper than I expect.

"What do you mean 'not lining up'?" she asks, setting her sandwich down with deliberate calm. "We've seen each other every day this week. We get along. Really well, actually. And we have dinner plans tonight. So I'm not sure why you're talking like he's already off the list."

I open the folder in front of me, not because I need it, but because looking away from her makes it easier to control the tightening in my throat. "I'm saying," I clarify, "that if something doesn't feel right—if the fit isn't as strong as you expected—you don't have to force it just because he scored well initially."

Her chin lifts. "It does feel right."

"Good," I say, and I mean it more than I'd like to admit. "Then there's nothing to worry about."

She hesitates then, just long enough for the air to shift. Something thrums beneath her skin—magic tightening rather than expanding, like it's bracing for something. When she speaks again, her voice carries a tone that's... off. Not unnatural, but not entirely hers either. Too smooth. Too practiced. Too certain.

"Actually," she says, settling deeper into the chair, "I came to ask for a favor."

The way she says it hits the room wrong, almost like a frequency my instincts can hear even if she can't.

"What kind of favor?" I ask slowly.

She folds her hands in her lap, her expression composed in a way that makes the unease inside me twist a little harder. "The next ball," she says. "Dorian wants to take me. He insisted, actually. And I'd like you to approve it. Officially."

My pulse goes sharp.

"He insisted?" I repeat.

"Don't make it sound strange," she says, brushing a stray curl behind her ear. "He said it's important to him. And after the week we've had, I don't see the harm."

The magic in the room pulses softly, a subtle ripple that brushes over my senses like a warning. Not loud. Not dramatic. Just... there. Wrong enough that every instinct I trust tightens in response.

"Francesca," I say quietly, "the original plan was for me to escort you to that event. Strategically, it makes the most sense."

"But this isn't strategy," she counters, almost too quickly. "It's a date. And I want to go with him. We've built something. It doesn't make sense for me to walk in on someone else's arm."

Her words line up perfectly—but something beneath them doesn't.

It's too firm. Too rehearsed. Too... guided.

I study her across the desk, trying to find the familiar patterns of her energy, the usual soft edges of her presence. Instead I find a slight discord, a faint pressure in the air around her that makes the back of my neck tighten.

There's influence here. Something shaping her choices. Something that isn't me.

"Fran..." I try again, softer this time, "are you sure this is what you want?"

She blinks, surprised by the question. "Of course I am. Why wouldn't I be?"

The magic in my office flickers once—barely noticeable, but enough to feel like a heartbeat skipping out of rhythm. I should say no. I should refuse outright. I should trust what my instincts are screaming at me. But she's looking at me with stubborn certainty, and the last thing I want is to push her into thinking I don't trust her judgment.

So I nod once, slow and reluctant. "All right," I say. "If that's what you want, then I'll approve the request."

She exhales like she's been holding her breath, a relieved smile warming the edges of her expression. "Good. Thank you."

But as she reaches for her coffee—her magic brushing the air in a faint, uneven pulse—the unease in my chest only deepens.

Because nothing about her request felt like Francesca. And everything about it felt like a storm building just beyond the horizon.

Chapter 27

Francesca

By the time I finish my makeup, the house smells faintly of jasmine and setting powder, the kind of soft, familiar scent that settles my nerves just enough to keep me from bouncing off walls. My gown hangs from the bedroom door—deep garnet tonight, fitted through the bodice and scattered with tiny iridescent beads that catch the light like magic trying to flirt. I smooth the skirt one last time and check my reflection. I look the part. I feel... close to it. Close enough.

The knock comes exactly when I expect it.

Dorian stands on the landing, framed by the glow of the hall-way lights. He's immaculate as always—dark suit tailored like it was stitched directly onto his frame, hair neatly swept back, a faint cologne that smells expensive and subtle. The kind of scent that doesn't announce itself so much as settle into the air like an invitation.

"You look incredible," he says, offering his hand as though we've stepped into one of those old-world romance films where everyone speaks in soft lighting and perfect delivery.

"Thank you," I say, slipping my fingers into his. "You clean up okay yourself."

He smiles, warm and polished, and leads me out of the building toward the sleek car parked at the curb. I'd almost grown used to his presence over the past week—our walks, our conversations, the gentle way he always made space for me at his side. Comfortable. Predictable. Steady.

Tonight, there's something else under the surface. A quiet charge in the air, like static waiting to choose where to land.

I settle into the passenger seat, gathering my skirt with practiced care. "We'll make perfect time," I say, glancing at the dashboard clock. "What did Sayer say the entrance window was? Thirty minutes from doors opening?"

Dorian pulls into traffic with a smoothness that borders on uncanny. "We're not going straight there."

The statement hangs in the air for a moment—light, casual, utterly out of place.

I turn toward him slowly. "We... not?"

He shakes his head, eyes on the road, posture relaxed. Too relaxed. "There's someone I want you to meet first."

A tiny pulse of magic flickers under my ribs, not sharp enough to hurt but insistent enough to get my attention. "Meet who?" I ask, my voice steady even as unease trails along my spine.

"My family," he says, like it's the most natural thing in the world. "They're hosting a gathering tonight. It's not far. They've been eager to meet you."

My heart stumbles a beat. "Your family. Tonight?"

"I told them about you," he says, tone warm but indisputably sure. "After the week we've had, it seemed appropriate."

Appropriate. The word lands strangely, like someone trying to translate emotion into legal terminology.

"I thought we were going to the ball," I murmur.

"And we will," Dorian replies, glancing at me with an easy smile. "After dinner. This won't take long."

My magic stirs again—restless now, curling beneath my skin in small, unsettled spirals. I smooth my hands over the skirt of my dress, trying to quiet the sensation the way I always do during the Season, but it doesn't drift away. It holds firm. Watching.

As the city lights blur past us, something heavy settles in my stomach. The car feels too quiet. Too insulated from the world outside. Too intentional.

"Dorian," I try, "I wish you'd told me earlier. I would've—prepared myself."

He laughs—soft, charming, practiced. "You don't need preparation. You're perfect just as you are."

The compliment should make me blush. Instead it lands like a statement someone has said a thousand times before.

The neighborhood he turns into is old-money elegant—brick townhomes with wrought-iron balconies and flickering gas lamps lining the street. Warm windows. Candlelit shadows. And somewhere deeper in the block, a house glows brighter than the rest, doors open, music spilling into the night.

A private dinner party. For his family. Magic presses at my sternum, almost like a warning.

"Dorian..." I begin again.

He slows the car in front of the home, his smile unwavering. "Trust me," he murmurs. "They're going to love you."

And for the first time since this whole ridiculous season began, I'm not entirely convinced that's a good thing.

My magic prickles the moment we turn down the secluded drive of a sprawling stone manor. Not a gentle flutter. Not curiosity. A sharp, protective spike—heat in my veins, pressure behind my ribs, the sense of something ancient stirring awake inside my chest.

I take a slow inhale, tamping it down the way I always do when the curse gets fussy. Maybe it's the old house. Maybe it's nerves. Maybe it's the fact that the driveway is long enough to have its own zip code.

Dorian parks beneath an archway of carved stone and kills the engine with a flick of his wrist. When he turns to me, his expression is tender—exactly so. Except something tightens behind it when he sees the way I'm gripping my clutch.

"You're tense," he says, tone light but carrying a sliver of irritation beneath the charm. " I told you, there's no reason to be."

"My magic's on edge," I admit, because pretending otherwise would be pointless. "This place feels... old."

"It is old," he replies with a smile that doesn't reach his eyes. "That's part of its legacy. Don't let it intimidate you."

"I'm not intimidated," I say, even though some part of me absolutely is.

He studies me a second too long, then his jaw ticks in a barely-there shift. "Francesca, they're going to adore you. Don't overthink this."

The sharpness in his voice is small but unmistakable.

I blink, surprised. "I'm not overthinking."

"You are," he counters, stepping out of the car and circling around to open my door. "You don't have to be afraid of every new thing."

A flicker of defensiveness rises before I can swallow it. "I'm not afraid. I just wish I'd known we were coming here first." My jaw tightens as I smooth an imaginary crease from my dress.

"It wouldn't have mattered," he says softly—but the softness feels thin, as if he's using it like a tool rather than a tone. "You look beautiful. You're charming. They'll welcome you."

He offers his hand. The magic under my skin pulses again—sharp, warning, instinctive.

I tell it to hush.

He's been kind all week. Gentle. Steady. Patient. Everything I should want in a match.

I place my hand in his. His fingers tighten just a shade too firmly, guiding me toward the grand front steps. The stone walls loom overhead, ancient and imposing, lit by sconces that throw long shadows across the courtyard. Music floats through the open door, elegant and distant, like it's leaking from another century.

With each step he takes, my unease grows—not loud, just persistent, like my magic is tugging at my sleeve, whispering pay attention.

I straighten my shoulders and breathe through it, reminding myself that this is a date. A meet-the-family dinner. Normal people do this. Normal women don't over analyze atmospheric pressure shifts and expect omens.

Dorian glances at me again, irritation flickering briefly in his eyes when he catches the tension in my posture. "Francesca," he says quietly, leaning in just enough for his breath to warm my cheek. "Please try to relax. It's important to me that this goes well."

There's something commanding in the way he says it—something that feels too practiced, too certain, too... expecting.

I force a smile. "I'll do my best."

He studies my face, then gives a clipped nod, satisfaction sliding over his features like a mask settling into place.

"Good," he murmurs.

We step inside together. And the moment the door closes behind us, my magic curls tight around my spine like a hand bracing for impact.

The foyer opens into a high-ceilinged hall lined with portraits—oil paintings of stern-faced ancestors who look like they'd scold the wallpaper for breathing too loudly. A long table glitters beneath an elaborate chandelier, already set for more people than I expect for a "small" dinner.

Dorian's hand at my back guides me forward, and my magic bristles again—an involuntary surge that feels like heat blooming beneath my skin. I swallow it down, shifting the tension into a smile as a woman approaches us.

"Francesca," Dorian says smoothly, "this is my mother, Elizabeth."

She is elegant in a way that makes the chandelier look under-dressed—pale silk, sharp jewelry, an expression that measures rather than greets. She extends her hand, cool fingers grazing mine.

"So lovely to finally meet you," she says with a saccharine smile.

My magic spikes hard enough to make my vision flicker—heat, pressure, the sense of wards shuddering somewhere miles away. I grip Dorian's sleeve to steady myself.

He frowns. "You're trembling."

"I'm fine," I lie, forcing air into my lungs. "Just... the room got too warm."

He doesn't look convinced, but he steps aside to introduce me to the next relative, then the next—names slipping past me as my magic snarls beneath my ribs. Not a misfire. Not an accident.

A warning.

A loud one.

And then it hits—like a bell inside my bones. Something has gone catastrophically wrong at the bakery.

My phone buzzes in my clutch before I even reach for it. One new message from Harper flashes across the screen:

That's it. Just the fire extinguisher emoji. Which is Harper's code for something exploded and it's still moving. The second I register it, the call screen lights up—Ellie. Video call. Frantic.

My stomach drops.

"Excuse me," I murmur, stepping away from Dorian and his hovering family before I accidentally level this entire ancestral mansion with emotional static. "I need—just a minute."

I answer the call with my back half-turned, lowering my voice. "Ellie? What happened?"

Her face fills the screen, hair frazzled, flour across her cheek like a war stripe. Behind her, the bakery looks like it's auditioning for a supernatural disaster documentary. A mixer is spinning on its own in the background. Dough is crawling up the wall. A tray of éclairs just... launches itself across the room behind her.

"Oh THANK THE MOONS," Ellie gasps. "Fran, the magic—your magic—is losing its mind. Harper's in the back throwing up shields like she's in a wizard battle. Miguel is trying to stop the baguettes from reenacting a jailbreak. Also I think the cinnamon rolls might be sentient now—"

Something crashes loudly behind her.

"Gotta go." She spins the camera, and for one horrifying second I see a cake levitating with murder in its frosting. "Please come home. Please. Please. Please."

She ends the call abruptly.

I stare at my phone for half a heartbeat before my instincts overtake everything else.

Dorian is beside me instantly, concern melting into annoyance so fast it almost trips the air between us. "What could possibly be so urgent?" he asks, his voice soft but laced with friction. "Did they run out of sugar?"

"The bakery," I say, already backing toward the front door. "Something's wrong. I have to go."

"You're overreacting—"

"No," I cut in, sharper than I intend. "Trust me, I'm not."

His jaw tightens. "Francesca this dinner is important."

"So is my family."

The words land between us like a stone dropped in still water—clean, irrefutable, unmovable.

And for a brief, brittle moment, the charm slips from his expression. But I don't wait for a reply. I don't have the luxury.

My magic is screaming, the wards back home flaring bright enough to hum through my bones.

I gather my skirt, turn on my heel, and walk out of the mansion without looking back—even though I can feel Dorian's eyes on me, cold and unreadable as stone.

Whatever tonight was meant to reveal... it's revealing something very different.

<h1 style="text-align:center">Chapter 28</h1>

<h2 style="text-align:center">Sayer</h2>

I should be enjoying the quiet. For the first time in weeks, my apartment is still—no files glowing on the coffee table, no reports piling on my desk, no frantic clients calling after making predictably catastrophic life choices. Just the soft hum of the city outside my windows and the steady rhythm of my own breathing.

Instead, I'm pacing the length of my living room like someone wound me too tight and forgot to release the tension.

I told Leona and Jackson I wouldn't attend this ball. It wasn't required, strategically or otherwise, and after the last event I needed distance—room to think, room to reset, room to pry Francesca out of the space she's taken up in my mind. They agreed, promised to keep an eye on things, said they'd text once they saw her arrive with Dorian.

They haven't texted.

Not one update. Not a single "she's here" or "he seems normal" or "everything's stable." Nothing.

I check my phone again. Empty.

I try to sit, but the cushions feel wrong beneath me, like they're pushing me back to my feet. So I pace instead, the wooden floor warm from the repeated path I've worn into it.

This shouldn't bother me. She's with Dorian. He's—technically—competent. He's passed every check so far, even though something about his records sits in my gut like a stone. But Leona is there. Jackson is there. I have coverage. A plan. A schedule.

It should be enough.

I drag a hand through my hair, restless energy scraping at the back of my mind. "She's fine," I mutter to the empty room. "She's with her chosen match. Nothing is wrong."

The words hit the air and fall flat. Something is wrong.

I can feel it in the wards layered around the building, the way they vibrate slightly—like a distant chord plucked just off key. It's subtle, easy to ignore if I were anyone else. But I'm not anyone else. I was built to sense these things. Taught to read the shift of magic in the air as easily as breath.

And right now, the magic feels restless. Unsettled. Searching.

I stop pacing long enough to stare at the drawer in my desk—the one that holds the locator spell. It's meant for emergencies. Clients in danger. Matches gone astray. Cases where lives hinge on seconds.

This isn't an emergency. Not yet.

I grip the back of a chair, grounding myself in the cool wood. I'm not going to use it. I refuse to be the unhinged cupid who stalks his own assignment through magic. I won't cross that line. I won't give whatever this is more space than it already takes.

But then the wards ripple again—stronger this time, a faint echo of Francesca's magic tugging across the city like a thread pulled too tight.

I swear under my breath.

My instincts have been gradually sharpening since the Council forced my wings free again—quiet, subtle, the old senses returning whether I want them or not. But this... this feels different. Like a pulse thrumming just out of reach, a call meant specifically for me.

Another ripple hits the wards. Sharper. Urgent.

My heart stumbles. Something's definitely wrong.

I reach the drawer before I realize I've decided to move. The locator spell sits inside, folded neatly in a small linen pouch. The second my fingers brush it, the magic hums in recognition—warm, electric, unmistakable.

I close my eyes, jaw tightening.

"I'm not supposed to do this," I remind myself. But the unease clawing through my chest doesn't care about rules or decorum or the thin line I keep trying to pretend exists between professionalism and... whatever this is becoming. I stare at it for a long moment, torn between instinct and discipline.

Then I let it go.

No. Absolutely not. I am not going to be that guy—the cupid-turned-lawyer lurking in shadows, tracking his own client like a lovesick amateur. Francesca has a date. A plan. A chosen match.

I have boundaries. Professionalism. Dignity. All the things Jackson keeps insisting I have in theory.

I close the drawer with a firm, decisive thud and turn away.

And that's when the wards in my apartment detonate.

Not loudly—the sound is more like a deep, vibrating boom from somewhere beneath the floorboards—but every protective sigil woven into the walls flares bright gold for a split second before collapsing into frantic pulses of light. The air snaps cold, then hot, then electric, like someone grabbed the entire building and shook it.

My breath punches out of me. Because I know that signature. Francesca's magic.

Not a whisper. Not a ripple. A full-blown distress surge.

I'm moving before my conscious mind catches up. My coat is in my hand. My keys hit my palm. The door slams behind me. I take the stairs two at a time, barely registering the echo of my own footsteps.

The moment I hit the street, the wards across the road ignite as well—every protective line I laid into the bakery's façade, years ago when Harper asked the entire Bellamy clan for backup during a particularly disastrous season. They flash in a sharp cascade of pink-gold sparks, outlining the shape of the building like a warning flare fired straight into the sky.

Something inside is wrong. Very wrong.

Traffic blurs around me as I sprint across the street, magic sharpening my senses whether I want it to or not. The bakery windows glow with erratic flickers—light, shadow, something moving that should absolutely not be moving.

Harper's voice echoes through the half-open front door, shouting instructions like she's commanding an arcane battalion. A mixer crashes. Someone yelps. Flour erupts into the air in a shimmering cloud. A tray flies past the doorway like an angry comet.

And there—beneath all of it—I feel Francesca.

Her magic surging. Defensive. Pulled too taut. My heart slams hard into my ribs.

"Francesca?" I call, already bracing for the explosion I know I'm walking into. "Where are you?"

Because whatever happened at her date tonight...

it didn't end where it should have.

And I'm not leaving until she's standing in front of me—safe, breathing, and nowhere near whatever set her magic on fire.

The moment I push through the doorway, the bakery feels like stepping into a magical riot. The air is thick with sugar, heat, and the frantic metallic clatter of enchanted appliances losing their collective minds. A mixer whips in circles on the counter like it's possessed. Dough balloons across the floor in slow, ominous mounds. A tray of éclairs ricochets from wall to wall like it's auditioning for an action film.

Miguel pops up from behind the counter, hair dusted with flour, apron askew, dodging an airborne éclair with the reflexes of a man who's lived through too many Bellamy seasons.

"VALENTINE!" he shouts the moment he sees me. "THANK THE GODS. We called her—she should be here any second! Whatever happened tonight? The wards have been screaming for the last fifteen minutes!"

Another éclair whips past his ear. He ducks again with a noise that might be a whimper.

I don't answer—can't, not while the magic crackles like a live wire under my skin. I tug lightly on the bond the assignment forged between us, finding Francesca's signature like a pulse through fog. It centers me—sharp, immediate—and for a breath everything in the room draws inward, aligning around that point of recognition.

And that's when it happens. My wings break free.

Not slowly. Not gracefully. They flare into the open on a surge of instinct, golden-white feathers unfurling with a force that knocks a few rogue éclairs out of the air. Miguel lets out a strangled yell—part awe, part horror—but the wings respond before I can think, channeling magic outward in controlled waves.

The room shifts the moment my wings unfurl. The air, charged and frantic a heartbeat ago, bends toward the pulse of magic rolling off them. The mixers, which had been rattling themselves into an early grave, slow as if someone dragged a calming hand across their gears. Trays that were spinning midair descend in gentle arcs, settling onto the counters with soft metallic clinks. The dough creeping along the floor shudders once and sinks back into an obedient heap, and even the rogue éclairs give up their aerial rebellion, plopping to the tile around Miguel's flour-dusted shoes like exhausted soldiers returning from battle.

I let out a slow, controlled breath and draw the wild energy inward, steadying the room one thread at a time. The wings ease behind me—not fully folded, not disappearing, but resting, the feathers settling into place with a faint whisper that seems to soothe the air more than any spell I could cast.

A hush follows, the kind that lingers after a storm breaks.

And then the door opens behind me, the bell above it chiming in a soft, almost delicate note that cuts straight through the quiet.

Francesca steps in, cheeks flushed from the cold, gown bundled in her hands like she ran the whole way here. Her hair is slightly mussed, her breath uneven, her eyes wide as they take in the aftermath.

She stops dead when she sees me—wings fully out, bakery frozen mid-chaos, Miguel staring between us as if deciding which one of us needs therapy more urgently.

And her magic... gods, her magic surges toward me in a wave of relief and recognition so strong it hits like a warm current across my skin.

"Francesca," I manage, though my voice comes out rougher than I intend, "are you—"

She meets my eyes, and whatever explanation she meant to offer slips away before it reaches her lips. I don't need her to say a word—the truth is written in the way her breath catches, in the tightness around her mouth, in the way her magic clings to her like it's bracing for impact.

She's not fine. Not even close.

And whatever she walked away from tonight... it didn't stay behind. It came with her, lingering at her heels like a shadow that hasn't decided yet whether it wants to follow or devour.

Chapter 29

Sayer

Dorian is already seated when I step into my office, and the sight of him there sets my teeth on edge.

He's taken the chair across from my desk—the client chair—his coat draped neatly over one arm, posture composed enough to look intentional rather than presumptuous. His hands are folded, his expression carefully neutral, his magic leashed so tightly it creates a faint pressure in the air, like a held breath that's been stretched too long.

He looks up as I close the door behind me.

"Mr. Valentine," he says evenly. "I assumed you'd want to discuss last night."

I don't acknowledge the greeting. I move past him, set my brief-case down, and take my time straightening the files on my desk. The ritual is deliberate—edges aligned, wards steady beneath the walls. This is my space. My rules. He doesn't get to rush this.

When I finally sit, I don't look at him right away.

"You changed the location of the date," I say flatly.

Dorian blinks once, then nods. "Yes. The original venue felt restrictive. Francesca mentioned she was uncomfortable with—"

"You changed the location without authorization," I cut in. "After already deviating from the approved plan earlier in the week."

His jaw tightens. "She agreed to go."

"You didn't tell her where you were taking her."

There's a pause—not long, but precise enough to register.

"It was a private gathering," he says carefully. "Low-profile. Discreet."

"It was unsanctioned," I reply. "Unverified. Unwarded. And you knew that."

His composure cracks, just a hair. "You're exaggerating the risk, *Valentine*."

I lean back, folding my arms. "You took a Bellamy with an escalating curse into a magical convergence no one cleared."

"It wasn't a convergence—it was dinner," he snaps, forcing a smile. "She wasn't going to drown in gravy."

"The wards across half the district disagree."

Silence settles, heavy and charged.

Dorian shifts in his seat, irritation bleeding through the polish. "Nothing happened. Besides, she left unharmed."

"She left destabilized," I say. "Her personal wards collapsed. Her magic spiked hard enough to trip external protections. And she ran."

"With respect," he says sharply, "you're projecting."

That gets my attention.

I lean forward, resting my forearms on the desk. The wards hum—not flaring, just listening. "You don't get to reframe this. You disregarded protocol, bypassed oversight, and gambled with someone you were explicitly warned required caution."

"I was giving her agency," Dorian snaps, the edge in his voice finally cutting through the polish. "She didn't want to be managed."

I lift my gaze to him, steady and unflinching. "You don't get to decide what agency looks like for her."

His jaw tightens. "She's not fragile."

"I didn't say she was," I reply, voice calm enough to make his temper stand out in sharp relief.

"You treat her like she'll shatter the second she steps outside your precious structure," he fires back, irritation bleeding into something hotter. "Like she can't survive without you hovering over every variable."

"I treat her like someone whose curse responds violently to emotional pressure," I say, leaning forward just enough to shift the balance of the room. "And whose magic destabilizes when pushed without safeguards."

"That's an assumption," he shoots back.

"No," I say evenly, holding his stare. "That's documented."

He scoffs, rising slightly out of his chair before forcing himself still. "You're compromised, Valentine. You've been circling her since the file reopened. Don't insult both of us by pretending this is objective."

The accusation lands hard—and he knows it.

I smile, cold and precise. "This became objective when you broke protocol."

His magic shifts—still suppressed, but no longer clean. Anger bleeds through in jagged pulses.

"You think you're the only one capable of protecting her," he says. "You think proximity makes you indispensable."

I slide a thin folder across the desk. The Council seal embedded in the cover warms faintly as it comes to rest between us.

"You're removed from the assignment," I say coldly. "Effective immediately."

He stiffens. "You don't have unilateral authority. And we both know I am the best match available."

"You altered the plan twice. Masked your magic. Chose an environment designed to muddy signatures," I reply. "And you took her anyway."

"I took precautions," he says, forcing a smile that doesn't reach his eyes.

"You underestimated her power," I answer. "And overestimated your control."

The wards along the walls brighten, firm and unmistakable.

Jackson appears in the doorway, arms crossed, silent but present.

Dorian's gaze flicks to him, then back to me. "This isn't finished."

"No," I agree. "It isn't."

I tap the folder once. "But you are."

That's when he snaps.

He's out of the chair in a sudden, furious motion, fist already swinging as he climbs over my desk. I duck on instinct, the punch slicing through the space where my head was a second earlier. My counter lands before he can recover—a clean, solid hit to the jaw that sends him stumbling back over the desk.

He glares at me, breathing hard, shock and fury warring across his face.

"Get out," I say quietly.

For a moment, I think he might try again. Then Jackson takes one step forward, and the calculation changes.

Dorian grabs his coat, magic snapping tight around him as he storms for the door, slamming it behind him with enough force to rattle the wards.

The silence that follows is sharp and wrong.

I don't move right away. I let the tension settle, let the implications finish forming.

That wasn't just anger.

It was fear.

And that tells me everything I need to know about what he was really doing with her—and why whatever he dragged into her orbit didn't stay contained. This time, I'm not trusting anyone else to stand between it and her.

I pace the length of my office until the space feels tighter than it should, boots scuffing the carpet in a rhythm that refuses to settle. The argument still clings to the air—Dorian's magic, thinned but not gone, sharp with the kind of tension that lingers when someone leaves cornered and angry. I tell myself to sit. I don't. My wings shift restlessly beneath my skin, keyed to a threat that hasn't finished announcing itself.

The door opens, this time with Leona's efficiency rather than a knock.

Francesca steps in carrying a cardboard drink carrier in one hand and a small paper bag in the other, already easing one of the cups free as she crosses the room. She looks composed in that deliberate way that reads as effort rather than ease, bakery warmth trailing in with her like a familiar ward. She sets the carrier on the edge of my desk and nudges a cup—and the fritter—toward me.

"Leona said you needed to see me," she says. "She also said you forget basic human functions when you're spiraling."

I take the coffee because refusing it would be obvious, and obvious feels dangerous after last night. The warmth grounds me enough that I finally stop pacing and lean back against the desk.

"Thank you," I say. "She's not wrong."

Her mouth quirks, but her eyes stay sharp. "I wanted to explain about last night—"

"You don't need to," I cut in gently, before she can wind herself tighter. "You don't owe me an explanation."

She pauses, surprise flickering across her face.

"What you walked into shouldn't have escalated the way it did," I continue. "That's on the process. And on me for not anticipating it sooner."

Her shoulders ease a fraction, though she doesn't step closer. "Okay."

I take a breath, choosing my words carefully. "I spoke with Dorian this morning."

Something guarded settles into her posture. "And?"

"He's no longer a contender," I say evenly. "Effective immediately."

Her brow furrows. "Sayer—"

"I know," I say, holding up a hand before she can build momentum. "And I'm not dismissing what you felt or what you were trying to do. But his actions crossed too many lines, and I won't recalibrate around someone who disregards safeguards."

She studies my face, searching for something. "So what happens now?"

"At the end of the week," I say, "there's Lucifer's ball. Masquerade. High visibility. Heavy warding. Enough oversight that no one freelances without consequence." I meet her gaze. "I'll escort you."

Her lips part slightly. "You."

"Yes," I say. "While we recalculate your matches and stabilize the field."

She tilts her head, considering the angle. "This is strategy."

"It is," I agree. "Public presence changes behavior. After last night, I don't want you anywhere unsanctioned or improvised. This keeps you in a controlled environment, with witnesses and limits."

"And you," she adds quietly.

"And me," I say without hesitation. "Where I can see what matters."

Her fingers brush the edge of the drink carrier, a small grounding habit. "You're asking," she says, not accusing. "Not ordering."

"I'm asking," I confirm. "Your choice."

She exhales, thinking it through, then nods once. "All right. But if this is strategy, I want transparency. No sudden pivots. No surprises."

A corner of my mouth lifts despite myself. "Agreed."

Chapter 30

Francesca

Morning arrives too bright for someone who barely slept. Thin bands of sunlight slip through the curtains, catching the steam rising from the mug cradled between my hands. I sit at the small kitchen table in my apartment above the bakery, hair still tangled from sleep, wrapped in an oversized sweatshirt that smells faintly of cinnamon and stress. My magic moves beneath my skin in slow, watchful spirals—not flaring, not settled, just awake in a way that makes it impossible to fully relax.

It's the day of Lucifer's Ball. The most theatrical event of the entire Season, which is saying something in a city where drama is practically a civic duty.

I should feel excited. Or nervous. Or at least properly focused.

Instead, my thoughts keep circling back to the same thing—Sayer, standing in his office yesterday, coffee in hand, voice steady as he told me I didn't need to explain myself. The way he apologized for how badly things had escalated. The way he said Dorian was no longer a contender, not with anger or triumph, but with quiet certainty. The way he framed escorting me tonight as strategy while still making it unmistakably my choice.

That shouldn't matter as much as it does.

I take a slow sip of coffee, then mutter into the rim, "Nope. Not doing this. Not today."

My magic hums in polite disagreement.

Footsteps on the stairs save me from arguing with myself further. Harper appears a moment later, curls piled on top of her head, eyes tired but sharp, a basket of warm cinnamon rolls balanced on her hip. Steam curls through the room as she sets it down.

"You alive?" she asks, scanning me like she's running a diagnostic. "Your magic's calmer this morning. Still moody, but not actively plotting against the appliances."

"I'm fine," I say, which earns me a look that suggests Harper has never believed that sentence once in her life. Especially coming from me.

Her gaze flicks to the corner of the apartment, where a small pile of offerings has accumulated overnight—a bouquet of red roses, a ribboned box, and a softly chiming crystal playing a looping violin melody. "Dorian dropped those off at dawn," she says flatly. "Again."

Of course he did.

For six days now, he's been trying—earnestly, persistently—to smooth things over while I've done my best to pretend he doesn't exist. Gifts appeared every morning, left without comment. Messages came every night, carefully worded and never answered. Check-ins followed, polite and frequent, as if enough consistency might rewrite what happened. He even showed up at the bakery the morning after, all concern and apologies, claiming he just wanted to make sure I was all right. I'd ignored him then too, busy wiping down counters while the air went tight around us. Harper stared him down like he'd committed a personal offense. Miguel dropped a bowl with enough force to echo. Ellie vanished behind the cookie display, whispering threats she absolutely meant.

Sayer had been there too—quiet, controlled, watching me with an awareness that settled low in my chest and made breathing feel optional. He didn't press. He didn't ask. He just saw me, and somehow that was worse.

Now I'm the one avoiding him, slipping upstairs when he walks in, trimming every interaction down to something neat and distant. He noticed. I know he noticed, because instead of giving me space, he started appearing every morning like a fixed point in my routine, leaning against the counter with his coffee and that infuriating patience, as if waiting me out, daring me to admit that things weren't as unchanged as I was pretending.

Harper nudges me with her elbow. "So. Tonight. Lucifer's Ball." She arches a brow. "Who's your escort?"

"Sayer," I say automatically.

She stills. Then her eyebrows climb so high they threaten to escape her face. "Oh."

"It's strategic," I add quickly. "He explained it. With everything going on, it makes sense."

"Strategy," she repeats, clearly enjoying herself. "Right. Nothing else wrapped up in that decision at all."

I glare. It does nothing.

She pulls out the chair across from me and sits. "Fran, you can rationalize it however you want, but your magic has opinions. Strong ones."

"It absolutely does not."

"Sweetheart," she says gently, "the mixer tried to melt the last time his name came up."

I drop my face into my hands. "That was unrelated."

"Sure," Harper says. "And I'm a dragon."

I lift my head and stare into my coffee, watching the steam curl. Dorian checks every box on paper. He always has. Calm, charming, attentive—everything a match is supposed to be.

But when everything fell apart, when my magic screamed loud enough to wake half the block, he wasn't the one who came running.

Sayer was.

Harper reaches across the table and covers my hand. "Just... be careful tonight. Lucifer's Ball amplifies everything—magic, emotions, instincts. And yours is already tuned a little too high."

"I know," I say quietly.

She studies me for a moment, then smiles, soft but knowing. "He'll be here soon."

I don't argue. There's no point.

He will be.

And as the day stretches toward evening, with Lucifer's Ball looming like a storm on the horizon, I'm forced to admit something I've been carefully avoiding—

I'm no longer sure if the thing making my pulse race is the danger waiting tonight... or the man who'll be standing beside me when I walk into it.

Or what part of me has already decided about him.

By late afternoon the bakery has finally settled—only the occasional shiver of magic rippling through the wards to remind me that my life is still one long cosmic punchline. The rest of the day passed in a blur of customers, deliveries, and Harper forcing me to eat something so I don't pass out at Lucifer's Ball. I spent most of it pretending not to notice when Sayer came in for his coffee, or when his gaze lingered a heartbeat too long, or when my magic responded like it had been waiting for him all morning.

Now, standing alone in my apartment, the sun edging toward the horizon in orange streaks, I try to steady myself. Tonight is a major event—the kind that can shift the entire arc of the Season. And I need to look like I have my life together, even if inside I still feel like a shaken snow globe.

I turn on the shower, letting steam fill the small bathroom in rising clouds. The hot water helps, unwinding the tight band of anxiety around my ribs, washing away the last remnants of flour and sugar that seem permanently fused to my skin in January. When I step out wrapped in a towel, my magic settles enough to let me breathe again.

The garment bag waits on the bed like it knows its moment has arrived.

I unzip it slowly, the fabric inside shimmering with quiet antic-ipation. The dress doesn't so much emerge as unveil itself—dark crimson silk threaded with charline that glows like banked embers beneath the surface. It's warm without heat, luminous without light, the kind of gown that looks alive in the periphery of vision.

I touch the bodice, and the magic woven into the threads stirs like a dragon exhaling beneath cloth.

This dress chose me.

Maribel said as much the day we fitted it. The tailor's giddy clap-ping still echoes through my memory as if she knew exactly what kind of moment she was helping create.

I pull it free and step behind the screen, slipping into the dress with care. The fabric glides over my skin like it remembers me—a second skin, a promise, a shield. When I step back into the open, the room shifts. Not dramatically, but undeniably. The mirrors catch the gown's ember-threading at every angle, the red deepening into a molten glow when my magic brushes against it.

The bodice hugs without constricting, forming around my shape as if sculpted there. The skirt moves like smoke when I breathe, soft and fluid, cascading from my hips in waves of crimson shadow. Embroidered accents rest along my collarbones, shimmer-flaring in response to my pulse.

For the first time all week, I feel beautiful without hesitation.

The accessories Maribel paired with the gown sit on the vani-ty—earrings of burnished onyx and fire opal, a bracelet threaded with grounding runes, and a delicate necklace with a single charm that glows faintly like the dying heart of a star. One by one, I fasten each piece, feeling the magic align with mine in soft, steady waves.

Harper slips upstairs just as I finish curling the last piece of my hair—dark waves pinned half-up with a spell-stamped comb that keeps loose strands weightless and curled.

She stops in the doorway, hand pressed to her chest. "Oh. Oh, Fran."

I swallow, suddenly unsure. "Too much?"

"Too much?" Harper laughs softly. "Sweetheart, you look like the reason poets drink and angels sing."

I roll my eyes, but warmth creeps into my cheeks. "It's just a dress."

"It's not," she says, stepping forward to fuss with a curl near my temple. "It chose you. And it makes you look like you walked out of your own prophecy."

I don't want to think about prophecies. Or fated matches. Or Sayer's wings unfurling like instinct the moment I walked into danger. I don't want to think about how the memory keeps replaying, quiet and persistent, catching in the back of my throat when I least expect it.

But tonight... tonight is big enough that I have to look the part, even if my heart is a battlefield.

A soft chime downstairs signals the arrival of a visitor. Harper glances toward the door with a knowing smirk.

"That'll be him," she says.

My breath stutters. "Dorian?"

"No," she replies, voice gentle but firm. "The one who actually makes your magic sit up and pay attention."

Sayer.

Of course it's him.

Harper squeezes my shoulder once before heading downstairs. I follow a moment later, the gown whispering across the steps like flame trailing behind me. Each footfall feels too loud in my chest, each breath too warm, and my magic—traitorous, eager thing—leans forward before I even reach the bottom.

I pause on the last step.

He's waiting in the entryway.

Sayer Valentine in a tailored black suit should be illegal. The fabric fits him like it was stitched with intent—sharp lines, dark silk, the faintest shimmer of charline woven through the lapels to match the enchantments threaded into my gown. He stands with his hands in his pockets, posture relaxed but alert, as if every sense he possesses is tracking the room the way a hunter tracks a shift in the wind.

His wings aren't visible, but I feel them anyway—some echo of magic settling in the air behind him like shadowed feathers folded out of sight.

And when he looks up...

The world tilts.

Not dramatically. Not like a swoon. More like someone grabbed the horizon and nudged it half an inch to the left. His gaze sweeps from my hair to the hem of my dress and back again, slow enough to feel, quick enough to make it seem accidental.

It's not accidental.

My heart stumbles in my chest, and my magic surges so fast the bracelet at my wrist warms in warning. I grip the railing, trying to ground myself, trying to smother the heat blooming through my ribs.

No. No, absolutely not. I cannot react to him like this. I cannot let my body or my magic get ideas simply because the man looks like temptation in a three-piece suit.

But gods, he does.

Sayer clears his throat, the sound low and quiet, but it slices through the crackling silence between us. "You're ready," he says, voice steady but a shade huskier than usual, as if the words have to fight their way past something he doesn't want to admit.

I step off the final stair, hoping movement will pull me back to myself. It doesn't. If anything, the space between us tightens, charged enough that I can feel the air shift. He's watching me with an intensity that borders on reverent—and I hate how easy it is to feel seen under that gaze.

"You clean up well," I manage, smoothing my palms down the sides of my dress because I need something—*anything*—to do with my hands. "Tailoring suits you."

His mouth curves, just slightly. "So I've been told."

We stand there a beat too long, neither of us moving, both of us pretending we're not memorizing the other.

My pulse hammers.

His jaw tightens.

My magic purrs like a delighted cat.

No. No, no, no. Absolutely not. I refuse to fall into this. I refuse to be the witch who ruins her life because a man looks at her like she's the only lit candle in a dark room. I'm going to a ball with him for strategic reasons, nothing more. I'm not thinking about the way his tie matches the ember-threading in my gown. Or the faint scent of cedar and smoke drifting from him. Or the way every cell in my magic is standing at attention like a soldier saluting their commander.

"Harper's right," he says quietly, almost as if he didn't mean to speak aloud. "The dress chose well."

I freeze.

His eyes hold mine for a heartbeat longer, something unspoken sparking between us, and it's too much—too bright, too real, too dangerous.

I swallow hard. "Let's go," I say, voice steadier than I feel.

He steps aside to open the door for me, his expression back under lock and key.

But as I move past him, my magic reaches for him like gravity itself has opinions—

—and for the first time all week, I don't know whether to run from this feeling...

or straight into it.

Chapter 31

Sayer

By the time we turn off the main road and follow the sweeping drive toward Lucifer's Ball, the sky has slipped into a velvet-dark purple, the kind of color that promises trouble and spectacle in equal measure. The venue rises ahead of us like something cut out of another world—gothic arches, obsidian pillars, thousands of floating candles drifting overhead like watchful stars. Even from the car, I can feel the thrum of layered enchantments pulsing across the grounds, more elaborate than any mortal palace and twice as temperamental.

But none of it compares to the woman sitting beside me.

Francesca's dress catches every stray light as we drive, ember-threaded silk shifting from crimson to molten gold whenever she moves. Her hair brushes her bare shoulder—a single tendril escaping the pins, curling like it's deliberately trying to ruin me. That dress was crafted to draw attention, to command it—but the real problem is that she doesn't seem to realize how utterly impossible she is to look away from.

I keep my hands on the wheel because if I don't, I might reach for her. Just a touch—her hand, her wrist, the soft line of her thigh where the fabric parts when she shifts. Anything. I've spent every day this week trying to rebuild the walls between us, and tonight she's looking at the world like a lit fuse wrapped in silk.

I inhale slowly, hoping the cold air from the vents will help. It doesn't.

She stares out the window as we approach, her magic brushing mine in soft, curious ripples that she has no idea she's sending. Or maybe she does. Maybe she feels it too. The connection tugging, tightening, insisting.

I pull the car into one of the reserved spaces near the entrance. The lanternlight spills across the hood and catches her mask—a delicate filigree piece of black charline and ruby crystal resting in her lap. She turns it over in her hands, fingertips brushing the edges as if testing its weight.

"This is really happening," she murmurs.

I can't stop the small, unintentional smile tugging at my mouth. "You sound thrilled."

"I sound... resigned," she says, but there's a tremor of anticipation beneath her voice that she probably doesn't hear.

I cut the engine.

The silence that follows is too intimate.

I get out quickly, trying to gather whatever fragments of self-control I still have, and open her door. She places her hand in mine—light, warm, careful—and the simple contact lights up every nerve in my body.

I help her stand, our bodies closer than necessary because the gown requires it, or at least that's the excuse I cling to. Her perfume drifts between us—dark berries and something warm, something like home, which is the last thing I need it to smell like.

Her mask hangs from my other hand. "May I?" I ask.

She nods, and I step closer—close enough that her breath brushes my throat. The silk of her dress whispers as she turns her face toward me, offering that last sliver of space between us. I lift the mask carefully, letting my fingers graze the side of her cheek as I settle it over her eyes and tie the charline ribbons behind her head.

Her breath catches.

Mine stops entirely.

For one brief, unguarded moment, her face is inches from mine, lips parted, lashes lowered. The air between us crackles with something too sharp and too real to pretend away. If I leaned forward an inch—just one—

Her magic surges.

Mine answers.

And I swear the entire world narrows to the distance between her mouth and mine.

I force myself to step back before I do something extraordinarily foolish.

"There," I say, though my voice is lower than I intend. "Perfect."

Francesca blinks once, as if steadying herself, then smooths her dress with hands that tremble only slightly. "Thank you," she murmurs.

I offer her my arm, and when she takes it, the contact feels like it echoes through bone.

Together, we walk toward the grand entrance of Lucifer's Ball.

And gods help me, I already know—

there is no version of tonight where I make it out unchanged.

The moment we cross the threshold into Lucifer's Ball, the world becomes a cathedral of light and shadows. Columns stretch upward like obsidian spines, draped in floating candles that orbit the ceiling in slow, deliberate constellations. Masked guests swirl across the floor—feathers, velvet, enchanted silks that shimmer like moonlit water—every movement a curated spectacle of magic and ego.

But Francesca steals the oxygen from the room the second we enter.

Her magic unfurls like a warm ember breeze, brushing against the wards, catching on candleflames, drawing quiet glances from witches who know better than to stare and mortals dumb enough to try. The crimson of her gown ripples with every step, charline thread catching light in small glints that look like sparks drifting from a fire.

If the point of a masquerade is to hide, she is doomed from the start.

And so am I.

She walks beside me, her arm looped through mine, posture regal without trying. My awareness of her settles into a low, steady thrum that blocks out every other presence in the ballroom—until he finds us.

Lucifer himself emerges from the shadows with the sort of dramatic timing that should be illegal. Tall, sleek, dressed in midnight silk with a half-mask of black glass that reflects candlelight like fire in water. His smile is wicked enough to be a brand.

"Well," he purrs, glancing between us, "if it isn't the most dangerously beautiful pair in the room."

Francesca manages a dry smile. "Lucifer."

"Darling." He catches her hand, bows extravagantly, and then shifts his attention to me. His smirk sharpens with interest. "Valentine. You clean up well."

"I try," I say, because I refuse to let Lucifer think I'm rattled.

He leans closer to Francesca as if sharing a secret, voice low and teasing. "You two look perfect together. Don't let anyone talk you out of it."

My pulse hits hard. Francesca inhales sharply beside me. And Lucifer grins like he's just thrown gasoline into a bonfire. Then, just as quickly, he drifts away, cape trailing behind him like smoke.

Francesca releases a breath she clearly didn't mean to hold. "He's impossible."

"He's not wrong," I mutter before I can help myself.

She goes still for half a second, and even through her mask I feel her react—quietly, deeply, in a way I don't let myself examine.

To cover it, I lead her toward the dance floor, and she follows without hesitation. The moment I touch her waist, her magic leans into mine like a tide caught in moon gravity. The first few steps are measured, careful, but then her rhythm settles into mine and we move as though we've done this a hundred times—fluid, precise, attuned in a way I feel low in my chest.

If I believed in destiny, I'd blame it for this. But I know better. Destiny doesn't feel this warm.

The waltz ends, applause scattering across the floor like sparks, and guests drift in to greet us—witches, fae, a few demons, each commenting on Francesca's dress, her magic, her presence, her connection to me in a way that makes my blood feel too warm beneath my skin.

She laughs it off, shoulders relaxed, eyes bright beneath her mask. She's luminous. Completely luminous.

I'm still drowning in the sight of her when her breath catches in surprise. She stands a little taller, focusing on something across the ballroom.

"I think I see Cassian," she murmurs—her older cousin, if I remember correctly, a Bellamy with the unfortunate habit of starting magical debates at formal events and winning them.

Francesca slips her hand from my arm gently. "I'll only be a minute."

I nod, schooling my expression into something that resembles composure. "Of course."

She touches my wrist lightly—a quick, instinctive gesture that feels far more intimate than she intends—and then disappears into the flow of dancers, crimson gown trailing like a ribbon of flame behind her.

Her magic lingers even after she's swallowed by the crowd, soft as breath against my senses. I exhale slowly, trying to shake off the afterimage of her warmth, but it clings like charline dust.

Leona and Jackson approach from the right, champagne glasses in hand. Leona raises a brow the moment she sees my face.

"Well," she says, "you look like a man who just discovered he's allergic to denial."

Jackson snorts. "Or he's finally realizing what everyone else has known for the past two weeks."

I glare at both of them because it's easier than admitting anything. "Behave. Both of you."

Leona clinks her glass against mine. "Absolutely not."

And as Francesca laughs with her cousin across the ballroom, the truth settles in my chest with unsettling clarity:

I am in trouble. Real, cosmic, no-way-out trouble.

The ballroom hums with magic and music, but my attention keeps drifting toward Francesca. Even from across the room, she stands out like a flame in a sea of candlelight, moving easily between conversations, her gown catching the warm glow in shifting ripples of crimson. Her cousin Cassian laughs at something she says, and she gestures with one graceful sweep of her hand—radiant, centered, completely unaware of the way half the guests have begun orbiting her like moths drawn to heat.

Leona nudges me lightly with her elbow. "You're watching her again."

"I'm making sure she's safe," I correct, though even I can hear the thinness in the excuse.

Jackson snorts. "Right. Just safety. Nothing else going on there at all."

I ignore him and shift my focus to what matters. "Any word from Dorian tonight? He was given an invitation."

"Nothing," Leona says, her expression tightening beneath the feathers of her mask. "And the deeper we dig into his background, the more my instincts tell me something isn't fitting the way it should."

Jackson adds, "Still no definitive red flags, but the silence from the Archives is strange. They're usually quicker than this."

I nod, though the unease in my chest is already growing before I can decide what to do with it. I glance back toward Francesca—and my attention sharpens instantly.

She's no longer with Cassian.

Another man stands at her side now, dressed in tailored black with an onyx-and-silver mask that obscures his face completely. There's something unsettling in the way the air bends around him—a magical presence that brushes against mine like a memory with the edges blurred. Familiar but distant, a sensation I should recognize but can't place.

His posture is relaxed, even courteous, but there's an intentional closeness to the way he leans down to speak to her. Francesca tilts her head to listen, though her smile has faded into something far more neutral. Her fingers drift toward the bracelet on her wrist, brushing the runes the tailor added for grounding. It's subtle, careful, and if I didn't know her magic as well as I do, I'd miss the tension gathering beneath her composure.

My pulse tightens. "Do either of you know who that is?" I ask, unable to look away.

Jackson follows my gaze. "No idea. Mask's too strong to read through. Could be a guest with layered wards."

"Or someone who doesn't want to be recognized," Leona murmurs.

The unease winds tighter. "I'm going over there."

I take a single step toward the dance floor—and, out of habit, glance toward Francesca one more time before committing to the distance between us.

I swear I look away for no more than two seconds—just long enough to tell Jackson to follow behind me—and when I look back, the spot where she was standing is empty.

No shimmer of red silk. No ember-threaded glow. No trace of her magic lingering in the air.

Just dancers moving in slow circles, the music rising in a swell, and a hollow space where she should be.

My chest goes cold.

Leona straightens beside me, her expression sharpening. Jackson mutters a curse under his breath.

A cold ripple works its way down my spine, the kind that doesn't come from nerves but from instinct—old, ingrained, unignorable. I look for her the way I've done a hundred times tonight, expecting that faint ember-warm pull of her magic somewhere in the room.

There's nothing.

No warmth. No spark. No residual hum in the space she just occupied.

It's like the air has been wiped clean of her.

Chapter 32

Francesca

The world shifts before I understand what's happening.

One moment I'm standing beneath the lanterns, answering a polite question from one of Cassian's acquaintances, and the next a cold sweep of magic brushes the back of my neck, so sharp it steals the air from my lungs. The ballroom tilts, the music distorts, and the gleam of crystal chandeliers smears into a streak of light. For a heartbeat I think I'm fainting, but the sensation is wrong—too deliberate, too precise, like someone folding a room instead of walking out of one.

When my vision steadies, I'm not on the dance floor anymore.

A narrow stone corridor stretches on either side of me, lit by guttering candles that throw uneven shadows across the walls. The air is cool and carries the faint metallic bite of old wards, the kind used to keep things in—or keep others out. My magic flares immediately, restless under my skin, responding to the confinement with the same distrust I feel rising in my chest.

"Great," I mutter under my breath, forcing my pulse to slow. "This is exactly the kind of night I was hoping for."

A soft rustle breaks the silence behind me. Footsteps follow—measured, calm, confident in a way that makes my stomach tighten. I turn quickly, gathering the skirt of my gown so it doesn't snag on the stone.

A figure steps into the thin circle of candlelight. The same black attire, the same onyx-and-silver mask from the ballroom, the same quiet pressure of magic held behind layered wards that feel too clean and too calculated. He looks like he could be carved from the shadows themselves—controlled, composed, completely unfazed by the fact that he has just pulled me out of a crowded event without so much as an explanation.

"You're safe," he says, voice smooth and entirely too calm.

"That's debatable," I answer, lifting my chin. "Most people don't teleport strangers into hallways to deliver safety tips."

He steps a little closer, hands loosely clasped in front of him, posture annoyingly serene. "You shouldn't have been alone tonight."

"And you shouldn't have been anywhere near me," I shoot back. "If we're handing out notes."

A faint amusement flickers through him. "Spirited. They did mention that."

"Who's 'they'?" The question leaves me before I can soften it. My magic surges again, pushing back against the tight weave of his wards, and a nearby candle sputters under the pressure.

Instead of answering, he studies me—really studies me—as if he's checking off a list only he can see. It makes something cold ripple along my spine.

"Take the mask off," I say quietly, evenly. "If you want to talk to me, you can do it face to face."

He doesn't lift a hand toward it. "Not yet."

"That's not reassuring."

"It isn't meant to be," he replies, and his voice slips into something colder, something that makes the corridor feel smaller. "Reassurance is Sayer Valentine's job."

The mention of Sayer hits me like a switch, sharp enough that my magic responds before my mind can catch up. The air around us crackles in a tight wave, and a hairline crack begins to travel through the stone floor near his feet. He doesn't move, but I see it—just for a breath—the way the shift catches him off guard.

Good.

Because whatever this place is, whoever he is, and whatever plans he thinks involve me—my magic clearly has other ideas.

He studies me for a long, deliberate moment before he speaks again, and when he does, there's no amusement left to soften the edges.

"You were never meant to reach thirty-five without a binding."

My breath catches. "That's not unusual. Plenty of Bellamys don't match by thirty. That's the entire point of the curse—"

"Twenty is expected," he interrupts. "Twenty is the beginning of the pressure. Twenty-five is still manageable. Even thirty can be brushed off as stubbornness, bad timing, or cosmic incompetence. But thirty-five..." His gaze sharpens behind the mask. "No Bellamy woman has crossed that threshold in centuries. Not since the beginning."

My magic prickles against my skin, uneasy. "Why does thirty-five even matter?"

"Because by then, the curse isn't just mischief and misfires. It becomes unstable magic under strain. And unstable magic—true Bellamy magic—is extraordinarily valuable."

A cold ripple of dread moves through me. "Valuable to who?"

"The Council of Thorns."

The name sounds like a cracked floorboard beneath my feet, something ancient and rotten trying to stay hidden. I've seen it in forbidden spell books, in footnotes nobody talks about aloud. A faction of bloodline purists obsessed with siphoning magic from old covenants.

I swallow hard. "They don't exist. And if they did, what do they want with me?"

His answer lands like a stone.

"They want the Bellamy spark—your spark—transferred before it binds itself fully to someone else."

"My spark?" The words scrape out dry. "I'm not a damn torch to be passed around."

"No," he says, "but you carry one. A lineage-light tied to the original enchantment that powers the Bellamy curse. It stabilizes magic, strengthens bonds, amplifies creation magic. Your ancestors wielded it to maintain balance between realms. Untamed, it's unpredictable.

Harvested..." He hesitates, voice dipping. "It can reshape magical power structures."

"And they planned to 'harvest' mine." The disgust in my tone is impossible to hide.

"Yes. Through Dorian."

Shock hits me so hard my magic flares, snapping against the corridor walls. "Dorian? He's... no. He's charming. He's—"

"He was assigned to you," the masked man says, voice gentler now. "Not as a partner. As a handler. Someone to keep you sweet, flattered, distracted, and unaware while your magic edged closer to the instability point the Council needed."

My stomach twists violently. "He wasn't my match."

"He was never intended to be your match. He was meant to guide you into a ritual when the curse reached its peak. But he failed. You were stronger than they calculated. Too independent, too magically aware, too... *inconvenient*."

I feel sick. "So they buried my file."

"They pushed Sayer over the edge. To the point he quit. Then they buried it the night you turned twenty. Moved it so deep in the archives that no standard Cupid could ever stumble across it. The delay was intentional. The goal was for your magic to spiral unchecked—to the brink of volatility—so the spark could be separated cleanly."

"And then Sayer showed up," I whisper.

A faint nod. "The moment you bonded, even slightly, the entire plan collapsed. Your magic stabilized. Your pathways shifted. And the ritual became impossible."

That hits me harder than the rest. Sayer didn't ruin the plan by interfering. He ruined it simply by *being near me.*

"And now?" I ask quietly.

"Now the Council is desperate. Your season ends soon. Your magic is too strong to control without your consent. And with Sayer in the picture—openly or not—you are no longer a predictable variable."

The candles flicker at the same moment my pulse does. "What do they want now?"

"You," he says simply. "Bound. Controlled. Or removed."

I stare at him, the weight of the truth settling like a storm on my chest.

"And who," I ask, "sent you to tell me all of this?"

His answer is low and uncomfortably earnest. "Someone who thinks you deserve to know the truth before you choose who to trust."

His posture shifts, not threatening, not comforting—something in between, something weighted by the fact that we've passed the point of pretending any of this is harmless.

"You need to make a decision," he says. "There isn't much time."

A cold knot forms beneath my ribs. "What kind of decision?"

"The kind that determines whether you walk out of here on your own terms or become exactly what the Council wants." His gaze, hidden though it is, feels sharp enough to pin me in place. "I can take you out of this corridor now, quietly, without anyone realizing you vanished. You'll have a head start. Protection. Enough time to tell Sayer the truth yourself and prepare for the next move."

"And the other option?"

"You stay," he says carefully. "And the Council will take what they want. They won't kill you—that would waste the spark—but you won't recognize yourself by the time they're finished."

A shiver runs down my spine, part fear, part rage, part magic rising hot in my veins.

"And why," I manage, "are you offering this choice? If you're working against them, why not just help me escape outright?"

"Because you're not a captive," he replies. "Not yet. And magic taken without consent fractures. It becomes volatile. Unstable. It dies. They need you compliant. I—" He hesitates for the first time. "I don't."

Silence curls around us, thick and pulsing.

"You're telling me I get to choose," I say slowly. "But if I choose wrong, everyone I love becomes leverage."

"That is the truth." His shoulders drop slightly, as if he doesn't enjoy confirming it. "And it's why you cannot stay here."

My magic thrums under my skin like it's ready to ignite the corridor.

"And Sayer?" I ask. "Is he in danger because of me?"

The masked man doesn't answer immediately, and that is answer enough.

Something snaps inside me—fear, fury, instinct, all woven together—and the corridor lights flare as my magic surges. The braid along my shoulder prickles as heat spreads outward, not fire exactly, but a pressure like a heartbeat expanding into every surface around me.

He senses the shift before I move. "Francesca—don't—"

But I'm already reaching for the oldest expression of Bellamy magic I know: a beacon spell. Not the kind used to guide lost children home. The kind used when witches vanished, when magic was stolen, when the world tilted too far off course. A witch light flare that calls to one person.

One bond.

One match.

One truth.

Sayer Valentine.

I focus on his name, on the warmth that steadies me whenever he walks into a room, on how my magic settles when his magic brushes mine. That feeling becomes the spell's anchor, the point I pour everything into.

The masked man lunges forward, not to attack, but to stop me—he knows exactly what I'm doing.

"Francesca's no—if you call to him, the Council will trace it—"

The magic bursts outward before he finishes the warning.

It tears through the corridor like a breath finally exhaled, a wave of red-gold heat that slams against the wards, ricochets, and punches straight upward through the seams of the building. The candles blow out in the shockwave, plunging us into darkness except for the faint, shimmering glow pulsing beneath my skin.

The masked man swears—an elegant, ancient-sounding oath laced with frustration. "You just alerted every damn power within a ten mile radius."

"Good," I say, breath shaking with adrenaline. "Let them come."

He looks at me in the dimness, half-shadowed, half-illumined by the fading afterglow of the spell. I can't see his eyes, but I feel the weight of his stare.

"You didn't choose escape," he says softly. "You chose war."

"No," I answer, lifting my chin. "I chose myself."

And somewhere far beyond this corridor— in a ballroom filled with music and masks— I know Sayer Valentine just felt me.

Chapter 33

Sayer

I 've walked the perimeter of the ballroom three times now, pretending not to look like a man circling panic. Every sweep of the crowd comes up empty. No crimson gown. No flash of ember-threaded magic. No sign of Francesca at all. The longer she's missing, the more tightly my chest draws, like someone winding a cord around my ribs one loop at a time.

Jackson and Leona fall into step beside me near the edge of the dance floor, their expressions taut enough to confirm they're just as worried.

"We found something," Jackson says quietly, voice low enough not to draw attention. "The Archives finally pushed through a sealed record. Dorian wasn't just vetted by the Council of Thorns. He's been actively working with them."

A cold weight settles in the base of my spine. "Define 'working.'"

"Assignments, reports, coded correspondences," Leona answers, slipping a folded charm-paper into my hand. "He's been their point of contact in the human realm for at least two years. We don't have the full picture yet, but it isn't good."

It shouldn't surprise me, but it does. I'd hoped my instincts were wrong. I'd hoped the suspicion clawing at me for days was just jealousy wearing a reasonable coat. But this—this fits too well. Dorian's perfect timing. His polished charm. His insistence on proximity. The way Francesca's magic always seemed muted around him.

I look toward the ballroom entrance again, ignoring the pulse in my throat. "She's not with him now. I checked every path he could've taken into the gardens."

"Which is another red flag," Jackson mutters. "He's here. His signature pinged the ward net twenty minutes ago."

I stop moving. "But she didn't."

"No." Leona shakes her head once, slow and grim. "No entry. No exit. No signature at all."

That shouldn't be possible. Francesca's magic is too strong, too distinct. Even masked, it leaves traces. But there's been nothing for the last half hour—an absence that feels like a hand pressing against my sternum.

I'm searching the crowd again when it hits me.

Not visually. Not audibly.

Through magic.

A sudden surge of heat spirals through my chest, sharp enough to rob me of breath for a heartbeat. It's not pain, not exactly—more like someone striking a gong inside my ribs. The sound echoes through every nerve I spent years training myself to ignore.

Leona grips my arm. "Sayer—you felt that too, didn't you?"

"Francesca," I say, but the word sounds wrong, raw, like it was torn out of me instead of spoken. The magic flares again, a bright, focused pulse that doesn't ask for attention—it demands it. It's familiar in the way lightning is familiar when you've been struck before.

Jackson takes a step back, eyes widening. "That wasn't a curse-flare. That was a beacon."

I know. Every part of me knows. It's a witch's call for help—a tether thrown into the dark meant for one person strong enough, bonded enough, chosen enough to catch it.

And I catch it.

Her magic slams through the barriers I've kept wrapped around my senses for years, tearing them open one after another until her presence floods me so completely that the ballroom might as well disappear.

This isn't a gentle spark. It's not Francesca laughing behind a counter or brushing flour from her cheek. This is her in danger, her magic stretched to a breaking point, her signature flaring like a flare hammered against the sky.

"Where is she?" Jackson asks, already reaching for defensive sigils.

"I don't know," I answer, but the certainty under the words feels ancient. "She's not here. She's nowhere near this ballroom."

The beacon jerks again, and my wings strain instinctively against the illusion, pushing for release. I feel Leona tense beside me when she senses the raw power starting to ripple at the edges of my control.

"Sayer…" she warns softly.

"She didn't walk out," I say, already turning toward the exit. "She was removed."

The words settle over the three of us with a heaviness that feels like a door slamming shut.

Another pulse hits—stronger, more insistent, threaded with fear she didn't voice but couldn't hide.

Leona's voice breaks through the ringing in my ears. "Do you know what direction?"

"Yes." The answer is simple, immediate, unshakeable. "She's north of the grounds. High wards. Somewhere underground or shielded."

"You can't go alone."

But the beacon pulls again—deep, magnetic, impossible to resist—and the idea of waiting even a moment longer feels like an unforgivable betrayal.

"I'm not going alone," I say quietly, already stepping toward the doors. "She called me."

And that is enough.

I push through the ballroom entrance, wings tearing free behind me in a rush of heat and air as the beacon flares again. Whatever corridor or trap or spell she's been pulled into, she's fighting her way out.

And she's reaching for me. Which means wherever she is— I'm going to find her.

The moment the ballroom doors close behind me, the beacon aligns like a compass snapping to true north. It threads through my ribs and pulls hard enough that I nearly stagger before I catch myself. Once I'm outside, the night air sharpens every instinct I've tried to bury for years. My senses stretch outward in a way I haven't allowed since the war—past the lights, past the wards ringing the venue, past the quiet glamour masking the grounds.

Francesca's magic is there. Thin but steady, like a single lantern burning in a storm.

The path to her isn't clean. Whatever corridor she's trapped in is layered under illusion spells meant to deflect celestials—especially former cupids who know how to read magic through walls. But her beacon cuts through those layers, a thread bright enough to tell me exactly where to push.

I move.

Not running. Not flying.

Something in between—a magic-fueled stride that eats ground too quickly for mortal senses to track. The trees blur, lanterns streak, and the cold night air whips past my ears as the beacon grows stronger, guiding me to a grove that shouldn't exist on these grounds.

A veil hangs there—thin, shimmering, silver-edged—and the moment I step through it, the world snaps colder. A warded passage materializes where open air should be, spiraling downward in a corridor of stone that feels ancient and wrong all at once.

Two guards materialize ahead of me, masked and armed with spears of condensed spell-light. They bark commands I don't bother parsing and move to block the way.

The first guard lunges. I pivot, catch the haft of the spear, and slam him backward into the wall with enough force to knock the breath from him. The second attempts a sigil burst—an immobilizing charm—but my wings flare instinctively, dissolving it before it can land. I sweep his legs and send him to the floor with a crack of magical backlash.

Neither stays conscious.

I keep moving.

Lights flicker overhead as if reacting to the raw magic bleeding off me. The corridor turns sharply, and more of them appear—three this time, then five more at the next bend. I don't hesitate. I haven't fought like this since the celestial lines broke in the last war, since I stood beside fellow cupids watching the sky tear open with rebellion and fire.

Tonight, it feels almost the same.

The guards attack with coordinated precision, but my instincts are sharper. A spear grazes my sleeve; I twist, step inside the guard's reach, and send him crashing into the next. A binding spell lashes toward my legs; I kick off the wall, wings snapping outward just enough to push me above its arc. Two more converge, and I knock them aside with the blunt force of a spell I swore I'd never cast again.

"Fall back—it's Valentine!" one of them shouts.

The name hits the stone like a thrown blade.

They hesitate.

I don't.

Another sigil bursts behind me—too close, too bright—and I throw up a wing to absorb the impact. The force stings, but it's nothing compared to celestial fire. I push forward, clearing the last of them as the corridor widens into a chamber that shouldn't exist beneath the ballroom.

The further I push down the warded passage, the more the air shifts around me—thickening, tightening, humming with the residue of spells that shouldn't be used in a place meant for celebration. My boots echo along stone, but the sound is swallowed quickly, as if the corridor itself has been designed to keep secrets trapped inside it. Francesca's beacon pulls harder with every step, threading heat through my chest that borders on painful. She's close. Too close.

The hallway spills into a circular chamber reinforced with runes I haven't seen since the celestial war, the kind meant to suppress magic rather than shape it. Three guards lie unconscious at the threshold, the aftermath of someone else's decision rather than mine. Whoever brought Francesca here didn't come alone—and they knew how to clear a path.

A lone figure waits in the center of the chamber, the dim rune-light catching the edges of his cloak as he turns toward me. The air around him carries the unmistakable pressure of layered wards—old ones, deliberate ones, the kind designed for personal protection rather than intimidation—and the way he holds himself radiates a calm so practiced it borders on arrogance. Whoever he is, he's been expecting me, and the invitation in his posture feels almost theatrical.

"Sayer Valentine," he says, and the sound of my name in his voice stops me more effectively than any barrier. "I had a bet going with myself on how long it would take you. You're a little faster than I expected."

His tone is familiar—too familiar. Something about the cadence tugs at an old place in my memory. My wings shift behind me, reacting to the undercurrent of recognition even before my mind can name it.

"Remove the mask," I say, voice steady. "Now."

He tilts his head in amusement, the gesture casual in a way that grates. "Impatient, as always. I suppose I shouldn't be surprised."

The flicker of familiarity sharpens until it's impossible to ignore, tightening in my chest like a hand closing around my lungs. I hold his gaze and repeat, quieter this time but with far more weight, "Take it off."

He sighs as if humoring an old habit. "If you insist."

With ease, he lifts the mask away. The chamber seems to tilt.

Lorian stands before me—older around the eyes, sharper at the edges, but unmistakably the same cupid I once trusted enough to fight beside. Memories slide into place whether I want them to or not: training halls, battlefields, missions where we relied on each other without question. And now here he is, still wearing the charm-mark that binds a cupid to service, still sworn to a system he clearly learned to manipulate rather than uphold.

He was never a deserter, never an exile quietly fading into obscurity. He stayed. He climbed. He hid behind neutrality while aligning himself with the one faction no cupid should ever touch. And the betrayal lands harder than the reveal itself.

"Sayer," he says with that same infuriatingly familiar smile, "you look like you've seen a ghost."

I stare at him, stunned fury simmering beneath my ribs. "You're working for the Council of Thorns."

"No," he corrects with a small, almost lecturing shake of his head. "I'm working with them. There's a difference. And given the number of celestial politics you've stepped away from, I've had quite a bit of time to rise through the ranks."

The revelation tastes like poison.

"You kidnapped her," I say.

"I escorted her," Lorian counters, voice smooth as a well-polished blade. "The Council has been waiting a very long time for a Bellamy witch to reach thirty-five. Do you have any idea how rare an opportunity she represents? Centuries of planning—derailed by your little flame of a witch sending a beacon in your direction."

My wings tighten, feathers heating with barely contained power. "Where is she?"

"In the next chamber," he says, gesturing toward two iron-bound doors behind him. "The ritual space is very secure. She's unharmed. For now."

Before I can respond, her magic pulses through me again—faint, strained, but unmistakably hers. It hits hard enough to make my breath hitch, not because of the force, but because of the fear threaded beneath it. She's still conscious. Still fighting. Still calling for me.

Lorian watches my reaction with the pleased detachment of someone observing a predictable experiment. "You know," he says lightly, "I always suspected that if you ever truly bonded with someone, it would be messy. I wasn't wrong."

"Move," I growl, stepping forward.

"Sayer, be reasonable."

"Move," I repeat.

He exhales through a half-laugh, spreading his hands as though indulging a stubborn child. "If you push past me, you'll trigger every ward the Council has placed on the ritual. You'll bring half their faction down on this chamber. You'll ignite a political incident the celestials aren't prepared to clean up. And"—he gestures lightly toward the door—"you'll destabilize her magic even further. Which, frankly, helps no one."

"Lorian," I say with a calm I don't feel, "I don't care."

He studies me then—not mocking, not smug, but something sharper, something that acknowledges the shift neither of us will be able to undo.

"I suppose you don't," he murmurs. "That's the trouble with cupids who get too close to their assignments. They start forgetting their place."

"I didn't forget anything," I say. "I made a choice."

"And so did I."

We stand in a tense, heavy silence. Her beacon pulses again, weaker this time, trembling at the edges. The sound of it—not audible, but magical—cuts through the chamber like a plea. It's enough to decide everything.

"I'm not leaving without her," I tell him.

Lorian's expression settles into something like resigned amusement. "Then I hope you're ready to break an extraordinary number of celestial laws tonight."

His wards flare.

So do mine.

The chamber seems to hold its breath.

And then I move.

Chapter 34

Francesca

The ritual chamber hums like a living throat—every breath thick with metal and old magic, every stone etched with sigils that pulse in time with a rhythm not my own. The room wasn't built to hold a Bellamy witch; it was built to drain one. The pressure around me presses in with the weight of a closing fist, trying to pin me in place, trying to turn me into something quiet and compliant.

They picked the wrong Bellamy.

I've been testing the wards since the moment the masked stranger shoved me in here. First small pushes, then harder spells shaped by instinct and anger. Every attempt made the circle tighten, every flare of magic drew more siphoning runes to life along the walls. They want me weak. They want me shaken.

Instead, the beacon sent everything snapping into focus.

Sayer felt me.

I know it—not through logic, not through hope, but through the unmistakable sensation of another magic brushing mine with the warmth of a hand offered in the dark. It should have destabilized everything. The curse should have erupted. The pressure should have turned explosive.

But the moment his presence grazed my magic, the spiraling stopped.

Clarity settled in.

My power no longer thrashes like a panicked animal; it sharpens, threads itself through the cracks of the room like water carving stone. I press my hand against the nearest sigil and let the magic pour outward—not wild, but intentional, the way I was taught in all those midnight lessons Harper insisted we practice "just in case." Self-preservation was always my talent. Tonight it's my weapon.

Heat builds along the stone where I push, and the runes flicker, confused by the resonance. They were designed to exploit instability, not harmony. The moment the bond steadied, the room lost its advantage.

Something slams against the outer door so hard the hinges shriek in protest.

He's here.

"Sayer," I whisper, bracing myself. "Please."

The wards surge in panic as the doors explode inward. Dust and candle soot swirl through the air, and through it steps Sayer, wings half-spread, expression carved with a fury I've never seen on him—furious, determined, and terrified all at once.

Relief hits me with such force my knees nearly buckle.

But the guards move quickly. Three converge on him, sigils primed, spells charged. Sayer meets them with fluid, practiced precision—deflecting one blast with the curve of his wing, dissolving another with a twist of his hand, stepping into a third strike so cleanly it collapses the guard before he hits the ground.

But more spill into the chamber. Too many.

A guard breaks from the cluster and lunges toward me. I shape a tight burst of magic and slam it into the circle's seam; the ward fractures with a sound like cracking ice. The guard falters, losing balance long enough for me to move. Sayer reaches me in the next breath, closing his hand around mine—not gently, not romantically, but like someone anchoring his entire world to a single point.

The moment our fingers touch, the room reacts.

My magic doesn't fight his; it aligns. It flows. It steadies into something sharper than anything I've ever channeled. Together, we shatter the remnants of the containment circle in a flash of ember-gold light.

The chamber erupts.

Spells collide in midair. Runes crack under strain. Sayer pivots with me at his side, the two of us moving in an almost instinctive rhythm—my shielding charm sliding across his wing, his counter spell opening a path for me to strike back. For the first time all season, my magic feels like mine. Better than mine. Stronger. Centered.

But we're still surrounded.

A binding charm grazes my shoulder; a blast of kinetic force shoves Sayer back a step. I gather another spell, but exhaustion starts to bite at the edges of my focus. There are too many of them, and the room won't hold much longer.

That's when the air shifts—cool, sharp, threaded with power that feels like a knife cutting through fog.

A flare of blue-gold brightness slices across the nearest wall, scattering guards like paper.

Jackson storms in first, already mid-incantation, smoke curling off his jacket like he barely survived whatever hallway he burned through to get here. Leona follows, elegant even in combat, her wards glowing like she's been itching to unleash them on someone deserving.

Jackson levels a spell at the nearest guard with an irritated flick. "We leave you two alone for five minutes."

Leona casts a shield that hits with enough force to rattle the sigils on the opposite wall. "Honestly, Sayer," she says, surveying the mayhem with exasperated grace, "you couldn't wait for backup?"

Relief washes through me—sharp, grateful, dizzying.

We may still be surrounded. We may still be outnumbered.

But we are no longer alone.

Chaos rolls through the chamber in waves. Spells collide midair, ricocheting off shattered runes and half-broken sigils, and the floor trembles beneath all of us as if the room itself is trying to decide whether to hold or collapse. Sayer keeps me close, pivoting whenever another blast arcs too near, and even in the frenzy of it, our magic keeps aligning, sliding together with frightening ease.

Jackson reaches us first, skidding across the broken circle as he ducks an incoming spell. "Move, both of you—Leona's got the exit ready."

Leona is already beside him, hands moving in tight, elegant arcs that trace a spell lattice I've never seen. Not a shield. Not an attack.

A warp-spell sigil.

A big one.

"Sayer, bring her here," she snaps, voice steady but sharp with urgency. "Now!"

Sayer doesn't hesitate. He guides me toward them as another wave of guards spills into the room, these ones far better armored and clearly prepared for a prolonged fight. The air thickens with fresh wards; the temperature spikes.

"Sayer!" Leona's voice cuts through the rising magic. "We don't have time!"

He pulls me fully into the sigil's center. Jackson plants himself at the edge, buying us seconds with a ward-wall strong enough to rattle the bones in my teeth. Spells crash against it one after another, explosions of color and heat.

Leona slams her palms together, sending a pulse of power rippling through the circle. The sigil snaps inward, bands of light tightening around us—hot, disorienting, electric—and the chamber blurs at the edges.

The last thing I see before the spell collapses is the doorway filling with reinforcements. Too many. If Leona hadn't acted now, none of us would be getting out.

The warp hits.

My stomach drops. The world folds in on itself, a moment of vertigo so sharp I nearly collapse, but Sayer's grip holds me upright as the magic drags us through a crack in space.

Light fractures.

Sound stretches.

The cold stone floor gives way to warm wood beneath my feet.

When the world solidifies again, we're standing in a wide living room filled with low lamplight, woven blankets, and the faint scent of cinnamon and old spell parchment. It's cozy in a way that feels almost absurd after what we just escaped.

The warp spell releases its grip all at once, and the world rushes back in—warm air, soft lamplight, the faint scent of cinnamon and old spell parchment. It takes my vision a few seconds to settle, long enough that I'm aware of Sayer's hand still firmly at my waist, grounding me like he's afraid I'll flicker out of existence if he lets go.

Jackson stumbles backward onto a couch, bracing himself with a breath that sounds like it's been dragged out of his lungs. Leona plants her hands on her knees, drawing in steadying air as if her body is catching up to the violence of the spell she just pulled off.

I take in the room slowly, trying to make sense of the sudden shift. Cozy furniture, quilts thrown over chairs, framed spell diagrams hung beside candid photos of the two of them laughing beside a lake. It feels deeply lived in, safe in a way that throws my nerves into confusion.

Leona straightens, swiping a loose curl from her cheek, then gestures around the space with a tired flourish. "Welcome to our living room. Shoes off, blood on the mat, and for the love of all things magical, someone please tell me none of you are about to pass out."

It's only then that I realize where we are—*their* home—and that realization settles somewhere warm in my chest, right beneath the frantic thrum of magic still humming under my skin.

I swallow hard, still trying to steady my breath as the last threads of adrenaline melt into a deep, exhausted tremor under my skin. Leona doesn't give either of us a chance to collapse in the hallway. She waves for us to follow, already shifting into that brisk, no-nonsense stride that means arguing would be pointless.

The house surprises me.

Warm lighting pools in corners instead of the harsh overheads I expected, and everything smells faintly of cinnamon and something herbal—sage or lavender, maybe. A row of photographs lines the wall: Leona and Jackson dressed for a solstice gala, Jackson triumphantly holding a giant mixing bowl like he just won a duel with it, the two of them laughing in front of a tiny lakeside cabin. It's lived-in and soft in a way that tugs at something in my chest I don't want to examine.

Leona turns into a room near the end of the hall, and when she pushes open the door, I blink at how comfortable it is. A neatly made bed, thick quilts folded at the foot, warm lamplight, a bathroom attached with towels already stacked and waiting. A first aid kit sits on the counter like it knew we'd need it.

"This is you for now," Leona says, setting the kit beside the bed with a thud. She hands Sayer a folded set of clothes, then offers me the same—soft shirts, loose pants, things meant for rest and recovery rather than presentation.

Before either of us can speak, she lifts a hand.

"No. Don't even try. I'm cutting off whatever denial either of you is about to attempt."

Sayer exhales, already bracing for impact. Jackson drifts to the doorway, leaning his shoulder against the frame as if settling in to enjoy the show.

Leona folds her arms, gaze flicking between the two of us with surgical precision. "You almost broke a Council ritual chamber. Together. Do you understand how insane that is? Do you know how many witches could survive even half of what you two just did?"

Heat crawls up the back of my neck. Sayer tries very hard to look undisturbed and fails spectacularly.

She presses on, relentless. "And then you come in here acting like coworkers who survived a minor inconvenience instead of people whose magic keeps grabbing each other by the soul."

"Leona," Sayer mutters, cheeks tightening.

"No," she repeats, utterly unmoved. "You will stay in this room. You will clean up. And you will talk. Because whatever is happening between you two is already in motion, and pretending you can ignore it is how people get manipulated, injured, or dead."

Jackson finally speaks, voice dry as desert heat. "Just for clarity, she means talk before kissing. Preferably. Not mandatory."

I groan into my hands. "Jackson, please."

"What? I'm supporting emotional honesty."

Leona taps the doorknob once, humming under her breath as a soft glow seals the lock. A ward settles over the frame—gentle but immovable.

"The door will unlock," she says, "when you two stop lying to yourselves and each other."

"Leona—" Sayer starts.

But she's already stepping into the hall, Jackson behind her, both wearing matching expressions of exhausted fondness and smug certainty.

"Good luck," Jackson adds, winking before he closes the door.

The click is final.

Silence blooms in its wake, warm and intimate and entirely too aware.

Sayer turns toward me.

I turn toward him.

And the locked door behind us hums like it knows exactly what kind of trouble we're both in now.

Chapter 35

Sayer

The lock vibrates behind us, sealing shut with Leona's unmistakable signature. The silence that follows isn't peaceful. It's thick and pointed, like the room itself is waiting for one of us to explode.

Francesca stands near the far wall, arms crossed tight, shoulders rigid, the faintest shimmer of defensive magic coiling along her skin. She looks like she's ready to bolt and punch someone at the same time.

I close the distance by a few measured steps, stopping just short of her space—close enough to catch every flicker of emotion across her face, far enough that the knot in my chest doesn't ease. It only tightens.

She beats me to it, spinning toward me with fire still clinging to her words. "You had no right," she snaps, voice rough around the edges. "No right to tear through that place like some celestial battering ram."

I let out a sharp breath and gesture back toward the door we came through, my wings giving a restless twitch behind me. "You called me," I shoot back. "*Or* did you miss the part where your magic screamed my name loud enough to rattle every ward between here and hell?"

Her eyes flash as she steps into my path, forcing me to stop pacing. "I didn't choose to call you. It was reflex. Panic. *Instinct.*"

"Instinct," I repeat, the word tasting bitter as I circle past her, dragging a hand through my hair. The air feels too charged, too tight. "Instinct doesn't aim blind, Francesca. It goes straight to whatever—or whoever—you trust most."

She pivots to keep me in front of her and jabs a finger into my chest, right over my heart. "That wasn't trust. It was desperation, and you don't get to rewrite it just because it fits *your* narrative."

I look down at her finger, then back up at her face. "Then you're welcome," I say flatly.

She recoils as if I've shocked her, throwing her hands up and turning away, pacing in the opposite direction. "Unbelievable," she mutters, running her palms over her face before spinning back to me. The space between us feels electric now, stretched thin and humming, like one wrong word might snap it entirely.

And the worst part is, neither of us steps back.

"You're alive," I say, stepping toward her despite my best judgment. "You're not siphoned, or bound, or gods forbid handed over to whatever ritual they intended. And you're angry because I didn't wait politely outside?"

"No! I'm angry because you keep acting like you're the only one allowed to decide what happens to me."

"You walked straight into danger," I shoot back. "Again. With a man who masked his magic, lied to you, and *literally* dragged you across dimensional space."

She stiffens. "He didn't lie. He omitted."

"He hid what mattered."

"And you think you don't?" Her voice sharpens, climbing with every word. She doesn't retreat; she advances, forcing me to give ground as she gestures between us. "You've been withholding things from me since the moment you walked into my life with that damn file. The wings. The deadline. The terms of whatever celestial punishment you're serving. All of it. You get to conceal half your existence, but the second I make one choice for myself, you're ready to start a war?"

My jaw tightens as I shake my head. "I didn't start anything tonight."

"But you sure as hell escalated it," she fires back immediately.

I rake a hand through my hair, frustration burning hot under my ribs. "If I hadn't, you wouldn't be standing here arguing with me."

She closes the remaining space between us until the hem of her gown brushes my legs, until her warmth is undeniable. Her magic flares with her temper, sparks skating along her fingertips before leaping toward mine like it recognizes me whether she wants it to or not.

"You don't get to play savior," she says, her voice dropping, breath uneven. "Not with me. Not when you're the one who vanished for fifteen years and then act surprised that my life didn't freeze in place waiting for you."

The words hit harder than anything thrown tonight.

"Francesca," I start, my voice softer despite myself, but she cuts me off without looking away.

"Do you have any idea what it felt like," she demands, "to learn my file was buried? To realize this wasn't just the universe being dramatic? That you—my supposed matchmaker—walked away while my curse spiraled and I was left managing the fallout alone?"

"That's not fair," I say, the edge in my voice cracking despite my effort to hold it steady. "I didn't know your file was next. I didn't know it was you."

Her breath stutters, just barely, and then the tears hit—bright at the edges of her eyes, threatening but not falling. She doesn't blink them away. She holds them there like they're evidence.

"But me," she says, voice cracking like someone just twisted a nerve straight through her chest. "Why does it matter if it was me or not? What difference does that make? If you didn't know, then why are you acting like—" She stops herself, jaw tightening. "No. You *are* hiding something. I can feel it."

I open my mouth, but she barrels on.

"And how could you let someone like Dorian slip through?" she demands, stepping in like she means to shove the truth out of me if she has to. "You're supposed to be a matchmaker, Sayer. You're supposed to see through people. But you didn't see *any* of that? You didn't feel a single thing wrong? No wonder you quit."

My jaw locks, heat flickering low under my skin. "That isn't fair."

"Oh, suddenly fairness matters?" she snaps. "Because it didn't matter when my file was buried for fifteen years. It didn't matter when a man with a masked signature dragged me halfway across a realm to turn me into some magical bargaining chip. It didn't matter when I kept telling myself you were distant because of the deadline—not because you didn't care."

"Fran—"

"No," she cuts in, breath shaking. "I asked you a question. If you didn't know it was me, then why does it matter so much now? Why—" Her voice catches like the truth is sitting just behind her teeth. "Why am *I* different?"

I don't answer fast enough.

That hesitation carves straight through her.

Her magic ripples in a way I don't like—too sharp, too defensive, too much like she's bracing for impact from something she hasn't even heard yet.

She looks away for a moment, swallowing hard, trying to pull herself back under control. "I can feel it. Every time you avoid something. Every time you look at me like you want to say something and don't. Every time you act like I'm important but won't admit why." She drags in a shaky breath. "I'm tired of trying to guess."

The anger in her voice softens—not gentler, but wounded in a way that lands far deeper than her shouting ever could.

"You didn't see Dorian," she says quietly. "You didn't warn me. You didn't stop it. You didn't do what a Cupid is supposed to do. And now you want me to trust you?"

I step toward her—slowly, deliberately, because her magic responds to pressure the way a flame responds to wind—dangerous when pushed, brilliant when coaxed.

"I didn't see him because something was masking him," I say, low and steady. "Something powerful. Something older. And hiding magic that well isn't normal matchmaking interference—it's sabotage."

She looks up at me through wet lashes, the bravest person in the room despite the way her voice almost breaks. "Then why didn't you tell me that?"

"Because I didn't know," I say, and this time there's no heat in it, just honesty. "Not until it was too late."

She shakes her head slowly, not in disbelief—worse. In disappointment. "You always show up a little too late, Sayer."

I exhale through my teeth. "I didn't know it was you. And yes, that changes things."

"Why?" she whispers.

Because my wings reacted. Because my magic recognized yours before I did. Because every instinct I've ever buried surged the moment your name touched my hands. Because the bond isn't just cosmic—it's personal. Because it's you.

But I can't say any of that. Not yet.

So I answer the only way I can without lying.

"Because you matter," I say, voice low enough that the walls feel closer. "Because this was never supposed to happen to you. And because I would burn down every council room in existence before I let them touch you again."

Her breath shivers, anger flickering into something softer—something dangerous in its own way.

But the tear that finally slips free tells me one thing:

Words aren't going to be enough. Not anymore.

The hurt in her eyes hits harder than anything she could've yelled. Not because she's angry—anger I can handle—but because she looks blindsided, like the pieces finally lined up into a shape she never wanted to see.

"It wasn't you," I say, stepping closer before I lose the nerve. "I didn't know your file was next. I didn't know it was sitting under fifteen years of dust. I didn't know your curse escalated without oversight."

Her breath trembles, but she doesn't move away when I reach up. My thumb brushes the tear threatening her lashes, and the sound she makes is small enough to shatter something deep in my chest.

"You deserved better than what happened," I continue, voice low. "You deserved someone competent watching your case. Someone who would've stepped in the moment the curse started shifting. Someone who would've made sure you didn't spend half your life waiting for a contact who never came."

Her jaw tightens as if she's fighting between outrage and heartbreak.

"And I wasn't there," I say. "I walked away. I left the system before I even knew they'd buried your file. Before I knew anyone hadn't assigned you a match. Before I knew they'd chosen someone for you without ever consulting you."

Her expression flickers. Hurt. Confusion. A pulse of magic pushes against my ribs like her body is reacting faster than her mind.

But I can't stop.

"If I hadn't quit," I murmur, stepping in until our breath mingles, "I could've found you anyone. Someone safe. Someone compatible. Someone the system didn't have to scrape from the bottom of an outdated archive."

My hand finds the back of her neck before I register the movement, fingers sliding into the loose fall of her hair, holding her like I'm afraid she'll disappear again.

"I don't deserve you," I admit, barely above a whisper. "Not after walking away from the job that should've protected you. Not after losing fifteen years that should've belonged to someone loyal. Not when the match they chose for you was so wrong it nearly destroyed you."

Something inside her breaks—not down, but open. Her magic hums like a heartbeat against mine. Her breath shakes.

And this time, there is no hesitation. I lower my mouth to hers and kiss her.

It's slow at first—gentle, coaxing, full of apology—but the moment she answers, the heat sharpens. Her hands curl into my shirt. My grip tightens at her waist. Her magic meets mine instead of recoiling. For the first time since this season began, nothing feels chaotic. Nothing feels wrong. It feels like breathing after weeks underwater.

When I pull back—just enough to speak, just enough to see the confusion and longing tangled together in her eyes—I say the truth that's been sitting like a stone in my chest.

"They chose for you, Francesca."

She freezes.

The warmth between us turns sharp in an instant. Her magic spikes against mine, not violently—but demanding.

"Sayer..." Her voice is barely a breath. "What did you just say?"

She steps back, eyes wide, breath unsteady, every instinct in her body turning toward the need to understand what I just revealed. And in that moment, I know the hardest part is still coming.

Chapter 36

Francesca

The words sit between us like something volatile, something waiting for the slightest spark to blow the entire room apart. My heartbeat climbs into my throat, my palms warm with the beginning tremor of magic, and I take a step back because if I don't put space between us, I might lose the thread of what I'm demanding.

"What choice?" My voice is sharper than I intend, but I don't soften it. "What did they choose for me? Stop dancing around it."

"Fran—"

"No," I cut in, pacing because standing still feels impossible. "No more vague explanations. No more half-truths. You said there was an error in my file. Fine. Then tell me *exactly* what error."

He follows my pacing with his eyes, tension coiling through his shoulders, his jaw tightening the way it does when he's preparing to say something he hates. "It shouldn't have happened."

"That's not an answer." I turn on him, heat rushing under my skin. "What. Error."

"Francesca, listen—"

"I *am* listening," I snap, stepping in, close enough that he has to look directly at me. "Now stop dodging me and start talking."

His hesitation is a physical thing, a weight in the air. He looks away—just for a heartbeat—and that's what breaks the last of my restraint.

"Sayer Valentine," I say, voice low and shaking, "if you don't tell me right now, the next spell I cast will *not* be subtle."

That gets him.

His gaze finds mine again, conflicted and pained and braced for impact. He draws in a slow breath, the kind that looks like it hurts to hold, and when he speaks, his voice is quieter than before—no less steady, just stripped bare.

"The error," he says, "was your match assignment."

My stomach drops. "What about it?"

He swallows once, the movement tight. "It listed... me."

For a moment, I simply stare at him, arms stiff at my sides, the air turning thick enough to choke on. It doesn't register at first—not the words, not the implication, not the enormous, terrible meaning sitting just beneath them. It's too much. Too close. Too ridiculous to be real.

When my voice returns, it's barely a breath. "You're saying the system matched me to you."

"It shouldn't have," he says quickly, pacing now because the confession has rattled him more than anything I've ever seen. "It wasn't supposed to. They don't pair matches to active cupids, and certainly not to ones who are about to quit. It was a glitch or interference or something deliberately altered—I don't know. But, your file named me."

The room tilts.

My magic turns over inside me in a low, rolling wave that feels like recognition and betrayal knotted together.

"Why didn't you tell me?" The question comes out softer, but the tremor behind it is sharper than any yell I could muster.

He drags a hand through his hair, frustrated with himself, with me, with everything. "Because it didn't make sense. Because it shouldn't have been possible. Because I... I didn't want that to be the reason any of this mattered."

The words land hard.

Too hard.

I take another step back because I need distance, oxygen, something solid to lean on that isn't him. "You let me go on dates," I say quietly. "You watched me try to find someone else while knowing—while thinking—that you were listed as my match."

"I didn't know until after the Council dragged me back in," he says, his voice tight with something like desperation. "I saw it the same night I opened your file. I didn't hide this for years. I just—" He stops, breath unsteady. "I didn't want to tell you until I understood what it meant. And I still don't."

My magic sparks at that, a flare of heat along my fingertips that feels dangerously close to something uncontrolled. He sees it, and his wings twitch behind him in an instinctive shift—not defensive, just attuned.

I hold up a hand before he can move closer. "Don't."

"Fran—"

"Don't," I repeat, forcing my voice to stay level. "I need a minute. I need to breathe, and think, and not be standing right next to the man who apparently got assigned to me like a cosmic clerical error."

His expression twists—hurt, restrained, already fighting himself.

"Is that all it is to you?" he asks quietly. "A mistake on a line?"

"I don't know what it is," I answer, and the truth of it burns. "And that's the problem."

Something inside me cracks—not loudly, not dramatically, just enough that the pressure behind my ribs shifts in a way I can't ignore. The heat rising in my throat isn't magic this time. It's anger. It's fear. It's the raw, humiliating sting of understanding something I never asked for.

My eyes burn before I can stop them. Not delicate tears. Not quiet ones. Angry ones. The kind that feel earned.

"Oh gods," I whisper, the words trembling as my hands find my temples. "All this time... all this time I was fighting it." I pace because standing still feels impossible; my body is too full, too restless. "The flare. The sparks. The way my magic kept reacting whenever you walked into a room. I told myself it was stress or the curse or the universe being an asshole—but no. It was *this*."

"Fran..." he starts, but I cut him off with a sharp gesture that sends my magic buzzing in the air.

"No." My voice shakes, but I don't hide it. "I went looking for a connection. I tried. I gave people chances. I blamed myself every time something didn't click. And the whole damn time—" I press a palm to my chest, breath unsteady. "The thing I was searching for was right fucking next door."

He flinches—not visually, but in that subtle way magic does when it recoils from truth.

The tears spill despite my efforts, hot and furious, as if they belong to the version of me who has been running in circles for years without realizing the map was rigged.

"I fought it," I say, voice raw. "I fought so damn hard not to fall into whatever this is. I told myself I was imagining it, that I was desperate for a solution, that you were just... convenient proximity." I swallow thickly, blinking through the blur. "But it wasn't that. Was it?"

He doesn't answer. He doesn't need to.

My breath shakes, and before I can stop myself, the question tears out of me.

"Was it me?" I ask, barely louder than a whisper, but the pain behind it feels enormous. "Was something wrong with me? Is that why you didn't tell me? Because you didn't want to be matched to the woman who couldn't find love for fifteen years? Because you thought the curse would make this messy or inconvenient or—gods—unworthy?"

His eyes widen, horror and denial rushing to the surface, but I'm already spiraling.

"Did you think I wouldn't want *you*?" I demand, stepping closer as my magic trembles in the air. "Did you think I'd reject you? That I'd laugh? That I'd run? Is that why you didn't say anything?"

He tries to speak, but the words don't come fast enough, and the hurt keeps pouring out of me.

"You let me go on dates," I say, voice breaking. "You stood there and sent me off with men who were wrong for me—dangerously wrong for me—while knowing you were on my file." My throat tightens on the next words, thick with tears. "Do you have any idea what that feels like? To be the one person in the world who wasn't allowed to know the truth about her own future?"

The silence that follows isn't empty. It's full of every unanswered question I've been carrying for years.

And when I finally look up at him, the anger twists into something quieter, but deeper.

"Why didn't you tell me, Sayer?" The question trembles out of me, soft and broken. "Why didn't you choose *me*?"

The room feels too small for the two of us, too full of everything we haven't said. My question hangs between us like a blade suspended by a fraying thread, and the longer he hesitates, the louder the ache in my chest becomes.

"Why didn't you choose me?" I ask again, quieter this time, because the louder version didn't get me an answer and the softer one... hurts more than I expected.

Sayer looks like the question physically hits him. His posture shifts, not retreating, but bracing—as if he's finally run out of places to hide the truth. He drags a hand through his hair, exhaling like he's about to walk into fire.

"Francesca," he starts, and the way he says my name already makes my eyes sting, "I didn't tell you because I didn't trust myself not to take advantage of it."

That isn't the answer I expect. Not even close.

He steps closer, slowly, carefully, like he's afraid I'll pull away. His hand comes up, hesitates for a heartbeat, then brushes the tears from my cheek with a tenderness that makes something inside me twist painfully.

"I've watched people cling to the wrong person for all the wrong reasons," he says, voice low and rough. "Magic. Fate. Fear. Obligation. I didn't want to be added to that list. I didn't want you looking at me and seeing a match because a system told you to."

I blink against the tears, but they spill anyway.

He keeps going, words tumbling out like he's finally lost the ability to hold them in. "I wanted you to have the choice. A real one. Without the curse pressing in. Without a deadline twisting your decisions. Without me standing there as the only lifeline in a storm you didn't ask for."

My breath shakes. "But... you still didn't tell me."

He swallows, jaw tight, eyes never leaving mine. "Because once I realized it was you... I knew it wouldn't be fair. To you. To the choice you deserved. And I knew I wouldn't be able to stay neutral if you so much as looked at me like you wanted something I couldn't give."

A tear breaks loose, sliding down my cheek. His thumb follows it, slow and careful.

"You deserved someone stable," he murmurs, barely above a whisper. "Someone who hadn't already run from the job that should've protected you. Someone who wasn't... me."

The words land in my chest like a stone dropped in water, ripples moving through everything I've been trying to deny. My anger blurs into something softer—hurt, hope, disbelief—and my magic lifts under my skin in a warm, aching pulse.

"So it wasn't because something was wrong with me?" My voice shakes through the question. "It wasn't because I was unmatchable or cursed beyond fixing?"

His eyes flash with something fierce. "Francesca, no. Never. There is nothing wrong with you. There never was."

My heart lurches.

He steps closer, close enough that I can feel his breath. "I didn't choose you," he says softly, "because the second I knew it was you... I realized how much I wanted to. And that terrified me."

My throat tightens around a breath I can't quite take.

"And I knew," he finishes, the words barely holding together, "that if I chose you for the wrong reason—even for a moment—I wouldn't survive choosing wrong."

Everything inside me cracks open.

All the fear. All the doubt. All the years of trying not to want too much or hope too loudly. I feel my defenses slip, slide, then collapse entirely under the weight of every truth we've been avoiding.

And in that moment, something in both of us snaps.

I reach for him at the same time he reaches for me, like our bodies finally stopped pretending they didn't know how to find each other. His hands settle at my waist, mine in his shirt, and the magic between us surges—not frantic, not chaotic, just unbearably certain.

The kiss happens like it was waiting for permission neither of us could give until now.

It's slow at first—warm, tender, almost reverent—then deeper, fuller, fueled by emotions neither of us are ready to name but both of us feel. His thumb brushes my jaw. My breath stutters against his mouth. His other hand slides to the small of my back, drawing me closer until the air between us is nothing but heat and want and the relief of finally, finally not fighting this anymore.

When he breaks away, it's only far enough to rest his forehead against mine, our breaths tangled, our magic humming in a shared, trembling rhythm.

Chapter 37

Sayer

My hands are already tangled in her hair, tilting her head back, deepening the kiss until everything else—Leona's wards, the Council's threats, the fifteen years we lost—dissolves into the sharp, immediate reality of her mouth under mine. She tastes like heat and tears and the profound relief of a truth finally spoken. This isn't just passion; it's a desperate, immediate claiming, a final surrender to a gravitational pull we both spent too long denying.

I break the kiss, desperate for air, and trace a line of fire down her jaw, my mouth finding the delicate curve of her throat. She shivers beneath my touch, a soft, involuntary sound escaping her that makes my grip on control fracture. The crimson silk of the gown is a barrier

I can't stand, and I pull her closer, my fingers finding the seam of her bodice, wanting nothing but her skin against mine.

"Gods, Francesca," I growl against her pulse point, the raw need in my voice undeniable. "We're done fighting. We're done talking."

"Good," she whispers, her hands sweeping down my chest, pulling at the loosened fabric of my suit. "Then stop talking."

I lift my head, looking into her eyes. They are dark and luminous, reflecting the intensity of the moment, and I see the same raw desperation that is currently consuming me. This is it. The point of no return.

My hand slides to the small of her back, and I feel the powerful, eager thump of her magic against my own. The connection is electric, thrumming with anticipation. Everything in the room fades, leaving only the sound of our ragged breaths and the frantic rhythm of our joined heartbeats.

I lean down again, trailing soft, lingering kisses from the curve of her jaw, down her throat, settling where her pulse races against the collar of the crimson gown. The silk feels impossibly soft, yet impossibly restrictive.

I want to take her here, now, in the middle of this room, on top of the blankets, with the scent of cinnamon and chaos still lingering in the air.

But a low, steady thrum of reason—Jackson and Leona's wards sealing us in until we 'stop lying to ourselves'—catches the edge of my focus. They forced us to stop and talk, and now, they've left us in a comfortable room with a locked door. We are here for a purpose. We just survived a council-sanctioned kidnapping and a magical battlefield. The thought of all the dirt, the soot, the sweat, and the sheer *mess* of the last hour is enough to make me pull back just slightly. She deserves more than a frantic, desperate collision on a bedroom floor.

I trace a slow, deliberate line back up her throat with my mouth, stopping just shy of her ear. "We need to clean up first," I murmur, the words a low, husky commitment rather than a question. "You're covered in soot, and I'm covered in the magic of people I just hit."

Francesca closes her eyes, a soft sigh escaping her as my hand settles firmly on her waist. "Sayer," she breathes out, the word thick with plea.

"I know," I whisper, pressing one final, meaningful kiss just behind her ear. "But you deserve soft towels and hot water, not another fight."

I slide my hand down, catching hers. The contrast is sharp: my skin rough, hers soft, the faint trembling in her fingers mirroring the frantic energy still coiling in my chest.

I lead her toward the attached bathroom, pulling the door open with my free hand. The room is immaculate—bright, warm, and blessedly free of any chaotic energy. I push past the impulse to lock the door behind us; Leona's external ward is more than enough security.

I turn the handle and the large rain-style shower head hisses to life, sending hot water spraying into the tiled stall. The steam begins to build instantly, filling the small space with warm, humid air that smells faintly of cedar and expensive soap.

I turn back to Francesca. She leans against the counter, watching me, the intensity in her eyes never wavering, and the raw vulnerability in her posture is more potent than any spell.

"Let me," I say, stepping closer.

I reach for the zipper of her magnificent, infuriating crimson gown. The silk thread catches the light, glowing faintly as I slowly pull the zipper down the line of her spine. It's an act of worship, not haste. The smooth metal slides down, and the heavy silk parts, easing away from her skin as the fabric pools around her feet, a shimmering puddle of molten gold and shadow.

She steps free of it, clad only in simple lace panties. The sight of her—unmasked, raw, imperfectly perfect—steals the air from my lungs. Her skin is pale beneath the ambient light, smudged faintly with soot near her shoulders and throat from the explosive end of our escape.

I let my gaze linger on the curves of her body, the soft swell of her breasts, the delicate line of her collarbones, the quiet hum of her magic just beneath her skin.

"Beautiful," I breathe, my voice thick with feeling.

I reach out and unpin the last few strands of her hair, freeing the heavy dark waves to fall around her shoulders. Her hands are already moving, reaching for the buttons of my ruined formal shirt. She undresses me—slowly, deliberately, until the expensive suit and the embroidered gown lie on the floor in a tangled heap of silk and charline.

When I finally stand before her, wings pressed close, only in my briefs, the heat of the room seems to concentrate between us.

I reach out, tracing the soot smudges on her shoulder with my thumb. My magic swells, not in threat, but in promise, warming the air around us.

"Come here," I say, grabbing her hand and pulling her gently toward the sound of the running water.

The steam is heavy now. I step into the shower first, then guide her in after me. The hot water hits her skin with a gasp, washing away the cold remnants of the stone corridor and the stress of the fight.

She leans her forehead against my chest, her body trembling not from cold, but from the sudden, intimate reality of the space we share.

I cup her face, lifting her chin until her eyes meet mine, and there is no more anger, no more doubt—only this powerful, undeniable truth.

"You are safe now," I promise, the words a vow delivered against her mouth. "You are mine. And I am never letting go."

And then, finally, I kiss her—long, slow, and deep—letting the hot water stream over us, washing away the last of the world's demands.

I pull back, just enough to catch my breath, my eyes dark with a hunger that mirrors hers, a primitive, consuming need reflected in the storm of her own gaze. The air in the small, steamy enclosure had grown thick, not just with water vapor, but with the potent, intoxicating scent of desire. "I've dreamed of this moment," I murmur, my voice a low, rough vibration that resonates deep against the delicate skin of her ear. The simple words hold the weight of weeks—or was it months?—of electric tension, of stolen glances and near-miss touches that had only amplified the inevitable connection between us.

I reach for the bar of soap, a simple, unscented white block resting on the porcelain ledge, and begin to glide it over her skin. This is no mere cleansing; it is an initiation. Starting with the elegant curve of her shoulders, my touch is both deliberate and tender, a slow, mesmerizing exploration that maps out the landscape of her body. I watch as the soap's slick, creamy lather blooms against her wet skin, a pristine white contrast to the flush that rises on her chest.

With each stroke, I learn every subtle curve and hollow—the sharp definition of her clavicle, the soft slope where her neck meets her shoulder, the taut muscle beneath. My silence is a promise, a binding contract of what is to come, communicated entirely through the language of touch.

My hands trail down, past the gentle arc of her neck, and she leans instinctively into my touch, her body seeking the heat of mine. I move with a reverence that borders on worship, over the swelling bounty of her breasts. A soft, involuntary gasp escapes her as my fingers brush the tender skin of her sternum, and I feel the quickened, fluttering beat of her heart against my palm. I watch her eyes flutter closed, savoring the small, breathless hitch in her breathing that tells me I have found the precise point of her surrender. I lean in, capturing her surprised, soft lips with my own, a slow, intoxicating kiss that tastes of water and want. We break apart, and I continue past the subtle dip of her waist, the creamy lather swirling like an erotic painting beneath my touch, closer and closer to her core. Each movement is a deliberate, agonizing delay, building the pressure, until I have created a long, tingling, fire-hot path in their wake, a luminous trail that marks her, that claims her, entirely.

I dip my head, tracing the faint outline of her hip bone with my thumb, the movement a silent query. When I finally reach the apex of her thigh, my fingers slide lower, finding the soft, slick heat waiting there. The sound she makes is a low, guttural moan—a pure, unedited wave of sound that tells me exactly how close she is to breaking.

My touch is feather-light at first, a brush, an exploration, a slow, deliberate circle that finds the small, taut bud waiting for my attention. She gasps, arching into my hand, her body suddenly tense, every muscle locked in a breathless coil of anticipation. I lean in, ready to claim this moment, ready to push her over the edge and watch the beautiful, chaotic release of her magic.

But as I press my thumb against her—finally, truly making contact—she moves.

It's not a retreat. It's an aggressive, beautiful reclamation of control. Her hands shoot up, grasping the sides of my head with a fierce, unexpected intensity, pulling my mouth down to hers with a force that makes my teeth click.

The kiss is sharp, immediate, and utterly consuming—a sudden, electric storm that blows away the tender exploration we were in. Her lips are open, demanding, and the subtle, insistent pressure of her tongue is a shock of pure, raw dominance. She doesn't ask for permission; she takes it, plunging us into a deeper, hotter space where apology and tenderness have no place.

My mind spirals, caught completely off guard. The subtle shift in power—the sudden, intense reversal—is more potent than any spell. She is furious, she is desperate, she is entirely *here*, and she is commanding this moment. The need to command back is a powerful, almost painful thrum, but the sheer force of her desire—her *claiming*—is exhilarating.

She breaks the kiss, pulling back just far enough that her eyes, dark and stormy with passion, look straight into mine.

"My turn," she says, the words a low, husky challenge that makes my entire body tighten.

Without waiting for my agreement, her hands, still slick with water and the residue of soap, glide over my chest. The move is deliberate, mirroring my earlier intensity. She presses her palm flat against the center of my sternum, right over the space where my magic coils, and the sudden heat of her touch sends a shockwave through my system.

Her focus is immediate, drawn to my wings, which are pressed close to my back but still visible, slightly damp and heavy with the aftermath of the fight. She traces the edge of a feather with a trembling finger, then, with a surprising amount of strength, shoves me back a step until my shoulders connect with the cold tile of the shower wall.

She takes the space I give her, stepping in close, her chest brushing mine.

Her mouth descends to my throat, but this time, it's not for a soft kiss; it's a hot, demanding line of kisses that trail down toward my collarbone. She uses her teeth, a sharp, playful nip that sends a flash of exquisite pain/pleasure through me. I let out a low groan, my hands instinctively reaching to cup her hips, holding her in place.

Her exploration continues, her mouth finding the damp, exposed skin of my shoulder and chest. The touch is a dizzying combination of silk and heat, and the sudden feeling of her desire focused entirely on me is almost overwhelming. The cold tile against my back only sharpens the heat that blooms everywhere she touches.

She pulls away, her eyes dropping to the flat plane of my stomach, and I feel a primal clenching low in my gut.

Her hand—the same hand she was just using to make my breath catch—slides down my soaked body, past my waist, until her palm settles, firm and hot, over the throbbing evidence of my desire.

The gasp that escapes me is ragged and uncontrolled, pulled from deep in my chest. Her magic flares in response, a low, triumphant purr that vibrates through my skin.

She looks up at me, a wickedly beautiful smirk playing on her lips, and in her eyes, I see the triumphant fire of a witch who has finally claimed what is hers. "You were right," she murmurs. "We're done talking."

Chapter 38

Francesca

The weight of his desire is an exquisite pressure under my hand, and the sound of his ragged, uncontrolled gasp sends a wave of pure, triumphant power through me. I keep my palm flat against him, my fingers wrapping around the hot, slick length, giving him just enough pressure to keep him desperate, but not enough to release the tension I'm deliberately building. I'm claiming this moment, not asking for it.

My turn.

I stroke him once, slow and deliberate, watching the powerful clench of his jaw as he fights for control. The look in his eyes—a mix of hunger, submission, and absolute devotion—is everything.

It's what I've been fighting for: not control *over* him, but shared control *with* him, where the rules of celestial bureaucracy and cursed matchmakers no longer apply.

I sink to my knees in the shower stall, taking him into my mouth, and the groan that rips from his throat is raw and desperate. I move on him, fast and practiced, bringing him quickly to the very brink of release, the warm water sluicing over us both as his muscles tremble under my touch. The soap, the steam, the water—they all amplify the heat between us, and I feel his climax building, ready to break.

I pull away from him, slowly. I stand up, letting the warm water wash the slick lather away from his skin, and lean in to give him a soft, quick kiss on his mouth. The moment his lips part, trying to deepen the connection, I pull my head back, deliberately, and step out of the shower stall, leaving the heat and steam and the raw, frustrated man behind the curtain of water.

A low, involuntary sound escapes him—a quiet, surprised whimper of disappointment that tugs at something deep in my chest. He reacts so completely to the sudden absence of my touch, and the immediate physical need is undeniable.

I don't look back. I grab one of the thick, plush towels Leona left for us, wrap it loosely around my body, and walk out of the bathroom. The warm air of the bedroom is a pleasant shock against my still-damp skin.

I hear the water shut off abruptly behind me. Good.

I walk to the bed, letting the towel fall to the floor in a shimmering crimson puddle—the color a defiant echo of the gown that started this entire night. I slide onto the sheets, watching the bathroom door as a shadow moves within the frame.

"Well?" I ask, my voice low, husky, and entirely too pleased with myself. "We've waited fifteen years for a match that was already made. We've fought through Council schemes and assassination attempts and your relentless denial. You and I, Sayer Valentine, are done with waiting."

He steps out of the bathroom—naked, wet, magnificent, his wings slightly ruffled and damp, the image of a celestial warrior just denied his prize. He looks furious, desperate, and utterly undone.

I smile, a slow, predatory curve of my lips. "If you want me," I challenge, my voice a soft murmur that promises everything, "you better come claim me."

The challenge hangs in the air, electric and thick. Sayer's eyes, dark with a banked fire, lock onto mine, and the hunger there is breathtaking. For a long, heavy beat, he doesn't move, as if testing the absolute limits of my command.

Then, the last vestiges of his control snap.

He crosses the room in three strides, not stopping, not hesitating, a force of nature finally unleashed. His wet body slams onto the bed, trapping me beneath the heavy, solid weight of him. I gasp, not from surprise, but from the sheer, overwhelming rush of pure physical connection.

"Leaving me alone in the shower, were you?" he growls, the question a low, playful menace. "That, little bakery witch, is a lesson you're about to learn I will not tolerate."

"You want me to claim you," he rasps, the words a rough promise against my ear as his mouth finds the sensitive curve of my neck. "Consider it done. And consider this the first day of your training."

His hands tangle in my hair, anchoring me, making the movement possessive, absolute. The kiss is deep and immediate, fueled by every piece of tension, fear, and desperate wanting we've collected since the day we met. My fingers finally find the heavy, damp mass of his wings, tracing the powerful, muscled curve of his shoulders, and the raw, tangible *him* floods my senses.

My magic surges in a desperate, eager response, mirroring the urgency of his kiss. It pours out of me, mixing with his—not in a gentle swirl, but a sudden, violent, beautiful fusion that makes the air crackle with heat.

He pulls back, his chest rising and falling, eyes blown wide and dark, still breathing raggedly. "Francesca," he says, the name a worship, a warning.

Then his mouth is on my throat, a warm, wet line of kisses trailing down the column of my neck, over my collarbone, and into the curve between my breasts. I gasp, a sound that's half pleasure, half protest.

"Hold on," I manage, reaching up to cup his jaw, trying to tilt his face back up to mine. "We can't be..."

He ignores me, a low growl rumbling in his chest. His hand shoots out, catching both of my wrists and pinning them against the silk sheets above my head. His grip is firm, inescapable.

"Shh," he murmurs, his voice rough. His other hand slides down, fingers finding the juncture of my thighs, slipping underneath to tease the sensitive skin hidden there. A sharp spike of electricity jolts through me, stealing the breath right out of my lungs.

A tremor runs through me, my back bowing toward him without thought, the entire world collapsing into the way he kisses me and the sure, grounding heat of his hand. His tongue is hot and wet, demanding a response my body is eager to give, and the subtle friction where his fingers tease my inner thigh builds a delicious tension low in my belly. It's an electric current, growing stronger with every slow brush of his thumb. My breath hitches again as he darkens the kiss, nipping softly at my lower lip.

The sensation intensifies, coiling tighter and tighter until I'm desperate for more. Just as I feel like I might combust, his hand moves again. He shifts his weight slightly, leaning back just enough to allow his index finger to slide easily, wetly inside me. A gasp rips from my throat, and I hear him groan, a low, guttural sound against my mouth. At the same moment, his mouth leaves mine, traveling down to latch onto my nipple, sucking and nipping with a gentle ferocity that makes my knees tremble. The double assault—the pressure and friction inside me coupled with the exquisite, sharp pull on my breast—is too much. My back bows further, and I cry out his name, a breathless, pleading sound.

I reach inward, sliding into the pulse of my magic—hot, insistent, already tuned to him. The moment I let it rise, it curls around his wrist where he's pinning my hands above my head, loosening his grip with a force that's gentle but undeniable. The energy slips between us like warm pressure, coaxing his fingers open before he realizes what I'm doing.

His eyes widen in surprise, but he barely has time to draw breath.

I push up from beneath him, twist, and use the momentum of the magic still humming through me to roll us in a single, fluid motion. His back hits the mattress with a low sound—half startled, half something else entirely—and I follow him down, settling astride his hips before he can reclaim the advantage.

Heat rushes between us, unmistakable, impossible to ignore. His hands come up instinctively, not to stop me, but to brace around my waist as if he's trying to decide whether to pull me closer or keep himself from doing exactly that.

His breath catches beneath me.

Mine shudders in answer.

The magic hums approvingly under my skin, a warm, reckless pressure urging me forward as I look down at him—flushed, breathless.

"Show me," I breathe. "Show me what you've been fighting."

Chapter 39

Sayer

I take her invitation like a soldier taking a final command. I lean forward, pressing up onto my hands braced on the mattress, and she hovers over my hard cock, her shadow falling across my skin. I reach up and curl my fingers around her hips, pulling her down slowly, carefully, until the tip of me brushes her wet heat.

I shift my weight, positioning myself between her legs, and the pressure of my body is an exquisite agony I welcome completely. I dip my head, looking deep into her eyes, and I see the last threads of my celestial restraint finally dissolve into pure, consuming passion.

Instead of pushing in, I let out a low groan and use the moment of friction to shift my weight entirely. My arms shoot out, catching the back of her thighs, and I pull, flipping her over so smoothly that she barely has time to gasp. One moment she's astride me; the next, she is pinned beneath my heavy, wet body, spread across the damp sheets.

I settle between her legs, pushing the tips of my wings just against the fabric of the sheet to anchor my position. She is breathless, stunned by the sudden, aggressive reversal, but her hands are already coming up to tangle in my hair. The hunger in her eyes is blinding.

I drive forward, an agonizingly slow, long slide of heat and friction. She cries out, arching up to meet the sudden, overwhelming fullness. It's tight, perfectly so, a profound, aching completion that steals the air from my lungs and the thoughts from my mind. The sensation is monumental, shattering every expectation I ever had of what a match—what *she*—feels like.

The connection is immediate, terrifying, and consuming. Our magic doesn't just blend; it ignites, a shared, catastrophic flare that pulses through the room. She clings to me, her nails digging into the damp skin of my back, eyes closed against the pure intensity of it.

I pull back—just a few inches—then thrust forward again, the movement deeper, more aggressive. The rhythm I find is desperate and primal, driving us higher, faster, pushing us both to the absolute edge of control. I hear her gasp my name, a broken sound torn from her throat.

"Mine," I growl, the word raw and possessive, driven out of me on a wave of pure need. "You are mine."

Her body answers the command, clenching around me, pulling me deeper into a space that feels engineered for this moment. I can feel the curse, the fear, the years of waiting, all of it dissolving under the relentless, overwhelming pressure of the bond finally completing.

This isn't just sex; it's a binding. It's the catastrophic fusion of two destinies that should never have been kept apart.

I shift one final time, a deep, earth-shaking thrust that sends her flying over the edge.

Her body convulses, an uncontrolled, shuddering wave that drags a scream from her throat. And then the magic comes. It bursts outward, a devastating, cleansing wave of pure ember-gold energy that slams against the walls, shattering the carefully placed wards holding us prisoner.

The bed shudders violently beneath us.

I follow an instant later, a low, guttural roar torn from my chest as I collapse against her, my breath hot on her neck. The power I release is colossal, a wave of warm, dark celestial energy that pours into her, sealing the break, locking the bond into place.

For a long time, we simply lie here, our bodies slick with sweat and water, our hearts hammering against each other, the air still thick with the residue of spent power. The broken ward-sigil hums faintly behind us—silent, finally, but irrevocably shattered.

I don't need to ask. I don't need to speak. We chose. And in choosing, we broke free.

Francesca's body stills beneath me, a deep, satisfied tremor running through her. The ember-gold light of her power recedes, sinking back under her skin, but the heat remains, a heavy, blissful weight that pins me to the mattress. I shift my weight, trying to ease the pressure on her, but my muscles refuse to cooperate. I am spent—not just physically, but magically, utterly undone by the force of the bond finally snapping into place.

My breath is ragged, hot against the damp skin of her neck. I press my face into the curve of her shoulder, inhaling the scent of her—soap, steam, and the sharp, clean smell of pure Bellamy magic. It's intoxicating, grounding, and absolute.

The silence is profound, broken only by the hitching of her breath and the frantic, echoing rhythm of our combined heartbeats.

"Sayer," she finally whispers, the sound muffled against the damp sheets. Her voice is raw, heavy with exhaustion and something that sounds profoundly new.

"I'm here," I manage, the words thick and husky. I lift my head just enough to look at her. Her eyes are still closed, her lashes dark against her flushed cheeks. She looks less like a witch who survived a kidnapping and more like a woman who just survived an earthquake—shaken, rearranged, and utterly magnificent.

She opens her eyes, and the connection snaps between us—not the painful magnetic pull of before, but a soft, warm certainty that settles deep in my chest. Her magic is everywhere now, woven into the sheets, clinging to my skin, nestled seamlessly within my own celestial power. It feels like coming home to a place I didn't know I was searching for.

A slow, utterly satisfied smile curls the corner of her mouth. She lifts a hand—slowly, as if it weighs a hundred pounds—and brushes the sweat-damp hair from my forehead.

"You shattered the wards," she murmurs, her voice filled with a mixture of disbelief and awe.

The room is still warm with the echo of everything we just did, our breathing finally slowing back into something human again. I roll onto my side and gather her in, pulling her tight against the length of my body. She fits there as if she was made for that space, soft and warm and trembling in the way that says she hasn't quite come down from the bond settling inside her. My wing curves around her on instinct, protective and sure, forming a cocoon neither of us seems inclined to break.

"You did that," I murmur against her hair, brushing a kiss there before I can stop myself. "Little bakery witch, that was all you."

She shifts closer, cheek pressed to my chest, her smile brushing against my skin like a secret she's choosing to share only with me. "We did it," she murmurs, voice lazy and satisfied. "And it was... *loud*."

A low laugh escapes me, one I'm too tired to hide. "That was fifteen years of denial detonating all at once." I trace the curve of her spine, feeling the shimmer of her magic quiet itself under my palm. "And the curse," I add, voice softer as the truth settles between us. "It's gone. I can feel it. Your magic isn't fighting itself anymore. It's... whole."

That realization knocks something loose in me — joy, awe, relief I don't quite know how to name. I shift up onto my elbow so I can see her face, framed in the faint glow of the broken ward at the door. "How do you feel?"

She drags her fingertips across my chest, drawing slow, idle lines that feel far more intimate than anything explicit could. Her smile curves knowingly. "Lighter than I've felt in years. And warm. Everywhere." Her eyes flick up to mine. "You?"

"Like I just ran a celestial marathon after a fifteen-year break," I admit, brushing my thumb along her jaw. "And like I'm finally breathing after a lifetime of holding my breath."

She laughs at that — soft, genuine, delighted — and the sound hits me like a spell I didn't bother resisting.

A more serious note slips into her voice as she shifts just enough to look at me fully. "So... now that we've survived a kidnapping, broken a ritual chamber, shattered half of Leona's security wards, and finally stopped lying to ourselves... what happens next?"

My gaze drifts to the door, where the ward flickers in weak protest, then back to the woman curled in my arms, her magic twined with mine in a way that feels irrevocable.

"Next," I say, letting the certainty settle deep in my voice, "we finish the season. We do it together. And we make sure no one—Council, Cupids, Thorns, or anyone else—ever gets their hands on you without going through me first."

Her fingers curl at my chest, not possessive, not afraid — just sure.

For the first time in fifteen years, the constant urge to bolt, to detach, to outrun the inevitable finally quiets. I'm not bracing for impact, not cataloging escape routes, not looking for the nearest door. The bond isn't something I'm fleeing from. The curse no longer hangs over us like a threat waiting to strike. And her—this woman curled against me, warm and steady and impossibly real—is no longer the thing I fear wanting.

She's the thing I choose.

At some point the heat between us softens, the adrenaline fades, and the quiet rolls in like a warm tide. Her breathing evens out first, her cheek resting on my chest, one hand curled just above my heart. I let my eyes close, only meaning to drift for a moment, but her magic settles over me like a blanket and pulls me under with her.

We sleep.

Not the restless kind I've grown used to — the kind where your body never quite relaxes because your mind is waiting for something to go wrong. This is the opposite. Warm. Heavy. Deep. The kind of sleep that feels earned.

When I finally blink awake, the room is different. Dimmer. Quiet enough that I can hear her breathing, the slow rise and fall of her ribs under my arm. My wing is still wrapped around her, feathers tangled in her hair. She stirs, stretching in a languid little arc that sends a ripple of awareness through me.

Her eyes flutter open, hazy and soft. "How long were we out?"

I check the faint light spilling through the drawn curtains. "Long enough that we're probably missing three meals and a dozen concerned texts."

Her stomach answers before she does — a low, unmistakable growl that pulls a laugh out of me. Mine echoes it a second later. She groans and presses her face into my chest as if that might hide the sound.

"No judgment," I assure her. "Considering what we've been through, hunger seems like the most reasonable response."

She lifts her head, hair tousled, cheeks flushed in a way that should not be legal this soon after waking. "We should probably eat before Leona breaks the door down."

"We should definitely eat," I agree, reluctantly unwrapping my wing from around her. The absence of her against me feels immediate, like my body hasn't caught up to the fact that we're moving yet.

We move slowly, limbs still unsteady, a quiet, half-awake humor slipping between us as we gather ourselves. She reaches for the clothes Leona left for her while I pull on mine, neither of us rushing, neither of us pretending this is anything other than easy. There's no awkwardness, no need to look away—just a shared, surprising calm that settles in as we dress, as natural and unremarkable as if we've done this a hundred times before.

When we're finally dressed, she pauses by the door, her hand brushing mine.

"You ready?" she murmurs.

"For food?" I say. "Absolutely."

She rolls her eyes, but the smile she gives me could unravel nations. I reach for the doorknob, the last strands of the broken ward humming faintly against my palm as if it's judging our timing.

"Let's go face whatever disaster is waiting on the other side," I say.

Francesca exhales, straightens, and slips her fingers into mine with a calm certainty that settles somewhere deep in my chest. Together, we step out.

Chapter 40

Francesca

By the time Sayer and I make it down the hallway, my hair is still drying in loose waves down my back, and the borrowed shirt of his I threw on is soft enough to make me want to curl right back into the bed we escaped. The house is warm with the unmistakable smell of cinnamon, toasted bread, and something savory that makes my stomach tighten with a very unromantic growl.

We step into the kitchen together, and the moment we cross the threshold, Leona looks up from the stove with the slowest, most knowing raise of her eyebrows I've ever witnessed. Jackson, seated at the table with a mug halfway to his mouth, freezes as if we've walked in carrying a live grenade instead of ourselves.

Neither of them speaks at first. They simply look at us—at our joined hands, at the faint glow still clinging to my skin, at Sayer's wing that isn't even pretending to fold properly—then back at the steaming platters spread across the table: fresh biscuits, scrambled eggs with herbs, glazed ham slices, fruit, and something that looks suspiciously like Leona's attempt at waffles.

She taps her spatula against the skillet. "Well. Good morning, or afternoon, or whatever part of the day you two decided to rejoin the living. Sit before the food gets cold."

Jackson gives a slow, stunned exhale and sets his mug down. "You know, Leo, I thought the magic spike earlier was just the house being dramatic. Turns out it was... other things."

Leona cuts him a sharp look. "Jackson."

"What? I'm not judging. I'm impressed. That was enough magical output to knock out half the neighborhood grid if we weren't warded."

I feel my face heat immediately, and Sayer clears his throat like he's attempting to mask a laugh. His hand squeezes mine in a way that makes my pulse flutter all over again.

Leona finally abandons her skillet, wiping her hands on a towel as she steps closer, giving me an evaluative sweep from head to toe. "You're glowing," she announces, not as a compliment but as a clinical observation. "That's either the bond settling or the curse evaporating. Either way, congratulations, I suppose. Also, stay hydrated. Magical exhaustion looks flattering on exactly no one."

"Leo," Jackson says, leaning back with a grin, "let the woman breathe for five seconds."

She ignores him completely, turning her attention to Sayer. "You look worse."

He lifts a brow. "Thank you."

"That was not a compliment," she deadpans. "You're running on fumes. Eat something before you face-plant. Preferably protein. The waffles are mine and therefore questionable."

"Hey," Jackson says, "they're not that bad."

"You didn't swallow," she fires back. "I saw you spit it in the sink."

He shrugs without shame. "I value my life."

I can't help it—the laugh escapes before I can swallow it, and both of them soften in a way that makes my chest warm. Leona gestures emphatically at the table.

"Sit. Now. Before your bond starts short-circuiting the salt-shaker."

Sayer nudges me gently toward the closest chair, pulling it out before settling beside me. The heat from the food hits me all at once—fresh biscuits still steaming, the buttery scent of scrambled eggs, the fruity sweetness rising from the platter in the center. My stomach clenches with an audible growl that has Jackson raising both brows in appreciation.

"There it is," he says, reaching for a bowl. "The sound of a curse breaking. And hunger returning with vengeance."

Leona snorts. "The sound of two idiots who didn't eat for nearly a day because they were too busy—" she gestures vaguely, mercifully skipping the details—"recalibrating their futures."

Sayer shoots her a narrow look. "You know, most people would open with 'glad you're alive.'"

"Oh, I assume you're alive," she replies, waving a dismissive hand. "The amount of magical combustion you two set off could've powered a small city. Death was the least likely outcome."

Jackson chimes in with a grin, "She's not wrong. I haven't felt a magical signature like that since the underworld summit of '17."

I bury my face in my hands. "Please stop talking."

"No promises," Leona singsongs, sliding a plate in front of me. "Eat. Then drink water. Then explain whether we need to reinforce the upstairs ward before one of you sneezes and accidentally opens a portal."

"Leona," Jackson says gently, "let them eat in peace."

She pauses... then sighs with exaggerated restraint. "Fine. Fifteen minutes. Then questions."

I meet Sayer's gaze, and he gives me a soft, private smile that makes my chest tighten in ways I'm not prepared to unpack yet. His knee brushes mine under the table, just barely, but enough to send a ripple of warmth through me.

For the first time in years, my magic feels settled. Balanced. Home.

Leona clears her throat loudly enough to break the moment. "If you two start glowing again at the table, I'm kicking you out."

Jackson laughs. "She's kidding."

"She is not," I whisper.

"No," Sayer agrees, grabbing my hand under the table with a quiet, warm certainty, "she absolutely isn't."

But hunger wins over embarrassment, and the four of us settle around the table—teasing, bickering, eating—and for the first time in a long time, the knot in my chest finally loosens. The food is hot and comforting, the kitchen humming with the kind of familiar noise that makes the world feel survivable again. Jackson keeps trying to sneak more fruit onto Sayer's plate, Leona keeps pretending she isn't watching our every shared glance like she's annotating it in her mental ledger, and Sayer keeps brushing his knee against mine under the table like he can't quite stop reaching for me even when he's pretending to focus on breakfast.

When we're finished, Leona shoos us out with the efficiency of someone clearing a battlefield. "Go," she insists, waving a dish towel like a conductor directing an orchestra. "Get out of here before one of you starts glowing again and the curtains catch fire. And hydrate. And don't do anything catastrophic until I run diagnostic scans on the upstairs ward."

Jackson leans against the counter, trying—and failing—to hide his grin. "Translation: she's happy for you. Now leave before she starts crying."

"I don't cry," Leona snaps, immediately blinking faster than necessary. "Ever."

I squeeze her arm on the way out anyway. She pretends she didn't like it.

The moment we step out onto the porch, the cool air hits my cheeks, a welcome contrast to the warmth still humming under my skin. The house door clicks shut behind us, and Sayer's fingers slip naturally between mine, his thumb brushing once along the back of my hand as if it's a habit he's had for years instead of hours.

Jackson parked Sayer's car at the curb—sleek, familiar, a grounding reminder that the world didn't actually stop while everything between us tilted on its axis. Sayer opens the passenger door for me, and I slide in with a soft exhale, feeling the last threads of magic settle quietly in my chest.

As soon as I'm buckled, my phone vibrates against my thigh with all the fury of a device that has been neglected far too long. When I unlock the screen, the notifications pour up in a dizzying cascade—missed calls, texts, group chat pings piling on top of each other until I lose track of which alert belongs to which emergency.

Sayer glances over as he starts the engine. "That bad?"

"Worse," I mutter, scrolling. "I think my sisters collectively broke the chat. And my parents tried to FaceTime me three times. I'm afraid to open any of this."

He smiles in that quiet, amused way he does when he's trying not to push. "You don't have to read everything now."

"No. But I need to say something." I tap into the family thread, the unread messages filling the screen in frantic blocks of text—WHERE ARE YOU, ARE YOU SAFE, WHY DID THE WARDS FLARE, CALL US IMMEDIATELY, FRANCESCA ANTOINETTE BELLAMY PICK UP YOUR PHONE.

I wince and type out a quick reply.

I'm okay. Long story. Meeting you all at the Bellamy house in an hour. Please don't panic.

Within seconds the typing bubbles appear, then disappear, then appear again, like the entire family is trying to answer at once and collectively losing the battle with sentence formation. I lock the phone before I can be tempted to read the responses.

Sayer puts the car in drive and pulls away from the curb. "One hour?"

"They need time to… brace themselves," I say, smoothing a hand over my knee. "And I need to look like I haven't been through a magical hurricane."

He shoots me a sidelong look that's equal parts warm and devastating. "You look perfect."

"That's your bond-induced delirium talking."

"No," he says with a quiet conviction that makes my stomach flip. "That's me."

I clear my throat before I melt entirely. "We should change. Separately. Quickly."

"Agreed."

His apartment building is just across the street from mine, so he drops me at the entrance before circling around to his. I take the elevator up to my place, shedding borrowed clothes on the way to the bathroom and pulling myself together with the efficiency of someone accustomed to magical crisis management.

A soft sweater, jeans, boots. Hair brushed into order. Lip balm instead of lipstick. Nothing dramatic. Just enough to say I'm alive and not currently exploding.

When I step into the hallway again, Sayer is waiting by the elevator, freshly showered and wearing a crisp shirt that absolutely should not look as good on him as it does. He smooths his collar once, more out of nerves than necessity.

"You're nervous," I tease.

His answer is immediate. "Your family terrifies me."

"That's because they care," I say, slipping my hand into his. "And because they don't believe in subtlety."

"That," he sighs, "is what terrifies me."

"Ready?"

He meets my eyes—steady, earnest, a little overwhelmed but not backing away. "For them? No. For you? Absolutely."

And just like that, the last bit of dread I didn't realize I was carrying eases into something warm and certain.

We head for the car together, fingers twined, magic quiet and content between us.

Chapter 41

Sayer

The Bellamy house doesn't wait for us to knock.

We barely make it up the front steps before the door swings open with enough force to rattle the hinge, and suddenly I'm face-to-face with an entire coven's worth of very determined women. Francesca's sisters fill the doorway in a wall of knitted cardigans, sharp eyes, and barely contained panic—Daphne, Juniper, Cassia—and behind them is a chorus of magic so strong it hums across my skin like static.

"Finally," Daphne says, grabbing Francesca's hand like she's checking for a pulse. "Do you know how many times we had to reset the wards because of you?"

Juniper circles around me, gaze calm but assessing, like she's conducting a magical MRI. "She looks intact. Breathing, conscious, no glowing runes. Good."

Cassia pushes her glasses up with unsettling precision. "You're an hour late."

"We said an hour," Francesca reminds her.

"And then we worried for exactly sixty minutes," Cassia replies. "Which makes you late."

Before I can decide whether speaking is a wise idea, someone else barrels into the entryway—her mother, Nyla Bellamy, a smaller but infinitely more terrifying version of her children. She takes one sweeping look at Francesca, then at me, and the expression that crosses her face makes me wish I had worn armor instead of a button-down.

"You," she says, pointing at me like she's selecting a target. "Inside."

I step forward because my self-preservation instincts apparently malfunction around this family. The instant my foot crosses the threshold, the wards pulse again, reading me, testing me, questioning whether a Cupid—former Cupid, technically—has any business in this house.

Nyla narrows her eyes. "You set off every bell in this place the last fifteen years, Valentine. The wards remember."

"I'm... aware," I say carefully.

Daphne snorts. "He's polite. That's suspicious."

Juniper tilts her head at me, gaze soft but uncomfortably knowing. "And he's bonded."

Cassia freezes. "Bonded?"

Every face swings toward Francesca.

Francesca lifts her hands like she's trying to calm a room full of magical cats. "We were going to explain. Just—not in the doorway. Or the front yard. Or before food."

Nyla crosses her arms. "Explain now."

She glances at me, and I can see the moment her courage flicks like a steady flame. So I do what I can—I step closer, my hand brushing the small of her back, grounding both of us in the truth we can't put off anymore.

"We're matched," I say, voice steady. "Fully."

Silence drops.

Heavy. Absolute. Wards vibrating with interest.

Then Daphne gasps so loudly I'm surprised glass doesn't crack. "I knew it. I *knew* it. Look at them—look at the way their auras are woven. That's not a match, that's—"

"A bond," Juniper finishes softly.

Cassia is already pulling a notebook out of nowhere. "I need timestamps, magical fluctuations, environmental triggers, and emotional context."

Nyla just exhales, a long, tired sound that somehow feels like relief wrapped in accusation. "I should have known the universe would send *you* back into this mess."

"Mom," Francesca groans.

But Nyla isn't looking at her—she's looking at me, eyes sharp but not unkind. "You'd better come inside, Sayer Valentine. There's food, and questions, and absolutely nowhere for you to hide."

Francesca threads her fingers through mine, her smile small but certain.

"Welcome to the family," she murmurs under her breath.

My heart does something stupid and traitorous in my chest.

The moment Francesca's mother releases us from the doorway bottleneck, the house dissolves into motion. Voices overlap—questions, exclamations, accusations, at least two demands for explanations—while cousins dart through the hall like magically enhanced projectiles. Someone's familiar hisses from the banister. A ward hums disapprovingly overhead.

She squeezes my hand once, a tiny warning and a tiny reassurance all at once, before tugging me toward the dining room.

The noise doesn't lessen. It concentrates.

Every Bellamy spouse—and her father—waits around the long oak table like a tribunal. Plates of food line the center in cozy, deceptive abundance: roasted vegetables, layered casseroles, warm bread, charmed honey butter that glows faintly gold. The kind of spread that would lull a lesser man into false comfort.

Not me.

Not with all of them lifting their heads at once to assess the intruder their daughters and wives herded into the room.

Francesca's dad rises first. Broad-shouldered. Quiet. The kind of man whose stare doesn't need volume to hit like a hammer. He gives Francesca a nod—warm, relieved—and then turns that gaze on me.

"Valentine," he says, as if tasting the name for structural integrity.

I incline my head. "Sir."

Across the table, Daphne's husband lifts a brow. Juniper's waves a greeting with his fork. Cassia's wife straightens in a way that reads like she's drafting an internal report on me.

Francesca clears her throat pointedly—once, loudly—to stop the room from dissecting me like a specimen.

"We're sitting," she announces. "Everyone can stare less aggressively once we're seated."

Her dad snorts. "No promises."

Chairs scrape back. I'm directed to the seat beside her—close enough for her knee to brush mine under the table. The room seems to collectively lean in, subtle as a tidal wave. Her mother appears with a pitcher of something citrusy. "Eat," she commands, in that tone mothers use when they're pretending this isn't a test.

Francesca murmurs thanks. I do the same.

But the moment plates are filled and forks lifted, every Bellamy at the table turns their attention to me with the precision of trained interrogators.

"So," Daphne's husband says lightly, "how long have you two been... involved?"

"Are you living together now?" Juniper's asks, too casually.

Cassia's wife adjusts her glasses. "Should we be expecting magical bond stabilization symptoms? I can run projections."

Francesca groans into her hands. "*Please* stop talking."

But her father just folds his arms. "I want to know what your intentions are with my daughter."

Six pairs of eyes pin me like a butterfly in a display case.

Francesca stiffens beside me.

I lay my hand on her knee—reassuring, steady—and meet her father's gaze head-on.

And just as I open my mouth to answer, half the wards in the house flare in overlapping tones—recognition, approval, annoyance—and everyone at the table goes still.

Francesca blinks at the nearest glowing sigil. "Oh no."

Her mother's eyes widen. "Oh yes."

Juniper's husband whistles. "Well. That answers at least three questions."

And every Bellamy in the room turns toward me with brand-new interest.

The moment the women drag Francesca out of the dining room—Daphne gripping one arm, Juniper shepherding from behind, Cassia muttering something about "unstable magical frequencies"—the house falls into a dense, watchful quiet. The door swings shut, muffling the rising storm of sisterly diagnostics, leaving only four others at the table.

Her father.

Three in-laws.

And me.

Every set of eyes settles on me with the polite intensity of a firing squad evaluating whether the target is worth the ammunition. The table, still laden with food, suddenly feels less like a family meal and more like a tribunal.

Her father leans back in his chair, arms crossed, gaze steady and assessing. "Alright," he says. "Let's talk."

There's no point dodging it. Not anymore.

"I love your daughter," I say simply, because anything less would be cowardice. "And I don't want to spend another second pretending otherwise. I've spent fifteen years holding myself at a distance I never should've kept."

Juniper's husband tilts his head, studying me like a man recognizing sincerity and weighing it against past stupidity. Cassia's wife sits straighter, eyes narrowing not with hostility but with calculation. Daphne's husband nods once, as if confirming a theory he's been holding since the moment I walked in.

But it's her father whose opinion matters.

He doesn't blink. Doesn't shift. Doesn't give me the emotional courtesy of easing the moment.

"And what exactly are your intentions toward Francesca?" he asks.

I meet his stare without flinching. "I want your blessing to propose to her. Tonight. When she walks back into this room."

The air tightens, every man going still.

I continue, steady and unshaken, "The ring is in my pocket. I brought it because I'm not leaving here uncertain. And if she says yes, I'd like your family's permission to hold the wedding at your Valentine's Ball."

Daphne's husband exhales a soft "well damn." Juniper's husband scrubs a hand over his jaw, half impressed, half startled. Cassia's wife mutters something about needing to revise the entire evening's timeline.

Her father doesn't react at all—not at first. He studies me the way warriors study a blade before deciding whether it will hold under pressure. There's nothing soft in his evaluation; only the fierce, unwavering love of a man who has protected his daughter her entire life.

"Are you certain?" he asks quietly, every word deliberate. "Not because the bond forced clarity. Not because the curse lifted. Because you choose her."

"I choose her," I answer. "Before the bond. After the bond. With the bond broken or blazing. I choose her."

A long moment passes—long enough for my heartbeat to feel like it's echoing through the walls.

Finally, her father nods once. Slow. Decisive.

"Then you have my blessing," he says. "And my expectations."

He rises, extends his hand across the table.

I stand to meet it.

His grip is firm, steady, and unmistakably a warning wrapped in approval. "You break her heart," he murmurs, "and I'll break your wings."

"Understood," I reply.

He releases my hand, and the tension in the room shifts—not gone, but changed. No longer suspicion. No longer defense.

Readiness.

Because the next time the kitchen door opens, they all know exactly what's waiting to happen.

The moment her father releases my hand, the room exhales—just a little—but the tension doesn't leave me. Not when I can feel the ring sitting almost painfully heavy in my pocket. Not when every footstep in the hallway sharpens something in my chest.

They settle, though none of them really relax. Her father sits again, posture upright, eyes fixed on the doorway as if he already senses the night shifting in ways even Bellamy wards can't track.

Then the first footsteps approach.

Her mother sweeps into the room, her expression somewhere between curiosity and mild suspicion—Bellamy trademarks. She takes in the suddenly composed men, the untouched food, the faint shimmer still clinging to the air where wards flared.

"What," she asks, hands on her hips, "is going on in here?"

Four sets of eyes slide to me. I straighten instinctively.

"Just talking," Francesca's dad says.

She gives him a look that suggests she believes exactly none of that. Her gaze skips to me, lingers just long enough for my heartbeat to trip, then she nods once as if mentally filing the reaction away for later interrogation.

Before I can speak, another set of footsteps shuffles in—light, impatient, unmistakably Daphne. She steps through the doorway still holding a half-dissolved diagnostic crystal, blinking as the ambient magic of the dining room flickers at her arrival.

"Okay," she says, scanning the room. "Why does it feel like you all had a meeting about something you shouldn't have had a meeting about?"

Juniper appears next, wrapped in that calm, cozy aura she always carries—though tonight it's edged with curiosity sharp enough to cut glass. "Mom said you're all acting weird," she says, leaning lightly against her husband's chair. "I see she wasn't exaggerating."

Cassia enters last of the three sisters who aren't Francesca, already flipping through a notebook filled with color-coded symbols and half-finished magical readings. "We need to talk about her energy output," she announces to the room, then pauses as she notices the tension humming under the surface. "Why do you all look like you're waiting for a bomb to go off?"

My pulse stutters.

Because I am waiting.

Not for a bomb.

For her.

Then the hallway goes quiet—too quiet—and a soft, steady tread moves toward the door. Every Bellamy at the table shifts, almost imperceptibly, like a flock sensing the wind change.

I'm on my feet before I register moving. And then she appears.

Francesca steps into the doorway, framed by the warm lights of her childhood home, cheeks faintly flushed from whatever magical evaluations her sisters subjected her to. Her hair has loosened around her face, eyes bright and searching, and the moment she sees me, something softens in her expression—just enough to knock the breath from my lungs.

The room starts to rise around us—questions, exclamations, another ward flickering—but it all fades beneath the single, quiet truth echoing through me:

This is the moment.

The moment her father blessed.

The moment I've carried in my pocket.

The moment I've waited fifteen years to stop running from.

And as she crosses the threshold back into the dining room, everything else falls away.

Chapter 42

Francesca

The hallway still hums faintly behind me when I step toward the dining room, the last remnants of the diagnostic spells trailing after me like stubborn glitter. My sisters peeled off one by one—Daphne muttering about "energetic spikes," Juniper fussing with a charm on my wrist, Cassia triple-checking her notes before declaring me "stable enough to rejoin the civilians."

I'm not sure any of that makes me feel better.

But none of it compares to the moment I cross the threshold back into the dining room.

Every head turns.

The shift is subtle, but it's unmistakable—the air changes. My dad and the spouses straighten. My sisters pause mid-step. Even my mother stills, her hands folded in front of her like she's bracing for an announcement she hasn't been warned about.

And then there's Sayer.

He's standing.

Not casually. Not politely. Standing like he lost the ability to sit the second I reappeared in the doorway.

His eyes find mine instantly, and something warm and impossibly familiar curls low in my stomach. There's a steadiness in his expression that wasn't there before, a quiet gravity that pulls me forward without a single word being spoken.

I manage a small smile—awkward, nervous, hopeful? I don't even know. "I'm back," I say, because it's the only thing that comes out.

Juniper nudges Daphne with her elbow. Cassia closes her notebook with a meaningful snap. My father folds his hands over his stomach like he's settling in for whatever comes next. The room is too quiet. Too expectant.

Something is wrong.

Or right.

Or both.

Sayer steps around the table as if moving through water, slow but certain, the space between us shrinking with each breath. He stops a few feet away, the glow of the chandelier catching the lines of his face, the faint silver threaded through his hair, the wings that stay politely tucked out of sight but somehow still presence the entire room.

"Francesca," he says, and my heart stumbles. Not because of the name, but because his voice sounds steady in a way that makes my pulse trip over itself.

Everyone is watching.

Everyone.

I should be anxious. I should be embarrassed. I should feel like a bug under a crystal dome.

Instead, all I feel is him.

And the quiet, trembling awareness that something is about to happen.

Something big.

"I have something I need to say," he continues, and suddenly my knees consider mutiny. "To you. And I'd like to say it with your family here. If that's alright?"

My mother covers her mouth with her fingers, eyes welling like someone just whispered the climax of her favorite romance novel directly into her ear. Daphne grabs Juniper's arm so hard Juniper yelps. Cassia leans forward, elbows on the table, already analyzing the moment in real time.

"Sayer," I whisper, caught between wonder and panic, "what are you—"

He reaches into his pocket.

And the room collectively inhales.

My breath stops.

My magic flares so sharply it tingles across my palms, gathering instinctively, overflowing into the air. Every ward in the house hums in sympathetic response. Even the chandelier brightens, traitorous thing.

Oh gods.

Oh gods.

He steps closer.

And kneels.

My heart nearly cracks open.

"Francesca Bellamy," he says, looking up at me with so much sincerity I feel it in my bones, "I've spent fifteen years running from something I never should have run from. And I'm done running."

The ring catches the light.

And so do my tears.

He holds the ring like it's something sacred—not because it's expensive, not because it's dramatic, but because it's mine. Because he chose it. Because he's choosing me.

And the world, for one suspended breath, stops spinning.

"Francesca," he says quietly, and the sound of my name in his voice feels like the gentlest unraveling, "I've loved you longer than I was willing to admit. I didn't know it was you I was avoiding. I didn't know it was you I was meant for. But the moment I realized... I never wanted distance again."

My throat tightens. My eyes burn.

I can't speak.

I can barely breathe.

He keeps going, steady as a vow. "You are the person I want beside me for every season. Every disaster. Every fight. Every ridiculous, chaotic thing that comes with your family and my wings and whatever the universe throws next." A flicker of humor warms his voice. "I want to be with you in every sense the bond offered us. Not because of destiny. Not because of magic. Because it's you."

My magic loosens inside my chest, warm and achingly calm. Not a surge. Not chaos. Just truth.

"I would like," he says, lifting the ring a little higher, "to marry you. With your family's blessing. And if you'll have me... to do it at your Valentine's Ball."

Somewhere behind him, Daphne sobs loud enough to scare a ghost. Juniper starts fanning herself with both hands. Cassia whispers, "I knew it," like she called bingo hours ago.

My father stands so abruptly his chair scrapes the floor. My mother presses both hands to her heart. Someone's familiar growls under the table, probably overwhelmed by the emotional pollution.

But all of it is background noise.

Because Sayer is still kneeling.

Still waiting.

Still looking at me like I'm a choice, not a cosmic obligation.

"Sayer," I whisper, trying to find words through the rush in my chest, "I—"

The rest doesn't make it out.

My magic gets there first.

It bursts outward—not violently, but in a soft, shimmering pulse that fills the room with warm gold and rose-tinted sparks, harmless but impossible to ignore. The chandelier flickers. Every Bellamy ward hums in approval. One of the bread baskets levitates three inches off the table like it's trying to clap.

Daphne shrieks, "SHE SAID YES MAGICALLY—SHE SAID YES!"

Juniper shoves her, "Let her speak!"

Cassia, already recording on her phone, murmurs, "This is excellent data."

And Sayer... Sayer looks up at me with the kind of smile that knocks the breath out of my lungs all over again.

I laugh through a tearful, breathless gasp and finally manage, "Yes. Yes, I'll marry you."

His exhale comes out like relief and devotion woven into one sound. He rises slowly, slides the ring onto my finger with hands that tremble just enough to make my heart twist, and the moment our skin touches, the bond surges—warm, steady, right.

The room erupts.

Daphne launches herself at me with a screech. Juniper pulls Sayer into a hug so fierce he stumbles. Cassia shouts instructions about arranging the wedding spreadsheet. My mother cries openly. My father wipes his eyes so discreetly he probably thinks no one saw. The men start offering congratulations with claps on Sayer's back that are a little too enthusiastic to be purely celebratory.

Through all of it, Sayer finds my hand again, lacing our fingers together as if the world is moving too fast and I'm the only thing he wants to hold onto.

"You have no idea," he murmurs, leaning close enough for only me to hear, "how long I've wanted this."

I lean into him, warm and breathless and overwhelmingly happy. "I think," I whisper, my forehead brushing his, "I finally do."

And with the Bellamy chaos swirling around us like the universe's own applause, I know—down to the very center of me—that this is exactly where we're supposed to be.

The Bellamy house dissolves into pandemonium the moment the ring settles on my finger. Plans erupt like fireworks—color palettes, guest lists, ward upgrades, ceremonial magic protocols—and I can practically see Cassia's brain rearranging itself around a new timeline. Every sister claims a role before I even catch my breath.

Somewhere between Juniper proposing floral illusions and Daphne debating whether a firework exit counts as "too on the nose," Sayer leans close, lips brushing my temple in a way that sends a shiver right down my spine.

"Come on," he murmurs softly, "before they start assigning seating charts by bloodline compatibility. We need air."

He's right. If we stay another ten minutes, I'll be wearing a veil and holding sample invitations.

I tug his hand and whisper to my family that we'll be back soon—hopefully before they accidentally summon a planning spirit. They barely hear me. Wedding fever has officially infected the living room.

The moment we step outside, the night air feels like medicine. Cool. Crisp. Blessedly quiet.

"You good?" Sayer asks, his thumb brushing the back of my hand.

"Honestly? I feel like I've been spun in the world's most enthusiastic cyclone."

"So... a Bellamy celebration mood."

"Precisely."

We head to the bakery, the sidewalks familiar beneath our steps. The bell over the door jingles as we enter, and the shift hits immediately—like the entire building has exhaled. Magic settles around us with a contented warmth, a low hum of peace rather than the volatile buzz it's lived with for the last fifteen years.

Harper notices first. She freezes mid-wipe of the counter, eyes narrowing, head tilted like she's listening to an invisible soundtrack.

"Fran?" she asks slowly. "Why does the bakery feel... zen? Did someone burn a cleansing bundle? Did Ellie finally smudge the mixers? Did we accidentally hire an exorcist?"

Before I can answer, Ellie pops her head out from the back. "Oh my gods, it feels calm. Like calm calm. Like 'the curse has been broken' calm."

It's then they spot my hand.

Harper's mouth drops open.

Ellie screams.

Miguel, standing behind the espresso bar, nearly drops a pitcher of milk. "Is that— is that an engagement ring? Is that a proposal ring? Did he—did you—WHEN—"

Harper reaches me first, grabbing my hand to inspect the ring with breathless awe. "I knew it! I KNEW something felt different today! Oh my gods, Francesca's this is huge! This is—wait." Her eyes widen dramatically. "Can I make the wedding cake? Please? Please tell me I can make the cake. I already have ideas. Tiered. Floral. Sparked. Maybe a floating layer. Possibly a flaming heart—"

"No flaming heart," Miguel interjects. "Not after last year's cheesecake incident."

Ellie swats him. "Let her dream."

I laugh, warm and light in a way I haven't felt in years. "Yes, Harper. You can make the cake."

Harper screams again.

Ellie also screams.

Miguel does not scream, but he definitely makes a noise that suggests emotional overload.

"We need supplies," Harper declares. "And meetings. And a list. And coffee. Lots of coffee."

"That's actually why we're here," I say. "We need nourishment for the planning committee. Whatever's hot. And caffeinated. And portable. I don't know if my sisters have stopped moving since the ring hit my hand."

Ellie is already packing a large pastry box. "I'll put in the good stuff. The stress-eating stuff."

Miguel pulls three large thermoses from under the counter. "Dark roast, caramel blend, and the witch-safe focus brew. Don't take the caps off until you're ready. I reinforced the spells."

Sayer watches the entire flurry of motion with a warm, dazed amusement, his fingers brushing the small of my back as if he's reminding himself I'm real.

"We'll bring everything back," he promises Harper as she loads the last thermos. "And we'll return in the morning."

Ellie nods fiercely. "You better. We're making a plan. Wedding week is serious business."

Miguel salutes us with a wooden spoon.

Harper clasps my hands, her expression softening just enough to make my eyes sting. "I'm so happy for you, Fran. Truly."

"Me too," I whisper, glancing at the man beside me.

When we finally step back into the night, arms full of coffee and pastries and the weight of an entire wedding on our shoulders, Sayer squeezes my hand. "One week," he says, voice low and warm. "We've got this."

My magic hums in agreement.

And for the first time in my life, the season doesn't feel like something to survive—

It feels like something to celebrate.

Chapter 43

Sayer

The morning of my wedding does not begin with champagne, vows, or anything resembling romance.

It begins at Cupid Headquarters.

Cold marble floors. Archways carved with too much symbolism. Magic drifting through the air like perfumed smoke—sweet, cloying, heavy with expectation. Of all the places I could be on the most important morning of my entire existence, this is the last one I would've chosen.

But ties must be cut cleanly.

Assignments must be closed.

And the Council needs its paperwork.

The main chamber hums as I step inside, the sound threaded with the kind of bureaucratic magic that makes my wings itch. A few junior cupids glance up, whispering to each other like they're not whispering loudly enough to be heard. They weren't here when I quit. They weren't here for the war. They only know the stories.

Stories travel faster than truth in this place.

Mara—efficient, sharp-eyed, and the only person in this building I trust to file things correctly—waits for me behind a polished desk stacked with glowing folios.

"You're late," she says without looking up, though her mouth curves just slightly at the corners. "Or early, depending on how one measures existential dread."

"It's wedding day," I reply. "I didn't realize dread was part of the recommended schedule."

She passes me a shimmering ledger. "You're getting married in a Bellamy house during the Season with a magically volatile bride. Dread isn't a scheduling suggestion, Sayer. It's a survival instinct."

I sign the first page anyway.

The paper pulses—the kind of pulse that marks the official close of a cupid's final assignment. Her name, glowing in soft gold, appears beside mine. Francesca Bellamy. Fully matched. Fully bonded. Full resolution.

A warmth moves through my chest, familiar and grounding. Not magic. Not obligation.

Her.

"Where's Lorian?" I ask, scanning the chamber.

Mara's jaw tightens. "Missing."

"Missing," I repeat, not even bothering to mask my irritation. "Convenient."

"He hasn't reported since the night of the ritual breach." She lowers her voice. "And the Council is pretending they aren't concerned, which means they're absolutely concerned."

I rub a hand over my jaw. "What's the working theory?"

"None they're willing to say aloud. I have three of my own, but all of them end with him skulking under a different identity or licking his wounds somewhere morally questionable."

"So the usual," I mutter.

She taps the ledger. "This part's yours. Initial here, sign there, promise you won't destroy any public infrastructure during your bonding surge—"

"I can't make that promise."

"—and affirm that you accept full completion of the Bellamy case."

I hesitate. Just long enough for her to notice.

"Cold feet?" she asks, arching a brow.

"No." The answer comes without effort. "Not even close."

I sign the last line.

The ledger seals itself with a faint shimmer, binding the magic, closing the case, and officially severing me from the work I once lived for. No more assignments. No more matchmaking. No more cosmic interference from a Council of people who hide their ambitions under the guise of neutrality.

It should feel heavy.

It doesn't.

Mara studies me for a long moment. "So that's it," she says softly. "You're free."

"I was free the moment I chose her."

She nods, something like approval softening her sharp edges. "Go. Before someone decides they need one more form."

I turn to leave, stopping only when she speaks again.

"Sayer?"

I glance back.

"Congratulations," she says. "Despite the chaos, the curses, and the political disasters... some matches really are worth the fight."

I don't have to answer. The smile that rises without my permission is answer enough.

Outside the HQ doors, the air is crisp and bright—the kind of winter morning that feels like a beginning rather than an ending. The bond hums under my skin, warm and sure, leading me back to the person who makes all of this matter.

One last complication remains.

Lorian.

And he will surface. Problems like him always do.

But not today.

Today is for her.

Today is for us.

I spread my wings, feeling them unfurl with a confidence that used to feel impossible, and take off toward home. Toward Francesca. Toward a future I'm finally done running from.

Jackson and Leona flank me like mismatched celestial bodyguards as we stand just outside the ballroom doors. The venue hums with layers of magic—Bellamy wards, celestial shielding, demonic ambiance that definitely wasn't in the original design. The music on the other side swells and quiets in alternating waves, as if the entire room is practicing breathing before the ceremony begins.

I'm not nervous.

I've survived wars, curses, cosmic politics, and Bellamy holiday baking season. I'm fine.

But apparently I look *unfine*, because Jackson eyes me the way a man watches a firecracker whose fuse has already been lit.

"You're breathing like you're about to argue in front of the High Court," he says, adjusting his tie. "Relax, boss. It's a wedding, not a cross-examination."

Leona snorts. "He would *absolutely* cross-examine if given the chance."

I roll my eyes. "I'm fine."

"That's exactly what people say right before they faint," Jackson replies.

"I am not going to faint."

Leona taps my chest—lightly, but with purpose. "Good. Because if you pass out before Francesca walks down that aisle, she will drag you upright using your wings as leverage, and I refuse to intervene. My dress is too nice for that level of chaos."

I try not to smile. It doesn't work.

They've been with me since the moment this mess started. Through every ritual, every scare, every stupid mistake I made trying to keep the bond at arm's length. And now, here they stand—Jackson in a perfectly tailored suit that probably cost more than my monthly rent, and Leona in a gown shimmering with spells subtle enough only witches notice—both looking at me like proud, exasperated siblings about to unleash me onto a future I should have claimed ages ago.

Jackson glances toward the grand double doors. "Lucifer's already inside. Pacing."

Leona shivers. "He said he's 'honored' to officiate. Do you know how unsettling it is to hear Lucifer sound sincere?"

"Yes," Jackson says dryly. "Because it means trouble is coming in a tailored suit."

I press my lips together. "He invited himself. What was I supposed to do? Tell the literal King of the Underworld that he's not allowed to conduct a wedding he claims to have invented the concept of?"

Leona deadpans, "Yes. Exactly that."

Jackson looks slightly worried. "He's definitely adding theatrics. I heard him practicing vows in the mirror. At one point the carpet smoked."

Leona groans. "We're all going to end up in someone's magical legal textbooks."

Despite everything, the knot in my chest loosens. The humor, the familiarity, the grounding presence of the people who've seen me at my worst and still showed up... it steadies me in a way no celestial pep talk ever could.

Jackson steps closer, adjusting my boutonniere with a quick, practiced flick. "Seriously though," he says quietly, "you're ready."

Leona nods, her expression softening. "And she's ready. You two have been orbiting each other for fifteen years. It's about time the universe caught up."

A breath I didn't realize I'd been holding finally releases. "Thank you. Both of you."

"No thanks needed," Jackson replies. "But we will accept cake."

Leona lifts a brow. "Second slice. Minimum. And I want the spicy frosting. Francesca better have included it."

"Pretty sure Harper threatened violence if she didn't," Jackson adds.

I laugh under my breath. "Cake is yours."

Jackson hears the shift in the music first. He straightens, glances at the doors, and nods once. "Showtime."

Leona squeezes my forearm. "Don't run," she says lightly, though her eyes are warm. "And don't let Lucifer monologue. He'll turn your five-minute ceremony into a full underworld sermon."

"I'll handle it," I promise.

She smirks. "You say that, but he *likes* you, Sayer. Which is concerning. And probably illegal."

Before I can respond, the ballroom doors begin to open—not fully, just enough for a flood of golden light and distant chatter to spill into the hallway.

Jackson pats my shoulder. "Walk in there like you're choosing her. Not fate. Not duty. Her."

Leona nudges me toward the entrance. "Go get your girl, Valentine."

I inhale, slow and steady, letting the warmth of the bond settle beneath my ribs, the certainty of it anchoring me more deeply than any magic ever has.

Wedding day.

Our day.

And whatever waits on the other side of those doors—Lucifer's theatrics included—I'm ready.

I step forward as the ballroom opens to greet me.

The ballroom is a universe unto itself.

Golden lanterns float in lazy spirals overhead, each one glowing with a soft pulse that responds to the magic in the room. The music shifts into something gentle, something anticipatory, and Lucifer—draped in a suit so sharply tailored it could probably cut someone—stands at the altar with the smug patience of a man who enjoys knowing he has the best view in the house.

Guests murmur. Wards hum. Children wiggle. Bellamys attempt to sit still and fail magnificently.

But none of that holds my attention.

My eyes stay locked on the staircase at the far end of the room—the one Maribel charmed earlier to "announce the bride's arrival with appropriate dramatic flair." I don't want to know what that means. I'm already on edge.

Then the lights shift.

Slowly. Deliberately. Like the room is taking a breath.

And when I turn back toward the staircase, every coherent thought slides out of my head.

Francesca steps into view like she was built from the same magic the lanterns were made of—soft, warm light catching along the crimson silk of her gown, each embroidered detail glimmering as if fire decided to learn subtlety. Her hair is swept back, curls falling in dark waves, and the moment her eyes lift and find mine, the entire ballroom fades into an unimportant blur.

Every inch she moves sends a quiet hum through the bond—steady, sure, welcoming. My wings tense beneath my suit jacket, fighting the urge to flare in instinctive recognition. I force them still. Barely.

She walks toward me, step by step, the gown shifting around her like living embers. People gasp. Someone cries. I don't pay attention to who. I only see her.

Lucifer clears his throat as she finally reaches the altar. "Do you want a moment to breathe, Sayer?"

"I'm breathing," I say, though my voice feels dangerously close to reverent. "Barely."

Francesca's smile tilts, soft and warm. "Hi."

I take her hands, anchoring myself in the feel of her skin, her magic, her warmth. "Hi."

Lucifer lifts his hands with a theatrical flourish that immediately makes Leona groan from her seat. "We gather today under the cosmic authority of love, chaos, and contractual obligation to celebrate—"

"Lucifer," Leona hisses. "Behave."

He sighs dramatically. "Fine." Then, in a perfectly normal tone that somehow feels even more outrageous coming from him, "We're here because two souls have finally stopped being stubborn."

Francesca hides a smile behind her free hand. I don't bother hiding mine.

The ceremony unfolds in a haze of warmth and color—Lucifer surprisingly sincere, Francesca glowing like she's lit from the inside, every Bellamy ward chiming softly in rhythms I've never heard before. The vows come next, simple and honest, the way we wanted them.

Francesca goes first.

She squeezes my hands, her voice steady. "You have been the most unexpected part of my life—and the most inevitable. You are the only person who has ever calmed my magic without asking it to shrink. You make space for me without making me smaller. And I choose you. Today, tomorrow, and for every season we're foolish enough to walk into together."

It hits me like it's meant to—sharp and soft and utterly dismantling. I swallow hard, grounding myself in the warmth of her fingers.

My turn.

"Francesca," I say, letting the words come without force, "I spent fifteen years pretending I didn't want what was right in front of me. I don't intend to waste a single day more. You're my calm and my chaos. My gravity. My home. You are the person I choose—freely, fully, without hesitation. And I will spend every day proving I deserve the life we're about to build."

Her eyes shine, bright and damp, and she laughs a little breathlessly. "That's unfair," she murmurs. "I wasn't ready for that."

Lucifer clears his throat loudly. "Vows complete. Rings exchanged. Magic harmonized. Anyone have an objection?"

Every Bellamy in the room glares at him like they're ready to throw him into a volcano.

He beams. "Marvelous. Then by the authority I definitely stole—"

"*Lucifer*," Francesca's mother warns.

"—I now pronounce you husband and wife."

Francesca barely has time to laugh before I lean in and kiss her.

It's not a soft kiss. It's not chaste. It's not careful.

It's everything we spent years denying—warmth, hunger, certainty, relief—colliding in a single, perfect moment that sends a pulse of shared magic radiating through the entire ballroom. Lanterns flicker brighter. Wards chime like bells. One of the floral arrangements blooms explosively, showering pink petals across the aisle.

Francesca laughs against my mouth, breathless and radiant.

When I finally pull back, she presses her forehead to mine, whispering, "We actually did it."

"We did," I murmur, brushing my thumb along her cheek. "And I'm never letting you go again."

Lucifer claps once, delighted. "Now *that* is how you start a marriage."

And as the room erupts into applause, cheers, and Bellamy-level emotional fireworks, I realize I'm holding the woman I've always been meant to find—

and I'm exactly where I'm supposed to be.

Acknowledgements

To everyone who stepped into the chaos with me — thank you.

Hexes and Heartbreakers is a love letter to messy magic, family curses, bad timing, and the kind of connection that refuses to be ignored. It's lighter in tone, sharper in wit, and still full of heart, and it exists because so many of you continue to show up for these stories with enthusiasm, patience, and trust.

To my husband, Ricky — thank you for grounding me when my magic (and my plotlines) spiral, for supporting every late night, early morning, and "just one more chapter" lie I tell myself. You are my steady constant, my calm in the noise, and the reason I can chase stories like this without fear.

To B. Wills and Charletta Benedict, my partners at Golden Light Publishing House — thank you for the laughter, the plotting, the absolute chaos, and the shared belief that stories should be bold, a little dangerous, and deeply human. Building this world alongside you makes every step of the journey better.

To my readers, reviewers, ARC team, and street team — thank you for believing in this book before it ever existed on a page. Your excitement, support, and willingness to champion indie stories make all the difference. You are the reason this magic gets to live beyond my keyboard.

And finally, to those who love stories about found family, stubborn hearts, and magic that refuses to behave — this one's for you.

Thank you for embracing the chaos.

— Yvonne Hamilton

About the Author

About the Author

Yvonne Hamilton is a fantasy author, world-builder, and co-founder of Golden Light Publishing House, where myth, madness, and meticulous storytelling collide. Based in West Virginia, she writes the kinds of stories that blur the line between beauty and ruin—realms forged in fire, characters stitched together with secrets, and worlds that refuse to stay quiet.

With a background in business management and data analytics, Yvonne brings the same precision she uses in spreadsheets to crafting sprawling universes filled with celestial bloodlines, shadowed magic, and rebellions that burn brighter than the stars. Her work—spanning dark fantasy, romantic thrillers, and multi-realm sagas—often explores redemption, betrayal, and the cost of truth in worlds built on lies.

When she's not writing, Yvonne can usually be found buried in coffee, orchestrating publishing schedules, or chasing down the next story that won't let her sleep. She believes good fiction should set something on fire—preferably expectations.

Also by Yvonne Hamilton

Flickers of Betrayal: The Unauthorized Rewrite

Keeper of the Forgotten Fantasy
No Vacancy for the Damned Book 1

The Breakfast Murder Club Series
Blades Over Breakfast – Book 1
Bullets Over Bourbon – Book 2 By B Wills

A Judgment of the Wicked Dark Romance
Ledger of the Damned Book 1